NO ONE

PRAYED

OVER

THEIR

GRAVES

NO ONE

PRAYED

OVER

THEIR

GRAVES

Khaled Khalifa

Translated from the Arabic by Leri Price

FARRAR, STRAUS AND GIROUX *New York*

Farrar, Straus and Giroux
120 Broadway, New York 10271

Printed in the United States of America
Originally published in Arabic in 2019 by Naufal, an imprint of
Hachette-Antoine, Lebanon, as *Lam yusalli 'alayhim ahad* (لم يصل عليهم أحد)
English translation published in the United States by Farrar, Straus and Giroux
First American edition, 2023

Library of Congress Cataloging-in-Publication Data
Names: Khalīfah, Khālid, 1964– author. | Price, Leri, translator.
Title: No one prayed over their graves / Khaled Khalifa ; translated from the Arabic
    by Leri Price.
Other titles: Lam yuṣall 'alayhim aḥad. English
Description: First American edition. | New York : Farrar, Straus and Giroux, 2023.
Identifiers: LCCN 2023001286 | ISBN 9780374601928 (hardcover)
Subjects: LCGFT: Novels.
Classification: LCC PJ7942.H343 L3613 2023 | DDC 892.7/37—dc23/eng/20230403
LC record available at https://lccn.loc.gov/2023001286

Our books may be purchased in bulk for promotional, educational, or business
use. Please contact your local bookseller or the Macmillan Corporate and
Premium Sales Department at 1-800-221-7945, extension 5442, or by email at
MacmillanSpecialMarkets@macmillan.com.

www.fsgbooks.com
www.twitter.com/fsgbooks • www.facebook.com/fsgbooks

10 9 8 7 6 5 4 3 2 1

NO ONE

PRAYED

OVER

THEIR

GRAVES

The Flood

Hosh Hanna and Aleppo—January 1907

The village of Hosh Hanna was completely silent when the storm hit and the Great Flood rose.

Within a few short hours, the houses of the small village were destroyed, its inhabitants drowned in their rags. No one survived apart from Shaha Sheikh Musa, wife of Zakariya Bayazidi, and Mariana Nassar. The two women clung to the trunk of a walnut tree caught between the iron columns of the lighthouse that guided boats through the depths of the river. Some fishermen rescued them and took them to a house in a nearby village, and by dawn, everything had quieted down.

Before Mariana Nassar lost consciousness, she saw the bodies of her mother, her father, and her four brothers and sisters floating on the surface of the river alongside others she recognized: her neighbor and her six children, the rest of her impoverished neighbors. She saw the corpse of Yvonne's fiancé—the girl was currently in Aleppo having her wedding dress made, oblivious to the rumors that her betrothed had deflowered her in his father's mill. The village priest was smiling as usual, and next to him was Hanna's son, not yet four years old, and his mother Josephine Laham, gripping him tightly. Their bodies rose and fell with the waves as if they were dancing.

Mariana had known most of the drowned. They were her students, her neighbors, family friends from the neighboring villages, her own friends. All the corpses passed by her. An entire life was buried in the river, and she wasn't certain she had survived herself. She closed her eyes in surrender, praying desperately to Jesus as she held on to the sturdy tree trunk caught in the lighthouse. She noticed Shaha next to her, clutching the body of her son to her chest. Later, the fishermen would succeed in extracting him from her arms only after a struggle.

Mariana saw cooking pots and rugs and beds, shards of large ceramic water pots mixed with roof timber, mirrors, bridal trunks, and other things she couldn't make out. Seared on her memory was the image of Shaha grabbing hold of her dead son when the waves tossed him near her, and the smile of the priest who had dedicated his last sermon to defending the honor of Yvonne and her fiancé, "the eternal lovers," as the fellahin of Hosh Hanna called them.

Zakariya Bayazidi and his friend Hanna Gregoros arrived in the afternoon after hearing news of the disaster. When the destroyed village appeared in the distance, they were horrified. Shaha was unconscious when he found her, and Zakariya couldn't believe that she was still breathing. Their son's body lay curled up in her lap, and they were still clinging to each other. Hanna was utterly stupefied—he thought for a moment that he had lost the power of speech. One of the fishermen led him down a narrow, debris-filled lane to the body of his wife, Josephine. She was paler than she had been in life, her lips closed like all the dead, and his son was next to her, rigid, his stomach distended like a waterskin.

Hanna trudged back along the river road, a familiar route. He stepped over the corpses of cows, sheep, and people. He climbed the long staircase to his room built a short distance away, and from the broad window he looked out over his village, transformed into silt and the remnants of things. There was no longer anything blocking his view over the remote distances. The river, which he knew so well, ran along as it had for eternity, demure and quiet, as if it hadn't done anything at all. The sunlight glittered on its surface like golden coins.

He reflected that once again he was alone, without a family. Entertainment and pleasure had saved him and Zakariya. If they had delayed their visit to the citadel with their friends, they would now be two bloated corpses reeking of mass death, that fetid smell that he would later try and fail to describe. He could not forget Mariana's words when she told him that Josephine had been terrified as her soul rose to Heaven, raising her hand and clutching at the air while her other hand gripped her son tightly. She had plunged into the river and resurfaced more than once before she drowned and became a corpse, meek and smiling, just as she had been when she arrived at Hosh Hanna for the first time and all the fellahin of the village saw her get down from the carriage. When Hanna insisted on asking Mariana about their last moments, all she said was that drowned people's features disappear, and they don't look at all like the other dead.

Hanna felt as if he were caught on a shadowy horizon, hearing the bones of perished beings shattering under his feet. Zakariya couldn't bear to see his friend so frightened, so he acted decisively. He arranged the village graveyard anew with the help of the fellahin from the neighboring villages, and he buried most of the bodies that the river had spat out onto its banks. He still knew them, even though their features were distorted. He knew their scars, the color of their eyes. He buried an intimate part of his life in their graves.

The graveyard was a vision of horror to Zakariya and Hanna as they looked at it from the window of Hanna's room. The graves of the Christians were lined up neatly next to the graves of the Muslims, and the graves of the unknown and the strangers were in a third orderly row. Other graves were left open to receive any corpses that the river had swept away to distant villages. The fellahin had spent three days digging graves according to instructions from Zakariya, who at that moment had no thought for anything other than burying the dead. He kept repeating that the dead would turn into a plague before long. He buried more than 150 bodies and was never truly rid of their cold touch and the smell. He hadn't known that the scent of death hangs in one's clothes, and that burial wasn't the least arduous task, as it had seemed to him when he was giving orders to the fellahin to dig the graves and sending someone to call a sheikh and a local priest to complete the requisite rites. The priest and the sheikh arrived, and both refused to pray over the unknown corpses, or those with features too distorted to be recognized. The sheikh said that it wasn't permitted to bury a person in the Islamic way or pray over their body if that person might be Christian, and the priest agreed—they had to confirm the religion of the body. But Zakariya went on burying them all in his own way, without bothering to pray over them, repeating that the dead lost their religious affiliations and became creatures without an interest in the affairs of Heaven.

It was ten days before Zakariya finished burying the bodies. He sat on the steps of Hanna's room and heard his friend sobbing. Exhausted, he reflected on their former lives. It was no consolation for him to see his sixty horses return—their ancestry had been lost when their pedigrees were drowned. They had come back to gather at the site of their stable, where only some wooden fragments and empty stone troughs remained.

Zakariya prepared two horses to pull the carriage and set off with Mariana Nassar and Shaha—but only after extracting a promise from Hanna that he would join them in Aleppo within a few days. Zakariya didn't look back when the carriage pulled away from the place that used to be known as Hosh Hanna. He wanted to forget the village that had become a graveyard. His horses ran behind him with bowed heads, dejected to be leaving behind the riverbank and their obliterated stables.

Zakariya couldn't make sense of the loss of his only child. He spent the whole journey in heavy silence and didn't reply when Shaha told him that the noise was hurting her. Before the flood, when she would lie naked beside him on the bed, she would ask him to close the curtain when the dawn's light pierced their window, saying that it wounded her. They lived, before the flood, in the certainty that everything would be all right, that they would have children who would inherit a love of horses, and who would be wounded by invisible things like light, air, and sound. But now, after the flood, they entered Zakariya's family home in the new quarter of Aleppo like a pair of orphans. They couldn't explain what had happened, neither to Zakariya's father, Ahmed Bayazidi, nor to his sister Souad, who knew that the flood hadn't just taken the son of her brother and his wife; it had also destroyed their passion and their love for each other. She said to her father, "We have to get used to them being ghosts, two invisible people." Her father didn't understand. He encouraged her to persuade her brother to open an 'aza and go to Hosh Hanna to bring back Hanna. Leaving him alone with the dead meant he would disappear like withered rose petals.

Zakariya left the business of caring for the horses to his groom Yaaqoub, who was already responsible for his second stable in the village of Anabiya. He didn't reply to Yaaqoub's question about recovering the pedigrees and paid no attention when Yaaqoub said, "What are the horses worth without a record of their bloodline?" When Zakariya returned to his room in his family's house at night, Shaha was asleep. He sat next to her on the sofa and looked at her for a long time. She had changed considerably. Surely it wasn't possible that witnessing death could turn you into another being within a few hours? Her laughing eyes were hollowed out, transformed into two pits of clotted blood. Her chest rose and fell with her agitated breathing, her lips clamped shut as if she were afraid that river water might leak in. Her large moist nipples had shrunk, and the gorgeous valley between her breasts had become a shadowless pit. He had never seen her like this before. Never again would she scold him for his frequent trips with Hanna in search of pleasure and women and card tables. She wouldn't laugh coquettishly when he calmly replied that horses love women and gambling and fun, pointing out, "You won't find purebreds in the houses of the frightened, or the misers, or the moneylenders." She used to conclude their little flirtation by asking him to describe the women whom the horses loved so much—but now she had surrendered to the image of death.

Shaha hadn't understood the relationship between horses and moneylenders in the early days of their marriage, but she liked the idea of it. She thought that pleasure and entertainment were the kind

Zakariya had introduced her to. When he saw her one night in the house of her brother Arif, she stole his heart with her slim figure and large eyes. Zakariya fell in love on the spot and exchanged some lingering glances with her, and later he whispered a plea to an intoxicated Hanna to make the marriage proposal for him. Arif burst out laughing when Hanna told him gravely that he was asking for Shaha's hand on behalf of Zakariya. Arif went out of the salon where his guests usually gathered, bringing his sister with him. He asked her, "Do you accept Zakariya, that outrageous wanton?" She said, smiling, "Yes." He went on, "You have to know he is utterly shameless and a complete buffoon. He has no respect for married life and will betray you with the first woman he trips over on the road to Afrin." She repeated her answer: "Yes, I will marry him." Arif had no idea what he was supposed to do in moments like this. He walked to the cupboard, took out his rifle, and fired a shot into the air. Then he sent for Mala Mannan to record all the terms of the dowry and marriage contract, and no one disputed any of the details.

Hanna felt that this novel event merited drunkenly staggering to his feet in the middle of the party and taking some gold liras out of his leather zunnar to present to Shaha as a wedding gift. Everything was very simple and joyful—"wonderful," as Shaha described it. Arif didn't care about the objections of his wider family, who would have preferred a Kurdish groom for the daughter of Sheikh Musa Agha. He didn't stint his sister and put on a lavish wedding for her, where he danced and flattered both Ahmed Bayazidi and Souad (whom he privately called "arrogant"). Souad was no more pleased by her brother's improvised wedding than she was by his marrying a girl from the countryside, even if she was the daughter of an agha, but the happiness of the bride and groom was enough to defer her criticisms. She knew, deep down, that this marriage was a declaration of Zakariya's permanent separation from his family. He couldn't care less what his relatives would say and delegated the task of informing them to his father who, for his part, was delighted. Shaha belonged to a large and powerful family, and by marrying her, Zakariya had put an end to his father's constant fear that he would be ensnared by one of those prostitutes at the citadel, whose shamelessness and licentiousness were the stuff of legend across the city.

After the wedding, which continued for three days, the married couple left Sharran trailed by large carriages crammed with gifts: rugs of virgin wool, embroidered cushion covers, Kurdish carpets made specially for Shaha's jihaz many years before, enormous copper cooking pans, and earthenware jars of goat cheese, olive oil, and cured meats, plus small things that Zakariya hadn't seen yet like Shaha's anklets and a heavy necklace of pure gold. And there was a carriage just for the married couple, pulled by a black purebred stallion that Arif had gifted to his friend and brother-in-law.

On their way to Hosh Hanna, Shaha said to Zakariya that she had loved him since she first saw him three years before. She used to look out for him among her brother's ever-present guests, and she could relate many stories about the moments he came to light. She said that she had put compresses on his forehead one day two years earlier when he had been struck with a fever. On that night of revelry, Arif had gathered his many friends for a party to mark the end of the olive harvest. In actual fact they were celebrating many things that had happened that year, most important of which was the return of his father's library to its rightful place, and the reconciliation that had at last taken place between Arif and his uncle, who had struck Arif with his shoe in front of a servant and called him ignorant after learning that he had sold the library to an Englishman who perpetually wandered the region that extended from Kilis to the Cathedral of St. Simeon Stylites in the company of an interpreter. This Englishman was interested in the theater of Nabi Houri, the ruins of the destroyed temples and churches in Barad, and the villages of Mount Simeon. Arif had regained the library only after great exertion. He had traveled to Aleppo, where the Englishman was staying in a residence belonging to the English consulate, and he ended up paying substantially more than what he had been given for it. Leaders of Arab tribes and Kurdish aghas mediated on his behalf and succeeded in striking a bargain for the return of the library, which was still in trunks, waiting to be sent to London. But three ancient texts written in Kurdish were missing, the most important a manuscript of *Mem and Zin* copied by Abdel Latif Bihzad, an adherent of the work's original author, the Sufi poet Ahmed Khany.

The library was welcomed home with a raucous celebration. Munshidun recited the odes of Ahmed Khany and Mala Jaziri for three days straight. Arif's uncle and Mala Mannan examined the books that Arif's Ethiopian servant, Mabrouk, had reordered and returned to their original places. Despite mourning the loss of the three unique texts, they were satisfied that the library was once again where it belonged: in the house built on a hill within Arif's estate known as Grandfather's House. It was an isolated residence composed of two spacious rooms that overlooked his vast olive groves.

At that party, Zakariya drank a lot of arak. By the end of the night, he was exhausted and suffering from sharp stomach cramps; his forehead was sweating, and his body wouldn't stop convulsing. Arif summoned a doctor from Azaz, but it didn't take much effort on his part to diagnose Zakariya's condition. He said that Zakariya had drunk like a mule, and his malady was just a fever that would necessitate complete rest and a few compresses soaked in an herb tisane. Arif conveyed Zakariya to a large room in Grandfather's House and instructed Shaha to change his compresses. She was delighted with this task—to find herself so close to him that their breaths mingled. When the servant Mabrouk went to bring the firewood brazier, she seized her opportunity. She looked at Zakariya for a long time, she inhaled him slowly, she took hold of his fingers and rubbed them, she wiped his forehead with her palm, and when he opened his eyes, he saw her as an angel hovering overhead. Just then the servant Mabrouk returned with the wood, setting it in the brazier. Shaha was embarrassed, rose from her place, and left, but she lingered at the door to smile at Zakariya.

The road to their house in Hosh Hanna was filled with Shaha's skillful storytelling. Half an hour before they arrived at the village, he pinched her breast. She leaned against him and said that his scent was what had caused her desire for him. Smirking, he asked, "What else apart from that?" She replied, laughing and reaching coyly toward his sex, "Don't you know that scent pierces my heart?" It was the first time she told him about the invisible things that wounded her.

A year after their marriage, her happiness was overflowing. She joined in telling stories and daydreams, and Zakariya loved her generosity and her creativity when it came to lovemaking. He was constantly surprising her, and she responded enthusiastically to his imagination, and to his peculiar tales of horses and women that he brought back from his trips with Hanna, her brother Arif, and the rest of their companions, all of whom adored uproarious parties at the citadel. Arif was the most resplendent of all the visitors there, obediently losing everything he won throughout the days of his visit. He would say that the gambler was a creature of eternal loss, and he liked this phrase so much he would reformulate it and repeat, "Gambling is eternal losing." Then he would roar with laughter, as always, and add, "A winner is a cowardly gambler and should be ashamed."

Zakariya and Shaha led a cheerful life in the few years before the flood. Whenever he went away with Hanna, he missed her. She enchanted him. She wasn't hostile toward the citadel, she didn't ask him to remain at her side, but after his marriage he didn't waste much time in the city. Leaving Hanna drunk in one of the many houses they were both familiar with in every city, he would depart at dawn and return to her weighed down with gifts and desires. She loved it when he called her by the names of his horses, and his trade expanded considerably when he added nine purebred Arabian stallions to his stable. A traveling broker had displayed them to him, saying that he was selling them on behalf of the sheikh of a large tribe who didn't want to give his name. Zakariya, who knew everything about the horses of his region, had dispatched his groom to the sheikh, who was staying in Khan Al-Wazir during his visit to Aleppo. Without mincing words, the groom had asked the sheikh if it was true he wanted to sell his nine horses, swearing to keep his secret. On receiving an affirmative reply, they had agreed on a price and the agent's percentage, and the sheikh had surrendered the horses' deeds. Zakariya never forgot the moment they made their grand entrance. He had long dreamed of the day that such horses would be in his stable to fill out its shortcomings and make it into one of the most important in the whole Vilayet of Aleppo. Horse traders made a beeline for him, and so did Bedouin sheikhs who loved horses, princes of distant regions, and foreign hobbyists who couldn't believe this outstanding collection could be found in a single place—and enjoying such a high degree of care. Their mangers were spotless, their saddles were hung on designated hooks like new clothes for Eid, and the spurs had the pleasant smell of gazelle leather. The stable was always clean, as the four grooms (who would also drown in the flood) used to take it in turns to mix the dung with straw and muck out every six hours. The horses drank water from huge copper basins inlaid with tin, just like rich people in the city. A long passageway separated the stables and the horses' overnight shelter from the large office. Composed of several rooms, its walls were filled with walnut cabinets, and lined up on the shelves of these cabinets, the complete files archived in a single register, were the biography and the bloodline of each horse, which Zakariya had delighted in writing out in his splendid calligraphy. Alongside this was a special cabinet where the pedigree of every horse was arranged, written on gazelle leather, signed and witnessed by seven people of good standing. (According to custom, Zakariya had memorized the lineage of the horses.) There was also a guesthouse attached to the stables, which had been expanded several times over ten years. And in the stables in Anabiya he kept several rare horses for breeding and crossbreeding. Everything was overseen by Yaaqoub, the most experienced groom in the region.

On their first night back in the family home, Zakariya sat on the sofa all night, watching Shaha as she drowned in uninterrupted nightmares. She had lost her magic; she had aged suddenly. He had always believed that coming back to the family home was a bad sign, a man losing his dream, especially if the place was tumbledown, dripping with the chronic illnesses of its elderly inhabitants, stinking of rot from being crammed full of old furniture and his father's detested files.

After the departure of Zakariya, who considered his friend's conversation about regret to be an evil omen, Hanna woke at dawn. He didn't want to think about his new life; instead, he let it seep away into the river that he had begun to see as a river that was new every moment. He brightened at the thought that he required very little: just a couple of cotton thobes and some garments he could gather in a single bag if he wanted to leave suddenly. Gone was his wardrobe of sumptuous English suits and European hats, custom-made shoes and perfumes and rich objects that reeked of his adoration of the good life—all drowned. He thought that the Lord wanted him to have a new life, one he could touch with his hand and heart. Hanna resolved not to regret anything he did from then on. Nothing would go back to the way it was, no matter how many times Zakariya said it; he himself was wagering that Hanna wouldn't be able to bear living among the meek, those who feared a bit of frivolity.

Hanna wouldn't listen to his friends who came from villages and cities, near and far, to assist and condole with him. They brought carts loaded with provisions for hundreds: clothes, cured meats, lambs, cages filled with chickens, bottles of wine and cognac, excellent tobacco, and money. Hanna was silent, wouldn't reply to any questions, and rebuffed all condolences. After a few weeks he refused to receive any of them. In his room, he pondered the meaning of death by drowning and wouldn't allow the gifts to be brought in. He asked his servant to bring everything to the caretaker of the church in the nearest village so he could distribute it among the few families that had stayed by the river. He begged Zakariya to tell their friends not to bring him anything else, as he already had everything he needed: olive oil, a little bulgur wheat, and some dried vegetables. But their friends wouldn't allow him to turn into a vagrant (or an imbecile, as they termed it), an ascetic who had renounced property and uproarious living. Everything could be replaced as long as there was still the thousands of dunums of his fertile lands, the olive groves that extended for great distances over the territory of Anabiya, as well as his great citadel and its gardens of 129 dunums planted with all types of trees, the khans in the souq, and the four splendid houses in Aleppo, only half a day's journey from this one-room dwelling, which, as he kept informing everyone, was more than sufficient for him.

Hanna felt like the flood hadn't just drowned his wife and son; it had drowned all his sordid and riotous past, his entire life. A desire welled up inside him for a new one. An image came back to him of Father Ibrahim Hourani, the itinerant priest who came to Aleppo every now and then and stayed in a large room attached to the Syriac Catholic Church. Hanna would greet him silently at Sunday mass, which he was assiduous in attending, compelled as he was to prove that he was still Christian and had not converted to Islam, as the rumors went. Once Father Ibrahim had blocked Hanna's path and told him, "You won't feel the power of weakness until you fall to the lowest point." At the time, he had no idea why this man, so venerated by the other worshippers, had stopped him. Hanna didn't leave the church after the prayers were over. He went to see Father Ibrahim, who took him by the arm, and together they went out into the city's streets. They sat in a nearby coffeehouse, and Father Ibrahim told Hanna that he had known his father Gabriel Gregoros very well. He had lived his entire life in fear of being massacred, of being forced to abandon his religion and convert to Islam. To be safe, he hid the money for the jizya tax in a place no one knew apart from Ahmed Bayazidi, despite Sultan Abdel Majid's Imperial Reform Edict of 1865, which relieved non-Muslim citizens of the Ottoman Empire from paying the jizya. Gabriel hadn't believed that he would never pay the jizya again and lived his whole life resigned to the imminence of his death, so when the massacre took place, he was expecting it.

Continuing to address Hanna, who was unusually submissive, Father Ibrahim said, "You are not like your father, but you will gradually transform into an exact copy of his original, and your wicked soul won't be saved unless you sink to the very lowest point and realize that everything you have ever done in your life has been mere mean-ingless ignominy." Hanna asked for his address, and Father Ibrahim replied quietly, "You may consider me a person with no address. I walk this earth in constant anticipation of my death." He wouldn't permit Hanna to question him further. He rose smiling and left him alone, turning onto the street that led back to the church.

"This is the lowest point that Father Ibrahim was talking about," Hanna said to himself. He felt that life was passing before him, slow, pleasant, and lightened of material things. Death was treading lightly alongside, invisible, reaching out his hand to help if life stumbled. Hanna left his room at dawn, walking slowly over the flat ground that used to be the village his father had founded more than thirty years earlier, which he named in honor of his youngest son. Hanna wished it would fall into oblivion forever, he didn't want anyone to remem-ber it, he wanted to go back to the image of the world as it was first created. He felt himself to be a child, reborn into another life with-out a past. He was a blank page expelling a memory, burdened down with the uproar and gaiety and pain of an entire life that was over now. Then he felt guilty and longed for his son and the face of the gentle wife who had endured a life with him. From the first day of their marriage, Josephine had never depended on his presence in their family life. She had gifted him to the distant wilds and the citadel of Shams Al-Sabah, with its endless caravan of women selling pleasure, with its troupes of musicians who played for days without stopping at the command of a party of landowners passing a winter immersed in gambling, with its sumptuous feasts prepared by Aleppan cooks who were adept at catering to the tastes of the little group that Hanna and Zakariya presided over. They would invite women from Aleppo, Da-mascus, and Beirut who had been hand-selected by a group of pimps throughout the year. In mid-December, the women would arrive at the citadel on the small hill overlooking the ruins of Barad, accompa-nied by trunks of sumptuous, exorbitantly expensive clothes, all paid for by the men. They were spread out among the chambers of the cita-del and would wander half-naked through the passageways, the large salon, the rooms, and the cellars tightly packed with bottles of fine wine and foreign drinks brought back by the men from their trips to Beirut, Baghdad, Damascus, Venice, Paris, Istanbul. They bought the finest alcohol from the Jews in Aleppo and sent it to the cellar of the citadel, whose every detail had been considered and chosen by Shams Al-Sabah herself: feather pillows, embroidered silk sheets, tall copper bedsteads furnished with mattresses of combed wool. She had gone to the trouble of selecting an individual color for the bedcovers in each of the nine rooms. The card table had been imported from London by a Jewish cotton trader from Aleppo. He had intended to open the first casino in Aleppo, only for his plan to fail before it began: the men of religion attacked him in a Friday sermon, and his friend Raoul the goldsmith begged him to abandon his project. The Jewish trader dropped the idea and sold the ebony table to Arif, who donated it to the citadel along with a china service, copper saucepans, and cutlery fashioned from pure, unadulterated silver.

Shams Al-Sabah didn't neglect a single detail. She understood that she was there at the pleasure of the elite, who didn't care what was going on in their vast lands, leaving the communication and defense of their interests with the governing classes to a group of lawyers and politicians. One of the men looking out for them was Ahmed Bayazidi, chief accountant of the Ottoman vali, director of the Ottoman Bank in Aleppo, and the dear friend of Hanna's father Gabriel Gregoros. Gabriel Gregoros came from a pious family, of which Hanna was the sole survivor. In 1876, every other member of the Gregoros family had been slaughtered at Mardin as punishment for the murder of an Ottoman officer who had tried to rape Hanna's aunt in broad daylight. The Gregoros family attacked the officer in the souq, dragged him off his horse, killed him, and threw his mutilated body in front of the governor's headquarters, threatening anyone who assaulted their women with the same fate.

Even after many years, Hanna's hatred and resentment for the three officers who had perpetrated the ensuing massacre was undiminished. He managed to have his revenge on two of them, but the

third, the leader of the garrison at Mardin, still lived. This man refused to mix with the populace, wore gloves in order not to touch
the fingers of those who greeted him, wouldn't accept gifts from anyone, and never betrayed his wife, who was described as the paragon of
beauty by everyone who knew her. And so the battle between the two
men remained unfinished. As the years passed, Hanna would convince himself that killing the first two officers had healed his thirst for
revenge, and he dismissed the idea of vengeance on the leader of the
garrison when he saw an old man getting down from his carriage in
front of the vali's residence in Aleppo.

And yet the outrage done to his murdered father remained the
hardest image in Hanna's life, and he never forgot it. It kept him
awake for long nights. He would choke suddenly in the midst of joy
and feel like he was suffocating. During these times, he would hide
himself away from his companions, and thoughts of revenge would
return in full force. He would imagine extraordinary deaths for this
haughty officer. Hanna thought he would order him to eat a sack of
salt, or he would drown him in a lake of piss taken from Zakariya's
horses. Hanna wanted him to have a slow death so he could relish it
and erase the shame that had accompanied him all his life.

Unlike this last officer, the other two had been susceptible to
Hanna's stratagems. They had loved parties, and he was able to hunt
them down easily by means of a well-known pimp. Hanna paid the
pimp a massive sum to lure the officers from Mardin to Aleppo, kill
them, and then disappear completely from the territory of the Ottoman Empire.

The officers died in the house of Nahawand, the most famous
courtesan in Aleppo, in the final years of the nineteenth century. She
slipped them some poison and made sure they were dead before she
and her pimp stole away at dawn in a carriage drawn by four strong
horses whose driver knew every back road to the village of Hosh
Hanna. Zakariya was waiting for them in Hanna's room. He paid
them a thousand gold liras and arranged for them to travel inconspic-
uously to Isfahan.

The day after, Hanna sat on his terrace, gleefully observing the officers' funeral as it passed by his house in Bab Al-Faraj. It caused him some pain to see Ahmed Bayazidi among the high-ranking officials in the mourning procession as it continued its journey toward the Umayyad Mosque. A few days later Zakariya hired a group of storytellers to circulate tales of the heroism of Nahawand, who had refused to spy on her people for the Sublime Porte, and the utter degradation of the two officers who, so the tale went, were homosexual and had used her house to secretly engage in fornication.

For several weeks after the funeral, Aleppo closed its doors early in fear of the state's retribution. Officers burned down Nahawand's house, which she had sold to a Jewish silk trader. They sought out her relatives but couldn't find any in the city. Everyone confirmed to the investigator that Nahawand was a Moroccan Jew who had come to the city a few years earlier with an Aleppan husband whose family couldn't bear her excessive beauty. He was forced to divorce her and marry a relative instead. She reneged on their agreement and stayed in the city, which she loved, and she lived in her pimp's house in Bahsita. She became famous among the young men of the Jewish upper classes as a coquette who could moan in three languages.

Hanna wanted to savor his revenge. He went out at night with Zakariya, and they walked the streets. It occurred to them to visit a brothel; they knew most of the ones in Aleppo. Zakariya suggested the secluded house of Um Waheed, located in a side street in the Nayal quarter. They craved the coffee of this kindhearted old woman who had tended to them when they were adolescents. Um Waheed welcomed them with warm kisses and told them the story of the homosexual officers, mocking the men for turning away from the local girls and putting their trust in a Moroccan Jew. Zakariya laughed out loud at hearing his own rumors repeated back to him, and Hanna was relieved to hear that Nahawand had safely left the city. Um Waheed asked Hanna if he would be staying overnight in his room, and she thanked him for the provisions that had continued uninterrupted, when their visits had not. Hanna was in the mood for a light dinner and a glass of wine, but Um Waheed was determined to present the girls she had working for her. (Um Waheed, for her own part, was nearing sixty.) She told the men about Sabah, a charming girl with bad luck who needed someone to look after her and who was more-over proficient in reading and writing in both Turkish and Arabic. Hanna was unprepared for how dazed he felt. He was intoxicated with triumph: later he heard that the story of the adulterous officers had reached all the way to the palace of Sultan Abdel Hamid in Istanbul, who ordered the investigation to be closed, Nahawand's punishment to be commuted, and the murders of the officers to be made a nonexistent event in the records of the empire.

Um Waheed knew that Zakariya was there for one girl in particular; with a wink, she dispatched him to the usual room where his favorite was waiting for him. Sabah came in carrying the china for dinner. She was exquisite—no more than sixteen—but Hanna's mood that night was troubled. He had dinner with Zakariya, who soon left to join his own favorite girls. Hanna promised Um Waheed he would visit again soon and spend the night in her house. Before he could leave, she told him that she wouldn't let anyone else near Sabah. He kissed her hastily, gave her a short message for Zakariya, and left.

Suddenly Hanna no longer felt any desire for any of the other girls of the brothels. Zakariya joined him at his house in Bab Al-Faraj at almost ten o'clock that evening. Hanna told him that he had been depressed when he left Um Waheed's house. Never before had he been so relentlessly assailed by the image of a woman he had seen only for a few moments. Sabah's innocent face (and her prominent breasts), her white skin, and her small mouth would never leave him. He considered going back to Hosh Hanna. He lay awake until daybreak, ruminating on how he might escape love and bondage, and repeating his favorite saying: "The best women are those you can forget after bedding them."

The following morning Zakariya left to inspect his stable at Anabiya; he knew what Hanna was like when he was drowning in delusions of love. Hanna sent his household servant Salih Azizi to Um

Waheed with a letter requesting to spend that night at her house. He
didn't delay his appointment, and when he climbed up to the upper
room, the women were awaiting his orders on the ground floor. He
asked for Sabah, who had known that he would come for her. She sat
facing him on the sofa but raised her gaze to him only when he stroked
her hand with his fingers. When he asked her about her previous life,
she told him that she didn't know who her family were. She had been
found at the gate of the Umayyad Mosque and had spent her childhood in an orphanage. There she had caught the eye of the wife of the
head of the vali's diwan, who brought Sabah to her house. She worked
there as a servant for ten years but was forced to leave when the master of the house harassed her. She didn't give many details of her life;
clearly she was the type of girl that Hanna adored: comfortable being
silent and asking for nothing more in return. Whores' stories were all
the same anyway, Hanna thought, and they had a long time ahead of
them for conversation. Sabah told him she was still a virgin and had
refused all of Um Waheed's clients: she would grant her virginity only
to a man she loved.

Sabah's voice was quiet, and she had few feminine wiles. She was
only a young, terrified girl, on her way to becoming a feebleminded
woman looking for a husband in a city that venerated fair skin and
broad hips. In this respect she was no different from the many rich
Aleppan girls who left their family home only to go to their husband's.
Her sentences were short and direct, and she frequently blamed herself for falling into a bottomless pit she could never escape.

Hanna made do with kissing her hand and stroking her skin as
she spoke. He asked her to change her name from Sabah—which
meant "morning"—to Shams Al-Sabah—or "morning sun." He left
her enough money to live on for a few months and easily came to an
agreement with Um Waheed. The girl adopted the name Shams Al-
Sabah from that night forward, and she began wearing a veil. She no
longer sat with the men like the rest of the girls. She had obtained her
objective—she would never be made available to clients.

As Hanna and Zakariya made their way back to Hosh Hanna, they spoke of their citadel, which was becoming clearer and clearer in their minds. "We will build the kingdom of pleasure we've always dreamed of," said Zakariya. Hanna nodded. "And we must build a stage especially for suicides." They had long discussed this dream, but this was the moment when they began to plan the details. A year earlier they had asked their dear friend Azar to reconsider their old dream, with which he had been familiar, and to help them design a whole citadel dedicated to the art and practice of pleasure.

Hanna hoped that the citadel would ease his anxiety and interrupt his endless stream of daydreams. In a cheerful tone, Zakariya concluded, "We will print money for our little nation, we will immortalize our memories on silver plates laid side by side in steel boxes, we won't erase our moments of madness, we won't live like a couple of misers hoarding gold for our sons to inherit after us. We'll leave them everything else, but the citadel will be the only place that's just for us." Zakariya and Hanna used to say, in all seriousness, that in a hundred years' time people would come from distant lands to enter the labyrinth of the citadel and try to break the riddle of it all. They were thinking of immortality—they didn't want to be remembered in history books as pimps for the Ottoman military, as liberators, or even as thinkers but simply as masters of the citadel of pleasure, every detail of which would be recorded in a special register only to be discovered after their deaths.

Their friend, Azar ibn Hayyim Istanbouli, had completed his studies in architectural engineering in Rome and returned to Aleppo two years earlier. He remembered the conversations about seas of pleasure that were constantly revolving between his friends Zakariya, Hanna, and William Michel Eisa. Even at school, the three of them would take every opportunity between classes to banter and laugh together. Azar used to think they were joking—that the citadel was just another one of their strange fantasies involving women, so he was taken aback when they came to his office in Jamiliyya and asked him to design the citadel, and to begin right away.

Azar listened as Hanna dictated his dreams slowly and carefully.

He turned Hanna's words and gestures into plans that he was constantly having to revise according to Hanna's daydreams, which went on for two years. The builders would work all day, hewing arches and huge stones, steadfastly refusing to answer the questions of passersby. Hundreds of laborers and dozens of carts conveyed boulders from the Kurdish mountains to the top of the hill where construction took place. Hanna was determined not to visit the site until the work was completely finished.

Zakariya felt his friend's intense passion for the citadel. He left the entirety of the building up to him but gave Azar instructions on the stable that would be attached to it, close to the hill, as well as the larger stable. Zakariya treated Hanna like a younger brother, indulging all his caprices, and Hanna never had to repeat a request. Since childhood, they had kept each other's secrets, swapping roles and faces when necessary. They had mastered the art of prevarication whenever they faced a rebuke from Ahmed Bayazidi, who always kept an eye on the scandals that were a constant feature of their lives since adolescence.

Azar begged Hanna not to go too far with his ideas. Stone wasn't a flexible thing that could be molded however they wished, and the design couldn't be altered after it was built: the place would be a single entity, like a body. It was designed as a labyrinth, easy to enter and difficult to leave. Curtly, Azar would point out that architecture wasn't like pouring a glass of wine between a lover's breasts. He would spend days in his office, listening to Hanna and Zakariya ramble on about pleasure and gambling and death and silver coffins. They spent many nights there, meandering around the large room and giving their thoughts free rein while Azar, knowing their penchant for strange ideas, recorded their conversations.

One night Hanna came alone and sat down on the sofa. The plans were half-ready. Azar had stopped making suggestions to his friends—he was resigned to their propensity to take things to extremes. But that night Hanna said he agreed with Azar's idea of a long staircase that wound between four statues of reclining couples in passionate embraces, but at the top of the stairs, he wanted to add one more statue of a woman. Azar didn't understand what he meant. Musing freely, Hanna described the woman he had in mind. As he spoke, he poured a cup of wine and lay back on the broad sofa. Azar took him aback by saying, "It's impossible to have a statue of Souad there. It would ruin the aspect." Hanna fell silent when he heard Souad's name. He was afraid of slipping into a conversation that would not be to his benefit, knowing as he did the strength of regard that Azar had for his friend Souad. She had cared for Azar like a brother, although she was younger than him, giving him embroidered silk shirts on his birthdays and listening to his worries whenever he needed a shoulder to lean on. Azar was angry that Hanna always ignored her despite loving her to madness; meanwhile William Eisa felt the same anger but encouraged Hanna to fall in love with someone else instead.

Azar was polite and shy. He didn't enjoy the raucous pursuits of his three friends, but he kept their secrets. After returning from Rome, he opened the office that his father had worked to establish for him while he was away with the help of the Jewish community in the city. Azar's place at the architectural college had been made possible through the intercession of Ahmed Bayazidi and the princess, Huda Shamoun, who had good relationships with men of influence. (She had persuaded the Italian consul to offer a full scholarship to a person of talent and formidable intelligence, a person like Azar.) Azar's family was poor, and his father worked at the Jewish orphanage. He had been one of the few survivors of the 1822 earthquake, in which twenty-five thousand people had been crushed beneath the wreckage of more than half of the houses in Aleppo. Hayyim Istanbouli would often gravely recite the tale of the earthquake and how he met Najib Bayazidi, Zakariya's grandfather and the father of Ahmed Bayazidi.

Hayyim, at seven years old, went out of his senses when he saw the corpses of his father, his mother, and his three brothers beside him, all buried under the rubble of the house they had shared with a Muslim family, who had been newly arrived from Beirut and renting a room until they could find somewhere better to live. In the other three rooms, there had lived impoverished families who had been settled there for a long time. None of them had any chance of survival when the earthquake brought their home down on top of them. Hayyim alone was left breathing. He didn't understand how it had all happened: how the roof had closed in, how the walls had sunk into the ground. Trapped where he was, the child tried to lie down in the narrow space. He would just wait for his mother to get up and wake him for his daily task of going to Sid Ibrahim's shop in Souweiqa Ali, where he worked as a servant. He passed a disturbed night; the sound of tremors and collapsing buildings was constant. At dawn, he discovered a small opening where the light crept in and crawled toward it. It was just large enough for him to squeeze his small body through, and he emerged out of the ruins. He was amazed at the silence. Hayyim walked all day, watching people who hurried to recover their belongings from their houses and fled toward the gardens that surrounded the city. He reached Bab Al-Hadid Square and spent his first night after the disaster sleeping by the old gateway. In the distance he heard women and children wailing. The weather was summery and the sky was red, and he fell asleep despite being hungry.

Most of the city's houses had been leveled. They had either sunk into the ground or caught fire, and caravans of people were moving to the distant gardens and orchards surrounding the city. Hayyim searched for food in the debris and found some cheese, olives, and a piece of dry bread. People were walking past him, paying him no attention. He found himself walking with them toward the city's outskirts. When they reached the gardens, he realized that the whole city had moved there. He thought everyone was playing; of course his family would get up once the game was over. He walked among the people looking for someone he might recognize, but he was just one of many homeless children. At the end of the day, he fell asleep under a large berry tree. In the morning, he decided he didn't like the gardens. He got up and walked back along the road he remembered clearly from the day before and found himself once again by the Umayyad Mosque.

Another child was walking behind him, fussing over his appearance. The child sat down next to Hayyim and asked him about his family. Hayyim tried to move his tongue but couldn't answer. Najib Bayazidi, Zakariya's grandfather, was ten years old and the son of a prominent family. He had been separated from his family when, along with thousands of other survivors, they left their house after the first tremors hit the city. Within a few days, Najib Bayazidi and Hayyim Istanbouli were firm friends. Najib led Hayyim to his family home. He still knew the way among the city's remains. The two children passed through houses that had turned into ruins. The roads were cut off, so they wandered through destroyed streets. They protected each other. They were blinded by intense flashes of lightning, followed by large fires. Najib opened his hands and recited the chapters he had memorized from the Qur'an. "Judgment Day has arrived!" he told Hayyim. Hayyim laughed and told him for the first time that his name was Hayyim Istanbouli and that he was Jewish. He had lost his way home but knew the shop of Sid Ibrahim, the invoice seller in Sweiqa Ali. Najib, seeing flames falling all around and the earth shaking again, repeated that Judgment Day was here. Hayyim asked if Judgment Day was a game that grown-ups played with children. Najib was taken aback at Hayyim's lack of fear and his utter indifference to what was about to happen to them. He explained that they were on their way to the Day of Reckoning, where they would see God and He would ask them about their deeds. "Relax, we're going to Heaven," he promised, kicking Hayyim. But then he realized he didn't know if Jews went to Heaven, and a thought occurred to him: "You have to be Muslim if you want to get into Heaven with me." "How do I become Muslim?" asked Hayyim. Najib took hold of his finger, raised it to the sky, and said, "Close your eyes and repeat after me: *I testify that there is no God but God and Muhammad is His prophet.*" Hayyim obediently repeated the shahada three times. He opened his eyes, and Najib Bayazidi was watching him gleefully. "Now you can come to Heaven with me." Full of innocence, Hayyim asked, "Do people reach Heaven by sky or by earth?" Najib thought for a moment, looking at the houses sunk deep into the ground. He pointed to one and said, "These special tunnels will bring carriages from the center of the earth to the sky." For good measure, he added, "Golden carriages, like Raoul the gold-smith's. Isn't he your relative?" Hayyim shook his head. He used to see Raoul getting out of his carriage at the synagogue. The rabbi himself would come out to greet him, and the family was spoken about with great respect. Lots of men from the community went to his shop in Khan Al-Wazir when they needed help. Najib nodded to show that he understood and said, "Yes, my father says that he's a big benefactor among the Jews and pays an enormous jizya."

Both children eventually tired and returned to the courtyard of the Umayyad Mosque to sleep. They woke at dawn to the sound of the mu-ezzin reciting prayers. A group of men were exclaiming "Allahu Ak-bar" and weeping with deep emotion. Their city had been destroyed, and the plague was everywhere. They spoke of divine punishment as they passed close to the two children hiding in their corner. Najid and Hayyim realized they were in a predicament: they had become vagrants mining Aleppo's ruins for scraps to keep body and soul together. They no longer knew the way back to the gardens of Khan Touman, where the Bayazidi family had gone—they were staying in the small wooden house they had built in their garden while their large house stood empty. The children weren't too concerned that most of the city had fled; it was fun to spend all day playing and walking through the destroyed streets, and their high spirits never flagged. They observed the destroyed citadel tower and the surrounding buildings that had turned into debris. Soon they stopped counting the number of days they had spent absorbed in their wanderings. They only became wor-ried when they saw the caravans of people coming back, as if the city's inhabitants were returning from a holiday. Suddenly they registered the immensity of the tragedy, witnessing the continual howls, the sad faces, the sheikhs and priests and rabbis asking for alms, talking about the great plague and the need to burn the bodies so it wouldn't spread even further. Najib and Hayyim kept wandering through the narrow lanes, which now stank of lime and burned flesh. Finally Najib was able to reach his family home and burst into hot tears when he saw his mother sobbing. Young men, Najib's relatives, were helping his father to clear the rubble, which was sorely needed, although it was possible to live in what remained of the edifice. Two days later Najib's father took Hayyim by the hand and led him to the Jewish orphanage where he would live for the rest of his life. He had no one left in the city, and when he grew up, he turned from a resident into an employee, responsible for the kitchen and for recording the charitable gifts of benefactors in a special register.

The two friends remained close and would reminisce warmly about their explorations in the city's ruined lanes and recollect their thrilling adventures scavenging for food in the debris. Hayyim couldn't believe it when he learned that his friend Najib had died from a heart attack before he was sixty-five. They had planned on living a long time, like all the earthquake survivors. But Hayyim's strong relationship with the Bayazidi family continued through its children, especially Ahmed Bayazidi, who never forgot his duties of visiting Uncle Hayyim to check up on him and caring for Azar, the friend and schoolmate of his own son Zakariya. It caused Ahmed deep pain that Uncle Hayyim died before seeing his son become a great architect. His whole life, Hayyim had been obsessed with avoiding poverty and the smell of the orphanage. His work there helped him to insinuate himself among the great philanthropists by offering them small personal services. With the small sums they gave him in thanks, he was able to buy a spacious house in installments as an office for his son.

Azar wasn't pleased to be entangled with the construction of the citadel. He was content practicing his role with architectural rigor and became obsessed with designing huge public places. For a long time, he considered designing an opera house, and a public library: he reflected that Mount Jawshan, overlooking the city, would be an ideal place for this project. But deep down he felt a peculiar pleasure hearing his two friends discuss the platform for committing suicide, and the boxes of cast silver. Their strange ideas kept him awake at night; in particular, he thought long and hard about the labyrinth. He sketched it out several times, relishing the challenge of making it simple to enter the citadel and difficult to leave.

Many long years later Azar would spend hours reminiscing with his friend Souad about the sleeplessness of those days. He was afraid for his friends, concerned that they were planning their own suicides. Hanna's tales of chivalry among the lost and the bankrupt meant nothing to him. Hanna would recount these stories with relish, enthusiastically relating the story of an agha who had inherited a large village beside Maabtaly from his father. He changed its name to Medinat Al-Joury, the town of the damask rose, and intended to plant hundreds of dunums with roses and establish a perfume factory on the Rajo road. But he lost half his fortune in a single night of gambling, and when he went back to his village exhausted, he was struck with the desire to return to the gambling table once more. In three nights he lost everything: his house, his lands, his village, his wife. He didn't move from the table; he just took out his gun and shot himself in the temple. "He was a courageous man," Hanna concluded.

In their gatherings, the rich landowners would swap stories about chivalry, loss, and reversals of fortune. Hanna mourned courageous men (as he called them) who didn't have an agent and father like Ahmed Bayazidi to protect them from folly. Ahmed Bayazidi had taken steps to guard Hanna and Zakariya against bankruptcy by distributing wealth in different places, dividing it up so it couldn't be easily accessed, such as the bonds and shares of the Manchester Company Bank that he had bought for Hanna out of the income from his lands, and for Zakariya from his portion of the family inheritance that Ahmed Bayazidi had decided to distribute years before his death. He registered the family house in his daughter Souad's name but maintained the right to use it. A man who spent his life among notebooks and numbers, he was always planning for the worst and taking precautions against it.

On his few visits to Aleppo, Hanna would sleep in Um Waheed's house. He no longer wanted to go to his own house in Bab Al-Faraj, and Souad would besiege him with glances whenever he visited the

family home. At Um Waheed's, Shams Al-Sabah would lie down next
to him and listen while he told her imaginary images of the citadel to
come; she would embrace him like a small child, and they would fall
asleep while his worries stole into her heart. She avoided foolish questions by not asking him anything at all. Wary of being treated with
pity, she told him several times that she was strong, not some feeble
thing, even if she was poor and of unknown descent and lived in a
whorehouse run by a retired lady with a kind heart, whose dwindling
influence was little protection against being spat on in the street.

Alongside Hanna, Shams Al-Sabah dreamed of the citadel that
would transform into a kingdom of pleasure. Lovers would write their
stories on its walls, gamblers would lose all they possessed and hang
on their own gallows like knights, without regret. Hanna's passion for
the idea of the suicides made her bold enough to tell him about her
dream of building a dais especially for the men who would honor the
citadel with their graves, and whose coffins would be cast from pure
silver.

Hanna liked the idea of venerating the suicides but wasn't as keen
on burying them in the citadel. Pleasure was opposed to death, after all.
There would be a special place in the citadel for each taste, he told her,
and all the time he secretly feared he would be disappointed. He briefly
wondered whether Shams Al-Sabah was like any other woman—that
a man would lose interest after sex. Right now he couldn't stop seeking out her uniqueness. If he kept her a virgin, he was sure that he
wouldn't lose his passion for the softness of her fingers, the smell of
her chest that reminded him of a wilted mother. After several nights,
Hanna admitted to himself that Shams Al-Sabah's smell was like his
mother's, and that keeping her a virgin would mean he could hold on
to her for longer. But day after day Shams Al-Sabah was turning from
a girl of pleasure into a mother. He missed her when he was away, slept
in her lap like a little boy, and spoke to her for hours about Souad.

It was pouring rain when Hanna arrived alone to receive the key
to the citadel from the head builder. He hadn't wanted the company
of Azar, who still had a long list of tasks for the builders before they

could finish their contract; he didn't want even Zakariya to share the uniqueness of this moment. Hanna wandered the citadel for hours. He turned a deaf ear to the head builder, who was very proud of having completed the two-year project, and asked him to wait outside. Hanna saw his dreams embodied in front of him, in a tangled place that wouldn't reveal its secrets to anyone. It occurred to him, when he saw the hall of the suicides, that its circular design (suggested by William Michel Eisa) would delight Shams Al-Sabah. The room was open to the large garden that lay to the west, where orchards of walnut, cherry, and olive trees stretched out into the distance. He spent some time sitting in the hall where the citadel's currency would be minted, before carrying on to the bedrooms, the dining rooms, and the gaming room that overlooked the distant vineyard and the olive groves to the east. His idea had been that everyone should see the dawn from wherever they were sitting. He didn't forget to inspect the nearby stables, which he thought Zakariya would be pleased with. After many hours of meandering, he emerged from the citadel happily. He had successfully undertaken a singular project, something that would never have occurred to any of his frivolous friends, landowners, or aghas.

The head builder felt Hanna's satisfaction: he didn't dispute the figures and dealt generously with the workers, inviting them all to dinner at a showa' restaurant in Bab Al-Faraj and tipping them handsomely. His eyes moved constantly, taking in the seven faces, each one glowing with deep contentment. He bid them goodbye warmly, although his own face was pale from the sleeplessness that had gripped him for three nights.

In the early autumn, Hanna arrived at the citadel. He stood and read the large plaque on which was engraved "1897," and underneath it the names of the four friends: William Eisa, Zakariya Bayazidi, Hanna Gregoros, and Azar ibn Hayyim Istanbouli. It was a message to all that the best days of their friendship were those they passed in school.

Hanna closed the door of the citadel behind him. Shams Al-Sabah stopped arranging the bed. She had perfumed the place, lit a wall heater, and poured out two glasses of wine. She was ready for her new life. She expected that night to grant her virginity to the man who had allowed her to share his dream, but Hanna was content with touching her fingers, embracing her in bed, and sleeping deeply until morning.

Until his marriage in the spring of 1900, Hanna did the same thing every time he visited the citadel. He took his dinner in silence, waved to Shams Al-Sabah to go to bed ahead of him, put on his pajamas, and held her in his arms without touching her further, content with a few light kisses on her cheeks, and then he would tell her about Souad. In the beginning of their relationship, she didn't understand this in the slightest. He didn't wait for her to guess and informed her coolly that she would remain a virgin if she wanted to be queen of this place. Silence settled, along with a profound understanding between the two of them. Shams Al-Sabah thought of the desires that now had to die within her—then of the madness of a man who would strike coins for an invisible country that had no army or bureaucracy, and whose inhabitants were a collection of men engaged in frivolity and reckless spending. Now he wanted to turn her from a novice prostitute into a mother for these men who were ten years her senior. Into *his* mother, she realized: she was the one he entrusted with his story of secret love, which no one else knew. After she went to live in the citadel, Shams Al-Sabah felt enormous contentment when she opened the door to the hall of the suicides. In the end, she decided, she liked the idea of remaining a virgin. The hall, spacious and beautiful, was perfect for the suicides to come. She breathed in deeply and told herself that the suicides wouldn't object to being adored by a young virgin like her, because they didn't carry the same burdens as the living. But it also occurred to her that the hall might remain just an idea—no one would kill themselves in this place.

After the flood, Zakariya's nighttime vigils, sitting beside a sleeping Shaha, were often repeated. He would gaze at her, reflecting that their happiness had plunged to the bottom of the river. His sense of things changed. Hanna didn't come as promised, and Zakariya was uneasy about leaving his lifelong friend alone in the desolate village.

He decided to go back again, determined not to return unless Hanna was with him. When he reached Hosh Hanna and entered Hanna's room, he didn't recognize him. Hanna looked like a beggar. His usually orderly room was filthy; the plates of food were moldy, and his bed stank of stale sweat. Hanna was sleeping on the ground, curled up in a corner. When Zakariya came in, Hanna looked up at him but didn't stand. Zakariya lay down on the bed without changing his clothes. He was tired. He slept for hours, and when he woke up, it was the middle of the night. He heard Hanna tell him that a new passion was growing in his heart. Zakariya went back to sleep, and Hanna sat in his usual place on the wooden chair all night, watching the emergence of dawn, the movement of the breeze, and the current of the river. He ignored the bodies that the river still hurled onto its banks from time to time—there were still many things in its belly. No one was looking for a loved one's body anymore, and there were no longer any places to confirm the identity of the drowned. More than a month had passed, and the flood was consigned to history.

Catching the bodies that the river tossed up gave Zakariya an excuse to stay close to Hanna. They spoke little. Hanna had always avoided long conversations. Since their childhood, he hadn't liked discussing anything that forced him to say more than five words at a time. So he needed Zakariya to stay close, but he didn't want to talk. He was feeling his new passion grow every day that passed. Zakariya would wake up in the morning, leave his friend alone in his room, and go outside. He walked alongside the river, catching the bodies that the river spat out onto its banks, and with the help of the fellahin and the fishermen, he would bury them and record their features, if the body still retained any. He numbered graves, stopped people from imposing on the new life of his friend Hanna, and undertook the facilitation of their pressing financial business.

He forced Hanna out of the room and ordered the servant to clean it and change the bedsheets. Zakariya was resolute. He didn't want anyone to take advantage of Hanna's moments of weakness, but the servant told him that his master hadn't allowed anyone inside for almost three weeks. He reeled off a list of the names of their friends who had come to offer their condolences, but Hanna wouldn't receive anyone except Arif Sheikh Musa Agha, who arrived crying like a small child, as he did the first time the news of the flood reached him, repeating the names *Ahmed, Josephine, Gabriel*. Arif was sympathetic and sensitive. He mentioned that on the children's last visits, he had taught them lots of Kurdish words, and the previous summer he had taken them to his house in Sharran so they could play in the vast meadows with his son Yousef. The children had come back three weeks later, full of Kurdish phrases, swapping curses, and giggling. It delighted Josephine and Shaha, who had begun to teach them the language.

Zakariya knew that no one could evade Arif—he would simply shoot the door open. The servant's excuses didn't convince Zakariya, but he wondered whether Hanna wanted to drown in putrescence. In childhood he used to punish himself whenever he committed an act he considered repulsive. He would disappear into the cellar, where he would sleep in mouse droppings and talk in a low voice like the meow of a cat. He would demand to be left alone and repeat his well-known phrase: no one in this world loved him. Souad, all innocence, would say, "But I love you, very much." Hanna would look at her and say, "Only you love me." She would steal some food for him and wouldn't tell anyone where he was. She considered it a perilous mission and always said that keeping secrets was hard, but committing to that practice makes us unique: we hate gossip and become more sincere.

Nine months passed after the flood. Hanna never went to Aleppo. Shams Al-Sabah asked Zakariya for permission to see him. He ignored her request at first and tried to dissuade her, thinking that he must go back to his life, but she was determined and agreed to Zakariya's condition that she see him only once, and from a distance. In the end, Zakariya decided that he needed the help of others to recover Hanna.

When Zakariya brought Shams Al-Sabah to Hosh Hanna, she saw Hanna looking out the window toward the remains of the village. He was a different person, someone she didn't know at all. He had become a very beautiful man and no longer seemed anxious. He was thinner and taller; he had lost a lot of weight. To her, he looked like an angel in the window frame. She sat on a rock to watch him, and at that moment she decided that she must see him and touch him, whatever the cost.

She took advantage of a temporary absence of Zakariya's and walked resolutely toward Hanna's room. Hanna was contemplating the shadow of the small trees that were growing again, their branches bursting into a charming green. Shams Al-Sabah had brought some clothes he used to like: blue silk pajamas, a blue shirt trimmed with lace, and a long cotton thobe she had woven him on the small loom that she had set up in the corner of the servants' hall to pass the time during the appalling vacuum of spring and summer, when Hanna and his guests went to inspect their properties, busied themselves with their family lives and the harvest, and traveled to Europe.

Shams Al-Sabah climbed the stairs leading to his door. She felt a terrible weight, as if she were dragging an iron lump in her feet. She thought of going back and giving up any idea of seeing him, but she was resolved to walk on, slowly. She knew on some level that it was the last time she would see him. She carried on steadily, staring up at the hill. She remembered stories of the toils of believers who throw resentment from their hearts on their journey to lessen the burdens of this world, losing a piece of their bodies. The path of the faithful is long, and when they reach the point of lightness and see the face of God inscribed on their deepest selves, they feel themselves dissolving into the vastness of the universe, becoming part of the heavenly bodies, a mote of dust from the moon, or a leaf on an olive tree that never loses its verdure. Deep within, she sensed another destiny lay in wait for her, concealed at the top of this hill which, slowly and doggedly, she finished climbing.

She reached the door, knocked, and waited. No one opened. She knocked again and heard his trudging footsteps. Hanna opened the door, and she stepped back, watching him for a moment, ready to be turned away. At that moment, he was the most beautiful man she had ever seen in her life. His eyes gleamed with contentment, and his body was slender, missing the deposits of fat that he had accumulated in recent years, which made him incline toward plumpness. At last he allowed her inside and embraced her tightly. Shams Al-Sabah passed out. All her remaining years, she tried to describe that moment but couldn't. Once she said it was like a slash of lightning in a rainy sky, and another time she said it was like the peacefulness of a corpse in the first slump of the eyelids after the soul has leaked out of the body. Eventually she stopped trying to describe it, saying, "What I went through then is impossible to express."

She threw herself onto his chest again. She had missed his embrace and wept silently. He closed the door behind her and resumed watching the sunset. She told him that Zakariya had prevented her from seeing him, and he replied that it had been at his own wish, but now he was happy she was there. The silence returned, heavy, between them. She sat down on a rug and watched his every movement. It really was a new life, she thought. He no longer cared for material things—had been freed from them, in fact.

Zakariya was furious with Shams Al-Sabah, but Hanna assured him that he had welcomed her and now wanted her to stay. He didn't ask her about her life, and he didn't care about hearing a list of the friends who had inquired after him at the citadel and offered to refurnish it to welcome him back. "Don't you miss the citadel?" she asked. He was silent, then lay on his bed and asked her to hold him. His scent was different, like a blend of fragrant plants. He fell asleep on her chest, and she held him as she used to. She decided that she hadn't lost him, but somewhere inside she realized that he would never live at the citadel again. His soul had gone wandering. Shams Al-Sabah had been incredulous when Zakariya explained that this level land filled with mud had once been the village of Hosh Hanna, and Zakariya no less so when Hanna asked her to stay with him.

She got up in the night and looked out the window. The world was silent and the river was bewitching as it ran along quietly. Faint lights glowed from the lanterns of the distant fishermen who were casting their nets. Dawn was approaching. She went back to bed and lay down next to Hanna. She hardly dared admit after all these years that to her, he was a different man from the Hanna she had once known, and she was no longer his mother. Hanna touched her breasts, took off her clothes, and kissed her for the first time, on her nipples. She reached for his sex, which was swelling and rising hard, and she felt its veins softly; she surrendered. She was crying silently when he entered her. This happiness had been delayed for more than ten years. She refused to let this opportunity pass her by; he was the lover she had been waiting for, for so long. He entered her in the peace of that dawn, unfastening her locks and opening the doors to another life whose shape she didn't know but that she desperately, shamelessly, deeply wanted. She felt none of the pain at losing her virginity that she had heard of from other women. A few drops of blood fell onto the sheet, and she fainted from the excess of sudden pleasure.

Shams Al-Sabah woke up less than an hour later. She got up, washed, changed the bedsheet, and lay down next to Hanna once more as dawn slipped through the window. He entered her again, and she was jabbering his name, moaning, squirming beneath him. She let him lead her wherever he wanted, and do to her body whatever he wished. His desires were strong, and he came in her more than once, which gave her a strange comfort. Images of the past years became mixed up, the hundreds of nights he had slept on her chest, when she had killed her feelings so that he could be her son. And now Hanna was shattering the solid, inviolable walls he had built between them over the years. His face was radiant, as if he had been thinking about her body for years.

Those nights were repeated over their first week. He slept with her every night, and she discovered pleasure for the first time, but Hanna didn't talk to her. He really thought he was no longer interested in sex, he felt intensely bored. In the second week, he kept remembering his mother. He described her white face and her tall frame, her large breasts. He was silent as he remembered her scent. He couldn't find anything that came close to expressing what his mother's scent meant to him. He said suddenly, "Like the scent of this dawn." He got up from the bed, washed, put on the cotton thobe that Shams Al-Sabah had brought him, opened the window, and resumed watching the dawn from his chair. The colors still dazzled him, red interwoven with yellow light. He thought that a new color was born every moment, and each new dawn was completely unlike the one that had died the day before. The taste of Shams Al-Sabah, to him, was also unlike the taste of any other woman. True, he no longer venerated her. He had ravished her virginity, and she would never be his mother again. But still, she wasn't like other women. Her skin was soft, and her black hair hung thick and glorious over her shoulders, just as he remembered from his old dreams of her. He thought for a moment that he might go down the steps, walk all the way to the citadel, marry Shams Al-Sabah, and have ten children with her. He would take earth and fill up the cellar for the suicides. After all, no one had ever committed suicide on his platform—it had just remained an idea.

Images of his future children invaded his daydreams in the third week. At the same time, he felt unparalleled triviality. It attacked him, stuck its tongue out at him, while bringing him back to the truth that he had discovered in contemplating the other lives of plants and animals and the vast universe. He said to himself that children were not like flowers, and men and women were merely troublesome fleas flying over the surface of the great river.

Hanna knew that now Shams Al-Sabah could live like any other woman. He had freed her from her promise to keep her virginity, and she had never planned to stay in the citadel if Hanna didn't return to her. She had everything she needed, and he would protect her from having to beg for work in some brothel. She had grown up at his side, she was almost thirty now, and she felt the full impact of having broken her virginity oath. She wouldn't be angry with him, but it wasn't easy to escape more than a decade of memories.

In the fourth week of her stay, Hanna refused to sleep with her. He left the bed to her and took to the ground, and she watched him all night until he fell asleep. His face glistened with sweat, and it was clear that he was suffering from continual nightmares. He smiled and frowned in his sleep, then flapped his hand as if he were getting rid of a fly, or as if imaginary ticks were stuck to his skin. Eventually he relaxed in his sleep, breathing regularly, and disentangled himself from his aba'. He would wake before dawn, and she would still be looking at him with the same zealous affection as she had whenever he was ill, and he would slide in next to her in the bed of his own room at the citadel.

On her last night, in the middle of October, the first downpour began. She felt that everything around her had revived, despite the deadly silence he had imposed on her for the last two weeks—he had been so distant in his transformation. The rain shower turned into a powerful storm. Suddenly Hanna got up from where he had been sleeping on the ground and slipped into her body. He was trembling with fear: the lightning illuminated the large room, and the thunder never stopped. It was like the night of the flood: the sky was shadowy, and the sound of pouring rain brought back his sense of loss. Shams Al-Sabah didn't waste this opportunity: she craved him. She undressed him and kissed his body and his sex, she made love as if he were going to get up from her bed and hang his noose with his own hand and die. She wanted to bid him goodbye for the last time, or open the door to their new life. All night she was intoxicated. The thunder and lightning only intensified her lust and his fear. She wanted to purify his body from the scent of those other countless women. The murmurings of their pleasure and their ecstasy rose and mixed with the sounds of the storm, which didn't die down until daybreak.

They lay together in their bed. When Hanna woke in the afternoon, Zakariya had arrived, but there was no Shams Al-Sabah next to him. She had left. He remembered that he had asked her to go back to the citadel. He stood up and wandered around the room. He asked the servant to clean the place thoroughly and went for a walk along the riverbank. Hanna felt that he had crossed the barzakh, and his soul could no longer bear squalor. Deep down, he felt his misery again. He bathed and threw away the clothes that Shams Al-Sabah had brought.

Perfectly happy with his mat, he no longer slept in the bed itself. He needed several days to forget what had happened, to return to taking in the smells of the river and the flowers that were growing this autumn. And when flocks of birds began to leave for other climes, his heart felt as if it had been reborn. It was the world that he wanted to cross over to and settle in, and the distance between the two banks was like the path of agony that Jesus had walked to reach his cross.

That night he was assailed by the memory of Josephine. When he had first seen her, it hadn't taken him long to decide that this tall girl, who prayed in church every Sunday and volunteered in all its charitable projects, would make a suitable wife. He liked her ascetism and the frank sadness in her eyes. And although her father wasn't a rich man, he had a good reputation.

Hanna approached her and said he liked her and was thinking of marrying her. His boldness shocked her, but secretly she already had a great deal of respect for him. He was somewhat notorious, and scandalous stories about him circulated among all the families of the city, but he was very generous to those in need and didn't abase himself to the patriarch or the vali and his men. He stated his opinions plainly, never lied, and didn't evade his responsibilities. Ultimately he was a brave, straightforward man, despite his dissolute life and the strange tales of women. She invited him to speak to her family, feeling as though she might collapse after these few words. She didn't complete her prayers and withdrew unusually early, but before she left, she glanced at him and smiled with a sadness that only enhanced her beauty, even though her knees were shaking. She couldn't believe what had just happened.

That same night Hanna asked Ahmed Bayazidi and Zakariya to go with him to ask for the hand of Josephine Laham. They arrived at the house of Joseph Laham at seven o'clock precisely. (Ahmed Bayazidi believed in the importance of being punctual.) As usual, Hanna left all the details to Ahmed Bayazidi, who was overjoyed that Hanna had chosen an alliance with a respectable man who thought of Hanna as an uncontested bridegroom. In later years Hanna discovered a hidden side to this man's personality. A great haggler, he plotted big projects and managed his properties in a different manner than his peers among the greedy landowners. He was committed to recognizing the thinkers of the city, supporting their projects of publishing newspapers (especially those that the Ottoman authorities had closed down), and opening clubs. His name was always mentioned next to the rich patrons of most of the liberal projects in the city. This image made him very popular, equally so among Christians, Muslims, and Jews, and they would often recount his attacks on the narrow horizons of men of religion. When donating to orphanages, he made no distinction in his material support whether it was intended for Muslims, Christians, or Jews. Meanwhile his unconcealed hatred for the Turks and the Ottomans made him popular with the nationalists who called for secession from the Ottoman Empire. They wanted to claim independence in order to become part of Europe, which was flourishing and whose ideas reached every corner of the world.

Joseph was a proofreader and editor for the newspaper *Al-Medina*, which belonged to a troop of minor public officials, and his passion for reading and studying manuscripts made him an important authority for thinkers, historians, and foreign enthusiasts who were interested in the history of Aleppo. He agreed with Hanna in many of his ideas and was confident that he would be a respectable husband for his daughter and wouldn't make her a mere servant. Ahmed Bayazidi required no prelude—he came straight to the point and asked for Josephine's hand, beginning a discussion of the jihaz and the marriage contract. Everything was easy, as it was Joseph Laham's policy not to ask honorable men details regarding their private lives. Within a few minutes, the zagharit rose from Joseph Laham's house to announce news of the engagement, which spread around every house in the city that same night.

A few weeks later Hanna and Josephine Laham were married in a simple wedding. After the ceremony, they attended a banquet that had been prepared for them by Zakariya at his father's house, and then the couple spent their wedding night in their apartment in Bab Al-Faraj.

They stayed there for a few days, receiving congratulations from friends and family, before heading to their house in Hosh Hanna. The servants had needed to work tirelessly to hide the traces of past nights of debauchery from the large house: the shoes, the women's underwear, and all the other remnants of Hanna's rowdy all-night parties. They lit incense in every corner to expel the perfumes of the dancers. Mariana didn't join in the party of the house's renewal and secluded herself in her family home. She felt tormented yet secretly satisfied at her defeat, as long as Souad Bayazidi, "that arrogant girl" as she called her, had lost Hanna as well.

On the way to Hosh Hanna, Hanna replied to Josephine's questions. He didn't equivocate and he didn't lie, and when she broached the topic of the citadel, he asked her to forget that place forever and fell silent. Josephine didn't understand what he meant. She was silent too and decided to consider the citadel nonexistent, as far as she was concerned.

Josephine felt liberated in the small village. She loved the life of the fellahin, she grew close to Mariana despite the girl's initial hostility, and she helped her teach the children. She looked after the affairs of the small church and listened attentively to the priest. She never waited to be asked to help meet the needs of poorer families, having always believed that the wound of pride was something that had no connection whatsoever with Christian morals. And she understood without a fuss that Shaha, as Zakariya's wife, was a fate she couldn't escape. But when she got to know her, she found in Shaha a wonderful companion who became her dear friend. She liked Shaha's savage temper, her limitless generosity, and her great experience in the ways of the world, and so Josephine let her arrange their lives as she liked.

Hanna enjoyed his marital bliss for a few months, then fled the house and resumed his trips and his pursuit of his shameless ways. Josephine didn't care. She felt instinctively that her husband was utterly shameless, but he was generous, and that was a quality she felt bound to respect in a man. He didn't probe too closely into things as other men did, which often made married life an unbearable hell. Instead, she could say, "This is my kingdom." All these fields, the great river, life far away from the slander and gossip of the families in the city. Deep down, she felt that in the end, he would come home.

Josephine was an ascetic in the matter of possessions. She didn't dispute the details of the jihaz and was content with a few thobes and a simple wedding dress from the collection of Madame Hassaniya. Souad was determined to sew it herself, and she helped Josephine select the rest of the items for the jihaz. Like Josephine, she couldn't care less what the city would say when they saw the small number of bags leaving the Laham family home. Souad offered herself to Josephine as a member of Hanna's family, and she displayed great enthusiasm for his wedding to a girl she regarded as miserable and abstinent. Souad had lost her last hope that Hanna would come back to her, and now she was determined to turn the page and to focus on her own life. He had to experience misery in order to be happy. She started to entertain the marriage proposals her father had put to her, stipulating only that his assistant Orhan and anyone from the family be excluded. Ahmed Bayazidi agreed—he hadn't wanted Orhan as a son-in-law anyway, having no desire for his daughter to live with a family of accountants. Their lives were dull, as regimented as the lines in their ruled ledgers. Still, convincing Souad of a fiancé wasn't easy. Her soul was crushed, and she wouldn't grant her body to a man who would be unable to expel Hanna from her depths.

After the flood, Zakariya returned to the family home, which was no longer used to his presence. The house, unusually, was neglected: the servant Margot had died, and Souad had negotiated with the family of their other maid, Um Kheir, tempting them with substantial compensation to take her away and care for her. Souad pointed out that she was going to get married, and there would be no one left in the house apart from her father. Souad succeeded in her negotiations, and Um Kheir moved to live with her nephew in a village close to Hama. Souad dismissed her father's anger when he discovered Um Kheir's absence; she argued that he could very easily make do with someone to clean the house and cook for him twice a week. Souad was preparing to marry Hassan Masabny in two weeks, and in a few days she would be thirty-three years old. Previously, everyone had given up the idea that any rational man would come to this city to ask for her hand—she had missed the boat. But she had always been sure she could determine the moment of her marriage herself. Men were all the same to her; she could find any one of them to fulfill this role. Her sufferings on Hanna's account were plenty for her. For Hanna's part, he had thought that his marriage would put an end to his desire for Souad, but he thought only of their unhappiness. She had him in a chokehold, and her fingerprints were all over his married life. When Josephine came to his bed, he knew that it was Souad who had guided her toward those openwork stockings and that nightshirt, who had pointed out that perfume to her. Neither of them could escape the other. She missed him and would wait for his carriage to pass underneath Sitt Hassaniya's atelier. She would watch it sway and rock slowly when it reached the neighborhood, and then she would see him get down and enter her family's house. He would be waiting for her below, but she refused to come. She was used to this pain. The few times he had come to the house unannounced, she treated him like a stranger; she was harsh, she wouldn't let him slink to her room like old times. She started to disavow their childhood as a boring story that no one would laugh at, should they even recall it.

On his last visit, two months before the flood, Souad told Hanna that he should treat her like a woman and a forsaken lover. She couldn't care less about moral justifications or fear of any sect. She spoke to him sternly, half afraid that he would be emboldened to grab her by the hair, fling her on the bed, and unceremoniously enter her. She always thought that she wouldn't fight him if that happened, she would simply surrender to those delicate hands she adored, but instead he would merely stand in front of her like a man robbed of his will. He enjoyed it when she raised her voice and insulted him to his face, listing all the ways in which he was a coward. He was intoxicated when she reached the point of talking about the bravery of William Eisa, who had undertaken an extraordinary feat, unlike Hanna, Zakariya, or even

Azar, who had married a Jewish girl whom Souad often described as stupid and lice-ridden, disregarding the fact she was the daughter of Raoul the goldsmith. Azar had married her because of sect, and because her father had helped him in his studies and afterward in establishing his practice. Souad was furious with Azar for marrying such a mousy girl. Souad remembered her well from the days when they sat next to each other in French classes, because she smelled of open drains. Hanna reflected on Souad's habits of expression. She loved and hated to the utmost degree, and her strength of feeling for her beloved friend Azar made her unwilling to accept any possible bride for him. They were all beneath his astuteness, his self-respect, his talent, which she described as "genius." The two of them had maintained a distinctive relationship since childhood. He would tell her every last one of his secrets, and before he went to Rome, he told her that he was humiliated to be the recipient of charity. His entire education had been financed by benefactors, and now he was traveling to Rome, and those same benefactors were shoving money into his pocket, just enough for cheese, tea, and a little food. She sympathized with him and understood how he felt. Instead she would go overboard in presents to him, sending shirts and trousers and suits to Rome, rather than putting any money in his pockets. To Azar, Souad was more than a patron or a sister. She sent him long letters cursing Hanna, who felt nothing for her, and Zakariya, who had pushed his friend into marrying a Christian girl. She described the city for Azar in his absence and wrote that she was waiting for him, that Aleppo without him was no better than a discarded onion peel.

Hanna knew his story with Souad would never be over. Even while she was preparing for her marriage, she didn't forget to give exhaustive lessons and precise instructions to Josephine, who trusted her and visited three times a year to renew her underwear and nightwear, all of which Souad chose. The shy Josephine listened closely as Souad instructed her on what she could do to keep her husband and make his life with other women a thing of the past. Josephine obediently learned to walk seductively on her way to bed. She faithfully repeated after Souad that men like Hanna wanted a whore in bed who would turn into an angel as she offered up breakfast and supervised the details of domestic life with a soldier's rigor. Men were reassured by women who dealt stringently with household matters.

Josephine would nod in agreement, but her shyness prevented her from doing any of this, and the provocative nightdresses remained folded away like cold shrouds. After her first son Gabriel was born, Josephine no longer cared for Souad's pronouncements on sex and happiness. She neglected her appearance, and like any other good housewife, she spent all day thinking about the Messiah and a life of virtue. She looked after her husband and his many and expensive things, his suits that were tailored by his own tailor, Monsieur George, who served only a small number of select clients. Monsieur George picked out various fabrics for them and made no bones of his opinions of the fashion fads that arrived in Aleppo via the city's foreign residents and the European fashion magazines that had begun to appear in the libraries. A constant fixture at the parties given by the European consuls, George used to say, "Why travel if all the world is coming to Aleppo, the capital of it all?" He had a flair for bold and unusual cuts and had no scruples about approaching any man wearing a suit he liked, asking him where he had had it made, and examining the fabric. His bonhomie put party guests at ease with his scrutiny of their clothes, and his modern ideas aroused admiration. He once criticized a well-known French tailor because the pocket of the French consul's suit clashed with the color of the material, but whenever he felt he was in an awkward position, he would simply change the topic of conversation to food. He would drift among the guests, glass in hand, offering his services gratis. Many large deals were struck between clients that he introduced to each other at one of his private dinner parties at the luxurious house in Farafra that he had retained, although Christians were moving from the inner neighborhoods of Aleppo to the neighborhood of Aziziya, and the Jews were moving to Jamiliyya.

After Hanna's wedding, the house no longer meant anything to

Souad. She spent most of her time in the atelier of her neighbor Madame Hassaniya, who taught her everything about tailoring and the
rapture of fashion design. Souad didn't like the prospective bridegrooms who came in quick succession to ask for her hand—she refused
even to see them. She asked her father to put a stop to Orhan, his Turkish assistant at the Ottoman Bank who followed her everywhere. He
wrote her letters and slipped them under the door of her room every
Friday morning when he visited his mentor to play chess. He sent
gifts to Sitt Hassaniya, hoping she would set up a meeting for him.
He dispatched a Jewish girl to curry favor with Souad and invite her
to her house, but Souad understood what was going on—she grabbed
the girl by the collar, spat in her face, and asked her to take her message back to Orhan. Souad declared he stank of mold and compared
him to a randy billy goat. She didn't read his letters and threw them
straight into a box with the rest of the tokens from her many admirers, the boys who would block her path and stuff them into her hand
while she walked on, not paying them the slightest attention. She no
longer waited for Hanna to come back to her but didn't want anyone
to occupy his place. She believed that love came only once, and anything else would be just a faint echo of it.

When Hassan Masabny came forward to ask for her hand after
the flood, he didn't block her path or send intermediaries to Sitt Hassaniya. He came out of his factory in Arqoub one afternoon, having
thought about Souad for months. He knocked on her father's door and
got straight to the point. Then he asked Souad whether she accepted
or would refuse, as usual. He didn't want to drag things out over the
next day, and so he requested a quick answer and concluded by saying time was short. Souad accepted without hesitation. She knew him
well: he was a boaster and talked with self-importance. Occasionally
he translated articles from English to flaunt that he was a worldly man
conversant with the latest writings from around the globe. He was an
intimate of the successive valis who controlled the city, and his family was a favorite with the Topkapi Palace; some of its members had
reached lofty positions in the sultanate. She liked the duplicity and

confusion created by his contradictory, ragtag collection of opinions. He would praise Arab nationalism but also wasted no opportunity to praise Sultan Abdel Hamid II and argue for a revival of the elevated ideals of the Ottoman Empire. He would donate to religious extremists who openly attacked Christians and Jews and demanded the return of the jizya tax, which used to be imposed on every Christian or Jew in the empire in order for them to maintain their religions. And at the same time, he subscribed to liberal, independent newspapers that attacked the empire's policies and called for the separation of religion and state.

Souad's acceptance shocked Ahmed Bayazidi. She had never admired shallow men, and she didn't trust this type of bumptious arrogance. Souad, meanwhile, was resolved not to give Hanna any cause for regret. She reflected that her decision to marry Hassan Masabny, a widower nearing sixty, would make Hanna think that Souad was still waiting for him.

Souad agreed with everything that the Masabny family suggested. She didn't argue the finer details of the jihaz; she had lost all enthusiasm for fine things. The flood, the 'aza, the death of her nephew along with Josephine and her son were offered up as a pretext for her behavior and accepted at face value by the Masabny family, who considered the wedding a declaration of influence and an opportunity to parade their wealth and power via relationships with statesmen. They were suggesting that the bridal residence be in Istanbul and that Sultan Abdel Hamid II make a personal appearance at the wedding of their son to give it his blessing.

Despite being absorbed in wedding arrangements, Souad tried to alleviate Shaha's suffering, which was making her increasingly worried. Shaha would wander the large house like a madwoman, and she believed that if she drowned in her dreams, she would inevitably die in reality. The faces of the dead leaked into her memories, and she simply couldn't believe what had happened. She missed Josephine, her dear friend. She left the house suddenly and appeared at the Syriac Catholic Church, looking for Mariana so she could ask her if it was true that all her neighbors and their children were dead. On hearing Mariana's response, she fell silent and asked again about Josephine and Gabriel, whose dainty movements she had loved when he imitated a galloping horse for her. She asked again about Yvonne, who had preferred to stay at her aunt's house in Aleppo. Shaha wept silently. She believed that the fishermen who had saved her had stolen her son—he hadn't drowned at all. Mariana was gentle and affectionate as she attended to her guest in the churchyard. The scars of loss had infiltrated Shaha's soul. She was going to lose her sanity, and kind words would be of no use to her. Mariana listened in silence until Shaha got up and left the church suddenly, without saying goodbye. She struggled to breathe, wandering the streets without caring that she was lost, or that men were staring at her and harassing her. She didn't know the way back to Ahmed Bayazidi's house, but she would mention the name to a carriage driver who would take her there and consign her to the care of Souad, who opened the door, paid the drivers, and never warned her brother's wife against getting lost again. She knew that no one could console a woman who had lost her son, her place, her bed that she loved.

Shaha stayed in bed for days at a time, making no reply to Ahmed Bayazidi's invitations to join him for dinner, or Souad's invitations to accompany her to the souq. She ignored her brother Arif, who asked her to come and eat with him at his house. She lost weight, and her face grew pale as an old owl's. Zakariya wasn't able to extricate his remaining family and friends from the disaster; they had all shattered. He asked Hanna to pick himself up off the floor and go back to his life that was waiting for him. Hanna listened, then asked Zakariya to leave him alone and take care of Shams Al-Sabah, who had left that morning. He didn't explain much of what had happened. When Zakariya asked, "Why didn't you let her stay near you?" Hanna replied, "I have been shattered."

After Shams Al-Sabah left, and Hanna woke at noon to find Zakariya beside him, he felt guilty; he had missed the dawn because of a woman. Now he would regain the freedom and solitude he loved. He went out in the afternoon and saw that Zakariya was upset that Hanna didn't look back at his friend—from the corner of his eye, Hanna saw his body was shaking from his sobs. *Yes, we have all been shattered*, Hanna repeated to himself as he continued with his solitary walk on the riverbank. He gathered some interesting plants, avoided people, sat down between a couple of nearby gravestones. He assumed they were the graves of Josephine and his son Gabriel. He felt a strange peace during the few hours he spent in the graveyard. Scenes from his life with Josephine and Gabriel came back to him. He missed trivial moments, those saturated with the decay of contentment. Josephine's attempts to seduce him always used to make him laugh: halfway through her performance, she would be shy and embarrassed, and she would flee his sight and go back to being that pious woman whom the Messiah had ordered to obey her husband. After Gabriel was born, she was suddenly transformed into a mother. Her breasts were full of milk, her face was innocent, her body smelled of affection. It was the kingdom of contentment that she had sought all her life. She was satisfied with Hanna's touches when he slept in her bed. He liked doing his marital duty and causing no harm to her transparent, rapturous soul.

The day after Shams Al-Sabah's departure, Hanna felt the softness of silence again. Pleasant breezes returned, the storm receded, and damp air came to him on the river. He went back to sitting in his favorite place by the window to watch the migration of the birds, then getting up wearily to go to bed. He would no longer shut the door in anyone's face—for him, they were merely transitory and their faces sparked no comprehension or feeling in him. They had become part of his past, which had begun to die, to be erased, and to drain out of his memory. The flood had destroyed his old life completely. New wishes gushed out between his ribs. He groped for them despite their vagueness, the vocabulary of a different life. His body became more vital, his heart more refined. Deep in thought, he reflected that dying wasn't so bad, as long as it didn't happen by drowning—he couldn't forget the faces of the drowned. Surely death wasn't always so malicious. The form of it changes from one way to another: it isn't enough for the heart to merely stop beating. Hanna thought about how people die choked with water, and he wished he had never seen Josephine and Gabriel's bodies. The drowned retain their essence from life, and Josephine had looked like the girl he had seen standing in the rows of worshippers, the woman he had approached and told he was thinking of marrying her, that same kind, pious face. Over Gabriel's face there hovered the severity of the grandfather whose name he bore. Every day he had grown into a miniature of his grandfather, a man Hanna hadn't known well. And so his son Gabriel was mixing the pages of his life: through his son, Hanna began to get closer to his father, to feel affection toward him. He was no longer that greedy, cruel man who spent half his life afraid that accountants and builders would steal his money and made frequent visits to Ahmed Bayazidi so that he could review every detail of his ledgers. Gabriel Gregoros didn't really believe that he would die one day, even as he waited perpetually for the massacre that would kill him, as Father Ibrahim had told Hanna. At the moment of his death, he was still planning several projects. Monopoly over the Aleppo-Mardin-Erbil trade line wasn't enough for him; he also dreamed of steamships going around the world bearing his company's mark.

Painful memories returned to Hanna, memories of overheard conversations and his father's papers, the symbols in which Hanna had spent three months deciphering. He had felt the misery of the whole world weighing upon him after he finished reviewing the final notebook. All they contained were figures, skeptical remarks about the trustworthiness of his agents, and musings about unfinished projects. There wasn't a single word about Hanna, his four siblings, or his mother, who, their servant Margot said, had taken a wrong turn: instead of going to Deir Za'faran and joining the nuns, she had married Gabriel Gregoros.

Hanna often remembered the day he discovered his mother's likeness in Shams Al-Sabah. Josephine was his mother's other face. Josephine surrounded herself and her children with amulets and saw the Christ Child fluttering over her blessings. Full of extraordinary joy, she told Hanna with a smile that faith had driven out all fear of death. He had looked with some sorrow at this woman who had surrendered to the blessing of death before she was even thirty. Despite her contentment, Hanna always used to think of her as miserable.

Hanna resembled them now, when he talked about death. He could see it, and it felt near. He didn't hate it. Instead, he focused on the full magnificence of the olive trees as they blossomed in his fields, and he recalled his astonishment at the beauty of the wild pomegranate flowers that he had seen in a meadow belonging to his friend Arif Sheikh Musa Agha. He used to wake early in the morning after a long night of debauchery and walk in the field around the large house, pushing his face into the pomegranate blossoms to inhale their scent, and in those moments he felt deeply happy. He felt as if he were joining them in the act of splitting open and turning into a small fruit that was growing every instant, never stopping. He used to think the pomegranate grew at night, and it would occur to him to leave his evening card tables and take his drink outside to examine the small pomegranate as it grew—but before long he was back to his amorous ardor, drowning in women's bodies. As he examined their nipples, which looked like pomegranate flowers, he reflected that women always share certain secrets with plants.

He liked the moments of spirituality that a woman's slender body would inspire in him, when he would reflect that she would age and her skin would wither, just like the pomegranate blossom that lasted till the end of the season without being picked. His memory came back to him, weighted with apprehensions. He simply couldn't believe in his own contentment, something he didn't dare express in front of the pious Josephine, who would always tell him that they had more than they needed, and he should try to extricate himself from the burden of his ever-increasing possessions. He believed her and understood the frequent donations she made to churches, charitable endeavors, and Mariana.

Meanwhile Josephine's happiness was tangible to him when she would watch the village children in the morning, carrying their slates on their way to school. And yet she was shy when the priest praised her to passing priests. Hanna didn't understand this kind of joy; he couldn't believe that a girl like her thought of others more than herself. She considered her life to be safe, and so it had to be offered up in the service of Jesus of Nazareth whose icons filled the walls of the house, along with paintings that the village schoolchildren had made, and even some from passing artists who knew her passion. They knocked on her door and sold her their hideous paintings, but for her it was enough that the painter had thought about the Messiah, even if only briefly.

From the window of his room, Hanna could see the shapes of the birds as they sought out warmer places. He compared their migration at the beginning of winter and their return in early spring, reflecting that birds had a homeland just like people and grieved when they left it. He thought that people, if they turned into birds, would become less brutal and selfish. If they lost language, they would become more tolerant, and less spiteful and mean-spirited.

He returned to his room at night and realized the error of allowing Shams Al-Sabah to visit him. The world he had escaped over the previous months had come back to him. He tore it up piece by piece and threw it off his shoulders, he hurled it into the fire blazing inside him that consumed thousands of images, people, ideas, and feelings, turning them all to ash.

The first night after Shams Al-Sabah left was hard. Hanna wept bitterly and was struck with his old anxiety. Images of her overlapped with images of the dozens of girls and madams who had passed through his life. Over the following days, he reflected that he had loved their surroundings more than the girls themselves: the damp air in their houses, the signs and their meanings, the smells, companions who weren't shy. The brothel-keepers and their charges didn't understand his nature very well and would often think at first that they had found the end of their quest in him. Hanna understood their desire—after all, they were women with long histories in the service of powerful men—but he didn't fit that role. He didn't want to stay in one place, sleep in one house, live in one time. He was in love with living in two times and two places and roaming among the houses of his friends. He was never tempted by a fixed address.

Before marrying Josephine, he hadn't lived alone. His large house was filled with the clamor of his friends; their carriages would halt, and the servants would unload their luggage, and the silent rooms would transform into a carnival of interweaving voices, musicians who played for days on end before others came to take their place, women who spent days at a time there and then went away to make room for other women from other cities. The house was some distance from those of the fellahin, cut off by a large grove of pine, poplar trees, and over fifty ancient walnut trees that bent over the river and veiled the view. The property contained a large garden stretching over thirty dunums, enclosed by brick walls. Zakariya's residence was nearby, and his stables were situated between the two properties, looking straight out over the river where anyone sailing past could see the horses lazing beneath the large trees and drinking straight from the river whenever they felt like it.

After Josephine arrived, the fellahin entered the house for the first time. They were taken aback by its splendor: the expensive furniture, the brightly colored armchairs and sofas, the large mirrors, the Persian rugs everywhere. They didn't know exactly how Hanna had brought all these things, but they remembered several carriages that had stopped and been unloaded over several days. Carpenters had then labored inside the house for three months, and many craftsmen had come and stayed inside until their work was done, then left without speaking to anyone. Hanna was obsessed with keeping his dealings mired in obscurity.

At first Josephine wandered through the house alone. A few days later her family joined her for their first visit and scrutinized the six bedrooms, the three large salons, the huge kitchen, the larder, and the three cellars. She felt she would be lonely there and would open the door at any time to the fellahin who came visiting. She paid for a two-room building to be built as a village school so that Mariana wouldn't have to receive students in her family's house. She said to Hanna, "I want the house to be less desolate." Josephine lived like the fellahat who brought her goats, sheep, chickens, geese, and cockerels.

The house soon lost its mystery and turned from a place where ghosts walked into nothing more than the house of a rich man. Josephine let the servants go, saying that it wasn't appropriate for a good Christian woman to have people serve her. She didn't refuse help from her fellahat friends, and in exchange she would look after their children, sharing with them in every detail of their lives.

Hanna was content. He gave up his house to her willingly—after all, the citadel was the only place arranged specifically for the lives of anxious men. A family couldn't live there: as a labyrinth, it respected the privacy of the individual, or so Azar kept repeating when he was convincing the head builder that the divisions between the rooms were intentional, and no room could have anything in common with another, not even a wall.

After Gabriel was born, Hanna felt that it was proper, marvelous even, that Josephine should have ten children to fill up the place. He liked hearing the sounds of Josephine chatting with her fellahat friends, as Gabriel cried, then giggled, like all children. Hanna used to wake up late and drink his coffee, play with Gabriel, who was trying to take his first steps, then observe the changes to the house. It had become a wreck. Gabriel threw whatever he could get hold of—he destroyed the big mirror and peed on the magnificent carpet. Joy was everywhere. When Gabriel reached his third year, he would wander barefoot by himself. All doors were opened to him, and the fellahin fed him alongside their own children. Josephine thought that this was the way things should be, that her child should live with the people.

Hanna would recall those days, when he had felt that Josephine was a wonderful mother. He almost lost his mind with happiness when she told him, three months before the flood, that she was pregnant again. He kissed her on the cheek and hugged her. He told Zakariya that they had to generate masses of children between them: nothing would fill their old age with love except huge numbers of sons and daughters. Zakariya agreed, but his mind was on his horses. He told Hanna that he would be forced to stay all month to wait for his foal to be born. Zakariya wasn't keen on masses of children, but he dreamed that one day he would own all the stables in the country. He was constantly plotting to buy stables that had failed and would pick up valuable horses at knockdown prices from people who had inherited them and didn't know their worth. After his second stable in Anabiya was full, Yaaqoub complained about the overcrowding and asked him to stop buying. Zakariya assured him that he would expand the stables three times over after he bought a house in the middle of seventy dunums of land that lay to the west of Anabiya.

Now alone, Hanna took hold of his window, reflecting how a small seedling when it was plucked out would still grow a complete life. He had lost everything but felt he was beginning to heal. He stopped crying, and felt himself getting better. Shams Al-Sabah had come so that he could feel regret. He knew that he was no longer suited for his old life but he didn't know the tenor of his life to come. In the end, he could always remain in this poverty-stricken place, spending his life helping the fishermen and the fellahin, recording his daily observations of nature. Nature knew no repetition, never resorted to the same vocabulary; every moment the rain was different and could never be repeated. Silence was what he needed. He had always thought that words made life dull and repetitive.

That night he slept soundly, his lusts gone. He remembered Father Ibrahim Hourani, who had been a guest of the village priest two years before the flood. Josephine had been eager to host him in her house, but Hanna couldn't understand how on earth she could be so enthusiastic to invite a man who had spoken so cruelly about Hanna's father. But when he sat in front of Father Ibrahim again, he saw on the priest's face the contentment that he was searching for himself. He wasn't like the greedy, cruel men of religion who loved power and intrigue.

Father Ibrahim refused to move to Hanna's house for the few weeks he would be staying in the village, content instead with the guest room attached to the church. He rode his mule every day, roaming over old monasteries that had fallen into oblivion. Once he went all the way to Ras Al-Ain and spoke when he was back about a church that had been destroyed one thousand three hundred years earlier, and whose remnants still formed part of the age-worn village walls. No one paid any attention to him apart from Josephine, whom he loved and blessed. Without preamble, Father Ibrahim told Hanna that he didn't like powerful men, landowners, rich men, or men of authority. Hanna didn't bother explaining that he was different. He made do with a few questions, and for the first time, he hazarded a conversation with a man different from himself. He confessed his misgivings regarding faith and apostasy; in front of Father Ibrahim, he cursed men of religion. Ibrahim smiled and told Hanna stories from ancient times that all revolved around a Christ-like figure, explaining how the resurrection of the Messiah was nothing but the transcription of this being who lives among us although we don't see him. Josephine loved the priest even more when he received confession from Yvonne, who seemed at ease after she went out of the church to greet the man who would soon become her fiancé, who was waiting for her at the crossroads. She smiled at him and left him standing there as she continued home. That night Father Ibrahim asked the village priest and Josephine to accompany him to ask for Yvonne's hand on behalf of this man. He put a stop to the mutterings and conjectures of the fellahin, which had been circulating ceaselessly ever since a young boy told a tale of how he had seen Yvonne naked in that man's arms in his father's mill.

Hanna still remembered Father Ibrahim—thought about him every day in fact. Back then, before Father Ibrahim left, their relationship had improved; their friendship remained uncultivated, but Hanna no longer listened apprehensively to his stern words. At the time, Hanna used to think that pleasure was the wellspring of life that had to be kept perpetually flowing. But now he understood completely what Father Ibrahim had said in their last meeting when he looked at him for some time and told him, "Don't kill your anxiety, let it flow from your ribs and spill onto the earth, where it will grow and bear fruit, or

NO ONE PRAYED OVER THEIR GRAVES 57

let it drown in this great river." And he pointed at the Euphrates, which at that moment was quiet and meek, like a beggar seeking alms.

As usual, Hanna woke at dawn, but he was troubled. Zakariya had told him that Souad's wedding was on Thursday. He imagined her as a bride in a white dress and was surprised that in that image she seemed a stranger. He thought about Zakariya's concerns, immersed as he was in the wedding of Souad, who was suffering from the overactive imagination that she had borne since childhood. He was surprised at the lean jihaz; he knew how much Souad cherished fine things. He couldn't believe that a single small carriage was all that was needed to transport everything she was bringing to her married life. In the family home, she was leaving behind Persian carpets and silk bedspreads, seven trunks of clothes, and gold necklaces and rings that she had designed herself. Her precious gold necklaces, the work of the golden-masked goldsmith, remained in place in the cupboard; some had been brought back for her from Istanbul by Ahmed Bayazidi, while others she had received as gifts from influential men. She left her family home like some oblivious girl, content with inviting only her aunt, Hajja Amina, and three girl cousins. She ignored the other women of the family and couldn't care less about their criticisms when they described her as a disgraced woman who kept company with strangers and boasted of her friendships with Christians, Jews, and girls who traveled abroad. Souad considered her wedding an ideal opportunity to cut off all contact with her gossiping relatives.

Zakariya considered the situation. In a few hours, Souad would be leaving for the house of her husband, Hassan Masabny, owner of a well-known textile factory in Arqoub, and he, Zakariya, would go back to his life. He had had many worries in recent times. He felt that Hanna was well on his way to being lost; whatever afflicted him, it was no longer an indisposition that he would rise from, but a deep transformation that he would have to live with, like a chronic illness. Then there was his father's devastating old age. A habitual early riser, the man was making every effort to retain his habits of drinking coffee, reading the newspaper, and criticizing the public calls for the separation of religion and state that he read there—between the lines, he could perceive the call to secede from the Ottoman state. But then he would plunge into a bout of forgetfulness and order his carriage driver to go to the post office with the letters he had already taken a short while before. The last of Zakariya's worries was his wife Shaha, who refused to come back to her family until it was settled where they would live. All these things worried him. The flood had destroyed all their lives with no hope of survival. He saw that the deep decay that continued to eat at the bodies and souls of the few survivors was also in himself.

Hassan Masabny had inherited his large house in the Farafra district from his father. He had renovated it so it would be suitable for a married life and imported everything, from gold-plated taps to a grand piano made specially in Italy and engraved with his initials. There were chandeliers from Bohemia, Persian carpets from Esfahan, drapes from Istanbul. Everything in the house was costly, and it satisfied Hassan's wish to enjoy property and wealth. Souad entered her husband's house lightly, completely uninterested in its trappings. From that first moment, she realized she had come to the wrong place with the wrong man. Initially, she committed herself to patience; she wouldn't break up the family, she wanted children. But within a few days she was irritated with her husband's ceaseless monologues about the history of each object in the house, and she was equally exasperated with his perpetual chatter about his love of chess, and the accounts of his daily matches with his friends in the coffeehouses of Jamiliyya. She soon felt trapped in the marriage, and trapped by her husband's four sisters, who kept a close eye on everything and interfered in every detail of the lives of their brother and his wife. Souad listened to them one after the other and resolved to turn them into friends, but before long she couldn't stand their fatuousness. They took turns coming unannounced and staying all day, intervening in matters of food and drink, never hesitating to comment on how the food was presented and the table arranged. After two months, Souad came down with a fit of total silence. She stopped observing even the minimal social decorum. She would open the door to some family member of her husband—he would welcome them and spend hours discussing the minutest family affairs, a well that never seemed to be run dry—and then she would leave her guests and go back to bed without asking permission to leave.

Souad considered becoming a snail, self-sustaining. She would leave the house without permission, and when she came back, Hassan didn't dare hold her to account. He knew, deep down, that he possessed only her outer shell, not her soul. He had taken her virginity, and she was recorded legally as his wife, but he never experienced the warmth he had expected from her. He had laid a wager on her love of objects, smothering her in gifts, but he would come across the boxes wherever he had left them, still unopened. Eventually he asked his sisters to stop visiting, thinking she might be suffering from the constant family banquets. She was relieved when his family stopped visiting, but she remained a snail, self-contained and self-sustaining.

After Souad left, the ruckus in Ahmed Bayazidi's house calmed down somewhat, but her sorrowful look backward as she climbed into the carriage, as well as Shaha's persistent moaning, left Zakariya no opportunity to think about the horses he had moved to the Anabiya stables. He wondered if Shaha missed the horses, too, and offered to take her on a visit with him to Anabiya. He guessed that leaving the house might help her to recover some of her vitality. He also needed someone to whom he could admit that he was afraid, and that his past was over and done with forever. Now he was like all the other survivors of the flood: a child with a memory wiped clean. Shaha agreed to the visit on the condition that they visit the citadel. Zakariya assented, and on the way there, Shaha was distracted, gazing out over the plains that she knew so well. Nothing meant anything to her anymore.

Shams Al-Sabah opened the gate of the citadel to them. When Shaha saw her, she was struck with a strange tremor. In silence, the two women reached a mutual understanding. When Shams Al-Sabah had come back to the citadel after visiting Hanna, she understood that her past had finished with the flood. She doubted she would be staying at the citadel for much longer, and no one would be able to protect her if Hanna kept talking for hours at a time about the color of swallows and partridges, and giving prolix descriptions of eagles. Now she invited Shaha to have dinner with her while Zakariya inspected the citadel. Everything was the same, but the bedrooms smelled of abandonment; no one had entered the citadel since the night of the flood, and about a year had passed since then. The workbench for pressing coins was stopped, and the platform for suicides was covered in dust. Everything was the same. Shaha expressed a wish to stay in the citadel. She told Zakariya that she would feel better there; it would be close to the horses, and to him, if he wanted to see her. Zakariya seized the chance to lighten her burdens. He would leave her to her affairs and go back and stay beside Hanna. From the first moment, he had wanted to escape Aleppo: when he had first left his family's house, he had sworn never to go back again. All his life he had hated the strict regime imposed on him by his father, who vaunted the splendor of a life that was minutely regulated and subject to reckoning. The family honor was apparently linked to the dog-eared notebooks that had been hidden by the family's sons in peculiar places that were soon forgotten by everyone, including the person who hid them. Before Zakariya left the citadel, Shams Al-Sabah asked him to take away the trunks full of silver. She didn't want the citadel to be a target for the brigands who already circulated fabulous rumors among themselves about the imaginary riches found in the citadel's vaults. He advised her to wait before making any crucial decisions; they had to wait for Hanna and consult him. She pointed out simply that Hanna was no longer himself. She went on, "The flood didn't just take the houses and the horses and the fellahin—it swept away the old Hanna and his past." Shams Al-Sabah concluded her address to Zakariya with some energy: "Yours, too."

Shams Al-Sabah herself didn't need anything. She had secreted away a small quantity of gold that would provide her with a respectable life. Three days later Zakariya mounted the iron gates on the citadel, carried away the silver coins in three large trunks, and hid them in his room in his family home. He left once more for the village of

Hosh Hanna and reached Hanna that night. The door was locked, and there was no sound from inside. The servant told him that Hanna had packed up some provisions in a small bundle and left and hadn't come back.

It was clear that Hanna had left only a short time before. The plate of boiled bulgur wheat hadn't gone moldy yet, and in the cupboard Zakariya found a nightgown that he knew belonged to Shams Al-Sabah, along with white cotton sheets stained with a few crusty drops of blood. For a moment, Zakariya was distracted, thinking how irrational it was to deflower Shams Al-Sabah after all these years. But he felt a glimmer of hope and hidden joy—his friend hadn't renounced women forever, evidently. He folded the white sheet and put it into his bag. The following day he went to visit Arif. He wanted his friend to convince Shaha to go back to her family home until their new life was settled, and to try to dispel the fatal images that afflicted her every night. Zakariya hoped that Arif's situation had improved by now.

On his last visit two months earlier, his friend had been unusually morose. Bandits had raided his farm and looted it, including all of Arif's savings that he had had in an iron box underneath his bedroom floor. Arif said that whatever they left, they had destroyed.

Arif hadn't told Zakariya the whole truth. He concealed from his friend that he had sold a large portion of his lands beside the river and bought shares in the Ottoman Train Company Ltd., an imaginary company that collected immense funds from train lovers. Arif had bought securities and shares in the Istanbul-Baghdad line and spent entire nights dreaming that one day he would own his very own train. But the company offices vanished suddenly, leaving behind a catastrophe for Arif and the other gullible shareholders, who couldn't believe the story at first. After they discovered the scale of the disaster, they fell silent. They couldn't find any means of retrieving their money from the fraudulent company—all its documents were forged. In two months, they had succeeded in collecting more than three hundred thousand gold liras. Arif's share alone was over twenty thousand.

Arif had never liked real estate and didn't trust banks, but he had been amazed when he saw a train for the first time during a visit to Istanbul. He couldn't believe that this awe-inspiring hunk of metal could run on iron tracks at such speed, and immediately he told himself that trains would be his downfall. He used to dream of a train carriage designed especially for him. He planned to take his friends on a trip from Istanbul to Aleppo, then from Aleppo to Baghdad, reeling off a list of the cities the train would pass through while his guests were wandering around in their nightgowns and cooking delicious meals in their compartments.

On that visit two months earlier, Zakariya had reassured Arif and his family about Shaha, saying, "Everything will be fine, they'll rebuild Hosh Hanna." Arif said it would be a mistake to live in a place teeming with all those graves, but Zakariya didn't want to debate it. He explained his point of view: the land where your loved ones are buried will haunt you—it's not so easy to leave it behind. Zakariya had always felt that anyone who wished to get away from their family should take their graves with them when they left.

Zakariya didn't stay a second night. He left his despairing friend, feeling that his own grief was more than enough to deal with. After Zakariya's departure, Arif stayed sitting on his wicker seat by the door of the salon, waiting for guests who never came. He considered his revenge on Azzouz Dara'ouzy, who had embroiled him in the deal. He took in the air silently and wondered how to recover the prestige of an agha. He was completely bankrupt and no longer had enough to keep body and soul together. He climbed the north road and stood on the elevation that looked out over his former lands. Returning to his room, Arif wept bitterly. He hid himself away in silence and wouldn't respond to the questions of Yousef, his son who seemed suddenly older; there was no longer much to do after losing his enormous properties, and the small land that remained wasn't enough to retain the family's former influence.

Now, returning again to visit Arif, Zakariya hoped that Arif had overcome his distress. He realized Arif's losses must be more than he had admitted; it didn't make any sense that he could go bankrupt in one night after the theft of a few hundred liras. The breeze was cool and refreshing, and the shy February sun gave Zakariya hope that everything would be better. He thought about Hanna. He was afraid of losing him; in recent times, he had learned the signs of a man about to cross the barzakh and renounce everything.

Zakariya arrived at Tel Arfad, and the horse broker told him that Hanna had passed through their village yesterday, but then had headed along the deserted north road, having refused to talk to anyone. The broker added that he had had some trouble recognizing him at first; Hanna was barefoot and even skinnier than before. The broker had thought he was a madman, one of the ones who wander the earth muttering about the soul and the barzakh. Zakariya knew it was useless to search for a man in the open country, but he continued north all the same. He asked everyone he passed if they had seen a man carrying a bundle of white sackcloth and walking barefoot—so the horse broker had described him—but no one had seen him. And so Zakariya arrived at the village of Sharran once again and knocked on Arif's door. His fourteen-year-old son Yousef opened the door and told him that his father was away, but he offered to put Zakariya up for the night. Zakariya considered this for a moment, but then said he would continue on to the citadel. Yousef informed him that he had seen Hanna two days earlier, close to Azaz. He had been walking barefoot and wouldn't accept Yousef's offer of help, but he was still the same powerful man.

Yousef wouldn't brook Zakariya leaving that night. He reminded him of the brigands who would see him as rich pickings; he would be forced to send escorts with him. Zakariya considered spending the night chatting with Yousef, who had grown a lot in the past couple of years; it was preferable to being escorted by guards with whom he wouldn't know what to talk about.

Yousef undertook all the duties of hosting Zakariya, behaving like a young and impecunious agha. The servant Mabrouk brought dinner, fed the horses, cleaned the carriage, and equipped it for the journey in the morning. Zakariya asked if he could sleep in the Grandfather's

House on the hill, which was now Yousef's, where he had taken his sketches and his books.

When Yousef was a young child, Arif had been afraid for him and circled his neck with protective talismans. Once he noticed his son sketching in the air and talking to himself. He sent for Mala Mannan at once and asked him for a hijab, an amulet for his son—not yet six and behaving like a crazy person. He lived in a world that wasn't earthbound, told strange stories about peoples whose homes were annihilated, and whose animals had become extinct. Mala Mannan listened to the boy with a concerned expression. He asked Yousef to come with him to his house. There he brought him into a large room filled with books and spoke with him for hours. Yousef was delighted to be speaking with a man who knew so much about books. He told the Mala that he hoped he would go to school, and in his dreams he saw himself living in huge cities. A few days later Arif Sheikh Musa Agha arrived with his friends Hanna Agha and Zakariya Bey, dragging a cart of provisions and gifts, but Mala Mannan asked them to share these things out among the poor. He whispered to Arif that Yousef would go on to great things. He assured Arif that his son wasn't suffering from an illness, but he had to send him to school. Hanna was filled with enthusiasm and enrolled Yousef at his own former school, entrusting him to the teachers' special care. Yousef started down a new path, but in the end, Arif's fear for his only son stopped him from allowing Yousef to remain so far away. He brought Yousef back to the village after his primary school studies, and immersed him in the concerns of the family land and its fellahin. But Yousef remained enamored of strange things. He no longer sketched in the air, but he never stopped dreaming of the other life he wanted to lead.

Yousef was still grateful to Hanna and Zakariya for taking care of him while he was at school, and that night he saw an opportunity to return their kindness. He told Zakariya he had been surprised when he saw Hanna, adding fervently, "Hanna has reached the truth." Zakariya ignored this comment, and Yousef left him to his silence and went back to daydreaming about his own life. When Zakariya dozed off, Yousef went outside to sniff the cold air. He decided that when his father came back, he would tell him about his uncle Hanna Agha's visit to the village of Bulbul, because he didn't believe the tale of the robbed savings—he knew the story of the train. He wanted to help his father, to give him an encouraging shake and assure him that what was left would be enough.

Three days earlier the fellahin had told Yousef that on the land Arif still owned in Azaz, they had found a large skeleton of an animal they weren't familiar with. Yousef didn't wait to hear the rest of the details. He climbed into his carriage at once and went to see forty panicked fellahin gathered around the skeleton of a strange beast over thirty meters long. Yousef examined it carefully. Its bones were still in good condition. He lost no time and asked the fellahin to think of how to lift it onto the carriage, but he was afraid that it would come apart in their hands. They all spent hours thinking how to move it safely and came up with only one solution. They placed the skeleton on a large wooden panel, and Yousef used the horses to drag it to Sharran. While this was being arranged, Hanna had reached Azaz and heard all the commotion about a skeleton. He stood watching from a distance, and when he saw Yousef busy alongside the fellahin, he smiled. Hanna's unexpected arrival was another miracle that Yousef took as a sign. Hanna regarded the skeleton thoughtfully and circled it several times. Then he told Yousef, "They are our ancestors whom we've neglected." Yousef didn't ask Hanna what he was doing in Azaz. He had already known about Hanna's transformation from overhearing his father talk with his friends, other aghas who had asked Arif Sheikh Musa Agha to intervene and help Zakariya in recovering Hanna and assisting him in his misfortune.

Yousef felt a deep spiritual kinship with the man who had paid out of his own money to send him to school, even though he had found the school's strict regime unbearable. He learned to read and write and in his father's fear seized an opportunity to go back to his village. He used to roam its meadows and pass a considerable time in the library of Mala Mannan, adding books he had bought in Aleppo to his grandfather's library. Hanna didn't keep him chatting long before he went on his way. Yousef followed after him and was taken aback when Hanna turned to him with a smile and asked to be left alone: in his sack he had some pieces of dry bread and a few raisins, and his heart would guide him along the path. Before he disappeared from view, Yousef saw him go downhill on the road toward Aleppo. In silence, he stood watching Hanna walking barefoot to nowhere.

The skeleton arrived after a long journey that took more than twenty hours. Yousef could find no place for it aside from the large room in Grandfather's House where he spent most of his time. As he cleared the jars of provisions away, Hanna's words about ancestors still rang in his ears. Arif was used to his son's peculiar hobbies, so he raised no objections. He had his own preoccupation: the noise of the trains that constantly echoed through his thoughts.

On the first night, Yousef was afraid of the skeleton that was sharing his house. Oddities provoke stories and superstitions, and all Yousef could think of was convincing the fellahin to halt the digging they had been engaged in when they had found it and prepare ground elsewhere. But at dawn, Yousef left his mattress and opened the door to the large room. Light was pouring over the skeleton, making it even more bewitching. He touched it, and just then he felt a deep kinship with this creature of legend. He resolved to never forsake the skeleton of his ancestors, whatever happened. He moved the last sacks of food in the room to a disused grain store, he repaired the wide window, he cleaned the place thoroughly. He wanted to stay close to the skeleton all the time. He was deeply contented. Gone was his initial fear that had spoiled the awe of having a dinosaur skeleton in his possession—or so he called it, even though he wasn't entirely sure that was what it was.

Yousef offered to take Zakariya to see the skeleton. Zakariya promised that he would see it on another visit, but just then he wanted to hear more about Hanna. He was unsuccessful in this, as Yousef was busy with his performance of being a real agha, issuing stern orders to Mabrouk, the only servant left. After the rich dinner, Zakariya kept himself busy until dawn and left at the first ray of sunlight. He guessed that Hanna had gone back to the citadel, and he arrived there three hours later. When the servant told him that no one had seen Hanna there, Zakariya continued on to Aleppo and arrived before midday. As he neared his family home, he heard the sound of sobbing and the voice of a muqry reciting verses from the Qur'an. All at once, he realized that his father, Ahmed Bayazidi, had died.

Zakariya blamed himself for being absent for the last five days: he had known his father was very ill and might not survive this time. He went inside the house and found Hanna presiding over the 'aza next to his own brother-in-law, Hassan Masabny. His cousins all rose, kissed him, and offered their condolences. It was clear that the burial had taken place at least a day earlier. He learned that Hanna had been with Ahmed Bayazidi on his final night. He had sat a silent vigil by the bed of the old man, who had become restless at the angel of death's delay; he didn't want his exhausted body to fester any longer from waiting. At the end, Ahmed Bayazidi spoke a few words to Hanna, who watched in silence as the soul rose and slipped through the gaps of the tightly locked windows.

Zakariya reached Hanna, who rose from his seat and embraced him closely. They both wept with a passion that the other men in the room, glancing furtively at them, couldn't understand; they deeply disapproved of crying so hard over an old man.

2

Sins

After burying Josephine and Gabriel, my blood was running beside me. It, and I, never crossed the threshold of the room, a place I loved more than anywhere else. This dwelling was very simple. Inside, there was a large bed and a carpet my friend Arif Sheikh Musa Agha gave me after a visit to Diyarbakir. I loved the outlines of colored peacocks inter-twining with long-beaked birds. They seemed haughty to me, suffering from chronic loneliness. And on the floor, there were a few cushions thrown down haphazardly, just the place where a man fleeing human-ity could rest. Four large windows looked out in every direction. Out of those windows I could see the destroyed houses of Hosh Hanna, the distant river, and the remains of the church and the cotton fields.

Before the flood, I had only slept in this room a handful of times. I had no need to escape from people. I adored the clamor of my friends all around me, and Gabriel's impetuousness, and Josephine's smile.

When Zakariya and I arrived at the destroyed village, I did not yet appreciate what the flood signified. And when I saw its effects, I couldn't believe it. I still don't believe it. I walked to this room without thinking, and I discovered it held three large mirrors that reflected a light whose source I couldn't identify: was it the moon, or the surface of the river, or the faces of the dead? In the large mirror, my face was repulsive, like a horned lizard's. I was so indescribably ugly, I spat on myself. In the morning, I threw all three mirrors onto a rock and heard them smash. I don't want to look at my face, ever again. Why look at a face that looks like that?

After that I was relieved. The room was bigger, and I slept for the first time in three days. In my dreams, I saw my ugly face again. My body was exhausted, the smell of death embedded deeply within it. Burial does not mean the end of death. For the first time, I felt the sensation of death circulating under my skin, roaming the spaces of my body. I was greatly comforted to think that I would die, and Zakariya would bury me just as he had all the corpses that I had avoided looking at. But Josephine's face remained impressed on my memory. She was mild, like she was during her life, which she had lived noiselessly beside me while I took no notice of her. She was walking to her grave on her own two feet; I, a coward, didn't follow. Josephine and Souad do not resemble each other in the slightest, but suddenly their images merged into a third face, a woman who resembled both Shams Al-Sabah and my mother.

My few hours of sleep became terrible nightmares. Every night I rose from my bed like the dead and walked through the room. I was frightened of going outside, of being ambushed by the river. Everything around me was a disaster. I couldn't explain any of this to Zakariya; it would only have increased his worries. He too lost his son, and on his broad, solid shoulders, he will carry all our pain that is still to come. I see him walking with his firm, powerful tread, like a mule. He is gathering up our memories so he can bury them.

Finally, I lay down on the ground. For the first time in a long time, I slept. Faces were streaming through my memory, faces of the living this time. I could smell Souad's scent, which is impossible to forget. Josephine's scent was more like a eucalyptus tree, and I don't know why she smelled that way. She was afraid of scandal and wanted to live like an ascetic, and so she did. She never cared for cupboards full of clothes, choked with possessions, she always gave them away. I didn't understand what she was telling me until it was too late. What do things do to us? They inter us and turn us into the dead, or something like them.

I was content and thought the nightmares wouldn't come back, but the blood flowing in my veins belongs to a corpse. I am still certain that my face is the face of a horned lizard from a bygone age. When I got up, I made coffee for the first time and sat by the window. The sun was setting. How entrancing, how bewitching is the sight of the sun as it sets. The color of the night changes every instant. I felt infinitely insignificant, as all the dead must feel when they are ensnared into living alongside people.

A long time has passed since the flood, whose thunderous waters swept me away and discarded me in the depths of the river. I have discovered the magnificence of living in water, delicate like everything here, nothing rigid around you, the touch of the plants that surround me, the soft skin of the fishes, the bed of water that I sleep on, the mud, the riverbanks; all tender, nothing like the hardness that surrounds me on dry land. I wander in that world, intoxicated by my new life. I feel for my horns and discover they have melted away, and a magnificent crown of flowers has sprouted in their place. It has a peculiar scent, like lemons, or cotton blossoms when they open at dawn. The scent envelops me, transformative. How lucky I am to live at the bottom of the river.

I get up every morning before dawn, woken by the murmur of my blood, and wait for the red of the sky to withdraw and become yellow, which in turn becomes mingled with blue. The sun rises just when it should, indifferent to the beings who go to war on behalf of the emperor, or a religion, or a political leader, or an ideology. The sun continues on, up the dome of the sky, and never repeats the same colors, and I am filled with bliss because I am here, in this moment. Every day I discover that my drowning in the river was a great act, so much so that the first time I left my room and walked on its banks, I saw pieces of my body fall off me. I didn't care, I am a plant that grows back. A new organ sprouts in place of my fingers, which were taken by a scavenging dog. We are eking out an existence on the remains of the dead, and I wanted that dog to do the same with my fingers. That dog I know well, he guards Zakariya's stables. I tossed my fingers to him and went on my way. Later I found myself sitting by the window, watching my fingers regrow, just as I watch plants that yesterday were no more than a few centimeters high and yet within a few days will have doubled their

*height and turned a different color. Perhaps they will fruit, and then I
will see a flower transform into a cotton boll, or an eggplant. There was
a time when I didn't think at all about the secret of this great death, but
now I feel a ghastly pleasure whenever I shed a new body part. I think
about the misery of my friends when I see Arif Sheikh Musa Agha's
carriage in the distance driven by his son Yousef, coming to my house
and bringing many things with it: broadcloth suits I can tell from the
color are English, made in Manchester (George must have sent them
again), jars of provisions, lambs ready for slaughter; in the same way,
I see my servant telling him that I live at the bottom of the river. I see
Yousef and my friend Arif, whom I love dearly, leaving sadly. It's quite
natural that Arif is depressed, still weighted down with a body as he is.
He dreams of trains, he walks on solid ground, he likes seeing his face
in the mirror. He is afraid of old age, of his sex shriveling. He told me
once sarcastically that old age is eating shit—impossible that it would
ever affect us, we lovers of the immortal citadel. I would laugh; I liked
the plain words he used in praise of pleasure, just as I used to like the
friend whose face would be drenched with tears whenever a certain female dancer performed until she went into a deep ecstasy and he felt
her body shaking the earth. He used to say to the women, "Don't dance
for our enjoyment, dance to rip our souls out of their fixed places." His
fervor growing, he would continue, "Be like my trains: storm hearts and
vast plains without a care." Afterward Shams Al-Sabah would try to
clarify for the confused women what Arif meant, although she herself
was somewhat at a loss how to explain the connection between trains
and women. In the end, she would simply tell them they were here because they were prostitutes, and she would instruct them, "Once you
come through that door, you should consider yourselves to have granted
your bodies to love."*

*None of my friends realize how hard it is to live on solid ground.
The road is filled with thorns. Day after day, I forget mirrors. My horns
turn into a crown of flowers that withers every night and regenerates
in the morning. I am flooded with scents on the breeze, I inhale them
deeply, I hoard them inside me, and just as I slough my fingers and*

hands and feet, I slough from within me an overflowing stench that has to be vomited up. I have vomited up the smells, but there are many that still mix with my pores. When I think of all these years spent cleaning my body with perfumes and covering it with fine clothes, I despair; I was no different from the living who want nothing more from their lives than to grow among solid things.

In the first month the nightmares never left me. The tableaux changed for me: Souad turned into a swallow, Josephine was a sweet female rabbit, and my mother was a wolf who nourished me from her body. The large, sumptuous houses I have lived in all turned to rubble, with all my possessions inside producing locusts and large brown ants with yellow wings. A world mixed inside me, and there was nothing left of what I used to live for. Now I am asleep at the bottom of the river, and no one will touch me. My body erases its parts every day and redraws them anew, like the sockets of the dinosaur skeleton that the fellahin gathered around, all of them terrified, apart from Yousef, the boy I have loved with all my heart, who was thinking only of how he could move the skeleton to his house so he could live beside it. I knew that he wouldn't drown it in the Afrin River. And it delighted me that Yousef thought this giant skeleton would be resurrected. That was on the sixth day of my journey to Aleppo, which I ended in good spirits. I no longer felt the agony of the road, nor its thorns; under my feet, the hard surface had turned into a wonderful, yielding softness, refreshingly cool. I felt as though two wings had sprouted on my back and carried me wherever I wanted to go.

After Shams Al-Sabah left my room, I was wonderfully at ease. My lusts had come to an end, they turned into something like the slime that slugs leave behind them when they pass over soft ground, beings I didn't look at much before the flood. Afterward, however, I spent hours pursuing them whenever I came across one. Their slippery bodies wallow in the dirt, leaving a slimy trail behind them. I said to myself that this was the happiness I aspired to: clinging to the earth, the soft soil, the fetid smell of plants that were here a short while before. In March, five seasons will have passed: spring, summer, autumn, and now a second winter. It is only right that I emerge from my shell and wander the earth. I like the thought of it. I will spend my entire life walking barefoot, nourished by the wonderful repasts of vegetables and dried fruits, admitting to myself that for the person I used be, his many possessions were never enough. They inspired a wish for vengeance, made him afraid of poverty. I was crammed full of things that still wound me, that throttle and choke me. Now a very little suffices me, even nothing at all; as long as there is river and wind and soil, I won't be afraid of anything. I am not a target for robbers and murderers; I am dead, and there is no use in killing a dead man. And the women I used to turn out of my bed after sex, who made me feel horrendously bored merely by looking at them, who were like old stockings to me—now I am crammed full of them. The remorse I feel . . . I wish I had been less uncouth. What is the point of building a citadel, and minting the currency of a nonexistent country, and promising coffins of pure silver to gamblers if they commit suicide after losing everything? What does it mean when you push your companions to suicide? It means that you are merely filth that should be cleaned away, turned into an inanimate lump. During her visit, I kept noting how Shams Al-Sabah looked at me in disbelief because she couldn't admit that I am not the person I was; but nevertheless, she is still the woman who is closest to me. All the times she embraced me I found that lost scent of my mother. Every day she lost her old character and became more like my mother. On our last night, she reverted back to the day we first met, a woman Um Waheed was readying for the selling of enjoyment to men of great wealth and power. I was grieved that she undressed and let me take her virginity. I wished that I had stayed the course and that the hateful smell of pus would slough off her soul. She tried to reclaim me, saying how much she loved me, how much she had waited for this moment, and I didn't tell her that I was corrupt, that I had ruined her life forever and turned her from a mother into a whore—maybe not entirely, but she is no longer sacred as she was, and she is no longer my mother. I have killed my mother. How painful it is, killing your mother. For the last time, I was seeking out what was left of the man I was—much of him remains. After she went away, I wept. I have lost only the outer layers of myself—I can still take pleasure in orgasm and the splendor of her breasts in the dawn light; I am still a being that resembles who I used to be. But I am choked with nightmares, and my mouth is stuffed with the corpses of dead fish.

When Shams Al-Sabah left, I didn't watch her walk into the distance. I felt that she would be the last of my crimes, but I wasn't sure. I heard Zakariya speaking about his horses and the changing seasons and almost asked him about the income of our shares in Barclays Bank in England, and our savings in the Ottoman Bank, but I stifled myself just in time. I didn't tell him that I have a dream that is becoming a vision. Every day brings me the same image: on our hill overlooking the village of Barad, there is a place buried in the ground, something like an ancient church, or a retreat where monks lived and fed on nothing. I have dreamed of that place. There I can live as I please, watching the sky and the rain and the nearby river. Yes, the Euphrates isn't far, and the River Afrin is less than an hour's walk. I have grown devoted to living by the river. I didn't tell Zakariya at first because I thought that it was an ephemeral vision, but it hasn't left me. I recall my mother's stories and Father Ibrahim's conversations about the ruined monasteries where monks passed their lives and devoted themselves to contemplation, and inactivity, and existence on the margins. It was an ingenious method of escaping the quandary that is living, given that they weren't able to live as a dead person, as I do. Yes, I haven't died, but I enjoy the distinction and privileges of the dead: my language of silence and the breeze that carries me like a feather.

I thought that staying here would turn me into an embalmed thing. I didn't think deeply about it, so long as I could return to this place. The road to Aleppo isn't long, but it is long enough for all the remaining parts of my body to fall off. I will cast my squalid soul, which has ruined Shams Al-Sabah and hundreds of other women, by the roadside. My passions won't have the force and strength to follow me—they will die and be annihilated. Yes, annihilated. I am as happy as a young child when I think that these lethal passions will be annihilated. I have put everything I need in my sack: a few dried apricots, tomatoes, and figs, and a piece of dry bread. I left my room at dawn, threw away my shoes, and thought, why not walk barefoot? I haven't touched the earth before. I could feel the soil—it was an enchanting sensation.

By the end of the first day, my feet were suppurating. The pain rose into my soul, washed it, threw out the filthy water, and buried the wretched thing in the depths of the earth. That first night, I spent outside. As I walked along the riverbank for hours at a time, I made the current my guide, by walking against it. Everywhere here is well known to me, I won't stray off course or have the pleasure of getting lost in this vast earth. My errors still burden me, new sensations overwhelm me. If I pass anyone on the riverbank, I avoid them and cover my face, so as not to be recognized.

I passed by the house of a usurer I once knew. On one occasion, he made it a condition that in order to be released from the mortgage on their house, Uncle Michel Eisa, who was our friend William's father, would have to pay interest for an extra year, and this he couldn't afford. We went to the usurer and offered to return his bond and take on his share of the property, but he turned us out. We were young and foolish, and we went back the following day. Zakariya put a knife to his side and told him to return the bond to Michel Eisa, who couldn't believe that we might kill a man on his account. Everything took place as we wished, and when we left, we spat on him: we did the same whenever we saw him afterward. We were so powerful, and now I am so weak. I am like a vagrant, walking along the bank of the great river that, in its omnipotence, killed all those people. We lie in wait for each other; I am not deceived by its docility, any more than it is deceived by mine. Deliverance from this putrid soul will require a long time; it is impossible for a chisel to hollow out and destroy a mountain that formed over centuries. It needs daily excavation, using calm, patience, persistence. I have been training myself in this patience, which I will need along my journey to bury my sinful self.

Hanna Gregoros
Deir Zahr Al-Rumman, February 1918

This text is one of the seven literary works that Hanna Gregoros wrote between 1918 and 1951 in Deir Zahr Al-Rumman, as dated in the original pages. It was accompanied by a story of two chapters entitled "Impossible Love," signed with the name Junaid Khalifa, and by many documents and photographs taken by the well-known photographer William Zakariya Bayazidi.

Khaled Khalifa found these works in his family home in Anabiya among many documents that belonged to Junaid Khalifa, his great-uncle. Khaled has freely rewritten these texts, including "Impossible Love," in his own style and included them in this novel.

Three works by Hanna have been omitted from this book. These contain long explanations about the flora and fauna of northern Aleppo and the River Euphrates. A text about horses and breeding methods containing instructive sketches, signed by Yaaqoub Al-Shughry, groom of the Anabiya stables, has also been omitted.

3

My Mother Is a Flat Bean

Hanna was eight years old when he stole a look out the window of their servant Margot's house at the procession that the inhabitants of Mardin had gathered to see. He was shocked when he saw the body of his father Gabriel Gregoros flung onto a donkey, his slack-lipped mouth stuffed with his own cut-off penis, while the inhabitants of Mardin lined up along both sides of the town's main road to spit on him, cursing all the while. Soldiers surrounded the procession, which turned along every alleyway in an orgy of public humiliation beyond anything Mardin had ever witnessed before.

The priest who had been dispatched from the nearby Deir Za'faran arrived at the office of the qaymaqam. The priest received the mutilated body so he could bury it on his own responsibility in the graveyard designated for Christians. The day before, he had buried the other members of the Gregoros family; the qaymaqam described the whole family as "criminal," because some members of it had killed an Ottoman officer and attacked the qaymaqam's residence, setting it on fire.

This image stayed with Hanna all his life. He didn't understand why people were spitting on a dead man, and the servant Margot didn't have time to explain that the people of Mardin had hated his father for a long time.

Margot was afraid. There were ceaseless raids in search of Hanna and his uncle and cousins. They checked every house in the town, including Margot's, where she had hidden Hanna in a large chicken coop. At night, she unrolled a small mattress for him among the sacks of lentils and bulgur wheat. She locked her door and begged him not to leave the cellar of the shabby little house. Margot was overwhelmed; she didn't have time to answer the questions of a terrified child, and she prayed to Jesus and his virgin mother, imploring them for help.

By the third day, the streets of Mardin had quieted. The soldiers withdrew to their barracks, and the three officers who had carried out the punishment without waiting for the qaymaqam's orders made sure to underline their victory by burning down Gabriel Gregoros's shop. They issued threats to the city, saying that anyone hiding a wanted person would be executed without trial, particularly stressing the name of Gabriel's son Hanna, whom Margot put in a large basket one night and carried out to a cart loaded with sacks of barley. The cart paused at her door, they climbed on, and at once it set off again along a side road leading southeast toward Amouda. The cart driver knew his route well. After he left the city, a signal was clear. He stopped when he reached the son of Mala Afif Husseini, who was waving a lantern, his brothers having lit a fire that the driver could see from a distance. The cart left the territories of Mardin, and Margot breathed out. She hugged Hanna and wept bitterly. Hanna raised his head and straightened up. He was refreshed by the night breezes and the sight of the wheat fields they passed through. He would always remember the way he artlessly reached his hand out, feeling how tender the ears of corn were as he brushed them gently throughout the journey. Eventually Margot tried to suppress her sobs, but she continued weeping in silence. It was a short distance, and the cart could have done it in half an hour or less, but the rustle of the green ears of wheat around the horses, and the heavy load of barley, made the journey last double that time.

When they arrived, Ahmed Bayazidi was waiting for the cart. Margot removed the cross from her neck and noticed the cross on Hanna's neck, which his mother had put there on the day he was born. It was large, made of pure gold, and stamped with his initial. She blamed herself for not having thought to remove it before. She dressed him in a white thobe and an embroidered woolen cap like the ones worn by Muslim boys when they went to pray in the mosque with their fathers. A little before dawn, they completed their journey to Aleppo in Ahmed Bayazidi's fine carriage, specially designated for high-ranking officials. Ahmed Bayazidi was worried, thinking about things that couldn't be reconciled, and was muddled by Margot's voice, constantly repeating the details of what had happened. He asked her to be quiet. He was angry that he hadn't been able stop the massacre, and deep down he was frightened. His career might be over; his enemies would exploit not only his close friendship with Gabriel Gregoros but also his own verbal attack on the qaymaqam of Mardin, which occurred in an outburst of anger after the vali of Aleppo defended the three officers and argued for the necessity of avenging the murder of an Ottoman officer. Those three officers had arrested every member of the family and executed them without bothering with a trial, and they issued a threat to the city's Christians that any reaction would result in further slaughter and the city being pulled down on their heads.

It was Ahmed Bayazidi's opinion that the qaymaqam should have prevented the massacre, apprehended the officers' murderers (among whom Gabriel Gregoros was not numbered), and put them on trial. That they were a group of thugs from the Gregoros family was no justification for these killings. Ahmed Bayazidi warned the qaymaqam of a Christian uprising in Mardin that would be followed by a popular outburst in every district, possibly even reaching the cities. He listed the times that the vali and the Ottoman officers had overstepped the mark in the last ten years, and he reminded him of the massacres that the vali's office had perpetrated in Mount Lebanon, Damascus, and Aleppo. The vali paid no attention to the opinion of his friend and chief accountant. He advised Ahmed Bayazidi to forget the matter and added that the European consuls were occupied with gaining concessions to extend the railways at the moment, and wouldn't stand up for the Christians even if they were exterminated to a man.

It was a long way to Aleppo, and Hanna's thoughtlessness might easily have ruined everything—he was a child, and children couldn't be trusted. Margot continued to be tense and afraid, even after they reached Ahmed Bayazidi's house in Aleppo. She still wasn't reassured that Hanna would be safe: she had seen for herself the rage of the soldiers as they cursed the Messiah and the Gregoros family and threatened to burn anyone who had any connection to the criminals. Few people knew that Margot's memory was still burdened by the massacre of Mosul, when the janissaries had attacked and slaughtered fifty Syriac Catholic families, pulling them out of their homes and throwing their bodies into an unmarked mass grave. She felt history repeating itself in every detail; she, like Hanna, had been a small child in 1834 and survived the massacre only by a miracle. There was no one of her family left apart from her brother Iskander, who had gone to Baghdad, where he would remain for the rest of his life, while Margot stayed behind with other surviving families from the Sharaqiyya neighborhood. She decided to walk west with no goal in mind and arrived in Mardin, lost and unprotected. She spent her tenth year in the house of a wealthy family, an orphan at their table, before Gabriel Gregoros took her on as a servant in his house.

A little girl with blond braids, she remembered her father's face and his thick mustache. But she also couldn't forget the sight of her family's corpses, her father's belly ripped open. She didn't talk about the massacre, but that didn't mean she had forgotten it. She only mentioned what happened on a few occasions. Her recollections of that massacre disturbed her master Gabriel Gregoros, but she kept telling Hanna about Syriac Christians slaughtered by the cruel janissaries, their bodies thrown into mass graves. She always used to say to Hanna that a corpse worries its murderer, who believes that it could rise up one day and avenge itself. For what does the resurrection of Christ mean, if not the resurrection of all victims? Although he didn't understand, Hanna was terrified of these stories and couldn't forget them.

Ahmed Bayazidi wasted no time. He gave Margot the choice of joining his servant Um Kheir or going back to Mardin. He said flatly that Hanna would live the rest of his life here, adding, "He has no one to go back to." Margot was upset by Ahmed Bayazidi's cold tone, although her master Gabriel Gregoros used to be much harsher; he fundamentally despised the weak and the servants. Margot didn't need much time to reflect. She was resolved never to leave Hanna alone with a Muslim family and believed that keeping Hanna a Christian was a serious matter, worth a sacrifice, and so she accepted Ahmed Bayazidi's offer of employment. The historical connection between the two families meant nothing to her; nor did their overlapping interests that extended back over more than two generations. She was in despair. She would never be able to save Hanna from Ahmed Bayazidi, a powerful man who was no one's fool, notwithstanding his austere appearance, his mild face, and his ponderous manner of speech.

Margot reflected that the church wouldn't allow the only heir of a rich Christian to be raised by a Muslim family, even though all his possessions had been forfeited. She believed that much of the gold was still in existence somewhere. She resented having lost her only opportunity to make Hanna her son; if only she had run away with him to Mosul, where the dregs of her family were, to put an end to the story. They would have believed he had been murdered, no Gregoroses left. But Ahmed Bayazidi had acted decisively: he reached Mardin the same day the officer was killed and tried every possible means of reaching an agreement between the Gregoros family and the officer's family but hadn't succeeded. He couldn't stop the massacre; on the other hand, he couldn't endorse the murder of a Turkish Ottoman officer (who also belonged to an influential family in Mardin) in broad daylight, even if it had been in defense of family honor.

The city was almost set on fire by the sectarian riots between Muslims and Christians: the murdered man's fellow officers saw the violence as an opportunity to reestablish dread and awe in a region where revolt had never really calmed. And the officer's family, who traded in lumber, saw an opportunity to claw back influence from the Gregoros family, which had enjoyed a monopoly on the trade line between the major trading posts of Erbil and Mosul after Gabriel Gregoros bought all the caravanserais of the old souq, soon adding to his acquisitions the shops of the Jewish traders in Khan Al-Arous. Within a few years, Mardin had turned into a transit hub for all kinds of wares, and the arrivals of goods from Aleppo never paused. Carts would unload textiles, glassware, henna, dried fruit, and lumber, along with weapons, twine, and dyes. Then other caravans would leave, loaded up with goods for Erbil and Mosul, and still others for Anatolia. The khans of Gabriel Gregoros never saw a pause in their incessant churn of goods and people.

The tempest eventually quieted down. Nineteen members of the Gregoros family had died, among them Hanna's uncle, his four brothers, his mother, and his little sister with the golden braids—the family was well known for its golden hair. The remaining Gregoros members, all from the poor side of the family, escaped through the fields and wandered the country, leaving everything behind.

Zakariya didn't hide his glee that Hanna had come to live with them in the big house. From the first moment, he shared everything with Hanna: his clothes, his new shoes, carefully placed in the corner of his cupboard, waiting for Eid Al-Adha to arrive. He begged Hanna not to accept living in a church orphanage, or going away with any member of his family who wanted to reclaim him. Zakariya had been lonely before Hanna came. He had reached nine years old without a brother, and his mother, full of fears for her only son, wouldn't allow him to visit his cousins or school friends. Souad, his sister who was not yet six, was still a small child who couldn't take part in his schemes for making paper kites in dazzling colors, or help him escape his parents' surveillance—especially that of his mother, who couldn't believe that he wouldn't die as all his brothers and his other sister had before they were two years old.

Hanna understood how things were for his friend Zakariya. He nodded gravely like a tiny gentleman and promised Zakariya that he would never leave him. Hanna took out a pin, pricked his finger, and reached it out to Zakariya, who did the same, and they mingled their blood, swearing to be brothers forever. Souad was watching them. She said that their blood was traveling to the sun now. They didn't understand what she meant, and as usual she didn't really understand the meaning of her own words, which always took everyone by surprise. After her peculiar utterance, Souad hugged them both and announced that she had witnessed their pact: they were brothers now, and they would share sweets and money. Zakariya got up, took out a bag of sweets from his cupboard, and gave it to Souad, who divided it equally between the two of them, declaring that now they were as alike as her father's carriage wheels.

The boys nodded in agreement. Souad told Hanna that she would allow him to take her bed in Zakariya's room, which was now Zakariya and Hanna's room. Then she left for her new room, only to return carrying a large bowl filled with rose-petal jam. This would help them grow tall, she said, grinning because they were both unusually short, unlike Azar, Zakariya's Jewish friend. She urged Hanna to take good care of her bed and went back to her room.

After that, Hanna no longer thought of leaving this beautiful house. After a few months, he even felt happy. Zakariya's mother, Radia Khanim, treated him with increasing affection and looked after everything for him. She was pleased: Hanna would be a charming and polite brother to Zakariya and Souad. She prayed for mercy on his mother's soul: described her to Hanna as a patient woman who had borne up under his father's difficult temperament, and did her best to forget the cruel way she had died. Radia shrank from gossiping about the dead; her own losses were more than enough for her.

In the early days of Hanna's residence with them, Radia Khanim noticed that Souad was bursting out with eccentric observations. One time Souad surprised her by getting up from the dinner table and claiming that she had seen a little elephant rolling around between the lentils in her soup. Radia and her husband exchanged a significant glance. She could no longer curb her fear that Souad had inherited her aunt Amina's ability to read fortunes. Ahmed Bayazidi didn't respond.

He too was secretly afraid that Souad might share his sister's fate: she was thirty now, and no one had yet dared to ask for her hand. He had gotten used to avoiding any mention of this and wouldn't comment on the course her life had taken.

The next day Radia took Souad to the sheikh, who made a protective talisman for her: he wrote out an incantation, recited it over her head, then folded it up and placed it inside an amulet pouch that went around her neck. Souad laughed while the sheikh was reciting, his hand shaking from his fear of Aunt Amina and her ability to see the future. Souad loved her aunt very much and couldn't wait for her to visit so she could tell her about Zakariya and Hanna, who couldn't sleep with their eyes open as she did. Full of dread, Aunt Amina hugged her. She didn't want her sweet-natured, innocent niece to inherit her fate of pain and torment. And she saw a bier coming closer: she didn't know whose death it foretold, perhaps even her own, but she saw death hovering around her family.

Souad went into Hanna and Zakariya's room to tell them that she hadn't liked the sheikh's clothes; he was nowhere near as elegant as Monsieur Jean, who used to visit Aunt Amina every Friday morning. She asked them to go with her to the river, and as usual, they had no choice but to obey her orders. The three of them crept furtively out of the house to where William Michel Eisa, Azar ibn Hayyim Istanbouli, and his sister Sara were waiting for them. They all followed Souad, who reached the river, took the amulet off from around her neck, cut the thread holding it closed with a small knife, and took out the paper on which the sheikh had traced triangles, incomprehensible symbols, and strange and mysterious words. She folded the paper to make a boat, went up to the river, and very gently placed it on the water. She asked them all to wave at the little boat as it drifted away.

None of them understood what was going on, but all she said was that she didn't need an amulet. She produced some sheets of paper, handed them out, and asked everyone to make their own paper boats. Hanna was enthusiastic about the idea: he wrote his mother's name on his and kissed the paper. Touched by this, Souad asked everyone

to write a message for Hanna's mother on their own boat, and they
enthusiastically agreed. Hanna was very moved by Souad's message.
After Zakariya wrote it down for her, she asked him to read it out
loud before she folded it into a boat, so he stood up and recited it for
everyone to hear. *To my beautiful auntie, Um Hanna. We miss you.
Don't worry, Hanna is living with us now.* Underneath, in his very best
handwriting, Zakariya had written, *We love Hanna, and he is our
brother now.* Sara sniggered as she read out what she had written—
that Hanna had stolen Zakariya's paper kite. Zakariya grabbed Sara's
paper boat and tore it up, explaining very seriously that Hanna didn't
steal and had even given Zakariya his own pocket money to buy paperboard to make into his kites. Once everyone was ready, Souad told
them to go down to the riverbank and send off the boats. Hanna was
moved when he saw the six boats plying the river. It was carrying
them to Heaven, and that night his mother would catch them up and
read the messages, just as Souad had promised.

When they arrived back at home, everyone was silently witnessing
Grandfather Najib Bayazidi's rage. He was heaping obscene curses on
Aunt Amina, who had gone to his room that morning, sat on his bed,
and said, "You have three days to live. You must settle your affairs."
She didn't wait for a reply. She instructed a coffin-maker to make
a walnut coffin that would fit a huge man and send it to her family
home in three days' time. After the body was buried in the ground in
its shroud, she told him, the coffin would be donated to the mosque.
Then she went to her own house to await her father's death.

Ahmed Bayazidi was afraid. He tried to listen to his father, who
was not yet seventy and enjoyed a robust constitution and an unnerv-
ingly sharp memory: he and his friend Hayyim Istanbouli still told
stories about the earthquake of sixty years earlier. It had come as a
surprise to everyone when he retired and told his son Ahmed to take
over all his work and his positions. Najib Bayazidi had suddenly decided he wanted to spend his time at his country house raising geese
and doves and reading tales of folk heroes to his grandchildren. (His
favorite was the warrior Abi Zeid Al-Hilaly.) He hosted his friends

and went on overnight hunting trips with them, where they would sleep naked like teenagers and discuss the gazelles they would shoot in the desert with their bows and arrows.

When he saw the children come in, Grandfather Najib broke off his ranting and stood up, frightened. He asked Zakariya, Hanna, and Souad to go with him to his house. He was teaching them how to raise doves and showed them the eggs that would hatch the following day. Souad in particular loved the idea and went out with him, followed by Hanna and Zakariya. Ahmed Bayazidi and Radia were silent. They knew that what Amina foretold happened, and she didn't talk about something unless it had come to her in a vision, but all the same, they hoped she had misinterpreted this time, as she had a few times before.

On the morning of the third day, Amina left her room and found her father strutting around in excellent health, laughing and teasing his grandchildren. He mocked Amina and heaped scorn on the coffin that the carpenter had brought. Taking a last look at him, she said, "You can turn the coffin I bought into a manger for your horses." Then she kissed him and left silently. As she walked away, she heard him declare that he would live another fifty years, but that night he fell asleep and never woke up.

Amina wouldn't walk in his funeral procession. She was tracking his soul as it rose closer to Heaven with every passing moment. She wept in silence for the death of her father, whom she had loved dearly, even though he had been very cruel to her in his final years. While his body was being prepared for burial, Souad said matter-of-factly, "Grandfather's disappeared." She had seen his body disintegrate and sink into the earth, and the shrouded coffin in the middle of the large courtyard now contained only his dense soul. When Hanna asked what his soul looked like, she said it was a bit like a huge bean. It poured out of the body's holes like smoke, condensed into a solid shape, and was buried in the ground.

Hanna didn't know what she meant. He looked at Zakariya, who shrugged to show that he didn't understand either. Satisfied with what she had said, Souad asked Zakariya to lend her his paper kite, which he gave to her willingly. Together, they took it to the roof of their house, where she held the string with both hands. The kite lifted into the air, and Zakariya was baffled when Souad let it fly away, but she said simply that Grandfather Najib had taken it out of her hand. Zakariya believed her. He held his little sister in high esteem—truth and imagination were mingled in her words—and he knew that the rest of the family warily regarded her as her aunt's heir.

Aunt Amina, notwithstanding her infinite kindness, was frightening. She only ever announced bad news, and the city's inhabitants avoided her. She lived alone in her father's house after his death, having refused to go and live with any of her four siblings for fear of ruining their lives. In any case, the place she occupied was just a fraction of the large house her father had divided among the siblings years ago. Ahmed Bayazidi, meanwhile, sold his portion and established a new family home in the new quarter, a large house befitting the director of a bank and a high-ranking official responsible for the vali's finances, the appointment he had inherited from his father.

Monsieur Jean Jazrawy, a great friend of Grandfather Najib during his lifetime, believed that Amina could read fortunes. She helped him plan his life. Every Friday morning he knocked on her father's door and, instead of going to visit his friend, walked to Amina's quarters next to the stable where the pair of horses lived. He drank his coffee while she searched the clutter of her awesome, terrifying memory for any record of him, and he waited for a sign, any sign, from her, that would tell him that he wouldn't die soon. When he was satisfied, he would leave her father's house and immediately seek out an act of recklessness to perform. He used to call Amina "the messenger of happiness." Grandfather Najib Bayazidi couldn't bear his friend's impudence and his daughter's fairy tales. He turned Jean out and told him not to come to the house again, but the man continued to be in touch with Amina by means of a Jewish girl whom he sent specially to bring him Amina's prophecies. Once Amina sent word to Jean via the messenger not to leave the house and to cancel his upcoming trip to Latakia with his friends. Jean couldn't believe it when the news reached him later that his friend's carriage had slipped into the valley after Jisr Al-Shughur and fallen all the way to the very bottom into a pine thicket where it was impossible to reach, and no trace of him could be found. A few days after that, Jean Jazrawy gave Amina a gold belt and emigrated to America. He had become jaded linking his life to Amina's prophecies and was afraid that one day she would knock on his door and tell him he only had a couple of hours to live. Amina returned the golden belt to him and shut her door, and after her father died, she stopped receiving anyone. She isolated herself with Hajja Nabiha, well known throughout the city for her piety, where she recited the Qur'an all day long and wept with deep emotion. Within a few years, Aunt Amina had become a fervent supporter of the ideas of Sheikh Abulhuda Al-Sayyadi; his star had risen in the vilayet, and his pupils had begun to circulate his ideas widely. But still, despite being associated with the sheikh, Amina's former reputation preceded her everywhere she went.

While the family was occupied receiving condolences for Grandfather Najib, marked by the apprehensive silence of the visitors who didn't know how to respond to Amina's prophecy, Zakariya busied himself with making a new kite: it was wonderful, and it flew properly. It occurred to Souad that if she let go of its string, it might return, just like the doves that her grandfather had been so proud of. He used to go with his friends to Idlib, to open the cages of doves, which fluttered out in a single burst of movement, and when the men returned to Aleppo, they would find that their birds had arrived ahead of them. So Souad thought that this new kite of Zakariya's would also come back, but she was slightly unsure, so she asked him, "Will the kite come back like Grandfather's doves?" Zakariya replied, "I don't know, but it might." He gave it some thought, then added, "William Eisa's didn't come back the time it got away from him, down by the river." Souad was excited as she took hold of the large kite's thread, threw it up into the sky, and let the thread go. When the wind blew it east, she saw it as nothing more than the hand of her grandfather—who had died only two days earlier—whisking it away. Souad was grateful to Zakariya, who had

allowed her to release the kite even though making it had been a difficult and costly undertaking. The next morning she told him that she
was sure the kite would come back like Grandfather's doves. Zakariya
was overjoyed to hear her say this and expected it to come flying back
through the window at every moment, but it never came. His mother
explained that kites don't come back, and his grandfather couldn't
possibly have left his firmly closed grave to catch hold of the string.
Hearing this, Zakariya was furious and headed straight for Souad. He
slapped her cheek and kicked her and said she had lost his kite and
made a fool out of him. Hanna rushed toward Zakariya and punched
him hard, bloodying his face. All this only took a moment or two.
Zakariya leaped on Hanna and hit him back, and Souad stepped between them. She was crying hard, and the two boys stopped fighting.
Hanna came up to the dazed Zakariya and hugged him, repeating
that he was sorry and begging for forgiveness, but he couldn't bear to
see Zakariya hit Souad.

Even after a year passed, Souad's eyes still filled with tears whenever she remembered that occasion. The following day, for the first
time, the three of them sat in silence. Zakariya brought out his portion of the sweets that his mother had handed out in memory of his
grandfather, and he held them out to Souad, begging her to take them.
He suggested that if they laid out hempseed and drink, the kite might
come back, just like the doves. After Grandfather's funeral, Aunt Amina had opened the door of the dovecote and set all the birds free. She
wanted to be rid of their excrement, but they came back at night to
roost on the roof. With no Grandfather to scatter grain and hempseed
for them and clean out their water bowls, however, they soon left and
never came back.

Souad quickly forgave her brother, and their reconciliation was witnessed by William Eisa, Hanna, Azar, and Azar's sister Sara. Alongside
Zakariya, Souad and Hanna busied themselves making a new kite,
brightly colored and even bigger than the last one. Souad got bored
with it after a few days, and Zakariya worked on it with only Hanna's
assistance. Aunt Amina advised him to use thick colorful paperboard.

Zakariya felt very proud when Hanna and Souad carried the finished kite, one on each side. It was huge and crisp and had thick hemp twine as a string.

On Friday morning, Zakariya walked with his friends to Mount Jawshan to fly the largest kite the city had ever known. Hanna and Souad defended him heroically against the derision of William Eisa, Zakariya's bitter rival in kite-flying. Their young friends kept telling them that the kite wouldn't fly, but Zakariya remained defiant, and when the kite lifted into the air, he felt his heart pound. The colors were beautiful in the sky, reflecting the rays of the sun. Souad was proud, and all the friends applauded when the kite dropped gently back to earth without mishap. William Eisa came up to Zakariya and kissed him warmly, and Azar whispered in William Eisa's ear, "You have to make a bigger one." Zakariya was exuberant and turned to his excited friends and boasted, "I'll make a new kite, three times bigger than this one." Then he gave the string to Souad and whispered, "You have to learn how to fly a kite." Souad was overjoyed, but even with Hanna's help, the string hurt her fingers. She managed to raise the kite, and it flew up high, but she was taken aback when Zakariya whispered to her to let it go, adding that their grandfather might need it—Aunt Amina had told him that Grandfather Najib's soul had risen into the sky. Souad looked at him. He was serious; he wanted his kite to fly away into the sky over the large city. It would pass over the lanes, the riverbank, and the orchards outside the city, and when it reached the graveyard, his grandfather's hand would catch it. He would read Zakariya's name and know that they remembered him and would send him more kites. Souad liked this idea. She looked at Hanna, smiled at William Eisa, Azar, and Sara, and calmly released the string—to the astonishment of their friends, who couldn't believe that she would do such a thing. But a moment later she explained that the colored kite was a greeting to Grandfather Najib and Um Hanna. The kite disappeared, to the amazement of all and a smile from Zakariya as he hugged Hanna, who was weeping quietly. He said, "I'll make a kite three times bigger than this one, and Souad will send that one to

Grandfather Najib and Um Hanna in Heaven too." Souad whispered gravely that he mustn't tell their friends that their grandfather's soul had slipped out of the grave and gone into the sky, and he nodded in understanding. He put his arm around her shoulders amid the commotion of the other children noisily making their way back home.

Hanna and Zakariya still remembered the tenor of those pleasant days, and Souad's guileless innocence and surfeit of imagination. She divided her life among several personalities and inhabited them with ease, effortlessly mingling her worlds and lives. She inwardly shrank from her aunt's fate—she didn't want to be like her. Aunt Amina had become a frightening wraith for the inhabitants of her own city. Men she didn't know would stop her and ask her their destinies, high-ranking officers would ask for appointments to question her about their fortunes, and her family didn't know how this tragedy would end. They loved her and were afraid that she would meet the dark fate that awaited a sorceress, whose image she was yoked to in people's minds.

After her father died and she retreated from life to stay at Hajja Nabiha's side, Amina felt more at ease. Her decision was made after her female friends held a large zar ritual to drive out the demons from her body and her deranged soul. They beat her, played the tambourines, and reached the summit of revelation. Amina was in the middle of them, sobbing violently, appealing to the saints, calling to them one by one. For hours, she quaked under the thud of tambourines until she fainted. When she woke up the next morning, she wept at the vision of Radia, her brother's wife, preparing to ascend the step of death. She burst into sobs and barricaded herself in her room.

Several months earlier Radia had asked Amina to accompany her to fulfill a vow. Zakariya was now ten years old, and he enjoyed good health and a strong body, and she intended to give thanks for his preservation by walking barefoot to the Umayyad Mosque. As they set off, Souad was beside them, delighted to be with her mother and Aunt Amina, who repeated verses she had memorized from the Qur'an all the way to the mosque. Hanna and Zakariya were walking in front, ensuring the road was clear of any large stones and thorns. They stopped people from even looking at the pious woman walking with bare feet, accompanied by a woman who hid her face behind a black burqa and a beautiful girl with a black covering on her head who was chatting about the ducks she had seen swimming in the river last month, which had turned into princesses! Radia arrived at the mosque, prostrated herself in front of the resting place of the prophet Zakariya, and said tearfully, "I have fulfilled my vow, and I want to make another." But Amina interrupted her, and she closed her mouth. Amina told Radia to be silent and simply pray, saying, "Vows are a bad omen. Zakariya will live a long time." Radia was overjoyed at Amina's prophecy; it was the first time that she had ever foretold joyful news.

Souad was agitated and excited and chattering rapidly as they all went home. Hanna asked her earnestly how she made up her stories. They had all been on the bank of the river together, but no one else had seen ducks turning into princesses. Just as earnestly, Souad replied, "Yesterday, when the two of you were walking in front of us and clearing the path for my mother, you were a hedgehog. But when we went home, you turned into a rabbit." Hanna didn't understand, but he, along with Zakariya, believed that when Souad grew up, she would give birth to a horse.

Within a few years, both boys were struck with an odd passion for going to the back alleys of Bab Al-Faraj with William Eisa, Azar, and Azar's cousin David, who knew every twist and turn of every lane, and where every Jew lived in nearby Bahsita. The boys would harass the young hawkers, trying to goad them into a fight. David's advice had been blunt: if they wanted to survive in the backstreets of Aleppo, they had to prove their strength. Over several days, David taught them the principles of knife-fighting. He was three years older than the others and worked with his mother in their neighborhood hammam in Bab Al-Nasr. David was famed among his friends for his mastery of weapons, knives in particular. Hanna stood in front of him, and David lashed out with a knife, ripping just Hanna's qunbaz without doing him any serious harm. He taught the boys this skill, which they picked up quickly. They kept sharp knives in their schoolbags, and at the slightest provocation from the other students, the four friends would range themselves in the corners like a gang and take out their knives—to the horror of their classmates, who fled in terror at seeing the blades glittering in the sunlight.

Before long they had become familiar faces in Bab Al-Faraj, whose alleys bristled with outlaws and pimps who sought clients in the crowded markets. Passersby would push the boys out of their way; they were young, and their clothes betrayed them as rich boys looking for adventure. They bribed David to let them sneak into the hammam and spy on the women there, but they found themselves disappointed by the heavy lumps of fat on the fleshy women when they removed their cloaks. David offered to let them watch the evening's clients instead, and they insisted on being allowed to spy on Huda Shamoun, the Jewish girl who was famed for her beauty and who came to the hammam in a procession with her beautiful companions. Huda Shamoun came from a rich family and adored exhibition and scandal. She brought her full entourage every time she appeared on the street: her driver, her maidservant, and three bosom friends. Men would gaze after her in a stupor as her carriage drove by, leaving a lingering perfume behind it.

After a moment's hesitation, David agreed. He opened the door to the corridor that led to the room where the fires were lit and told them to be absolutely silent. Huda's carriage arrived, and she alighted. David signaled to the four friends to take turns at the peephole that was just big enough for a single eye, and they almost shredded each other with their knives in their dispute over whose turn was next. Meanwhile Huda's maid and her friends had removed their clothes, and the smell of perfumed soap filled the air. The boys finally agreed to draw lots, but their raised voices had betrayed their location. Huda's personal bodyguards surrounded the boys, took them by the scruffs of their necks, and threw them out of the hammam. To the bodyguards' surprise, the boys didn't submit as they had expected. They took out knives and waved them in the guards' faces. Passersby who had stopped to take a look couldn't believe the skills of these mere children as they faced down the guards. When the boys saw that William Eisa was bleeding from his nose, they rose up as one and stabbed one of the guards in the stomach. Rather than ending the battle, this merely intensified it; the brawl ended up spilling over into the nearby streets of Bab Al-Faraj, until a police patrol intervened and arrested everyone. The yazbashy couldn't believe that these thugs were schoolchildren, one of them the son of the respected Ahmed Bey from the Bayazidi family.

The families of Huda Shamoun and Ahmed Bayazidi intervened to save the boys from police custody before they were transferred to the judge. Huda Shamoun demanded to see them in her house after they were released. When the boys entered the large salon, their clothes were torn, and they looked like a bunch of reprobates. She asked them what they had been doing in the hammam, and Hanna answered at once, "We wanted to see you naked."

Huda Shamoun scrutinized the boys thoughtfully. They were scrawny and far from fully grown. Considering their impertinence, she asked, "Why?" Zakariya replied, "You are the most beautiful woman in Aleppo." William Eisa chimed in, "In the world, even." Azar, abashed, said nothing. He was thinking about what would happen when he went home—his father would never forgive him and would beat him with a worn-out leather strap. Hayyim would often remind Azar that his scholarship was paid for out of the Jewish poor fund and also by his friends, the sons of rich men and blithely indifferent to their own wealth.

Huda felt an unfamiliar happiness. She forgave them on the spot, kissed them, and shook hands with them. She asked Azar to stay behind so she could mediate with his family, and her carriage driver took them all home. Huda Shamoun was preparing to marry the Italian vice-consul, Simone Giovanni. The agreements were all concluded, her jihaz was receiving its final touches, and she didn't have time to reflect on the reckless adventures she would have liked to enjoy with these ruffians. But she never forgot Hanna's sensual lips as he told her that they had done it all just to see her bathing naked.

The carriage arrived at Ahmed Bayazidi's house. Zakariya wasn't afraid; he whispered to Hanna to hurry inside and let him deal with his father. It was late, and it had been an exhausting day. They had slept under watch and been spat on by the guards. The door was open, the house completely silent. Souad hurried toward them in tears and hugged them. She said that their mother had died and her soul was rising out of the house. It wouldn't be long until dawn, when her soul would leave the city and become a huge flat bean.

Radia Bayazidi was a God-fearing woman, slight and short. There was a strange light in her eyes that had only been extinguished in her last moments. She spent most of her time thinking about her three dead children, and she had been struck with the delusion that she would never be blessed with a child who could resist death. She couldn't believe it when Zakariya reached his fifth year, and she was terrified of any slight illness that befell him. She made incessant vows until the day Amina told her that promises were a bad omen and Zakariya would live. Radia Bayazidi lived her life in the shadows, and from her own mother, she inherited the advice not to interfere with the Bayazidi clan. She used to describe them as a collection of people who lived their lives in notebooks and ledgers: people didn't exist, to accountants. And neither her father nor her husband had evaded that legacy of the family that adored numbers.

When Zakariya reached fifteen as a strong and sturdily built boy, she was reassured. She couldn't believe it when his voice broke, and Souad turned twelve. Around this time, Radia was cured of her fear that Souad had inherited her aunt's legacy. Souad had strange ways of expressing herself, but she was a cheerful, laughing girl, despite suffering from an "overactive imagination," as the doctor described it after examining her—Radia had expressed fear of a mental defect. Souad's condition would be easy to treat; it would be enough to live among stupid people for a short while, and she would forget everything and become a realist who would see a river as a river and not as a herd of elephants rolling around a hilltop. In Radia's last days, she was secretly pleased to see Zakariya and Hanna causing her husband headaches; she didn't want her son to be like the rest of his family, reined in and disciplined from childhood.

The school administrators sent for Ahmed Bayazidi. They complained about the two schoolboys who carried knives into the classroom while the headmistress of the girls' school praised Souad's politeness, intelligence, and cheerful spirits. Radia wanted a different life for her son, far from the ledgers of cringing accountants. She always believed that finance was the worst profession a person could practice; it gave him an inflated sense of his self-worth, like her brothers and her father and her husband, who all fell over themselves to praise numbers and the riches of their clients. But Zakariya wasn't like them. He threw his clean clothes into the bottom of the cupboard. Like his friend Hanna, he couldn't care less about new things. She used to look at him with pride, and the older he got, the less she felt the need of summers in Ariha, where the soft air helped her to endure her bouts of asthma.

Hanna and Zakariya never forgave themselves for leaving her to die alone. The servants, Um Kheir and Margot, hadn't noticed that their mistress hadn't woken from her afternoon nap until Souad asked Margot if her mother was up. Souad had been avoiding her father, who was furious when he came home from his office, cursing Hanna and Zakariya. But Margot, who had gone into Radia's bedroom, came out terrified and said, "It's as if she's dead."

Souad couldn't believe that her mother had died. She kept waiting for her every day on the step to her room. Hanna would sit next to her and tell Souad that her mother had gone where his mother had, and each of them would be very glad that the other was there. He told her his memory of his father, and added that he didn't know where his mother was buried, and he never saw her dead. After a long silence, he asked Souad, "Does death bring happiness to the living?" Souad considered this and said she didn't know, but death was definitely a lie, it was like a game of hide-and-seek. She wasn't brave enough to tell him that she had seen her mother the night before in a vision, crossing the courtyard, carrying her white shroud, and smiling. She was delighted at having turned into a bean. Souad couldn't control her tears. Hanna hugged her, and Zakariya tried to cheer her up. He told her, "You're our mother now." She nodded in agreement, remembering the day her grandfather had died, five years earlier, and recalling how he had turned into a very big flat bean. Before she went up to her room that evening, she asked Zakariya to help her make the biggest kite he could. The misery their mother had lived through while remembering her dead children was more than enough; now their mother's soul deserved to fly with the most resplendent colors.

Hanna embarked on his fifteenth year, and his seventh living in the Bayazidi family home. Ahmed Bayazidi's battle with the church over custody had come to an end only a few months earlier. This battle had exhausted him, particularly the occasions when Hanna's distant relatives would come to his office and, with overweening confidence, demand to see the secret accounts of Gabriel Gregoros and his family. They haggled over which portions of his estate they had an illusory claim to, and spoke to him rudely, and tried to persuade the church to reclaim Hanna and put him in a Christian orphanage. But Ahmed Bayazidi, as was his wont in pitched battles, turned his patience to his advantage. He always believed that time brought an accumulation of errors on the part of one's enemies, cracks that eventually revealed themselves so that one could sweep in and deliver a devastating blow.

Ahmed Bayazidi drew on all his connections to maintain custody of Hanna, the sole remaining child of the Gregoros family, but the matter was put to rest only with the intervention of Aunt Amina, who exercised her covert authority. She wrote to Abulhuda Al-Sayyadi who, from his origins as a Sufi dervish banging a tambourine, writing out protective amulets, and collecting alms for the poor, had become a man ravenous for power. His already considerable local influence expanded, he drew closer to the sultan, and he rose in rank until he reached the position of Sheikh Al-Islam of the Ottoman Empire, one of the inner circle of Sultan Abdel Hamid II and his court at the Sublime Porte.

In her letter, Amina explained Hanna's story and requested that the sheikh take steps to issue an order from the Sublime Porte itself to the vali to cease harassing her brother. After such a prolonged and bitter battle, Ahmed Bayazidi was taken aback by an invitation to meet the metropolitan, who promised an end to the issue of Hanna's custody and to drop all claims to the Gregoros estate, in exchange for a written pledge from Ahmed Bayazidi that he would never attempt to convert Hanna from Christianity to Islam.

Ahmed Bayazidi believed that he didn't have long to live and worked hard at protecting Hanna's property from the greedy and the ambitious. Everyone wanted to plunder his inheritance, and so distant relatives challenged the judgment from the sharia courts that granted Ahmed legal custody of Hanna, insisting that it wasn't possible to grant custody to a Muslim of anyone or anything related to a Christian. The church obligingly agitated for the issue to be raised all the way to the Sublime Porte, but after three years they fell silent. They understood that the relationship between the two families was intricately entwined, not the usual relationship of a landowner and trader with his accountant and agent. Moreover, they suspected that Ahmed Bayazidi secretly retained his Christianity, although more than a century had passed since his grandfather converted to Islam.

One morning soon after Radia's death, Ahmed Bayazidi inspected all his rooms. Everyone was asleep. He sat at his favorite table to drink his morning coffee, felt the refreshing April breeze. He went back to his library; there were piled-up letters from banks he had invested in. So far his returns weren't numerous, but they might double if he abandoned his caution. He reflected that if his friend Gabriel were still alive, he would tell Ahmed to buy bonds in a new treasury offered by the British government. Ahmed Bayazidi wouldn't take responsibility for a risky matter such as this—he would freeze everything until Hanna reached twenty, and then he would deliver to him all

his wealth. Ahmed Bayazidi had saved more than half of Hanna's liquid funds from being smuggled, and more than half of his property
from the clearing of the Sublime Porte. What Hanna already had was
enough, but Ahmed Bayazidi was determined to uncover the fate of
the ten thousand gold liras that Gabriel had converted into sterling
and deposited in an English bank five years earlier. It was the last payment Ahmed Bayazidi saved from the liquidation of his friend's warehouses in Aleppo, which Gabriel had protected by registering the title
deed in the name of his friend—Ahmed Bayazidi. He secretly blamed
Gabriel for letting a bunch of crooks from his family play havoc with
the Gregoroses' relationship with the rulers.

Radia's death gnawed into his bones. He grieved her loss deeply.
She had been his dearest companion, and now he was alone; he enjoyed good health and would live out the rest of his long life among
servants. He was troubled to see Hanna and Zakariya in the prime
of youth and so utterly heedless. He was aware that they were well
known in the back alleys of Bab Al-Faraj, and he decided that he had
to put a definite stop to this chaos. But then his thoughts grew muddled as he heard the sound of his servants, Margot and Um Kheir,
squabbling again. They never paused their endless debate around the
Messiah and the Prophet Muhammad, repeating the same words over
and over; they both possessed an astounding capacity and energy for
prattle, as if they lived in a world cut off from humanity.

He had suggested that they separate so that each woman could live
in her own room—he could build a new room in the large courtyard.
But they refused: their fight had become an integral part of their lives.
Souad intervened to resolve their dispute even though she was still
very young. They listened to her, but their voices would soon be raised
again in an unending dispute about the two religions. Um Kheir
never passed up a chance to invite Margot to convert to Islam, saying,
"I am thinking of you, I want you to go to Heaven." Margot would
summon up everything she had learned about Jesus and his disciples,
and about the lives of the saints, and would whisper to Um Kheir that

converting to Christianity would bring her joy. She would promise in a low voice that if Um Kheir did convert, it would stay a secret, just between them.

Before they fell asleep, Margot would remember her youth and tell Um Kheir about the young men who used to wait for her to pass so they could have the boon of a single glance from her. As usual, she concluded by reminiscing about a Kurdish youth who used to play at being a knight and ask her to elope with him. But she would always say to him, "If you go with me to the priest and announce you are a Christian, I will run away with you at once." Hundreds of times Margot retold stories about Muslim youths, Kurds and Arabs and Turks, who had fallen in love with her but couldn't overcome the barrier of apostasy to renounce Islam and become Christian for her. On long winter evenings, Um Kheir would reminisce about her lovers too. She would say that they were three Christian youths, one from a well-known family, but she held her tongue regarding their names. They used to follow her when she went out to the market with her mother, and they would hold vigil under her window at night. Margot would nod understandingly and say, "How could a Christian bear to leave the religion of Jesus, son of Maryam, and convert to Islam?" Um Kheir would fly up in a rage, and Margot would laugh and say she was joking. Then they would commiserate with each other for the bad luck that had made each beloved by beautiful young men from another religion, and after a brief silence, the women would fall asleep in neighboring beds.

After Radia died, Margot became more stern. She suffered from constant nightmares and still believed that holding on to Hanna's Christianity was worth sacrificing her life for. In truth, she was poor and had nowhere else to go. She dreamed that Hanna would grow up and take her with him, and they would both travel to some other place where she could hang her pictures of Jesus and the saints whose stories she collected, and at night she would tell these stories to Hanna's children. They would be the opposite of their father, who had been raised by Muslims and was so terribly bored by her tales of the lives of the saints that he would fall asleep. She decided that she would take Um Kheir with them because despite everything, the woman had a good heart, and she was an excellent cook. Margot loved Souad, who felt great affection for her in return. Margot made sure that Hanna was covered with a blanket on cold winter nights, and on the way to school in the morning, Souad would tell the boys that Margot was happy because she had seen Jesus hovering around Hanna in his room the night before. The boys would look at her, and Zakariya would ask, "Just around Hanna?" Yes, she would reply. The boys sniggered as their thoughts went down paths that Souad would never have imagined; they had lots of indecent stories they had agreed they could never tell her.

The boys grew up and felt increasingly full of life. They both enjoyed a little buffoonery, and a shared love of mischief brought them even closer. No one could believe that these adolescents could come up with so many wicked ideas. They spent a long time gazing at Souad while considering whether to throw her into the large pan or dangle her from the well rope. They went out in the evenings to walk around their new neighborhood in Farafra, knock on William Eisa's door, and turn into the neighborhood of Bab Al-Nasr, where Azar Istanbouli lived. Then the four of them would emerge into the night like hungry wolves. They thought long and hard how to make themselves into a story the city would be unable to forget.

Hanna and Zakariya couldn't care less about their religions. If they were asked, Hanna would sometimes reply that they were Christians, and other times that they were Muslims from the Bayazidi family. Zakariya never objected to or corrected this information; they were pilgrims headed for the backstreets of Bab Al-Faraj. Meanwhile they often alarmed Azar and William Eisa with their ideas. When the owner of a coffeehouse in Jamiliyya threw them out and wouldn't give them any coffee because they were too young, Zakariya and Hanna vowed they would burn down the coffeehouse, but they forgot the incident in a few days. They were sixteen when William Eisa took the group to a brothel in the Nayal district. The oldest by a year, William acted as the leader; he whispered to the madam, Jamila, that it was Hanna and Zakariya's first time experiencing the magic of sex. Jamila's practiced eye saw that this was a momentous occasion for these four ruffians whose exploits with Huda Shamoun were now notorious throughout the city.

She led them to some beautiful girls and whispered to them to take good care of their clients, who would be rich pickings—Jamila knew exactly who they were. And so the girls looked after their four clients, who didn't have any money on them. William Eisa promised Jamila that the bill would be paid in double, as he did on subsequent visits, but she reached her limit when for the fourth time, she opened her door and found them all standing there, asking to see their girlfriends. She threw them all out, and the following day she marched into Ahmed Bayazidi's office at the bank and presented him with a bill for dinner and three full nights with four girls. Ahmed Bayazidi paid up, left a substantial tip for Jamila, and issued a threat that if she ever welcomed them again, he would burn down her house, adding that he knew an important Turkish officer who frequently patronized her establishment. Jamila continued on to Azar's family home and spoke with his father Hayyim Istanbouli, who waited for his son to come home that night and then hung him off the roof by his legs. He spat on his son and spoke the words that rang in Azar's ears: *No one studying on charity has any right to visit a whorehouse.* He beat Azar ruthlessly, shut him up for three days in the orphanage storehouse, shaved his head, and told him he could choose between staying away from his idiot friends or being sent off to school.

Souad couldn't understand her father's rage that night. The scandal was dealt with and in the past, just like the many other scrapes he had been forced to intervene in personally. But that night he was different, stern, and he pointed to the details of Jamila's bill on which she had written the item *alcohol*. Zakariya looked at his father innocently and said, "It was just a bottle," and then fell silent. In the following days, when Azar evaded Souad's questions, she understood that they were hiding a secret from her, but she was absorbed in consoling her friend Azar. He was crying, saying goodbye to his friends, telling them he would never see them again. But the next day he was at their rendezvous as usual.

Everyone was surprised when Ahmed Bayazidi brought in an architect to construct a wall to separate Hanna's room from the rest of the house. Ahmed Bayazidi said it was impossible for a young man to live in a house with a girl who was about to embark on adolescence, but in truth it was a preventive step made to forestall the gossip of the Bayazidi women, and the sheikhs who would waylay him and ask if the Christian Hanna was really a brother to his own children. Zakariya and Hanna didn't like the idea at first, but they soon found it an opportunity to be liberated from the strictures of the house and wished their room were even more remote. Souad was upset by their removal; she saw they were becoming more distant and keeping secrets from her, but she resolved to follow behind and wouldn't let them disappear. When she reminded them that she was their mother now, they would laugh and, for a moment, felt that she really was occupying that role fully.

Two years later Zakariya and Hanna mischievously told Souad that they were thinking of going to Paris and living there for a while. Hanna pointed out that they already knew Turkish, and they wanted to join her in Madame Claude's classroom to strengthen their French. Souad waited for them in the afternoon to go with her to Madame Claude's enormous house in Aziziya, the new and rapidly expanding quarter of Aleppo. Madame Claude gathered girls from rich families and taught them French and the basics of European etiquette, which had become à la mode among the upper classes. Souad waited for some time and was furious to discover they had lied to her. Instead they were preparing for a new adventure, having found the key to the box of gold pieces that Radia had left Souad, which Ahmed Bayazidi kept in a cupboard along with his precious ledgers. The boys stole three large gold coins, and William Eisa helped them persuade his uncle the goldsmith to buy them for half their value.

Hanna asked William Eisa to book Jamila's house for the entire night. Azar bowed out; his father's words about living on charity had cut too deep. The remaining three decided they would share all five girls who worked in the house, and they wouldn't disclose their identity beforehand. That night they knocked on Jamila's door, and when she opened up and saw who her clients were, she glared daggers at William Eisa. She turned them away, but Zakariya jammed a foot in the door before she could close it. They pushed their way in to where the smell of incense and perfume wafted throughout. Making a swift calculation, Jamila asked them to pay in advance and to keep absolute secrecy. Zakariya paid her and left her a generous tip to hire some musicians. Jamila considered these rich boys to be easy pickings: raw young men, sons of notable families who had fallen in love with whores, represented a fortune for any brothel in this city. She apologized for going to Ahmed Bayazidi's office and didn't tell them about his threat, which she hadn't taken seriously.

The three of them discovered their passion through the eyes of the shameless women, in the scents of their perfumed rooms. The girls danced and sang with their clients as if they were friends. William Eisa had to make do with one girl, having sex with her hastily before he was forced to leave. He couldn't spend the night away from home, where his father imposed a strict regime upon him, and he was also afraid of the anarchy that reigned over the city at night. Meanwhile Hanna and Zakariya decided to spend the whole night in the arms of the girls, who suspected that women would play a significant role in the future of these reprobates.

It was the first time Hanna and Zakariya had fucked with such utter debauchery. They were freed from their childhood. They forgot all about Ahmed Bayazidi, who got no sleep that night as he kept moving between his own house and the room that Hanna shared with Zakariya. He smelled danger. At dawn he went to the vali's residence. The Turkish officer on duty knew him and, on hearing his request, instantly understood the situation. He dispatched ten soldiers to accompany Ahmed Bayazidi, and when they reached Jamila's house, Hanna and Zakariya were slumped in a drunken slumber, having enjoyed every girl in the house. Jamila was tired and couldn't be bothered with their demands to keep going, so she had left them and gone back to her bedroom. She startled awake in terror when she heard an insistent banging on the door. When she opened the door, she saw Ahmed Bayazidi in front of her. The soldiers searched the house and arrested the girls and Jamila. Hanna and Zakariya struggled back into their clothes and climbed into the carriage displaying a total lack of concern. Once home, they slept late and felt they had been reborn the night before, little boys no more. Hanna made up a story for Souad that they had spent the night in a shrine in Bab Al-Nasr. Their souls were purified, they had sung odes in praise of the Prophet with some other munshideen. Souad was full of praise and added that her friend at Madame Claude's was the daughter of a great musician, and he could teach them music. The boys enjoyed elaborating on this tale for Souad, who was gullible enough to believe them.

That night Ahmed Bayazidi sat at the dinner table, trying to conceal his rage while Hanna and Zakariya ate nonchalantly. Abruptly, he asked his son if he wanted to inherit the accounting profession. He cast a vicious look at Hanna and asked if he wanted to be an employee at the bank: after all, it was a necessary first step toward his future and the management of his properties. Zakariya and Hanna replied shortly that they were thinking of a different future.

Ahmed Bayazidi stood up, looked them each in the eye, and declared that he wouldn't allow them to ruin their lives. His anger rose as he declared that they would join the army; moreover, he would ask the vali to send them under escort to the Ottoman Military College in Istanbul. Many rich families sent their sons to this establishment, to safeguard their influence and instruct their scions in cruelty. A week later Ahmed Bayazidi entered their room and asked them to pack their bags: in three days they would be going to Istanbul. He stressed that Hanna's admittance had not been easy because the college didn't usually accept Christians. After that Ahmed Bayazidi went inside the large house for a short nap, and when he woke up, Zakariya and Hanna were nowhere to be found. Souad was crying heatedly and kept saying that they had gone to Paris, and she begged her father to send her too so she could stay close to them—their French was terrible, and without her they would surely get lost in that huge city.

When they left Aleppo, neither Hanna nor Zakariya had thought very hard or made much of a plan about anything at all; they had arranged everything hastily, having only just realized how serious Ahmed Bayazidi was in his threat. In Hanna's pocket there was a letter of recommendation that Azar had requested on their behalf from Huda Shamoun, who had by now married her Italian vice-consul but still kept herself apprised of news about her four admirers.

Zakariya took care of everything. He stole the remaining gold from his mother's box: it wasn't much, but it would help them live somewhere for a year, maybe less. He knew that if they stayed in Ottoman territory, Ahmed Bayazidi would find them, even if they went underground, so they made their way to Beirut, boarded a ship to Venice, and found things greatly eased for them when they showed a letter of recommendation from the Italian vice-consul to the travel agent. He had been suspicious at first, but the letter of recommendation transformed these boys into valued customers; perhaps they were on a secret mission for the Italian government. Hanna and Zakariya couldn't believe it when the ship sailed; they were at sea and had no idea what they would do in Venice. The captain invited them to a private dinner with other important passengers. He asked them how they knew the vice-consul, and Hanna replied, "Family friend," then fell silent. They enjoyed the mystery they had cast over their dealings with the travel agent. They had dinner and drank the captain's finest Tuscan wine, flattered the other guests, then rose and took their leave. For the rest of the voyage, the passengers continued to talk about the inscrutable mystique surrounding those two young men. Hanna and Zakariya reflected that they were foreigners now, and as such they had to be careful; at the same time, they were absolutely delighted that they were on their way into the unknown.

At this point, Hanna and Zakariya were almost eighteen years old. Zakariya was tanned, tall, and broad-shouldered, with a flour-

ishing mustache; at first glance anyone would think he was a wres-
tler. Hanna's eyes were calm but keen. He was of medium build, with
soft hair and fair skin. Adding to their intrigue, they wore the same
outfit, betraying that they were brothers even if they didn't look at all
alike. From the moment the steamship left port, they knew that the
ship's crew would be looking for them, and they had to be sure that it
wouldn't be so easy to catch them. They invented a new family history
that took into account their Aleppo accents, and having learned from
experience in Bab Al-Faraj not to trust fellow voyagers, they took the
precaution of dividing the gold between themselves and keeping it secreted away in leather zunnars wrapped around their waists. Mostly
they assumed the character of two young men on a mission, and on
occasion they played the role of two naïve, impoverished boys working
on behalf of other unnamed men. Their entire journey was spent in
the same clothes. Although they thanked the captain for looking after
them, they kept their distance from him. The journey passed peacefully, apart from two robbery attempts and a fight with a drunkard
who accused Zakariya of pestering his wife. He took a knife from his
pocket and attacked Zakariya, who easily evaded it. It wasn't hard to
gain mastery over the drunk man, and the next day Hanna went over
to him as he slumped dejectedly in the corner and invited the man
to join himself and Zakariya for breakfast. They found him to be a
good-hearted man from Baghdad who was fleeing a tribal blood feud:
he had not wanted to take this voyage. The three men settled their
differences and exchanged apologies. The man spent the few remaining days of the voyage peaceably drunk, telling them about his life in
Baghdad. He avoided talking about his wife, who only rarely left her
cabin, and on those occasions Zakariya would studiously avoid looking at her while Hanna joked with her. Hanna and Zakariya found
it hard to say goodbye to him; they liked him very much in the end.
They wished him a safe journey to America.

At last they reached Venice, which was teeming with people. They
quickly rented two rooms in a hotel in Piazza San Marco, close to
the cathedral. The first six months were spent moving between hotel

rooms and temporary accommodations. They presented themselves as
horse traders. They didn't understand the first thing about breeds and
bloodlines and couldn't tell the difference between a stallion and a
mule, but it was the least grueling of employments. Years afterward
Zakariya would still remember the story of the horse thief who presented them with purebred horses stolen from the stables of a wealthy
farmer in Tuscany; he was offering the horses for half their value on
the condition of shipping them to Aleppo. Zakariya inspected the five
horses, circled them as he had observed experts do, and opened the
horses' lips to confirm their age. The boys understood each other with
a single look that the deal was no good and gave the pretext that the
horses weren't purebreds. The man took a gospel out of his pocket
and swore an oath on it that the horses were purebred, but the documents of their lineage were lost. Hanna and Zakariya left the warehouse filled with stolen goods, wishing a pleasant evening to the horse
thief's family.

Middlemen swarmed around the pair, and they took their time,
relishing it. They behaved like seasoned traders, in no hurry to contract a deal. They spoke to brokers, examined horses in the stables of
wealthy families and faded princes on the verge of bankruptcy, and
had dinner at the tables of dukes where they discussed politics in weak,
barely comprehensible French. At night, they slept with dancing girls
who loved their generosity, their indolence regarding anything like
hard work, and their inclination toward laughter and entertainment.

After they had been in Venice for a few months, Azar wrote that
he was on his way to Rome and would be in Venice in two weeks.
This made them think of William Eisa: if he stayed alone in Aleppo,
it would soon be the end of his dream to become a great artist. They
wrote to him and asked him to come by any means, they could book
a passage for him, and here he could work on his projects. They also
asked him to spy on Ahmed Bayazidi and tell them how he was. They
wrote too about the bewitching city, and Zakariya sent a portrait of
the two of them in Piazza San Marco, signed by a street artist, who
had sketched it in return for a meal at a Sicilian restaurant.

When William Eisa received the letter, he was incredulous and his eyes filled with tears of joy. But he reflected that his friends were in another world. William was now employed in the factory of Hajj Sobhy Mufti, thanks to his father Michel Eisa, who worked there himself as an expert dyer. William wrote back that he was waiting for them to return. He charged Azar, who was departing Aleppo and would reach them in a few days, with explaining about his work in the factory. His family relied on the money it brought to their household, but he might be commissioned to go to Istanbul or Manchester. He couldn't find much to add—only that there was a Christian girl he was thinking of proposing to, but she was more of a believer than was strictly necessary.

Hanna and Zakariya couldn't believe their eyes when Hanna opened the door and Azar was standing right in front of them, bag in hand. And Zakariya was even more incredulous when Azar told him that Ahmed Bayazidi knew where they were and had started a rumor that had gone around all of Aleppo that he and Hanna were studying art in Venice.

Hanna and Zakariya never found out how Ahmed Bayazidi had learned where they were, but they believed Azar when he said that Ahmed Bayazidi was sure they were in Venice, saying that it was natural for a man like him to know. The pair welcomed their beloved friend, and in his honor they held a riotous party at one of the brothels they frequented. They offered him a Brazilian girl, but she ended up falling to Hanna's lot that night. He admired her figure, and her breasts, and her piercing gaze. The three friends spent a month together before Azar went to study architectural engineering in Rome and was immersed in an entrancing new world. By this time, Zakariya was trying to conceal his growing passion for horses. The magnificent creatures had stolen his heart, and he learned everything he could from Uncle Idris, the Libyan groom who had settled in the city thirty years before and now worked in the stable of Duchess Katerina Gumani, a noblewoman who enjoyed Hanna's and Zakariya's frivolity. She spent hours talking to them about how much she adored Aleppo, but they learned the real secret of her interest in them when she took a letter out of a binder on her bureau. It was a letter from Huda Shamoun made in reply to an inquiry from the duchess, in which she praised Hanna, Zakariya, and their families and asked the duchess to look out for them.

Hajj Idris was generous with his time, explaining to Zakariya in detail how to identify various horse breeds, how to learn their age, and the importance of lineage. He even told Zakariya that when Arabs lost their horses in raids and battles, they sent their hajja, their deed of pedigree, to the victor so that the horses' lineage wouldn't be lost. Unable to lie anymore, Zakariya confessed his new passion to Hajj Idris and his new idea that horses might become his profession. Hajj Idris encouraged him to secure his first deal, saying, "Remember, horses don't like misers or the meek, and you won't ever find them in the house of a moneylender." It was the phrase that Shaha memorized later on, without understanding what it meant.

Meanwhile Hanna spent his time wandering. He took long walks in olive groves and vineyards, or took a carriage and roamed all day. Whenever he was outside the crowded city, he felt great purity and serenity. After six months of living in Venice, they rented a large house and a servant who spoke excellent Arabic to facilitate their affairs. They no longer felt like strangers, having found friends who eagerly joined in their frivolity, and the pair hosted uproarious parties. They traveled to Rome, Florence, Sicily. Azar spent most of his holidays with them, but in general he was kept busy with his studies, which he took seriously, as was his wont. The letters from William Eisa never stopped. He told them about Aleppo and his upcoming plans, mocked the girl he was supposed to have married, and related the details of his first trip out of the city—he was going to Istanbul to carry out some projects for Hajj Sobhy Mufti's factory.

Venice was, above all, a way-stop for two runaways with no aim in mind. As Zakariya discovered his love of horses, Hanna had some painful moments remembering Souad. Her image was constantly at the forefront of his mind, and he couldn't believe she was the girl who was most present in his thoughts. She was there in his dreams, and when he wandered in the nearby meadows or through the streets interwoven with canals, he saw her face everywhere. He reflected that if he stayed in Venice for much longer, he would turn desperate. Meanwhile Zakariya spent most of his time with Uncle Idris in the horse market, learning about horses and their habits. A world of joy opened its gates to him. He came back every evening exhausted and weary, and he would instruct Hanna how to tell English horses apart from Arab horses, a subject Hanna couldn't care less about. He was looking for his own self, and every moment he drew closer to the idea that he would spend his life seeking endless, inexhaustible pleasures. He was intensely frustrated when he realized that after a woman left his bed, he couldn't bear for her to return. But still, Souad never left him, and the last image of her before they left remained fixed in his mind: a girl suddenly grown up, whose breasts had rounded in an instant, she was asleep in her bed, and from the door left slightly ajar, he could see her uncovered chest. And an image of her standing in the courtyard watering the plants, her tresses loose . . . to his shame, images of Souad blended with images of momentary girls, and he felt troubled.

He rented a gondola and toured the rippling alleys of the city. He went out to nearby villages and wandered through their lanes, looking for some meaning to his life. His body continued to grow, and he felt its weight. He was missing Zakariya, who spent most of his time with Hajj Idris learning how to care for the four horses he had won in a gambling bet (although he lied to Hajj Idris, telling him he had bought them from a stable in Florence). The horses were good, but they didn't carry the mark of rare stock that Hajj Idris spoke so fervently about. Zakariya learned to feed them and treat their minor ailments.

One day Zakariya took courage and knocked on the doors of famous stables, presenting himself as a horse trader. He was astounded when at last Hajj Idris was permitted to take him on a tour of Duchess Katerina Gumani's entire stable. It all seemed to be on another plane altogether; it was a grand hotel for horses, not merely a stable. At that moment he resolved to do the same thing on his return to Aleppo. Meanwhile Hanna discovered a new passion of his own; he spent hours in St. Mark's Cathedral, sitting alone and staring at the ceiling. On other occasions he returned to pray with the other worshippers, never speaking with anyone. For the first time, he thought about the Messiah, whom Margot had always portrayed as an angel and the guardian of innocent children. In those few weeks, he thought deeply about the different religions and their meanings. A single question wandered through his head: what if people lived without religion, or any gods at all?

Despite Zakariya's new passion, and the uproarious parties, and Hanna's wanderings in the countryside around Venice and Padua, his hours-long conversations with the fellahin, and even the occasional moments he joined them in prayer as a fellow Catholic; despite his anxiety that grew with each night, and his never-ending questions about the meaning of religion and tolerance, and his examination of olive oil presses as he tried to understand the difference between each type; despite their riotous, unruly life and their sense that they would never go back to how they were when they first arrived in Venice; despite all that, they were essentially without ambition. They believed that life was one long continuous game, but they believed that if they decided to live here much longer, they would have to arrange their lives differently. They received a letter from William Eisa telling them that his work had moved to Istanbul and inviting them to visit him there, but they decided to go back to Aleppo instead. A year and nine months had passed in their absence—it was a long time. They missed Souad, and the house, and the city. The gold pieces would run out in a few weeks. They calmly plotted their life to come. Hanna was twenty and could take control of his property if he convinced Ahmed Bayazidi that he was a serious-minded young man who could hold on to it. Zakariya was deeply gripped by his passion for horses; the discovery of the existence and nature of these magnificent creatures had worked a mysterious sorcery he couldn't describe. He would always remember his first teacher, Hajj Idris; he would never forget his calm words telling him that whoever lived with horses became like them. Images of vigor and honor and power were very seductive to a young man like Zakariya, and most important of all, it would permanently preclude him from accounting, the historical family business.

Hanna had planned out his life. He wouldn't stop asking questions, and because he had no answers, he would live as a drunkard, lying intoxicated in the arms of women—nothing equaled the pleasure of being extinguished in a woman's embrace. They didn't give much thought to Ahmed Bayazidi's scrutiny; they would live in independent houses and manage their own lives. Zakariya knew that separating from the family wouldn't be easy, but it was necessary. On their last night in Venice, the pair spent hours discussing their future. They thought that it was the first time they had spoken like adult men, and this new image came with a burden of sadness, a farewell to a childhood that was now very distant. Their days in Venice left an indelible impression on them. For years afterward, they would reminisce about their time in the city that couldn't tempt them to stay but that turned them into something different from the young men who had arrived there. Back then, they had been still in their childhood and considered laughter a profession. Before deciding to return, they had briefly considered spending the rest of their lives away from Aleppo, but they were horrified at the mere thought of it. Hanna was more enthusiastic about going back than Zakariya, who had begun to build good relationships with horse traders. Hanna didn't mention his longing for Souad, whose image had never left him for a single instant.

On the way back, they weren't afraid of anything. The few gold pieces they had left were not enough to be a temptation for thieves, and they were more experienced this time in dealing with the sailors and the other passengers. They spent most of their voyage reminiscing about their surprise whenever Souad had calmly tossed out another of her strange sayings, and how she had believed all their peculiar stories and the lies they had concocted just for her.

They had missed Aleppo, which they finally reached one autumn evening in 1892. Souad opened the door, and they were both thunderstruck. Since they left, she had become a tall, beautiful girl of seventeen. She hugged Zakariya hard and was embarrassed as she greeted Hanna in a more aloof manner, then noticed the two horses, which Zakariya also suddenly remembered. He took his leave and disappeared for a couple of hours to place them at a khan for animals until he could find a suitable place to keep them.

Hanna stayed behind in the courtyard. He couldn't believe what had happened. Souad looked at him ardently. She was a different girl, nothing like the old Souad, who had still been growing. At that moment, she was the most beautiful girl he had ever seen in his life. Margot hugged him and spoke to him in Syriac. Hanna didn't understand why she would speak Syriac with him in front of Souad, who had no knowledge of it. Souad left them and withdrew to the kitchen. She would prepare coffee, and they would have a long time to talk about the last two years.

On her way to the kitchen, she felt his gaze pierce her. Her body was on fire, and she was embarrassed. She shut the door to the kitchen and burst into tears. She took her time making coffee to give herself a chance to believe what had happened, that their return was real, and all the while Hanna was standing in the courtyard, speaking Syriac with Margot and teasing Um Kheir.

Zakariya came back, delighted with the two expensive horses that he had bought through the mediation of Hajj Idris. The trader he bought them from didn't usually sell these lineages, but had indulged Zakariya in exchange for a vow that they would grow old in his stable. The trader added that tender Aleppo hay would suit these horses very well, as would living in a great city far away from the light-headedness of Venice, which had become occupied by foreign traders.

Souad had always known Hanna and Zakariya would be back before long. She told them that her father had banned her and the servants from even mentioning their names in front of him, but he hugged them both warmly as soon as he saw them, forgetting his former warnings to the servants and to Souad. He treated them as friends rather than dependents, and within a few days he asked the church to send a witness to his lawyer's firm to attend the transfer of Hanna's property. Ahmed Bayazidi retained the right of administration, however; he still feared Hanna's recklessness. Everything was concluded quickly and quietly, but the city mined every detail of it for gossip for a long time. Ahmed Bayazidi accompanied Hanna on a long tour of the properties he had been able to save from the authorities in his famous negotiations, and when they reached his extensive lands in the village of Hosh Hanna on the banks of the Euphrates, Hanna thought it would be a perfect place to live. With a wave of his hand, he indicated that here would be his large house, and next to it Zakariya's house, and there would be a stable in between them. For a few moments, he saw a large village in Hosh Hanna, not just a farmstead of six houses built by Mariana's father and his family who worked as fellahin on the Gregoros lands. Mariana's father had retained his title of wakil, and he hosted Hanna and Ahmed Bayazidi for a night. Mariana couldn't stop gazing at Hanna in amazement. Having him in her house was the realization of a distant dream. She had heard his name every day in conjunction with never-ending rumors: he had converted to Islam, run away to Italy with a prostitute, gone mad, been imprisoned for immorality. His face didn't display any of the cruelty that her fellahin uncles had spoken about. Mariana was seventeen and seemed like a grown-up woman. She had learned to read and write in a school that the priest had set up in the church at Maazouza, three kilometers from Hosh Hanna, and Mariana used to walk there every day to attend classes.

While on the road, the two men spoke freely. Ahmed Bayazidi wanted to become acquainted with the new Hanna, who was charming and responsive. Hanna promised that he wouldn't disobey orders in the future, and without any fuss, he said that he considered Ahmed Bayazidi to be his father. He also spoke to Ahmed Bayazidi about their experiences in Venice without reserve, and he didn't hide his craving for women. On behalf of Zakariya, he asked Ahmed Bayazidi to give up his dream of passing his profession on to his son. He could pass the throne to any one of his nephews who were passionate about continuing the family legacy, but Zakariya loved horses, and they loved him. He also claimed that he and Zakariya shared a passion for farming and horses. Finally, he asked Ahmed Bayazidi to do whatever he liked with the liquid cash, adding with an embarrassed chuckle that he and Zakariya would repay Souad in double for the gold they had stolen.

Ahmed Bayazidi was relieved, his anxiety over. He made plans to distribute Hanna's liquid capital (which wasn't much). In his life, he had seen many reckless landowners and heirs of wealthy families go bankrupt and live in wretched penury. Life, to him, was a never-ending reckoning. Poverty terrified him; he had known too many people who had spent their old age in pain and humiliation. And so his voice quavered as he shared with Hanna what he knew of abject poverty, underscored the value of ambition, and repeated his habitual praise of property. He spoke respectfully of how Hanna's father had doubled his own property five times. Hanna didn't flatter the man whose fears were growing as he approached middle age. Hanna spoke about his father, how his life had been abject and lowly despite all his property. Gabriel Gregoros had conspired with corrupt men of religion and easily bribed functionaries, all to gain a monopoly on sea transport. "Now it's all gone," Hanna said simply. Now all he had was the blood feud on behalf of his mother, his brothers, and the little sister whom no one but Hanna remembered. Ahmed Bayazidi was frightened when he heard Hanna talk about reigniting the blood feud for the first time. He thought of how it would never end, and he begged Hanna to forget about exacting his revenge. He insisted that the story of three officers who had murdered Hanna's father was a fabrication with no truth to it whatsoever; his death was the result of a mistake by unknown savages, and it was the Gregoros cousins who had killed the officer. Hanna interrupted him to say that the mere fact that he was an Ottoman officer who wanted to rape a respectable girl was enough—he deserved death. Hanna added that no one with Syriac blood running in their veins would forget the massacres perpetrated by the Ottomans against Syriac Christians. Despite himself, Ahmed Bayazidi was pleased when he heard Hanna talking with such vehemence about being Syriac; he was aware of the rumors that he was trying to convert Hanna to Islam, and he hoped Hanna's new phase would help to avert those suspicions.

The two men didn't discuss the blood feud again. Throughout the month he spent traveling with Ahmed Bayazidi, Hanna tried to reassure him and avoid provoking him. He was indebted to this calm man who had saved him from an unknown fate. He knew that Ahmed Bayazidi had held on to Hanna's property for him, raised him, and given him a wonderful brother and sister in Zakariya and Souad. (But on some level, he changed his mind; after all, Souad wasn't his sister.) He had been kind to Hanna, who couldn't imagine his life without his inheritance. He shared many characteristics with his father, but he was less covetous, more generous, and more of a realist.

The story of Gabriel Gregoros—or what parts of it he had been able to gather from people who had known him—confused Hanna. At the same time, he felt some hidden pride in him. Gabriel Gregoros hadn't abandoned his people at a time when Christians lived as second-class citizens. They didn't have the right to walk on the sidewalk and had to step off it if they met a Muslim; they had to wear special clothes that differentiated them from Muslims; and above all, they had to pay the jizya tax for every Christian individual who wanted to keep their religion. Gabriel Gregoros used to pay on behalf of poor families who had no money, and he donated secretly to those in need. But on the other hand, Ahmed Bayazidi provided Hanna with a summary of Gabriel's theory that the road to power must be walked over the bodies of your victims. This linking of power with victims troubled Hanna's thoughts for several nights. He thought Ahmed Bayazidi had raised Hanna to resemble himself, rather than Gabriel, who had bequeathed to Hanna the attributes of life among the powerful. However, Hanna wanted to see his path strewn with the bodies not of his old enemies but of new enemies: anyone who would thwart his ambitions of owning the world. The blood feud was a powerful hidden desire of Hanna's, and he believed it would heal his wounds. Hanna tried to explain his theory about victims on the road to power, and revenge for the past, to Ahmed Bayazidi, but he ended up remaining silent. He realized the conundrum of explaining his notions to a man taught by accounting ledgers to doubt everything and trust only figures and their final outcomes.

Hanna still remembered when Ahmed Bayazidi had taken him to church for the first time. At fourteen years old, his first appearance had been a momentous occasion in Christian society, especially as there had been rumors that Hanna had been forced into Islam. Afterward, when he started to attend mass every Sunday, he got to know several Christian families who would smile at him and, once back in their homes, gossip about the nonsense he got up to with his Jewish and Muslim friends in the backstreets of Bab Al-Faraj. The priests were delighted with him, and families threw their daughters into his path. Hanna was indifferent to their hypocrisy, of which he was well aware. After he returned from Venice, he was assiduous in attending prayer. He was no longer content with Margot's equivocating stories about the massacres that left mass graves of Christians in their wake. He wanted to know more about the history of his family, about the history of the Christians in the region and the struggles between Christian sects— and he wanted to lessen the rumors that still dogged him.

Soon after he came back from Venice, he wanted to leave Aleppo again. He felt under siege there, hunted by eyes and rumors. His past antics with Zakariya, William Eisa, and Azar encouraged many people to invent stories about them. He ignored them all, but the advice and moral exhortations he received everywhere irritated him. He told Zakariya he wanted to move to Hosh Hanna, saying, "There we'll be free. There we can escape this hypocrisy." Crucially, they would also be far from the watchful eye of Ahmed Bayazidi, who decided he had won his battle with his son Zakariya and his friend Hanna. As usual, he had wagered that time would be his ally, and he had waited for them to grow up so they would fully grasp the profound import of power, property, and stability—although he hadn't expected them to leave the pleasures of the city to go and live on the banks of the Euphrates.

Zakariya also dreamed of a large stable, like the stable of Duchess Katerina Gumani. They lost no time and soon moved out to the village. Zakariya was glad of his friend's decision. Together they planned their houses, the stable, and new houses for the fellahin who would move closer to the fields.

Hanna's anxiety rose in that period. He felt as though life had him trapped. From the large room he had ordered to be built on the hill, he watched the village that grew every day and observed Zakariya's strenuous efforts to turn the hamlet into a town brimming with life. He relied on the stubbornness of his friend, who worked tirelessly for a year to persuade the rest of Hanna's fellahin from the neighboring villages to live in the village. Zakariya designed houses for himself and Hanna and a stable for his horses. To the plans that he brought with him from Venice, he added many ideas that no one knew about apart from Hanna, who had begun to be cheered by being away from the rigidness of Ahmed Bayazidi, but still close to Aleppo and the towns of Azaz, Afrin, and Antab—and most of all, by the fact that they were living on the riverbank.

A new life awaited them both. Hanna left his room on the hill and moved to his spacious house. He liked the large library overlooking the river; a man could live in total independence in such a place. Zakariya's house was like his, but its back door opened onto the large stable divided into eight sections and with enough space for eighty horses. Zakariya didn't forget a single detail; he excelled at anything that required patience, or a long discussion with the craftsmen and laborers. Together the friends walked in the village alleys and were content to concoct stories as they sniffed the smell of cooking and fresh bread that wafted into every corner. Mariana's father was pleased at the thought of all the fellahin gathering together. He had grown old and was no longer capable of going around to gather them for the farming and the harvest. Mariana meanwhile was determined to catch Hanna's eye. She gathered the young children in a room in her family's house to teach them reading and writing. Hanna was pleased as he saw his life developing in a different way. He thought he could achieve something, a lot even, that he wasn't just another worthless heir to a fortune. He was indifferent to Mariana's maneuvers whenever she waylaid him to discuss matters relating to the children's education or the general improvement of the lives of the fellahin. He agreed to her suggestions and wasn't at all tempted to gaze overlong at her peculiar earrings or her sharp face.

Assiduous in attending Sunday prayers at the nearby church, Hanna would exchange respectful greetings with the priests and supported their plans to help Christian families in need. When he saw small children singing hymns in unison, he was flooded with happiness. He increased his contributions, offered gifts to outstanding students, and felt like he was part of this ambitious community. They in turn regarded him with great respect and didn't believe the stories about his decadence. Before his marriage, Hanna was uneasy that Mariana accosted him so frequently and instructed his wakil, Mariana's father, that no one was allowed to knock on his door; he wouldn't risk anyone disturbing his rest and spying on his private life.

Of course, people still circulated the old stories about him and wrote to the vali, denouncing him as an infidel, but Ahmed Bayazidi was lying in wait for his enemies. One day he said to Hanna, "You can't be an angel in a world where devils dwell." And he explained his approach of resembling others in order to fit in. He pointed out that being different might cost Hanna his life, then without preamble suggested he consider getting married, saying, "Marriage lessens your uniqueness. It gives you great strength; having relatives makes a man one person within a group."

Hanna didn't know why he treated Souad, one of those closest to his heart, with such cruelty. He could no longer go inside the Bayazidi house whenever he wanted, as the pretext of visiting Margot wasn't enough. They had grown up, and Ahmed Bayazidi could no longer bear gossip or stares from those who wondered what right this outsider had to enter his house. In the end, Hanna was not family. Hanna felt deeply constricted—he wished he could stay a child and be close to her. Eventually, Azar's sister Sara helped them to meet by themselves while her father was away; she arranged a few meetings for them and kept their secret.

When Hanna saw Souad standing in the courtyard of Hayyim Istanbouli's house, he felt awkward and embarrassed at betraying the family that had raised him. They had lost their innocence. Hanna wasn't brave enough to hear whatever it was that Souad was going to say. She told him that while they were away in Venice, she had spoken to him every night, and now she would repeat all the words she had had to say then. She was eighteen now, bewitching and elegant, nothing like the naïve young girl she had been. He drank coffee with her in Azar's room, who would shortly be returning to Aleppo, having completed his studies. Hanna was overwhelmed with confusion as Souad looked at him steadily. She was waiting for him to say something, and he was also waiting to hear her say what she had been thinking over the past three years. But they both avoided this subject, exchanging only a few cautious words. At their second meeting, Souad fumbled her way to the wall that he had raised between them. Despite his silence, he was flowing in her blood. She reflected that silent love lives alone, like a wayward, blind child. She felt trapped inside the chasm of pity she had avoided all her life.

Whenever Hanna used to visit Zakariya and Souad in their house, he would be absorbed with inane things, such as getting up and plucking dried leaves off the basil. Souad would watch him, displeased. She was expecting some initiative from him. Every moment she could feel his breaths drawing closer to her and was determined not to wait much longer; she would lead him where she wanted. She could feel his longing for her, and she read his desires.

And yet every time they met, something would rescue him. Once he was waiting for Zakariya to finish bringing some of his belongings so he could take them to Hosh Hanna. Souad poured her second cup of coffee and waited for him to finish removing the dead leaves from the house plants. In the middle of his task, he heard Margot sobbing in the servants' room and immediately hurried toward her, but before he reached the door, Souad told him bluntly that he was in denial, and selfish, and unworthy of love. Furious, she left him and went to her room.

Hanna didn't understand what had just happened. He looked at Souad's retreating back. She didn't turn around. As he walked to Margot's room, he felt worthless, that his heart was black and hateful. When he first came back from Venice with Zakariya, he hadn't noticed that Souad was waiting to tell him about her life and her studies and how much she wanted to go to Beirut. And he had also neglected Margot, whose lap he used to sleep on, who used to comb his hair and tell him about Jesus, who loved innocent, truthful children because they were made in His image. He trudged to the servants' room, opened the door, and was taken aback to see that Margot was dying. Now an old woman who couldn't get up, she was clasping a statue of the virgin in her hands and pleading with the Lord to be allowed to die. Um Kheir was warming her feet and comforting her, asking her to be patient and to take heart.

He sat next to Margot's bed in silence, but he was still thinking about Souad. Images of her now mingled with images of her as a small girl, such as the time he had told her that people turn into their favorite animal when they die. Souad had clapped her hands and said, "I want to be a dog." He burst out laughing at her response, and when she asked him what his favorite animal was, he said without thinking, "A fish." Thinking she would never see him again if that was the case, she suggested that he become a cat instead, so they could stay together. Souad had always considered him part of her life, but after his return from Venice, Hanna and Zakariya had occupied themselves with their new life, separate from Souad, Margot, and the family. They even stopped replying to Azar's and William Eisa's frequent letters. The latter had told them that he was running away from everything and devoting himself to art: he wasn't enjoying life among cotton skeins and the ceaseless activity of dockworkers.

After their return, Hanna and Zakariya spent their time on constant trips in search of women and horses, utterly sincere in their belief that they were doing it all for the sake of others. Hanna saw

Margot only very briefly now and then; he hadn't asked about her health, he hadn't put a room aside for her in his big house. Now he asked for her forgiveness, and she said, "Take me to the orphanage. I want to die among my fellow Christians." Deep down, she thought that dying in a house of Muslims would bring shame upon her sect. In response, he suggested taking her to his house in Hosh Hanna: there were lots of women there who could wait on her, but he couldn't persuade her—she had made her decision. She said she had become worthless garbage, smelly and fit only to be tossed into a pit some-where. But until then she wanted to live in a place where she could hear Christian prayers and be surrounded by pictures of Jesus. She said that when people die, the last image they see goes with them into the sky, and when the Messiah is resurrected, He sees that image in their eyes. Margot wanted a picture of Jesus to be the last thing she saw. But Um Kheir didn't stay silent. She took Margot's hand and whispered that she would fill the wall with pictures of Jesus, and they would make sure Christian prayers were recited for her every morn-ing. She wouldn't let Margot feel estranged from her religion. Um Kheir was very emotional: the two women had shared this room for thirteen years, had spoken thousands of times on every possible sub-ject, had fought and made up a few minutes later. But Margot did not respond and looked pleadingly at Hanna.

He felt helpless. He couldn't persuade her to go with him. He left at night and walked to the church, knocked on the door of Metropol-itan Basilos and told him about Margot. The metropolitan pointed out a home for the elderly that was run by the church and escorted him there. Hanna was shocked to see so many wretched people in one place. The bedsheets stank of pus and disease. The old people were sitting on their beds, gazing at the icon of Jesus that hung on the large wall. Most of them were old women who were living out their lives here after surviving a massacre or a failed marriage; some were women whose families had abandoned them. The conversation with the supervising sister didn't take long—she promised to take care of Margot—and he didn't forget to tell Mariana's father to send a quantity of provisions that would last those poor, forgotten women for a year at least. Hanna visited Margot whenever circumstances allowed, but Um Kheir came every day with food cooked especially for her, and the two of them carried on their usual conversations. Margot shared the money that Hanna had given her with Um Kheir, and if Um Kheir was absent for more than a day, Margot sent for news of her, to be reassured that she was well. Margot died before the winter was over, and Hanna never forgave himself because he wasn't at her funeral. His visits to Aleppo had grown painful during those months. He thought of Souad all the time; every street reminded him of her and their childhood. When he approached the new quarter, his heart would sink, and when he sat in a coffeehouse in Jamiliyya with his friends, he remembered when she had led them to Mount Jawshan and then to the orchards around the city. She always used to warn them to be careful. Her face came to him like a guardian angel. Losing her was unbearably painful, but he couldn't do anything about it. Often, crazy ideas occurred to him; he had never liked being rational. Zakariya wouldn't stop Hanna marrying his sister, and as for Ahmed Bayazidi, it wouldn't be long before he passed on—but could he convert to Islam for her? At times he felt like he could kill himself for her, but at others he felt like an abominable coward. He avoided talking with her. He had nothing to say.

Hanna still remembered Father Ibrahim, who returned to Aleppo around this time. Father Ibrahim welcomed Hanna and praised his morals, which the Christians spoke about. Hanna told him briefly about his travels, asked him about love and whether Jesus could forgive a man who changed his religion for a woman. For the first time, he spoke as a Christian clinging fast to his religion; he had never felt that he belonged to any group that claimed him. Father Ibrahim treated this young man's anxiety with affection. He calmed him, saying, "There is no way of combining atheism and faith. They are two different sides of a void, and you cannot stand on both at the same time. Doubt is a leap into that void, which has no form or taste." Hanna didn't know at the time just how apposite Father Ibrahim's speech really was, but he realized that he couldn't hide the passionate love for Souad that was overflowing from him that night. He walked to Um Waheed's house, which was not far from the church, knocked on the door, and asked to be left alone in his room; it was kept aside for generous clients like him.

After Ahmed Bayazidi had carried out his threat to Jamila and forced her out of Aleppo, her girls were made homeless, and Um Waheed's star rose. Her house soon became a meeting place for the elite. It wasn't long before Zakariya and Hanna knocked on her door and became patrons. The first time she saw them, she said that she and her girls had been waiting for them for some time. Without conferring, they agreed to sample Um Waheed's fare: the most beautiful girls in Aleppo that night. She wanted some good-looking young men for her house, saying, "The secret of happiness is youth and beauty." She didn't want to become a pimp for a bunch of old men who spent their nights with the girls reminiscing about what their penises used to be like.

Zakariya and Hanna easily reached an understanding with Um Waheed. They joined her club and introduced most of their friends to it. Arif Sheikh Musa Agha arranged to meet them there, and he introduced them both to other members of his vagabond clique. Um Waheed wasn't stingy about sending girls on special assignments to Hosh Hanna, where they would spend several days at outrageous parties and return loaded with gifts, provisions, and money.

Um Waheed didn't like the sad light she could see in Hanna's eyes around this time. One morning as she joined him for breakfast, she said love couldn't hide itself. Hanna thought about Souad's face and its sharp contours, her firm lips, her breasts. His constant desire was continually mixing up two eras, two different images. No one could have expected that the innocent child to whom he had been a brother would turn into this strong, beautiful girl, who had made Orhan, her father's new Turkish assistant at the bank, the laughingstock of the city. She would ask him to wait for her in Bab Al-Faraj Square, and there he would wait for hours though her carriage never passed. When he flirted with her again, she did the same thing. Whenever he visited the house to play chess with his mentor, Ahmed Bayazidi, she would cast a scornful glance at him. She wouldn't raise her head-covering, and she criticized his clothes and their colors that matched too well. She asked him to give himself over to Monsieur George's full discretion; he would improve Orhan's taste and teach him that white silk shirts were a good choice for bank employees and beloveds but not for lovers. He didn't understand, but he agreed fervently. Her self-confidence turned other men into wrecks as well. They would dispatch their mothers to examine her for a betrothal, but the mothers didn't like her strength or impertinence in criticizing them; even the ones who had asked her aunt Amina to intercede in the courtship would flee after the first meeting, in which Hajja Amina did her best in the role of the absent mother.

On the way to Hosh Hanna, Hanna reflected that he would pay a steep price to stop caring about the beauty who had grown up so close to him. He refused to be embroiled in a marriage to a Muslim girl. Recently, he had begun to feel exhausted. No one believed that he didn't want to live in a single place, that he felt as though he were double and perfectly capable of living in two places at the same time, or living in one place at two different times. He often mixed his past with his present. In this vein, he was cheered by his decision to live by the river, while Aleppo would remain the city of his secrets. He bought a house in Bab Al-Faraj and loved watching the shadow slink from the shutters of the windows that looked out over the large square close to Bahsita. He wanted a place no one knew about other than Zakariya, and no one would know when he went to Aleppo or when he left. A succession of good seasons reassured him that his lands were doing well, and even Ahmed Bayazidi was pleased at the way Hanna was managing his wealth; he wouldn't die bankrupt. Nevertheless, Hanna couldn't bear cringing and bowing to a bunch of corrupt officials. He delegated that task to Ahmed Bayazidi, who sent costly gifts in Hanna's name to the vali of Aleppo, the chief of police, and the judiciary, and none of them spurned his offerings. Hanna didn't object to this method of managing a relationship with state officials, but he didn't want to see them in person; he hated them all deeply. Slimy and shallow, they spent their lives in a cycle of mutual satisfaction. He had briefly considered reviving his father's dream of a huge financial empire but felt trapped at the thought of dealing with such hypocrites. He thought of money and authority as slices from a cake of corruption, which would inevitably draw flies. And in any case, nothing equaled the enjoyment of being lazy in the morning.

On his next few visits to the Bayazidi family a month after removing to Hosh Hanna, he avoided Souad when she joined them for dinner. She ignored him too, went to her room as quickly as possible, and didn't come out until morning. Hanna decided that he wouldn't allow her to hate him; he couldn't have endured that. He considered their childhood the happiest days of his life, when his life had been filled with joy and she had been a true sister to him. At times, he used to feel Souad was his daughter, and other times she had behaved like a mother. She was the only person he had really missed when he was in Venice. Zakariya had missed her too, and they had spent entire nights reminiscing about their childhood.

One morning he risked visiting the house while Zakariya and Ahmed Bayazidi were out. Um Kheir opened the door to him, and he walked to Souad's room, knocked on her door, and asked her to join him for a coffee. She allowed him to enter and closed the door behind him. Hanna felt he was in a different era. It wasn't the room he and Zakariya used to sneak into to put gifts under her pillow. Back then they used to hide under her bed and make animal noises to scare her when she slipped into bed. She would startle, and look for the source of the noise, and leap about with delight when she found them under the bed. They would join her on errands, and Hanna would buy her anything she pointed at, and in return she shared everything she owned with him. She was their spoiled little girl. That morning he looked at her for a long time. He gazed at her face, her figure, her breasts, her hips. She was wearing a tight dress. She had been about to leave for Sitt Hassaniya's atelier, and there was a French book upside-down on the table, a novel by Alexandre Dumas. Souad lost no time.

She told Hanna that even in her worst nightmares, she had never imagined that he and Zakariya would leave her alone. She had waited for them and cried the entire time they were in Venice. He attempted to justify himself by arguing that the city wouldn't allow them to live as they had when they were children. Everyone was hunting the family, they couldn't continue meeting at Hayyim Istanbouli's house until Azar's return. He went on and on, talking about the unjust city and the endless gossip, but Souad didn't want to talk in general terms. She told Hanna that when she thought of him, it wasn't as a sister but as a woman. She added she was a woman now, and no longer a little girl. Hanna was overcome with confusion. He wanted to recover his cheerful demeanor, but he couldn't. He was drowning in sadness, a feeling he was very familiar with, and stayed silent. Souad went on: the women he visited would pollute his soul. She reminded him that she wasn't his sister and therefore she wasn't mahram. He drank his coffee calmly and asked her to listen closely. He didn't care what designation she gave herself; he wanted to talk to the girl she used to be. At this, she interrupted and said the past couldn't be recovered, adding, "Those boats have gone out onto the river of Paradise." He was afraid of her confident tone but continued regardless, recalling that when men were stranded in some desolate place, they talked to themselves, or they sang. Hanna spoke about how tired he was. He felt his words had no meaning as his complaints went on and on. Souad was looking at him, and he wanted to say that he thought about her for days on end, but he found the alteration in their relationship—in her changed designation—utterly terrifying. He couldn't separate the image of her as a child from the image of her today. He spent the time chattering about her father, who increasingly seemed like an old man to him, constantly mumbling about being afraid of retirement and old age. She replied simply that her father had grown a little older, and he missed both Hanna and Zakariya. She didn't give him a chance to recall stories from their not-too-distant past. She took a freshly ironed shirt from her cupboard, presented it to him, and said it was his birthday gift. She added in a tone of rebuke, "For my sake, don't wear it in a whore's room." She went out, tying her milaya securely, and Hanna smiled. He contemplated the shirt of embroidered silk and noticed that her initial was embroidered there, her signature that she had made it.

Sitt Hassaniya's atelier was next door to Souad's family home, and Ahmed Bayazidi didn't prevent her from being trained in dressmaking. He regretted not having been brave enough to send his daughter to study in Paris; when her friend Nadima Basmaji planned to study law at the Sorbonne, Souad seemed curious about the idea of accompanying her, although nothing came of it in the end. Hassan Basmaji was proud of his daughter. Relatives and old friends opposed him and used to ask if he knew what his only daughter was up to in that country of infidels. Eventually he became a recluse and vanished from sight among his books. In the end, he died grieving, still defending a woman's right to education. He endured the mockery of bigoted sheikhs who attacked him openly, accusing him of spreading vice and calling for mixing the sexes. He could make no reply to the gangs of zealots and bigots who patrolled the city's streets on the lookout for lapses of virtue, wishing to impose sharia by the authority of the swords in their hands. Hassan Basmaji considered fleeing the city, but he relished seeing his enemies so furious. He spent little time with his remaining friends. Their number had diminished in any case, and only one of them dared accompany him at Eid to visit the graveyard. On the day of his funeral, many were surprised at the hundreds of unfamiliar people who came to pay their respects. After he was buried, Ahmed Bayazidi said to their mutual friends that they all had been vile cowards when they let their friend Hassan Basmaji plunge into battle alone, and he had paid the price of their silence.

Souad didn't want to leave Aleppo and be away from Hanna. Here she saw his image everywhere. She knew that silent love turned the heart into a piece of shriveled quince, but she secretly told herself that a dried-up quince was better than a dead heart; there was still hope that its veins would be revived and it would flourish once more. Souad found a passion in the atelier of Sitt Hassaniya, who openly cursed the hypocritical men of religion. She despised them and considered them unnecessary. She wasn't afraid of them and always told their listeners that if she opened up her box of scandals, there wouldn't be a single imam left on his minbar. She was in her sixties and still elegant and lighthearted. Her first husband had been her cousin, an important official in the administration of waqfs. She spent three years with him before asking for a divorce, describing her life with him as "shit." The virtuous sheikh didn't dare hold her back; she accused him of liking boys and of stealing the interest on the waqfs of the Umayyad Mosque. Then she married Abdallah Youzbashy, a fabric trader, who loved her but died at the age of forty. He left her a sickly, asthmatic child who didn't live to see his fifth birthday. After that Hassaniya remained alone; her love story with Abdallah Youzbashy would last her an entire lifetime. She described their warm nights frankly to her girls, telling them provocatively, "He drank wine from my shoe." He also taught her the difference between colors and types of fabric. Eyes gleaming, he would take some cloth and describe the type of thread and the dye that was used. He would say to Hassaniya, "Touch it. Silk, soft as a woman's newly threaded thigh." He loved drawing on unusual images that stirred Hassaniya. He left her a shop in Khan Al-Jumruk that she ran herself without relying on agents or middlemen, and a huge warehouse filled with all kinds of fabric in the middle of his meadow in the village of Khan Touman.

Souad would always remember her teacher Sitt Hassaniya: she taught her everything she knew. And in return, she considered her student Souad a rare treasure. She loved Souad's taste, ideas, and dreams, her beauty and her strength. Sitt Hassaniya used to say, "This city hasn't produced a girl like her in decades." (It was her custom to exaggerate praise of those she loved.) So when Souad embroidered a white silk shirt, Sitt Hassaniya knew she had fallen in love with Hanna, the kind of love from which there would be no return. And she believed it was impossible to save someone who had fallen like that.

She let Souad be and didn't share her opinion until a few years later, when the two of them were alone in the atelier. Souad's face, in the light coming from outside, was entrancing. Sitt Hassaniya told Souad she had made a mistake in falling in love with a man who adored prostitutes, and went on, "One woman alone, no matter how beautiful and strong she is, can never defeat an army of prostitutes, because they are women too. They have dreams that normal, fearful women don't know about. And Hanna has an army of them in his possession." Souad nodded when her teacher spoke in this tone. Sitt Hassaniya knew she was remembering dreams that had been buried alive. She never told Souad that the dresses for Um Waheed's girls, which Souad had designed with her customary artistry, had been made at Hanna's request.

But Souad knew. She was excessively quiet as she focused on a buttonhole. She said to herself that his fingers would unfasten this button, and he would be even more aroused when he saw the neckline. He would be dazzled by the beauty of this revealing black dress. Hassaniya felt Souad's torment double when she arrived before all the girls in the early morning. She made her coffee and sat by the window, longing for a man's fingers to reach out for hers and enlace them—together they would run off at dawn to the nearby riverbank. Once after she and her father returned from a visit to Hosh Hanna, Souad was silent for days. She couldn't bear what she had seen. It had even made her ill, and she lay on a bed in the small atelier among swatches of fabric. She didn't want to stay in her house, she didn't want to see the doctor. Hassaniya thought she would probably die. The words that were stuck fast in Souad's throat had to be extracted, because those few phrases were choking her. Suspecting what ailed her, Hassaniya forbade Um Waheed's girl to come into her atelier. Souad lost a quarter of her weight and often spoke about dying. These were the symptoms of a fatal love, Hassaniya well knew, and she knew also that it would take more than a chamomile tisane to ease the words out. But eventually Souad told her everything. For the first time, she felt like a mangy mule, humiliated, a nothing. Her soul had disappeared, her body felt riddled with pus, and she wished it would be burned along with the city's waste.

Everything had come about because after Hanna moved to his village, Souad decided to persuade her father to visit Hosh Hanna. She
said that Zakariya and Hanna would be pleased at the surprise, and
Ahmed Bayazidi could assure himself that everything was as it should
be. Her father tried to get her to forget the idea, but she was determined. She wanted to spend Hanna's birthday with him. Her father
was hesitant but agreed despite his misgivings. He wanted to be welcomed in both his sons' houses, and on a deeper level he wanted to put
an end to Souad's attachment to Hanna without a tragedy.

After arriving in Hosh Hanna, Hanna had decided to throw an
extravagant celebration. He invited his friends to his large house,
and Zakariya told them that there was no obstacle to the celebration
lasting an entire week. Everything was as it should be: the horses in
Zakariya's stable were increasing, and the harvests had been excellent. Um Waheed, as usual, perfectly comprehended their needs, and
she sent six girls to dance, sing, and strut naked in the large salon.
Their elegance, and the masks they wore till the last moment of the
night, were bewitching. His friends were not outdone by elite landowners, who had been selected with extreme caution from among the
ill-reputed, the spendthrifts, the pleasure-seekers. They came with
their servants, their guards, and their cooks, followed by a collection
of girls from famous brothels of Mosul and Baghdad.

The guards fanned out around Hanna's house, while Zakariya let
the servants, guards, and cooks sleep in his house and moved in with
Hanna. The barbecue and the dining table were left open in the garden for seven days, and they were refreshed three times daily by the
various cooks. The servants would roam between the tables dotted
around the garden and rooms picking up plates and empty glasses. In
that week, Zakariya and Hanna lived out their old dream of refram-
ing the very notion of Paradise.

At the height of the party, Hanna was shocked to see her standing in the doorway to the salon. The guards hadn't been able to
prevent her from entering. The band was playing dancing songs.
Hanna came up to Souad, who ignored all the shameless debauchery

she saw all around. His embroidered white silk shirt was stained with lipstick and wine. She reached out and ripped it, slapped his cheek, and left with Mariana, who had taken her there, in full awareness that it wasn't an entirely appropriate moment. Zakariya had passed out, and Hanna didn't know what to do but weep. Souad went to Mariana's father's house, where Ahmed Bayazidi had chosen to spend the night after hearing the sound of music coming from Hanna's house, and seeing the carriage drivers of "those clowns" occupying Zakariya's house. He understood they should leave at once; it wasn't a good time, and he didn't want to see a nightmare that might haunt him for years to come.

Hanna withdrew and spent the rest of the night alone. When he woke up the next morning, he went out looking for Souad and Ahmed Bayazidi, but they had left at dawn, dejected. Hanna went home and carried on with the party as if nothing had happened. He was happy that his lifestyle was no longer secret; now Ahmed Bayazidi and Souad knew all about it. Deep down he felt that he had insulted them, but it had been unintentional. She would forgive him, and perhaps it would even excite her. His mind a jumble, he told himself that it was just a silk shirt, so what if it was torn.

On the seventh day of the party, Zakariya couldn't stop exclaiming, "This is Paradise. These women are even more beautiful than houris," gesturing to the women who had woken up and gathered around the dinner table. Zakariya went on, "Heavenly wine is no match for this wine, and this scenery—" He looked at the clear blue spring sky and searched for adequate praise, but couldn't think of anything to say except, "We're living in Paradise." Hanna's friends gave him costly gifts and praised his exquisite taste. That night, after their guests had left, Zakariya and Hanna dreamed of their citadel, which was within sight of being finished. They remembered their dear friend William Eisa, who was supposed to be with them. Zakariya informed Hanna dryly that William Eisa had turned into a functionary; soon he would marry any Christian girl his father chose, and that would be the end of his brothel visits. Hanna remembered that he hadn't read William

Eisa's recent letters and rebuked himself. He took them out and began to read, guilty at neglecting his friend. The last letter was a collection of yarns about their childhood, in which William Eisa recalled Souad, Zakariya, Azar, and Sara. In the last line, he told Hanna he was thinking about leaving Hajj Sobhy Mufti's company and devoting himself to painting. He spoke movingly about his life, which he was squandering on meaningless pursuits, and about his desire to welcome the next century, only a few years from now, as an entirely new man.

Hanna realized that he had become indifferent and uncaring. He suddenly felt a violent longing for his friend, whom he hadn't seen for years. He got up, folded the letters, and replaced them in a drawer in his bureau, then left the house and went for a walk along the riverbank. The open space and view over the fields gladdened him, but he couldn't forget Souad's slap, which echoed in his depths.

4

Impossible Love

A novel by Junaid Khalifa,
follower of the Imam of the Lovers, Salih Aisha Azizi

PART I

Istanbul was preparing to welcome the new century within a few hours. William Michel Eisa opened his windows that looked out over the spacious courtyard of Maggie's house to air the room and get rid of the smell of oil paint. Maggie was telling her Greek neighbor about the sheikhs of the Eyüp Mosque, who had been banging their tambourines for six days now, announcing that Judgment Day was arriving on the morrow. Maggie's neighbor wasn't listening to her; she couldn't understand why Maggie didn't also believe that the new century would be nothing but perdition. Judgment Day would come before the new century arrived, and everything would be over. She had donated all her savings to the church, because what good would a single gold piece do her on the day of reckoning? She was in a frenzy of excitement that Christ was coming, and exclaimed how lucky she was that she would see Him bless her with her own eyes. Maggie was shocked to realize that her neighbor wasn't listening at all, and shouted, "What good will that gold do the church if Judgment Day is coming?" Maggie didn't want to talk to herself; she raised her voice even further and informed her neighbor that she was mad to have given away the precious gold pieces she had earned from working as a servant. Maggie's neighbor paid her no attention; she was in ecstasy, pressing her hands to her chest and swaying back and forth as she bade farewell to the last

evening she would ever see. Jesus would rise, and she would welcome
Him in just a few hours. Maggie spat on her, incredulous at the hyste-
ria that had overcome the city. Everyone was talking of Judgment Day.
She spotted William Eisa sneaking out the door and yelled after him
not to come back late from his parties. As she shut the window, the
neighbor was still swaying on the spot, embracing the spirit of Jesus
whom, she said as tears poured over her cheeks, she could see hovering over the blessed city of Istanbul even now.

William Eisa paid no attention to the city that was chattering
about Judgment Day in every corner. He was thinking of his immense
foolishness seven months earlier, on a day he would always remember,
when he had made a decision freely for the first time in his life.

The weather had been unusually hot for Istanbul in the middle of
May. On that day, William Eisa resigned from his job as a supervisor at
the freight company of Hajj Bashir Mufti. He handed over his responsibilities to a new employee and went to Eminonu, where he bought a
warm bread roll, sat on the bridge, tore up the bread, and threw it to
the fish. He reflected that living like this would suit him. He wouldn't
spend his life as an employee afraid of risk and adventure, and he
wouldn't strive to win the admiration and approval of his teachers or
his bosses. He wouldn't finish studying to be an accountant. The future that his father, an expert dyer in Hajj Bashir Mufti's factories, had
planned out for him was destroyed in moments.

He continued on to Cihangir and bought some tubes of oil paint, a
new paintbrush, and a primed canvas from a small shop that sold all
the necessities for calligraphy and painting. He kicked a pebble in the
street. He had always believed that kicking pebbles signified a crum-
bling of obligations—a respectable bureaucrat couldn't kick pebbles,
whistle, or urinate on a street corner. He softly hummed a Turkish
song he liked as he bought white cheese and potatoes and walked back
to his lodgings in the Karaköy quarter.

There he closed the door and for the first time found himself in
front of a blank canvas. He wouldn't leave his room, for which he'd
already paid the year's rent. He would enjoy lazing around, thinking,

writing down his daydreams, and sketching the paper kites he and Zakariya used to make, which dazzled the city. He had always wished he could make a living from painting. He wrote to Hanna, Zakariya, Souad, and Azar telling them how happy he was, because he had thrown his old life into the sea along with his worn-out shoes, but apart from Souad, they replied to his letters only three months later. Souad always responded to his letters, which were delivered to her by Sara, Azar's sister, who was now David's wife. Souad encouraged William Eisa to paint and recalled memories from their childhood when he would produce astonishing paintings in minutes, especially the painting of the paper boat he had sent out onto the river. In another letter, she reminded him of the portrait he had made of a beautiful woman looking sadly at her destroyed kite. She reminded him of the time he asked her to sit on a chair in the courtyard of her house, and he sketched her on a large piece of cardboard: the picture was recognizably of Souad despite its gloomy air. Souad still kept that picture hanging in her room, next to a portrait of Margot and Um Kheir reading the gospel and the Qur'an; notwithstanding the trite concept, Margot's face expressed her constant worry over Hanna, who seemed to be looking at her, smiling, from the corner of the painting.

William Eisa still remembered the moment he arrived in Istanbul nine years earlier. He loved this city for no particular reason; he would get lost in its streets and observe the seagulls and the boats as they crossed the Bosporus, and he watched the painters and calligraphers in Beyazıt Square for hours at a time. A few months after his arrival, a Greek friend, an employee at the same company, took him to museums and the houses of painters who were exhibiting their work to the public. On his day off, William Eisa would wake up and go out to wander in the streets, and he could easily spend hours watching a painter or a calligrapher hard at work. Every time, when he left them engrossed in their work and walked away, he was frustrated at the thought that he would never be able to stop betraying himself. He would never paint the melancholy pictures that ceaselessly flowed through his mind's eye.

On the day he handed in his resignation, he was exuberant. Without any planning, he painted a small picture of a Turkish dockworker, his emaciated face laying bare his deep-seated misery. Within a week, he had completed three more paintings. One, a large one, showed a group of Russian sailors drinking in a bar by the port. He was pleased when he contemplated the colors, and the drunk, benevolent faces—he had always believed that no sailor could visit a bar unless he was friendly. He picked up his paintings and left his room. As he went by, Maggie was looking at him, afraid but deferential. He had often told her that he was going to give up accounting to become a painter, and now after resigning, she hadn't seen him leave his room for a week. He hadn't asked for any help. She thought he was becoming more of a puzzle; certainly normal people didn't behave in such a way. William Eisa assured her that everything was fine, that he was finally making his only dream a reality. He would never go back to being an employee or a bureaucrat—instead he would spend his life dreaming of strange things.

A few months later he brought his paintings to his Greek friend, who was still angry at him for handing in his notice and passing up the opportunity of a lifetime. The Greek man looked at the paintings and said, "You left a job at the company on account of this rubbish?" William tried to explain the pictures, but he was miserable. His friend didn't want to listen—he was planning his own future. He would advance all the way to director of accounts, he would marry, he would have children and teach them Greek, and he would smile when he took a souvenir picture with his family in front of the gate of the Dolmabahçe Palace. William Eisa was silent. He finished a glass of cheap brandy and quickly left. He rushed to the post office in Beyoğlu and sent the paintings to Sara's address with instructions to get them to Souad, without leaving a word in the parcel for her. Souad would understand the message he was sending, and she would distribute the paintings accordingly. William Eisa felt liberated. He was freed from the weight of the paintings that had been exhibited for the past six months in small galleries in Cihangir. The gallery owners, after taking one glance at them, would grimace and advise him to paint the land-marks of Istanbul instead of the face of a Turkish girl, or a drunk Russian sailor, or a mysterious woman who looked like one of the city's tubercular prostitutes. These subjects were not right for any of the art collectors in this city, not even the foreign hobbyists who were in love with exotic private scenes, such as women in a public hammam, or conjurors breathing fire for a sultan. No one cared about dead mice in a warehouse that stank of hemp.

It was rainy. As usual when he found himself alone, he walked the interweaving lanes. He didn't shelter under an umbrella. His life was pointless unless it was soaked with rain and scorched by scattered lightning. With immense relish, he kept repeating certain words as if he were writing a story about a man who resembled himself: strange, alone, afraid—the feelings that had attended him all his life. The rain paused briefly, and he found himself on a stone bench overlooking the sea, beside one of Hajj Bashir Mufti's warehouses. He knew this place well, its hiding places and its guards. He had spent months here making inventories of the cotton bales prepared for export to Manchester, but it meant nothing to him anymore.

William Eisa sat on the bench, absorbed in watching the colors of the sea that were almost gray. The rain returned in torrents, but he didn't get up. He was lingering in a moment of stability, something he missed. In the early evening, he went back to his room and once again began to paint his depression. The image of the dead mice filling the floor of the warehouse was still in his mind. In those moments he felt he had found the road to ruin that he had been looking for.

In the final days of the nineteenth century, he was so hungry that he staggered from dizziness. His remaining money would last a few more weeks if he limited his expenses. He hadn't thought before of how much paints and canvas cost, but despite everything he was finally happy. He had received a long letter from Souad thanking him for the "wonderful painting of the Turkish girl," which she had kept for herself. She praised the other pictures too, which she had given as gifts to Zakariya, Hanna, Azar, and Sara.

Three days earlier William Eisa's Greek friend had left a message for him with Maggie asking him to come to the house of Hajj Bashir Mufti, owner of the cotton and textile company, in the afternoon of the last day of 1899. William Eisa was waiting for that meeting; he wanted to obtain a remuneration that the director had denied him. After that, he would stop off at the market to pick up some pork for Maggie from the Italian shop in Beyoğlu; she had invited him to join her and her friends for a party to welcome Judgment Day, in mockery of the Christians who had thrown all their savings into the church coffers. Before William Eisa left for his appointment that morning, Maggie said, "Make sure you don't miss the party! This moment won't come again in our lifetime."

William Eisa put on his suit, which was still new. He felt completely weak. He liked Maggie's idea of welcoming a unique moment with a raucous party that she had begun preparing a month ahead of time. She invited Greek musician friends and a few of her old friends, mostly Christian Turks working in small public roles, or Greeks over sixty who were still lighthearted and loved dancing. They would reminisce about their past with deep grief and plot how to return to their villages in Greece, but year by year they moldered away in the big city, turning their hands over and remembering that most of their villages had been burned to the ground by Ottoman troops. The rest of the guests were lodgers in the house.

William arrived at Hajj Bashir's house, which occupied a large ground floor on the corner of two intersecting streets and looked over the back garden of the Madrasa Galatasaray. The clock was showing eleven o'clock. The snow hadn't stopped since the night before, and the city was white, its streets full of the smell of coal emitting from chimneys. The servant Sitt Khadija opened the front door to him. William Eisa knew her as well as he knew the house; for years while he worked at the company, he had spent much time reviewing the end-of-year accounts with Hajj Bashir, who didn't conceal how much he enjoyed speaking with this young man, brimming with ambition just like his father Michel before him—a man who loved his work, never betrayed his teachers' trust, and displayed an ungreedy spirit.

When William Eisa arrived, the candles in the hall were slowly melting; Hajj Bashir liked to light perfumed candles during the day. The servant led him to the warm salon, where Hajj Bashir was sitting close to the window that overlooked the garden. His daughter, Aisha Mufti, sat next to him. Hajj Bashir welcomed William warmly and embraced him. William greeted Aisha shyly and sat on the nearest sofa. He tried to remember the words he had been planning on his way there. He couldn't quite believe it. His stomach had dropped, and his legs felt as heavy as if they were tied to a boulder. Aisha Mufti was so close to him he could smell her breath. He bent his trembling head, thinking of how to ask for his reimbursement. He raised his head and looked at Aisha Mufti frankly, then returned to studying the designs on the carpet.

Aisha had been suffering from the ennui of the cold winter as she gazed out the window at the snow that never stopped falling. She stole a look at William Eisa, paying no attention to her father's gestures that she should leave and go to her own quarters. Instead, she invented a story about William Eisa's sister and her fiancé so she could say something to him, and they spoke about his sister as if they were friends. Hajj Bashir felt himself in an awkward position. He was expecting an emissary of Sheikh Abulhuda Al-Sayyadi for lunch, and after performing the midday prayer together, they would discuss an important project for which Hajj Bashir was requesting Abulhuda Al-Sayyadi's support in order to obtain approval directly from Sultan Abdel Hamid II.

William Eisa had initially thought that he would stay for half an hour, ask for his compensation, and leave, but he forgot everything. His feet wouldn't take him anywhere. The servant came in with cups of tea, and after a few minutes she came back and announced the arrival of Sheikh Mahmoud, ahead of time. Hajj Bashir got up quickly and led Sheikh Mahmoud to the library. For a few moments, a thick silence fell, but the men were gone long enough for William Eisa to raise his eyes to Aisha Mufti's face and look directly at her. She was looking straight back at him. Her lips were trembling, her heart was thudding, her feet, too, would not move, and her body was assailed by an incomprehensible tingling.

Aisha Mufti very much wanted to get to know William Michel Eisa. She wasn't afraid of her desire for him, or his dubious reputation, stories of which were circulated among the Aleppans. The women of the city would spread whispers about William and his friends, their immaturity and their love of whorehouses, their legendary all-night debaucheries. The eyes of upper-class girls would take on a strange gleam as they spoke about glasses of wine spilled onto bodies—the bodies of prostitutes as they danced naked all night long. Aisha reflected that not all of what was said could possibly be true; but in any case, she found the rumors exciting.

While the two of them were alone, she asked him straight out if he liked the women of Istanbul better than the women of Aleppo, asking with composure, "And which are better: Jews, Muslims, or Christians?" It was a hint that she knew who he was, but William Eisa was almost swooning as he stared at her beautiful face, her lips, her round, full breasts. He couldn't speak. He burst out that he and his friend Azar were nothing like Hanna and Zakariya—he had always been too cowardly to join them in their amusements—and added somewhat incoherently that a city like Aleppo always needed gossip. He asked her suddenly if she was attached, and fell silent. Time passed slowly. From the open door, he heard the voice of Sheikh Mahmoud raised in prayer and Hajj Bashir loudly repeating the words after him.

William Eisa worried that Aisha would never cross his path again, and she felt trapped in a story whose ending it was difficult to predict. She felt faint. Without quite knowing why, she asked if he was familiar with the house, and he replied with a nod. She told him that she slept in the room next to the servant's, away from her father's bedroom and library, which occupied a separate wing of the house, and he caught her message. Gathering his courage, William Eisa lost no time and

proposed that she run away with him for a little while that night to
Maggie's party to welcome in the new century, adding that Maggie
was a Greek friend of his who could help them. Aisha didn't think
for long; she liked the idea, although she was afraid—it wouldn't be
easy to escape from the window and wander the streets of Istanbul at
night.

He didn't linger after that. She told him that her father went to
sleep after evening prayer. They agreed on a signal: she would wave a
lantern from her bedroom window three times if she agreed to meet
him. Maggie would be waiting for her in a carriage next to the back
gate of the garden of the Madrasa Galatasaray. If the lights of her
room were out, and she didn't come after half an hour, the carriage
would go on its way and everything would be over.

Hajj Bashir came in after his prayer. He asked William Eisa to join
them for lunch, but William Eisa bowed out politely. He bid goodbye to Hajj Bashir, who said that he had left William's remuneration
which he had forgotten to ask for—in the company's office. William
Eisa thanked him, and before he left, Hajj Bashir said that William's
father Michel was very worried about him. He suggested that William Eisa reconsider and come back to the company, adding that he
could choose where he wanted to work. Hajj Bashir said they were an
honorable family that had never betrayed his trust and praised his father, who had worked for him for thirty years. He went on to speak of
William's dedication to art, but by this point William Eisa just wanted
to leave. His whole body was sweating, and he wasn't sure that his legs
were capable of crossing the few meters to the front door.

Aisha Mufti couldn't believe what had just happened. After he left,
she withdrew to her room. Hajj Bashir thought she was ill—he couldn't
understand how else she could have grown so pale in just a few moments. She assured him that she was fine; it was only that the cold
was frightful, and staying alone in the house for a week had made her
depression even worse. She didn't like Istanbul, which she was visiting
for the first time in her life; she preferred London and Paris, where she
had greater freedom.

At first glance, Aisha seemed like a naïve girl living out a dream of romance, but this appearance belied a woman who loved adventure and strange stories. Her family had prepared her to be a girl of her era, suited to a husband from the upper class, a high-ranking state official destined to be a vali or an industrialist of great ambition. She acquired a good education, in contrast to her close friends and companions who married early, many before they were fifteen years old. She mastered French easily and began to plot a different life for herself, confident that she could impose her wishes on her father, who adored her. He ignored the way the hijab slithered off her hair whenever he accompanied her at the invitation of one of the consuls; her name was always on the list of invitees for their perpetual carousel of events.

Hajj Bashir Mufti would look at his daughter proudly as she spoke French with the wives and daughters of the diplomatic corps and confidently put forth her opinion encouraging girls' education. The diplomats and their families used to boast of her presence at their parties, and they called her by her first name without any honorific and allowed her the same familiarity with them. They said that Aleppo was changing and more should be done to ensure it was saved from the Ottoman legacy that continued to drag it down. They whispered these opinions, and Aisha Mufti would agree, going so far as to assert that Aleppo's future lay with Europe.

These were only a few short words whose deeper meaning she didn't fully understand, although they left a marked impression on those gathered around her. But now, on her first journey outside Aleppo to Europe and Istanbul, she had begun to understand what Europe meant. She was tired. She closed the curtains of her room and slipped into bed. Her body had to stop shaking; of course she wouldn't escape and join someone with as terrible a reputation as William Eisa on the eve of Judgment Day. She slept lightly and woke up feeling more tranquil, but still she got up before afternoon prayer. She saw Hajj Bashir reading the Qur'an and speaking about the "blessed sheikhs" who were banging their tambourines to announce Judgment Day. He suggested they go to the market and have dinner at Eski Locanda, a restaurant often patronized by wealthy families. She excused herself and asked the servant to heat her room. She kissed her father and teased him, wishing him a happy Judgment Day.

Aisha Mufti couldn't quite believe herself when she rose from her bed to get her gold-embroidered abaya. She didn't really believe that she was waiting for eight o'clock. Having assured herself that her father had been sleeping in his room for the past half hour, she sought out the key to the back gate of the garden. From her window, she could see the carriage that had stopped. She lit the lantern, waved it three times, climbed out of her room, crossed the garden, and got into the carriage, where Maggie was waiting for her, smiling. She had a kind face, and Aisha felt as though she were in a delicious daze, as if a strange force were pushing her toward an abyss, but she was soon absorbed in studying Istanbul at night; it was unusually crowded for such an hour, but this was an exceptional day—all of humanity was taken up with it. It was strange to think that a century would end in just a few hours, although deep down she wasn't so sure that life would be all that different in a new century. She realized Maggie was telling her that William Eisa would be a great artist one day, and he wouldn't forget his promise to paint an icon of her saint that she could donate to the church in Thessaloniki where she was baptized.

Maggie spoke constantly throughout the short journey, while Aisha nodded in agreement, her eyes fixed on the streets, which swirled with chaos. Soldiers had been deployed on most street corners, and a group of men and women were walking and speaking loudly in a language that she didn't understand but guessed was Bulgarian or Greek. Cake vendors and kashtaban players provoked an uproar as usual, hunting out gullible patrons. From her seat, Istanbul seemed to be a cheerful city, in complete contrast with the sullen image she had observed over the previous few days. When she got out of the carriage, William Eisa was waiting for her by the front door. He had been sure she would come; he loved this type of foolhardy, bold girl, whose appearance belied her true nature. Maggie ordered the carriage driver to come back at midnight and went straight to the dance floor, where the musicians were playing Greek dancing songs. Aisha realized that she hadn't yet spoken a word. She tried to say something but couldn't. William Eisa led her to his room and left the door open. The room plainly revealed the occupation of its inhabitant: open tubes of paint, unfinished canvases, remnants of tobacco and tea, chaos in every corner, summer socks and an old coat, and a painting of himself and his friends flying Zakariya's paper kite. She recognized Hanna and smiled, but they both stayed silent, and without stumbling over words, they left the room. William Eisa toasted everyone's health and danced vigorously to the beat of three santouri players. His heart was laughing, his soul was flying, touched by Aisha, who by now found pleasure in the idea of silence. She didn't say a syllable but joined in everyone's madness, nodding and smiling, observing the faces of the fervent dancers. She felt it was all for her.

At a signal from William Eisa, which she caught easily, the pair slipped out of the uproar, and soon Aisha found herself next to him in a carriage that left Karaköy and reached Madrasa Galatasaray. The place was crowded—over a hundred dervishes were banging their tambourines and chanting in one voice, halting for a few moments in the street whenever their leader made a certain gesture with his hand and dancing, oblivious to the people watching them in astonishment. They were concerned only with Judgment Day and felt the earth pulling away from beneath their feet. Aisha Mufti watched them from the window of the carriage, and when it jerked to a stop in the traffic, she was thrown into William's lap. The coachman mentioned that it would be the new century in five minutes. Aisha Mufti leaned on William Eisa's arm, and he seized his chance. They got out and hurried into a narrow side street, and he kissed her on the mouth. It was her first kiss. Her body was set on fire. She hung on to his neck and kissed him for a long time, not caring what might happen.

From where they were, they could discern the madness of the city. Church bells were ringing, the sound of weeping and dancing music was issuing from distant houses, and the owners of the halted carriages simply sat and waited for the traffic to ease. Aisha shook in

William Eisa's arms, and he instantly took her back to the carriage. He ordered the coachman to turn toward Hajj Bashir's house. Aisha stayed silent all the way, and William Eisa drowned in her perfume. He was breathing in the city anew; it was a new century.

As she reached the house, Aisha Mufti couldn't believe it had all gone so smoothly. Her eyes were cloudy, her heart beat painfully, and her face was pink. She felt like a monstrously huge pelican, but one flying lightly in the sky over an enchanted city. When she opened her window, William Eisa was standing where she had left him on the opposite sidewalk. She saw him through the snow, which hadn't stopped falling all night.

She couldn't bear seeing him on the sidewalk like a vagrant. He fixed his gaze on her window, and she signaled that she would open the door for him. She didn't realize she had been struck with excruciating madness. She didn't think for a moment about what she was doing. She wanted him in her warm bed.

She led him by the hand to her room. Reflecting that dawn was still a long way off, she assured herself that her father and the maidservant were asleep, then went back to her room. He was waiting for her, half swooning, and she threw herself into his arms. He held her close, inhaled her perfume. He couldn't part from her for even a minute. Her long white face, and the black locks that hung from beneath her hijab, made her irresistible.

She changed her clothes and put on a scarlet silk thobe. She felt she had been looking for exactly this man. She wasn't some lost girl, but one who knew exactly what she wanted from him and from life in her faraway city of Aleppo. She still couldn't believe she had kissed him so warmly at the moment they welcomed the new century, but she feared nothing; his lips had tasted delicious.

The city had quieted down by now, and the sounds and the voices, the silent night, the empty streets, all disappeared. Inside the warm room, Aisha was walking on tiptoes. She drew his face to her lips and thought how it was impossible to dwell on the past—after all, an entire century had just come to an end. Next to her, William Eisa was

thinking that he was a different person. He could hear his ribs cracking. He would have to leave before dawn, but he didn't want to leave
her alone. If he took her by the hand, they could walk to Aleppo, their
city, and live by the river in a small boat.

As dawn approached, she pointed out that he had to leave. He rose
and embraced her again, then cautiously followed her through the
halls. When he was in the street, he felt like screaming. The sound of
the dawn call to prayer sounded as he walked home. Here and there
a few groups of people were sheltering from the still-falling snow. He
arrived at his lodging, and the chaos of the house betrayed the scale of
the evening's party. William Eisa threw himself down onto his bed, but
he couldn't sleep. He felt as though his guts were disintegrating, and an
intense cold crept into his joints. Fearing he was dying, he tried to get
up but couldn't. His deep groans woke Maggie, who was still drunk.
She brought him a hot drink and fell asleep on a chair next to his bed.

When she first met William Eisa, Aisha Mufti had thought that
he would do for a mild flirtation and nothing more. Perhaps it would
be the adventure she hadn't dared have with the French youth she
had met at a reception held by the French consul in Aleppo, who
had suggested she come to Paris and work in his small theater company. Alarmed at the mere idea, Aisha had left him without another
thought and started a conversation with the consul's wife. Her adventures with other men had been insignificant, not much more than a
brush of the hand or a squeeze of the palm. With William Eisa, she
had felt her soul crumble underneath his lips.

She woke at ten in the morning. The servant had prepared her
breakfast three times, and her father had left early to tend to his business affairs. The servant gave her a letter that a Greek boy had brought.
She opened the envelope, stood up quickly, and left without explaining
anything to the servant. When she arrived at William Eisa's lodging,
she found that he was delirious, and Maggie was weeping silently at
his bedside. The doctor who examined him assured them, however,
that it was merely a bad cold, and he would be up and about in a few
days.

William's illness was Aisha's opportunity. Every morning she came to nurse him. He ignored her many questions about his past and told her that there were withered pomegranate groves in his memory, and paper kites that didn't fly. He took her hand, lingering over every movement, and asked her to leave him to his fate. Every moment she felt that he was sweeping her away; it didn't seem possible that a man like him would lie about his feelings. He wept if she was late, and on his second night, he couldn't sleep for thinking that they were standing together on a boulder rolling to the edge of the world.

Hajj Bashir made no objection whenever Aisha went out to get to know the city and took the maidservant with her (who would then go to visit her relatives, leaving her mistress to her own devices), but he grew concerned about his daughter when he saw she was permanently distracted. He assumed she was missing Aleppo, but her silence took on a different aspect when he told her that they would leave for Aleppo in three days' time; after all, it had been three months since they had left the city. Aisha was disconcerted and couldn't say that she didn't want to go back to Aleppo. She dreaded her upcoming separation from William Eisa, but she took it as a good omen when he got up from his bed, having regained his health. She had grown attached to the house and had become a friend to Maggie, who loved her back and allowed her all the time she wanted to look after William. His small room was drowning in incomplete paintings, his clothes were sadly neglected, and his things were scattered everywhere, but she held the vessel of his soul, which steadily filled drop by drop, and when the vessel overflowed in her hands, she thought that the world could no longer go on as it had.

On her last night in Istanbul, William Eisa slipped into Aisha Mufti's bedroom. He received the signal through the back door that she had left open for him, and already knowing the way well, he arrived at her room. He shut the door slowly and deliberately but wasn't slow to reach her; he embraced her and kissed her deeply. She felt deliciously dizzy. She wasn't sure why she had surrendered to him, but much to her surprise, she found that he swept her away like a flood.

He was the kind of man she had dreamed of, the object of scandal who had lived most of his life among prostitutes, who knew about love and women, who was bold and utterly heedless of his reputation. He tore to ribbons the morals of the city and the reputation of his conservative family, he abandoned stability and secure employment to live in the gutter, he painted oddities and savored the taste of life. Yes, he was her ideal man, her eternal beloved, and nothing would keep her away from him.

William Eisa was an attractive young man, tall, with strong features and bold eyes in a tanned face. Combined with his natural elegance and his experience pursuing women, it was impossible for a girl like Aisha Mufti to resist him. He took her clothes off gently and laid her down on the bed—he wasn't in any hurry, the night was still just beginning—and she reminded him that she was a virgin and wanted to stay that way. He spoke about love as a lover; she believed him and felt that she was nothing like the girl she had been before she laid eyes on him. Something inside her had shattered and couldn't be mended. Her body, every part of her, was no longer the same. Everything in her life had changed. The moment she had spent years waiting for was close. She surrendered to him, and he held her close, kissed her overflowing breasts, her stomach, her ankles. She wasn't shy of her nakedness; she had inspected it in the mirror and could see how splendidly her limbs were formed, just as he told her. He spoke to her fervently about his dream of painting the faces of the itinerant hawkers in the alleyways of Aleppo. He wanted her to share his dream. They spent that last night together clinging and naked, talking about the canvases he would paint, for her.

Aisha Mufti believed that she deserved such a partnership. She gave no thought to the difference of religion between them; she told herself that the adventure was worth it. She had found a great aim to work toward, she was infatuated with his lips, she waited for his kisses and his bewitching words about the maze he would lead her into. They would spend their lives tasting the honey of love and dreams. She felt herself capable of doing anything in order to live with this man and his runaway imagination. She had always despised the apathetic, well-brought-up men who came to visit her father in his big house and spoke about laudable morals, and whose fathers alluded to the possibility of making an offer to his daughter. But her father, who had promised her not to say anything on the subject of marriage before she turned eighteen, would suavely make his excuses.

Before daybreak, the couple both wept. They felt that their separation was impossible. She let him have all the beautiful clothes he had taken off her body one by one, and he left her all the sketches he had made in her room on her handkerchiefs; to Aisha Mufti, their gifts were equal in importance. They agreed on a means of correspondence as soon as she reached Aleppo. William Eisa assured her he was ready to convert and become a Muslim for her, and her father would never refuse their marriage. Hajj Bashir had liked him very much during all the years he had worked in his company and had always had praise for his trustworthiness; for his part, William Eisa admired her father's love of art, his open-mindedness and liberality, and his lofty dreams that he told to all without fanfare.

Before going to the dock to say goodbye to her from a distance, William Eisa sent a telegram to Hanna, asking him for help in arranging his correspondence. He explained everything in a longer letter and wrote a second letter to Souad, laying out his relationship with Aisha Mufti and asking her to make her acquaintance. He wanted to tell the whole world his love story.

As Aisha Mufti prepared to board the boat back to Aleppo, she was a long way from William Eisa, but she could sense he was around somewhere, watching her. She scanned dozens of well-wishers before she saw him standing in a distant nook. She boarded the ship and waved at him; she felt as though his breaths were brushing her throat. He didn't move from his spot until the ship had disappeared from sight. His knees felt weak as he walked along the dock, not knowing what to do with himself.

Back in Aleppo, Hanna read the letter and laughed scornfully at his friend, who had become attached to a Muslim girl hundreds of kilometers away from him. But he ordered his servant Salih Azizi to leave off his work overseeing the fellahin and temporary house servant; he would move away from Anabiya and live in the servants' room at the bottom of the stairs in Hanna's house in Bab Al-Faraj, and he was to devote himself to the task of a go-between. Whenever a letter was placed in an iron box hung by the door, Salih Azizi would take it, put it in a special envelope on which he was to write the name *Hanna Gregoros*, and then send it to William Eisa's address. He would receive William Eisa's letters and put them in the same box, leaving the lid unlocked.

From the first letter, William Eisa admired Aisha Mufti's powerful eloquence. She was no naïve little girl; her first visits to Europe with her father had taught her that the world was vast and filled with wonderful things, and she simply refused to repeat the life of her sisters, who were drowning in the misery of children, family chatter, and stifling traditions. After she came back to Aleppo, she thought long and hard about what had happened. Distracted and alone most of the time, she received and wrote letters every day.

Salih Azizi delighted in his new life as a go-between, far away from the drudgery of the fellahin, the harvest, and the planting. He crossed the city every day, went to the post office, picked up the letter from abroad and left the letter he had to send, and went back to his room. It was an easy job, and he reflected that this was his chance at building a life here, far from Anabiya. For the first time, he tried wearing a shirt and trousers. He walked a bit clumsily at first, but within a few weeks he was used to his new clothes. He escaped his cumbersome shirwal trousers, and he no longer cared about his family in Anabiya, to whom his visits grew fewer and further between. He was no longer the singer of the harvest who used to lead the long caravan of workers to the fields of lentils and vetch, urging them to work with his never-ending songs. His voice was sweet, and by flirting with the girls and praising the men, he would arouse the workers' zeal, cheering everyone as they melted under the June sun in the enormous fields.

In the first month, he didn't know anything about the letters and their contents. One day he peeked out and observed a young man putting a letter into the box and quickly running off. Salih Azizi thought his task must be a mysterious and dangerous one if Hanna surrounded it with all this secrecy, giving him this task exclusively (along with many warnings and instructions), and paying him a monthly salary for it. Salih Azizi began to feel, in some vague way, that he was part of some great conspiracy. After less than two months, an employee at the post office asked him what the big secret was in these daily letters that Hanna Gregoros sent to his friend William Eisa. He whispered to Salih to be careful; perhaps the two of them were hatching a plot against the vali.

Salih couldn't respond to the quickfire questions of the post office employee, but he instantly felt he had to protect his master from the injurious suspicions of these minor public employees. He said that Hanna and his friend William Eisa were in the leather trade, and these letters related to their business. But on the way home, he turned William Eisa's letter over in his hands. He suspected that the matter was related to a woman.

That night he thought he could actually feel the strong words in the envelope searing him with their heat. He finished his work and hurried to the house of a man he had met several times in the coffeehouse, where a large number of effendim would sit in a circle and question him on everything. He was a humble man who taught children in his house by the entrance to the coppersmith's market, and he studied ancient manuscripts. Salih knocked on his door and waited apprehensively until a young pupil opened the door for him. Salih asked for Muallim Junaid Khalifa, and the pupil made way for him unhesitatingly. Salih asked the teacher to teach him reading and writing.

Junaid Khalifa scrutinized the young man, who seemed like a rustic trying to become urbanized. Without allowing him time to say anything, Salih announced that they both came from the same village, Anabiya. It transpired that Junaid Khalifa knew Salih Azizi's family and spoke highly of his grandmother. Salih Azizi offered his services to Junaid; he was willing to do any odd jobs, clean the classrooms, chop firewood. The taciturn teacher asked him to join the class the following day. Salih Azizi was twenty-three years old, short and sturdily built, and his eyes gleamed with a keen intelligence. Junaid Khalifa was astonished at his prodigious capacity for learning, and within a month he could read simple words. He withstood the mockery of his classroom peers who were all young children, and in three months he could write simple sentences without making any mistakes. He was always ready to carry out tasks without being asked; he cleaned his teacher's house, tarred the roof, fixed the water spouts, isolated the well, brought the young students to school, and delivered them back safely to their families after their classes.

The first time Salih Azizi dared to open a letter from Aisha Mufti to William Eisa, he felt dizzy as he read the words, most of which he understood. A woman was writing to a man who couldn't possibly forget her powerful phrases. *Come and pick my flowers. My pillow is soaked with tears of longing. Without you, I am a leaf whirling lost on the surface of the river.* Those and several other lines stuck in his mind, and he learned them all by heart.

He couldn't sleep that night for thinking of how he could see Aisha. He couldn't imagine what her words could mean to a man living so far away from her. The following day he bought a large notebook and copied the entire letter into it. He knew it was an idiotic and foolish thing to do, but he couldn't resist the temptation of reading it again in the quiet of the night before slipping into bed.

William Eisa missed Aisha and felt increasingly constricted. Every day he circled Hajj Bashir Mufti's abandoned house, imagining the hand of the enchanting Aisha Mufti opening the gate for him. He noticed the plants withering in the garden; evidently even the servant was no longer there. He walked aimlessly in the streets, asking himself what he was doing away from her. His money had run out, and in two months he wouldn't be able to pay his rent. His paint would run out long before that, and no one cared about the canvases stacked up in his room. His daily letters gave him great energy. Seeing him at a loss, Maggie refused to give up; she persuaded the caretaker of Karaköy

Church to employ William to restore the icons that had been stored in their vaults for centuries. The repetitive work, the rudeness of the other painters working on restoring the icons, and life in the church vault were not to William's taste. He wasn't enough of a believer to appreciate the world of churches and monasteries. He wanted to draw fellahin in the fields and sailors in bars.

He gave himself the liberty of living free from obligations. This is what lovers need: plenty of time to reflect on love. He wrote to Aisha that he would come back to Aleppo to spend the winter close to her; he could no longer bear breathing the air of a city whose nights they were no longer sharing.

Salih Azizi had copied nineteen letters into his notebook before it occurred to him to follow the young servant boy who collected the letters. The boy never heard Salih's footsteps behind him, and Salih watched as the boy went inside the huge gate of a large house more like a small palace, surrounded by high walls. He already knew it was the palace of Hajj Bashir Mufti. He spent the whole night circling the house and spotted Aisha opening the window of her room. Fair-skinned and tall, she was wearing a cotton nightshirt, and her hair was loose and uncovered. Salih's knees buckled, and he staggered—he had never seen such captivating beauty in his life. He hovered around the house for days. Once when she left the house in her carriage, he drifted after it. At a certain point, the carriage stopped and she got out, wearing a hijab but with her face uncovered. He followed her, feeling that this was his girl, the one he had been dreaming of. She passed close to him, utterly indifferent, and he was seared by the scent of her perfume as she went into the house of Sitt Hassaniya the seamstress. It wasn't difficult for Salih to connect William Eisa with Souad Bayazidi, who worked in Sitt Hassaniya's atelier. Hanna had often sent him to Ahmed Bayazidi's house, loaded with the choicest baskets of cherries or figs, and later on he had sent baskets of walnuts and grapes to Sitt Hassaniya's house as well.

When Salih stopped attending Junaid Khalifa's lessons, the teacher sent a young pupil to Salih to ask if he was all right, but the young boy didn't understand Salih's words, which he repeated faithfully back to his teacher. Junaid Khalifa thought that his student, who sent word that he had turned into a breath of wind crossing the room of the beloved, had been struck by a passion of some sort. When he saw him a few days later, Salih was a different person from the one he had known, babbling something baffling about love and annihilation. He told his teacher, "Ya Muallim, can you believe that yesterday I was kissing the little finger of my beloved, and today I am a small button on her thobe, and tomorrow I will be the dust slipping into her night-dress to inhale the perfume of her breasts."

William Eisa was greatly relieved at his decision to return to Aleppo. He wandered Istanbul all day, paused by some shabby fisher-men, and observed their exhausted faces. He read Aisha Mufti's new letter until he had memorized it; then he sat in a teahouse in Beyoğlu and wrote pages back to her. He sketched the faces he had seen for her, saying, "Yesterday I dreamed of you. I therefore have no news, but this morning I circled your father's house seven times, like the Hajj pilgrims do in Mecca." He went on writing and sketched her some large seagulls. He sealed the letter and tossed it to an employee at the post office in Galatasaray, who took it and teased him, wondering aloud what the real name of the letter's recipient might be. He wanted the whole city to know his tale. Without hesitation, William Eisa told him they were Aisha's letters, but he didn't say "Mufti." The employee nodded sympathetically.

When William Eisa looked in the mirror after a long time, he was alarmed. His eyes were hollow, his body even skinnier than before. His blood seeped away into deep valleys. Nine months had been enough for him to disintegrate. He didn't leave his room until he had finished packing his suitcase. He tucked in six paintings for Aisha and left the rest for Maggie, who was devastated he was leaving. He woke her be-fore dawn to say goodbye. He was ready to leave; a city whose skies didn't embrace her breaths had no value for him. Maggie understood his longing and burst into tears. He left quickly to post his last letter, in which he wrote that he was on his way to her: "On the surface of the water I walk, carried by wings of regret. How can my cruel heart have surrendered you all these months, leaving me to be snapped at by wild beasts and torn at by birds of prey? You will be mine alone, and I will be yours alone, even if I am a lifeless corpse." Aisha wept and counted the minutes till he would arrive. Words were no longer enough. She stayed in bed for hours, suffering from imaginary illnesses, but she knew he would come, and she thought she would stay in his arms for an entire century, inhaling the smell of his chest, staying beside him until the end of the world. He boarded a steamer to Iskenderun and sat in a chair for the whole length of the journey, all three days of it, with his gaze fixed on the same point on the horizon. He wanted to torture himself. He nibbled the few bread rolls that Maggie had wrapped up to keep hunger at bay along the way: she knew that he had nothing apart from a few Turkish mecidiye that would barely cover his ticket.

Aisha Mufti's appearance at Sitt Hassaniya's house turned Souad's life upside down. On her first visit, she kissed Souad and introduced herself. Souad had already written and invited her to the atelier, having received the whole story from William Eisa. Aisha was a precious gift to Souad. She was a girl who had traveled outside Aleppo and toured Europe and Istanbul; like Souad, she was strong, confident, afraid of nothing. Without wasting time, Souad told Aisha all about her childhood with William Eisa, Azar, Hanna, Zakariya, and Sara. Aisha Mufti, for her part, told Souad about faraway curiosities, and the two soon became close friends, exchanging confidences and frequent visits.

When Aisha told Souad the date that William Eisa would be arriving, Souad assured her that she would devise a way for them to meet. Whenever she recalled their childhood, William Eisa was the most refined and the most intent on pleasing her. She was determined to help her old friend and the girl who had become her close confidante.

The day after William Eisa arrived in Aleppo, he moved to Hanna's house in Bab Al-Faraj. He had spent his first night back at his family home and couldn't take any more of his father's speeches about how he needed to go back to being an accountant at the company. Souad went to Hajj Bashir Mufti's house to get Aisha and bring her to the Bayazidi family home. Then she sent word to William Eisa. Ahmed Bayazidi was away, inspecting his summer house in Ariha. She set up the cellar that would one day hold her mannequins. She encouraged Aisha Mufti to lose her virginity and whispered to her that the only one who deserved that honor was the man she loved. And when Aisha Mufti asked, "Have you done it?" Souad said regretfully that the person she loved was a coward who fled from love, and added that she had fitted out the jihaz of the bride whom he would be marrying in a few weeks. Aisha understood she was talking about Hanna. Every day Aisha Mufti felt a deeper kinship to Souad, whom the other women of the city described as arrogant, cruel, forceful, and impossible for a man to live with unless he was a killer. Sometimes they would go further and say she would stay a spinster if she kept refusing the prospective bridegrooms who thronged her father's office, most of them scions of wealthy families of note.

At their first meeting, which Souad ensured would be uninterrupted, Aisha Mufti asked William Eisa, "Do you want to pluck my flower?" Aware that he was risking a catastrophe, William Eisa simply said, "Yes." He looked at her wildly, hardly believing that he was touching her. He picked her up in his arms, laid her down on the floor, and greedily kissed her every pore. He was delirious, and Aisha was half-faint from ecstasy. She took hold of him and pulled him to her body; she wanted him to dissolve inside her. A few hours took them to distant realms, they felt their craving for each other would never be extinguished, they couldn't be apart. Aisha Mufti surrendered to him, and he wanted to condense the last nine months to nothing. A lover's yearning can't be extinguished—its flame and heat can only increase. Aisha was shocked to find that evening was falling when she heard Souad's voice telling them she had to get back to her family's house before dark.

After Aisha Mufti went home, she went straight to her room. She felt a bottomless yearning. She waited until nine o'clock when everyone in the house was asleep and went outside onto the terrace. She saw that William Eisa was hovering near her house, concealing his face and looking at her from a distance. He stayed there until midnight, when he waved at her and left. For the moment, he was utterly heedless of what might happen.

They continued to meet: Azar's sister Sara rented a small room for them in a house attached to a printing press in Bab Al-Nasr. The Jewish landlady rented out five rooms to poor families, but allowed this one to be rented out for romantic assignations; it was where Sara usually brought her clients. She was a highly skilled professional go-between, tasked with keeping lovers' secrets. She was assisted in her work by her husband David, who still worked at the hammam, where he kept the fire in the boiler stoked and acted as a guard. Souad was eager to help the lovers; she asked her servant to stay in Hassaniya's atelier, arranged some cuts of fabric, and accompanied Aisha to the door of the Jewish house. Both women were wearing heavy wraps and impenetrable headcoverings, and they had two children in tow, whom Sara had borrowed for them so that they would look like two women on their way home. On some level, Souad wanted to express her gratitude to William Eisa, her childhood friend whom she was forbidden to see now that they had grown up. Now they had only letters, and some fleeting encounters, to sustain their friendship. She used to write to him about her pain and Hanna's abandonment of her. William Eisa was supportive of her idea to found a sewing atelier of her own. He encouraged her in her dream of organizing a fashion exhibition, and he offered her some designs he had painted of unusual dresses. Souad loved them. He had always drawn her dreams for her. He felt a deep affinity for her and was a repository for her secrets.

Souad also, quite sincerely, wanted the relationship between Aisha Mufti and William Eisa to be a success. When her father went away on a sudden trip, she invited them to the house and arranged everything well. She guarded them, careful that nothing unexpected should ruin things or compromise the couple. They crept into the cellar, which had been Souad's favorite place for years—where she stored fabric and trunks filled with her own fashion designs. She was afraid to draw her dreams, which William Eisa drew for her. Souad made the cellar into an ideal place for the lovers' secret meetings, and they buried their secrets in that shadowy place. Aisha would come at ten in the morning, drink coffee with Souad, and then leave her to wait for William Eisa, who would slip inside through the unlocked side door and cross the courtyard, whose every chink and crevice he knew from childhood. Souad would bring them a plate of fruit and nuts, some Indian incense, and a jug of rose petal sherbet. Then she would make sure no one disturbed them.

William entered the cellar where Aisha was waiting for him. She put her arms around his neck and kissed him ravenously. She was no longer afraid. She spent three hours in his arms and whispered to him to take her virginity, but he hesitated. He told her that after returning from Istanbul and dealing with the continual problems with his family, he had begun to think of how they could stay together forever. When she was beside him, he felt that everything would be all right. He drew back at the last moment, gazing at her pink sex. Within him, he could feel a bottomless chasm filled with everything that belonged to her: her scent, her voice, her hair, her words of lust, her dreams. He would say later that love is being filled with the details of a woman who can drive out all the others from within you.

William Eisa had to endure the mockery of Hanna, Zakariya, and Azar for his theories, and for his romantic speeches that made him sound like one of those feeble-minded lovers who spent their lives droning on about their beloved, pining for them in separation, and who finally ended up as mystics in some zawiya or other, preaching about intangible desires. Bereft of the glow of the lover, they turned into lunatics. But at the same time, they realized that William Eisa was serious about this relationship, and it wasn't just a passing whim. For the first time, Hanna reflected seriously on the danger of what William Eisa was doing, but after conferring with Zakariya and Azar, they all resolved to stand by their friend.

While taking dinner together, William Eisa's friends promised him everything would be fine. Hanna would clear the way for them to be joined. Hajj Bashir Mufti was no bigot, and the complex knot composed of her uncles, and Michel Eisa's religious family, would be dealt with using calm and patience. Without question, it was not easy for a Christian to declare himself Muslim in order to marry a Muslim girl, but Hanna was confident he would find a way to resolve the problem. In recent months, he had felt himself to be in the best position he ever had been. Strong relationships connected him with the most important pillars of authority: the vali, the judiciary, high-ranking officials, and both Christian and Muslim men of religion. In the end, he had become a man for all. He was fascinated by the games played by the great, but he didn't want to compete with anyone and often would suddenly disappear from view, only to reappear in the midst of a heated battle to offer his opinion and intervene in its outcome.

When Aisha returned from Istanbul, she was a different girl than before. She helped her sister arrange matters for her four children and shared aspects of her father's work; she reviewed accounts and sometimes visited the textile factory, ignoring the glances from the workers, who were baffled as to why she was there. She would reassure herself about the conditions of the female workers, give an opinion about the dyes (which she had recently taken an interest in reading about), then spend her free time with Souad, chatting in a secret code only they understood. She was preparing her jihaz, and Madame Hassaniya insisted on using the finest fabrics. She didn't like drowning in things—and in this she was supported by Souad, who said that a few things would be enough—but Aisha nevertheless didn't hide her passionate conviction that those few things should be precious. She loved nightdresses embroidered with gold thread and insisted on a set of sterling silver spoons. She was carefully considering every detail of the objects that would form her enchanted world with William Eisa.

She visited orphanages and didn't scrimp in her donations to the mosques that cared for orphans and the elderly. She volunteered to teach the girls French and joined a group of women concerned with the affairs of the city, who would meet and loudly deplore the pervasiveness of ignorance and make plans to educate the children. They swapped books that came in the post from Paris and Beirut and supported the journalist reformers who spoke about women's rights. They would send letters to the newspapers, wishing to have a share in editing them.

Her father felt very proud; Aisha Mufti had grown up just as he had wished. But nevertheless, he was afraid for her, and he worried that if he died, the family would descend on her and tear her apart. He no longer had any contact with them apart from rare occasions. His siblings would criticize him and recount in lurid detail the gossip that was spread around the city about his daughter: her wild recklessness, her lack of respect for order. In their censure, they included his own connections with the group of Abd Al-Rahman Kawakibi and those atheists and heretics who had raised their voices in recent times to the extent that they demanded reforms to the religion itself. Hajj Bashir Mufti wanted a successful marriage for his daughter, one that would protect her from the rumors that dogged her, just as they had dogged her friends over the years. But he couldn't manage to convince her about any of the young men who tried to gain her attention.

Aisha entered her eighteenth year in the year they returned from Istanbul. She grew even more beautiful with her slim frame and the long neck she had inherited from her aunt, an icon of the city. But Aisha was warmer than her aunt, a little shorter, and her soft white skin came from her grandmother, a native of Aleppo. She still remembered the sad look in her grandmother's eyes when she picked Aisha up in her arms and muttered that when she grew up, her charms would burn men's hearts to ashes. Everyone in the family took the grandmother's words very seriously at first, but they were soon forgotten after Aisha grew up at a distance—her father had quarreled with his siblings and his cousins about her grandmother's substantial estate, in a judgment that was famous throughout the city, but especially among the shops of the Souq Al-Khaish.

The women of Aleppo said that Aisha Mufti, who came from a family of women all famous for their beauty, had drawn on the best of everything they all had. But her high spirits were not to the taste of those women who were occupied with perpetually swapping information about prospective brides. Aisha's name was taken out of circulation after she refused the mufti of Antioch's grandson, a recent graduate of the medical college in Istanbul whose father held an important post in Yıldız Palace. No one braved the path to her family's door after that, and the city circulated the details of her reaction to the costly gifts. Reportedly, she had said to him, "You may buy chairs with legs made of gold, but not the heart of a woman who was born on the surface of a river, and who has given herself to the deepest seas."

No one understood what those words meant, but the conversations lingered over the gold, painstakingly worked and stamped with the name of the Armenian goldsmith with the golden mask whose rare pieces the upper-class women of Istanbul, the sultan's capital, thronged to buy.

The autumn passed as William Eisa set up his life in the city. He was still moving between his family's house and Hanna's house in Bab Al-Faraj, looking for a place to turn into his own studio. He thought of renting a house that would serve as a nest for a married couple. Every Monday and Thursday, Aisha Mufti woke up early, ordered the servant to prepare breakfast for her nieces and nephews, and supervised a special lunch for her father, who suffered from rheumatism. At the same time, she would leave and go to Sitt Hassaniya's house. From there she would slip out with Souad and Sara, walking ahead of them to be sure that the way was free of surprises, and when they turned into Khandaq Street, she would walk behind them to be sure that no one was following them. The women would arrive at the Jewish landlady's house, where William Eisa would be waiting. Soon the couple began to talk about arrangements for their engagement. Hanna, Zakariya, and Azar had promised to help and offered all the required support; they were mindful that William Eisa's change of religion would be a disaster for his family. In addition, Hajj Bashir's approval was not guaranteed; he wouldn't want to clash with the Christians or cause riots.

On the way to meet William Eisa as usual, Aisha relaxed in her seat. She was thinking pleasant thoughts about being loved, when she heard a shout from the driver of a carriage whose path had been blocked as it tried to turn into a side street. Aisha put her head out of her carriage. Her own coachman was apologizing to the military coachman, even though he had done nothing wrong, and he was being reproached with ugly words and threats. Hikmat Dashwali, Ottoman officer, got down from the carriage and saw Aisha. He looked at her for some time. He ordered his coachman to drive on but couldn't sleep that night. He had heard about Aisha from his aunts, but he simply couldn't believe the self-assurance he saw in her eyes.

His aunts were not at all keen on his choice. They said that men were afraid of headstrong girls, and Aisha Mufti was very headstrong indeed, as well as being a fool who behaved with unseemly frivolity and had no respect for the weight of tradition. She wasn't a suitable choice for a powerful officer in the inner circle of Sultan Abdel Hamid II, for whom illustrious appointments were expected in the near future. In the previous few months, Hikmat Dashwali had heard many stories about Aisha Mufti. He had met her by chance by the port in Iskanderon as she was disembarking from the steamer that had brought her from Istanbul. It was a short encounter, but he noticed how confidently she dealt with the porters who carried her bags. She was accompanied by her father, and when she took his arm and walked to her carriage, she was like a princess. He saw her self-assurance and her beauty, and he couldn't believe that any man could be afraid of a woman. Of course, a man like himself—one who had scraped Armenian bodies along the streets of Edessa, waged war for years, and curbed all the protests against the sultan in Anatolia—would never fear a woman. The name of Hikmat Dashwali alone was enough to strike terror into the hearts of the fiercest adversaries. He didn't wait for long. Aisha Mufti's face gave him sleepless nights. He had initially been convinced by his aunt's argument that he should look for a bride among the families of men close to the sultan, and that she should preferably be Turkish as well, but on the day he met her again in Khandaq Street, he felt Aisha Mufti was the woman he had been looking for. It was decided. He knocked on the door of Hajj Bashir Mufti and asked for his daughter's hand without preamble, adding that Sultan Abdel Hamid II himself would be pleased to hear that the hajji had accepted his proposal. The message was clear and was reinforced the next day when the vali came to Hajj Bashir's house. In a smooth tone, the vali praised the lofty morals of Hikmat Dashwali, hinting at his elevated lineage and his roots in Aleppo, and he mentioned Hikmat Dashwali's grandfather (counselor to Sultan Abdel Hamid II) and uncle (confidant of the vali of Damascus). Without waiting for Hajj Bashir's response, the vali decided that the engagement contract should be completed on the coming Thursday.

Aisha Mufti felt a powerful shudder contract her body as she fell into a snare she couldn't evade. When she shared her dilemma with her close friend, Souad asked her to be calm, although Souad already knew of Hikmat Dashwali and despised him as much as he had despised Hanna, Zakariya, and Azar from their school days. Aisha was sure that the encounter had destroyed all their lives; if she refused him, he would arrange some false charge to throw her father in jail, and he would mutilate her. It had happened before, to a Bedouin girl whose family had refused to marry their daughter to the commander of the Ottoman army in Mosul, and who couldn't escape his revenge. After deciding they could no longer bear the nonstop harassment, they moved to Aleppo, but before they reached the city, their way was blocked by a group of masked men. They slaughtered the family's horses and herd of goats, and they kidnapped the girl and took her back to Mosul. They raped her over several days and left her for the janissaries, who also took turns raping her until she died three days later, and they threw her corpse into the Tigris.

Aisha felt a horrifying pressure. It wouldn't be easy to find a way out of this predicament. She listened to Souad, who advised her to flee Ottoman territory and live in Europe if she was prepared to see this adventure with William Eisa through to the end. In the meantime, Aisha Mufti became a fiancée and couldn't leave the house without permission. The verbal letters that Souad carried every day remained the only means of communication between Aisha Mufti and William Eisa.

William Eisa wrote ardently, saying that he wouldn't abandon her, they would escape together, and he confirmed that he had arranged everything they would need and his loyal friends would help him. Every night after their engagement, Hikmat Dashwali came to his fiancée's house, where they would sit on the large terrace overlooking the rose garden and throw pebbles into the nearby river. He imposed his wishes on her and walked in front of her with a firm tread. Aisha stayed silent and exchanged agonized glances with her father, who felt he was offering up his daughter to be raped. Hikmat Dashwali even ordered the servant to move the dining table out onto the terrace to enjoy the spring breezes. He behaved with an arrogant self-importance, determined to destroy Aisha's haughtiness before the wedding, and he relished his dominance, which was made clear by the submissive conduct of Hajj Bashir Mufti and the way he made no objection to any of the officer's opinions or suggestions.

Aisha Mufti tried to escape from Hikmat Dashwali's ardor, which increased by the day. He told her that he was a candidate to be an important man in the sultanate, and he would strive with all his might to serve his august sultan. He aimed to prepare her to become a very important lady when the sultan chose him for an eminent position in Istanbul. She nodded and flattered him and stopped herself from murdering him. One day she said that he should think long and hard; he still had a chance to relinquish his decision. She spoke about her difficult temperament, and her chronic epileptic fits (an invention). But his attachment to her only grew stronger. The day before she ran away with William Eisa, she told him that neither of them was suited to the other, but she was surprised when he stood up, red-faced. Before he left, he asked her father to have the marriage contract ready for Thursday night, in three days' time. His decision was final.

That night Aisha Mufti put on a black cloak, covered her face and eyes with a burqa, and got into the carriage that was waiting for her in the dense cypress thicket by the riverbank. Everything was prepared for her to cross Aleppo and leave the city. Hanna and Zakariya had readied everything and acted with the utmost secrecy. The carriage left the city before dawn and climbed the rough roads to avoid the main routes to the village of Sharran, where Arif Sheikh Musa Agha was waiting. Zakariya was driving the carriage that went into Grandfather's House, where William Eisa waited for her. Meanwhile Hanna was supervising all matters and ensuring their comfort from a distance.

Aisha Mufti had burned her boats. Neither Aisha nor William Eisa lost time in asking about the best route to escape the territories of the sultanate. Before Zakariya and Hanna returned to the citadel on their way to Aleppo, they conferred with Azar on how best to smuggle William Eisa and Aisha Mufti to Paris. Zakariya knew the route well and suggested they live in this house for a few weeks, away from prying eyes, until the caravans of Hajj pilgrims started to arrive. A caravan would take them to Al-Hudayda in Yemen, and from there it would be easy to take a steamer to Venice, where they could make their way to Paris. Aisha Mufti relaxed. She was no longer afraid. Arif left them a lot of food and provisions, and Zakariya sent them one of the best horses from his stable, to be at their disposal if they needed to flee.

Aisha Mufti spent the happiest days of her life in that small house away from humanity. The road to the house was guarded by armed fellahin stationed by Arif Sheikh Musa Agha. She would wake before dawn, make her coffee, and open the window to watch the dawn and see the distant plains, the carts, and the fellahin. From her window, she saw things and people as small dots, moving in the fields. She had breakfast and woke William Eisa with a kiss on the lips. Like any good fellaha, she looked after the chickens, watered the seedlings of beans, okra, and watermelon in the farm, then went back to the room and slipped into bed next to William Eisa, who felt that happiness was living with his beloved Aisha. He was enthusiastic about running away with her to Paris; there he would paint the canvases he dreamed of, and he would design huge theater posters. He was dreaming of the many things it was impossible to do in Aleppo. They planned their

life and often spoke about the future, both unafraid. They were in total harmony, and he had no opposition to her wish to be married in
Venice. There she would give him her virginity and become his wife.
The days passed quietly in that house, but in Aleppo, the storytellers
had composed their story, and new details were added to it every day.

Before her departure, Aisha Mufti had left a short letter for her
father. She begged his forgiveness, because she had hidden her love
for William Eisa from him. She said that death would be easier for her
than life with a shallow, arrogant murderer like Hikmat Dashwali.
She assured him that she was somewhere no one could ever reach her,
and when she had a permanent address outside the empire, she would
inform him, and he would be proud of her.

Those few words caused this kind man, so unlike most of the inhabitants of his city, to overflow with love for his daughter. He had
concealed many of his own wishes in order to be able to live alongside
his peers, and he had grown used to living a double life. He didn't
dare express himself, and in his most candid moments, talking with
those he loved, he admitted to being a coward. He had spent his life
in denial of his dreams. He admired the strong men who openly criticized the men of religion for fawning over the sultan, but he himself didn't dare miss Friday prayer at the mosque or the sermons of
those sycophants, and he never refused a request to donate to their
mosques or their organizations. He reflected that Aisha had given
him the push to rid himself of his duality; she had a different destiny
from her wretched sister, who had married early, and he had never
paused along the path of her education. He had encouraged her to
learn French and maintain friendships with liberated women, and he
never reprimanded her for her clothes, which were nothing like those
of the other women of her family.

After he read her short letter, he felt dizzy but relieved. He thought
he had been saved from his dilemma. There were people who could
help him—how would he explain his predicament to them? He had
recited the Surah Al-Fatiha over his daughter, and Hikmat Dashwali
and the vali witnessed the agreement. It had been decided that the

vali and the mufti would come to his house to contract his daughter's marriage that very night.

Hajj Bashir Mufti put Aisha's letter into his pocket and went to see his friend Ahmed Bayazidi. He closed the door behind him and held out Aisha's letter, but it did not have the effect he had intended. Ahmed Bayazidi told him that the vali wouldn't allow him to escape his dilemma. He suggested going to the mufti or sending a telegram to his friend Abulhuda Al-Sayyadi in Istanbul, but he admitted his doubts that even Abulhuda Al-Sayyadi would intervene to oppose the Dashwali family. When Hajj Bashir Mufti accepted his suggestion, Ahmed Bayazidi found no way of excusing himself from accompanying his friend to the mufti, who listened to Hajj Bashir in silence.

The mufti's silence augured ill. The only thing he suggested to Hajj Bashir Mufti was to try to disappear from the city, if he wanted to live. This wasn't merely a case of a girl refusing a bridegroom—this was an insult that the Ottoman officers in Aleppo wouldn't overlook. Within hours, the city was circulating the tale of Aisha Mufti, who had run away with a man. Hikmat arrived at Hajj Bashir's house with his soldiers and pounded on the door. The servant opened up, and they barged into the house, searching every corner of every room. The house was half-empty. Hajj Bashir had already packed up his precious things and his papers and left the city with his other daughter and her children. Hikmat Dashwali and his troops seized all of Aisha Mufti's possessions, set the building on fire, and didn't leave until they had made sure that the whole sumptuous house was reduced to ash.

Everyone thought the blazing fire would extinguish Hikmat Dashwali's rancor. Instead, he strode across his office and felt a void between his ribs. Aisha Mufti had smeared his honor in the dust, but he also missed her. He felt a violent love toward her, even as he recalled her quelling words and the messages she had tried to send him. Burning down her family's splendid home wasn't enough for his pox-ridden honor. His victory in this city wouldn't be complete until he had recovered her and tamed her. Search parties of soldiers raided the houses where he guessed they were hiding. When they entered Ahmed Bayazidi's house, he didn't scream in their faces. Drawing on his experience as a high-ranking official, he submitted calmly to the soldiers, who dealt roughly with the old man. He was tired of complaining. He had always considered it luck that fate had never yet put him in conflict with an unprincipled Ottoman officer famous for butchery, one such as Hikmat Dashwali. Over the years, Ahmed Bayazidi had been exposed to countless intrigues and machinations, but he always managed to keep ahead of the storm, and he knew that it was impossible to confront someone who was capable of killing in cold blood. When at last, the soldiers left his house, Ahmed Bayazidi didn't seek an apology; he was simply relieved the storm had passed. Aisha Mufti had thrown a heavy stone into a stagnant, putrid pool—the city would be set on fire in hours, and he could no longer try to quell the flames. The next day, having verified the matter, Hikmat Dashwali circulated the name of William Eisa as the accomplice of Aisha Mufti. The story became even more titillating for the storytellers, who spoke about the great love story between a young Christian man well known for his philandering, and a Muslim girl. The city recalled the old tales of Hanna, Zakariya, William, and Azar and their dalliances with prostitutes. The story came to settle in its initial contours, a tale of forbidden, impossible love. The young girls of Aleppo sighed as they listened to the hastily concocted details of the historical meetings between the lovers in the house of the Jewish woman, who admitted her role; Hikmat Dashwali searched the house and interrogated Sara and David. The girls talked about the scented handkerchiefs exchanged by the couple; the soldiers sought out and confiscated every silk handkerchief they could find that bore the name *William Michel Eisa* in Latin characters.

Christians protested against dragging the name of William Eisa, son of Michel Eisa, into this scandalous story. The metropolitan complained to the vali and warned him that sectarian rioting might set parts of the city alight if the officer Hikmat Dashwali continued to violate the sanctity of Christian houses on the pretext of searching for his bride. But the vali, who secretly relished a state of chaos, had no answer for him. He considered the matter outside his mandate, claiming that he couldn't stop a man looking for his wife. The vali's men leaked several false stories about investigations being undertaken by the authorities, accusing the lovers of disturbing public order, conspiring against the state, and communicating with political groups that aimed to destroy the system of Islamic morals.

The campaign of house raids within Aleppo continued for a number of weeks. On the pretext of searching for Aisha Mufti, a search of all houses was undertaken, especially the houses of Christians, and six people were arrested for possessing illegal weapons and pamphlets that incited revolt against the sultan and called for Arab nationalism.

As all this unfolded, Hanna and Zakariya were resting in the citadel, collecting all these stories, assessing the situation as if they were on a war footing. Prepared for a real battle if soldiers stormed the citadel, the issue was no longer how to smuggle two friends across the border but how to evade the civil unrest that was shaking the foundations of the hitherto tranquil city. Young men and women defended Aisha Mufti and her reputation, and others demanded retribution for the disintegration that had begun to spread throughout the city. A newspaper that described the officer's engagement to Aisha Mufti as "a forced marriage" was shut down and the journalist led away to prison—a place he was already familiar with, and where for the hundredth time the authorities tried negotiating with him to stop agitating against the corruption of the men in the sultanate, especially Abulhuda Al-Sayyadi, who had risen to the rank of Sheikh of Islam, one of the closest of the close to Sultan Abdel Hamid II.

As they were drinking and contemplating the distant plains from the citadel's balcony, Hanna said to Zakariya that Aisha Mufti and William Eisa had thrown a lit match and would end up burning down the city. Many people had taken advantage of the story to assert their own points of view. Aisha Mufti was no longer the nice girl their friend had fallen in love with; she was a symbol of emancipation for those who espoused liberation from the Ottomans and a joining with Europe. For supporters of the Ottoman Empire, on the other hand, she was the result of overly permissive weakness and deserved nothing less than death. Zakariya was of the opinion that the story had to run its course before the couple could be smuggled out: you can't smuggle a legend, as he said. He had readied everything for the dangerous journey that William Eisa and Aisha Mufti would undergo before reaching Al-Hudayda in Yemen. Hanna urged him to ask their friend Huda Shamoun for help in reaching Venice; if she was on their side, their journey to Paris would be easy.

It was settled that Aisha Mufti and William Eisa would travel in a Christian pilgrimage convoy to Bethlehem, and from there they would follow the road with a caravan of Muslim pilgrims heading to Mecca for the Hajj. From Mecca, it would be straightforward to reach the border with Yemen, where they would be welcomed by the Italian consul, who would grant them the necessary permissions to board an Italian steamer. As soon as they boarded the boat, they would be safe, under the protection of the Italian government.

Zakariya worked out every detail with Hanna: the convoys they would join, the fees they would have to pay, the forged papers that would be easily obtained, in which Aisha Mufti was called Maria and given Hanna's family name of Gregoros. In the convoy to Mecca, she would be Souad Bayazidi. Hanna guessed that Aisha's accent would betray that she was from Aleppo, and so all the papers came from the civil register in Aleppo, stamped in the proper way, so there would be no doubt of their veracity.

The letters William Eisa exchanged with his friends Hanna and Zakariya were written in a code they were familiar with and were carried back and forth by trusted men who would go to Arif Sheikh Musa Agha's farm in Sharran and bring back the replies on the same day. In the last letter, everyone agreed they would join the Christian pilgrimage convoy that would leave Jisr Al-Shughur on September 25. William Eisa and Aisha Mufti were relaxed about it all and were taken by surprise when, shortly before the appointed time to leave the place where they had briefly lived in such tenderness, Ottoman soldiers and a group of janissaries surrounded the village and stormed the house. None of them spoke Arabic. William Eisa had no time to draw his weapon. He understood everything when he saw Arif Sheikh Musa Agha's men in chains, but in the same instant, he was determined that he and Aisha could still survive. They jumped from the window and fled through the vineyard, but the soldiers' shots rang out faster than they could hide. Certain of having killed them, the soldiers withdrew. They didn't dare to arrest Arif Sheikh Musa Agha, whose property had sheltered the fugitives and whose men had guarded them; the agha had been waiting for an occasion such as this to declare open rebellion.

After the soldiers had retreated, Hikmat Dashwali dismounted from his horse and looked at Aisha, smeared in blood. He couldn't bear to look into her eyes for long. He realized he was in a predicament. The Christians would never shut up about the murder of a Christian youth, and the foreign consuls would consider it a major issue, especially at that moment, when there was conflict brewing between the English, the French, and the Italians over striking deals for railway concessions. Nevertheless, he felt that he had recovered his lost honor, and leaving the couple where they lay, he went away. When he reached Aleppo, he received an order to transfer to Astana. And so Hikmat Dashwali left Aleppo on the first of November 1901. The city was silent as if it were in mourning. He passed Hajj Bashir's house; although it had been reduced to ash, the walls and the marvelous ornamentation were still visible. People in the streets avoided looking at his carriage. But the story wasn't over. Arif Sheikh Musa Agha lost no time taking the bodies to the citadel himself. At the sight of the bodies lying in the carriage, Hanna wept bitterly. He and Zakariya decided to bury them in the nearby fields. From her window overlooking the fields, Shams Al-Sabah watched Zakariya dig two graves under a large walnut tree. Hanna and Zakariya placed the bloodstained Aisha Mufti into a coffin, on which Zakariya had carved her full name, and they let the coffin down into the grave calmly and patiently. They did the

same with their friend William Eisa. Shams Al-Sabah saw their tears
as they kissed him for the last time and threw the flowers they had
picked themselves from all over their vast territories onto the graves.

PART II

Salih Azizi couldn't bear it when William Eisa ordered him to pick
up his bags and unpack them in the guest room at Hanna's house.
Deep down, he felt he himself deserved Aisha; he loved her more than
William Eisa did; he would carve open his own chest and offer up his
bleeding heart to her; he would gouge out his eyes so she could use
them to see through, should she wish. This was what he believed: love
was giving a piece of your body to your beloved.

At night Salih Azizi often knocked at the door of Junaid Khalifa,
his teacher, exhausted and gabbling incoherently about love, and passion, and Aisha, and death. Once he told Junaid that he was thinking
of killing William Eisa. He said, "I will pour molten lead over his
head, and that will be it." He took a large lump of lead from his pocket
and concluded by saying gravely, "No one will be able to take Aisha
Mufti away from me." Junaid Khalifa let him rave on, bored by the
strange ideas his friend kept returning to. Junaid eventually realized
that Salih just wanted to talk to someone who knew the story of his
love for Aisha Mufti. Several times Junaid had tried to dissuade him
from his impossible dream by approaching the topic rationally and
laying out all the differences and obstacles that lay between him and
Aisha Mufti, but Salih simply didn't hear advice he didn't like. He was
intensely annoyed by this approach—he was sincere in everything he
said to Junaid. When Salih was alone in his room, he took out his
notebook and wrote letters to her. He never sent them: he wanted to
remain concealed, living in her shadow. At night, he would go out and
circle her house. He knew she wouldn't see him, but he would imagine
her there, behind that window, sleeping in her bed. He imagined her
in her opulent surroundings, and he would watch the darkened win-

dow for hours, waiting for any chink of light. Exhausted, he would go home before midnight and reread her letters, most of which he had copied down in his notebook.

One day he waited for her. She got down from the carriage and walked toward the door of Sitt Hassaniya's atelier. He came right up to her, wanting to say something, anything, to her. She stopped and waited for him to speak, but he was mute. Her looks pierced him, full of energy and strength, and her perfume wafted toward him. His look of weakness bemused her, and she continued on her way. A pin fell from her hair as he watched her go. Afraid that Souad would give him an order, he swooped on the pin, scooped it up, and hurried away. Now he had something of hers. After two streets, he stopped and decided he should tell her the truth. She should know that he was her one true lover whose life she had changed forever. For the first time, he was afraid of what might happen, and it occurred to him that when men were struck with overwhelming, giddy, passionate love, they grew fearful and filled with gas and empty words.

William Eisa's return made him lose hope. That night he wept alone, like a lonely wolf in the wilds. He could hear William Eisa moving around at dawn and making his coffee. Salih was in his room downstairs, listening to William Eisa whistling. He had every right to be happy; anyone who was loved by Aisha Mufti might as well be a king. Salih couldn't endure being anywhere near William Eisa, especially after he left his family's home and took up residence in his friend Hanna's apartment close to the brothel of Bab Al-Faraj, bringing all his bags, canvases, and paints with him. The area was just right for someone like William Eisa: movement never stopped here, the sound of music came from the house in Bahsita until dawn, and the carriages never stopped serving the clients of the prostitutes.

A few days after William Eisa settled in Hanna's house, Salih packed up his belongings and went to Junaid Khalifa's house. He asked permission to stay the night while he arranged his affairs. He had few possessions: a large bag containing three small notebooks, some pens, two shirts, and a collection of odds and ends—nails, a piece of soft wood, lots of dirt, some pieces of fabric picked out of the rubbish, and a magnificent hairpin that was clearly very expensive. He had a large number of envelopes, and a blue silk shawl that had been carefully looked after and wrapped in a piece of leather to protect the perfume it still held. And a large painting, meticulously wrapped. Junaid opened it and looked at it for some time. It was superb. The deepest feelings of a lover became part of him, mingling with his very blood, and he wasn't surprised when he saw William Eisa's signature in the corner, but he didn't understand the value of the other objects. It wasn't long before he heard Salih inform him of his decision to stop working as a servant for Hanna. He couldn't bear his rival ordering him to clean the room or bring him some food from the restaurants nearby, any more than he could bear it when he watched Aisha Mufti slipping into Ahmed Bayazidi's house, and William Eisa creeping in after her through the door that Souad left open for him.

Junaid Khalifa agreed to share his lodgings for the night. He soothed Salih with an offer of assistance, saying, "Tomorrow we will talk for longer, and we'll arrange somewhere for you to stay." It occurred to him that by keeping him close, he might alleviate Salih's loneliness. But in truth, Junaid Khalifa was also exhilarated by finding himself part of a story that was almost a fairy tale, full of enough secrets to burn down the city. He was stirred by Salih's transformation from naïve provincial fellah to servant who wanted to be part of the city, and then again to lover in a tale of impossible love. He reflected happily that things should always happen this way, in a life worth living. And at the same time he was drawn in by the letters that Salih had copied into his notebook, so that he wanted him to stay close by.

Junaid Khalifa spoke with the owner of the house, who informed him there was a small cellar beneath the quarters that he shared with other lodgers. He bought a woolen mattress, a blanket, a pillow, a mat, and a water pitcher. Salih Azizi said these things would be enough for him, went into the cellar, and left only rarely. He spent all his time sitting cross-legged on the mat, watching a spider weaving its web in a corner. Junaid asked him what his plans were, and Salih replied,

"I am cleansing my heart," and then fell silent. He ignored Junaid's invitations to loaf around the city like other young men. Although Junaid had a habit of asking questions, he was forced to relinquish them in this instance by Salih Azizi's long silence. Salih stayed alone in his cellar, suffering from a desperate yearning to see Aisha. All of a sudden one day, he went out and walked toward her house. Several patrols were circling as he went on his way to Sitt Hassaniya's atelier, by Ahmed Bayazidi's house. That was the day he discovered the Jewish woman's rooms, and as he observed Aisha then William enter, he realized that Aisha was meeting her lover in that house. He thought he would go mad if he kept following her tracks without ever getting hold of her. When he left Hanna's house, he had stolen a shawl from William Eisa's room as well as the canvas that he found in a corner behind the wardrobe. He knew that William had hidden the painting from Hanna, who would stop by once in a while with Zakariya and Azar. On those occasions they would spend the whole night eating dinner and talking in hushed voices, and then the three friends would leave and William Eisa would stay by himself, dividing his time between painting, wandering, and having assignations with Aisha.

The night that Aisha disappeared with William Eisa, Salih returned to his room, frustrated and defeated. He had seen Aisha get into a carriage driven by Zakariya that headed north. She had escaped, and he had lost her scent. Losing the scent of one's beloved turns the city to ash. The streets no longer hold any meaning, nor does the sky, the buildings, the rain, or the wind. Everything vanishes with the beloved. Salih's sense of loss was acute. His head was a cacophony of images and ideas, but he felt powerless. He fell to thinking about where Aisha might have hidden with William Eisa. He reflected that Hanna wasn't stupid enough to receive them at the citadel: it was too well known. The carriage was heading north, so it would no doubt take her to Zakariya's stables in Anabiya, or Arif Agha's farm.

The next day Junaid Khalifa brought food and chattered about the rumors that were circulating the city: Hikmat Dashwali, the Ottoman officer, had lost his fiancée, who had been abducted and disappeared from the city. Salih didn't mention that he had seen Aisha leaving in a carriage driven by Zakariya. He almost slipped, more than once, but he preferred to keep the secret. Eventually Junaid withdrew to his room, leaving Salih alone, staring at a spider.

At dawn, Junaid woke up to a powerful blow on the door. When he opened it, he saw a group of soldiers spread out over the court-yard. They brought Salih out from his cellar in irons and took him away to prison. They threw him into a cell and flogged him. In the middle of the night he was summoned by Hikmat Dashwali, who sat in a chair facing him and asked him directly where Aisha was hid-ing. Salih looked at him, wide-eyed and stunned. He replied that he didn't know. Hikmat Dashwali asked about the letters that Salih had taken to the post every day, and Salih replied calmly that they were Aisha's letters to William Michel Eisa. On being returned to his cell, he thought he wouldn't survive. Hikmat Dashwali hadn't dared to interrogate Hanna and had made do with his servant instead. On each of the ten nights he spent in the cell, Salih thought long and hard about disclosing the couple's secret hideaway, which he now knew was Arif Sheikh Musa Agha's farm. On the day after their flight, he had gone out at dawn, hired a mule from Khan Al-Qadary in Bab Jinan, and toured the farm, which he knew well. He spotted Aisha's silhou-ette at night; she was far away, but Salih couldn't mistake her. He had stayed looking at the lit window until the light went out at midnight and considered forcing his way into the house, but there were guards everywhere. On the way back, he had thought that if Aisha went abroad and he lost her scent once again, life would lose all its savor for good. If Hikmat Dashwali were to find the place, he would bring back Aisha and kill William Eisa. A man like him would never marry a girl who had run away with a Christian man, whose story the whole city knew by now, and Salih started to hope that Aisha would soon be unattached once more. He harbored a deep hatred both for William Eisa and for Hikmat Dashwali; as far as he was concerned, both of them wanted to snatch his beloved away from him. The whipping he received daily at the hands of the torturers in his cell had no effect on his silence, but on the tenth night, after his hatred reached its zenith, he asked to see Hikmat Dashwali alone. He recited Aisha's letters to William Eisa, which he had learned by heart, and he carefully observed the rage in Hikmat Dashwali's eyes as he repeated whole passages at a measured pace. He wanted the officer's heart to overflow with rancor so that he wouldn't be content with merely arresting William Eisa—he would have to kill him. Then very simply, Salih told him the way to Arif Agha's farm in exchange for a pledge that he would be released immediately and Aisha Mufti wouldn't be killed.

On the day of Aisha's and William Eisa's murder, Junaid Khalifa went into the cellar and burst out every detail of the news that had rocked the city. Against Junaid's expectations, Salih received the news without noticeable surprise. He already knew it all. Drowning in grief, he reflected on his betrayal. After leaving prison, he had gone to Anabiya. He didn't stay long in his family's house; he changed his clothes, borrowed a mule from a relative, and went on to Sharran. On the way there, he unexpectedly saw Arif Sheikh Musa Agha driving his own carriage, heading for the citadel. He saw Aisha lying in the back, dead. From a distance, he watched Zakariya dig graves for the two lovers under the walnut tree. He wept bitterly and felt a gaping void open in his chest. He continued on to Aleppo, went to his room, and thought he deserved to die instantly. His life was worthless now, and he was smeared with the filth of treachery.

The next morning Junaid left him to go to work at his new employment at a newspaper printer, but when he got home, Salih wasn't in the cellar. Salih took to going out every morning and wandering through the lanes of the city, muttering things no one could hear. He stood by the barracks waiting for Hikmat Dashwali to come out and go to his aunt's house in Bab Al-Hadid, where he lived. The barracks guards found it odd that he walked behind Hikmat Dashwali's carriage, then stopped some distance away and watched him go inside. He neglected his clothes, and his long, unkempt beard made people think he was a madman, or the father of a prisoner; men were often looking for their sons in the barracks prisons. Eventually, Salih noted

with surprise one day that Hikmat's well-guarded carriage was heading out of the city, and when he asked one of the cavalrymen where
they were going, he replied they were accompanying their commander
to Istanbul. That night Salih returned to his cellar, worn out. He made
no reply to Junaid's questions and went back to staring at the spider.
He felt he was just a traitor and nothing more, and had been living a
delusion. He had abandoned Aisha and never told her of his love. She
should have known that he adored her, but instead he had handed her
to her murderer. He felt a horrifying emptiness inside that could not
be cured by anything other than revenge. Salih began to regret letting Hikmat Dashwali leave the city. He imagined that he could have
stabbed him, despite the intensified guard that had accompanied him
in recent days, which made it impossible to get anywhere near him.
Just making the attempt without being allowed near him would have
been enough to strike terror into the Ottoman officer's heart. Salih
wished he could send that message, so that he would be added to the
story of Aisha Mufti and her relationship with William Eisa, which
the city never stopped embellishing with fabricated details.

Hikmat Dashwali was indeed afraid of vengeance for the killing of
William Eisa and Aisha Mufti. Death could come for him from any direction, when he least expected it. The young couple's vengeance would
be steep, and now that the story had become widely known, it would
follow him and would never let him sleep. Rifles can't kill rumors or stories. He knew he would never be able to live in Aleppo again. This was
different from his work quelling the continual uprisings of the Armenians. Here he was a murderer, and nothing would stop the mufti and
the Eisa family from exacting their revenge. He knew the families,
and his status as an officer of note, even one who was close to Sultan
Abdel Hamid, would not protect him. He strengthened the guard
on his aunt's house and was escorted by six cavalrymen whenever he
crossed the city. He spent most of his time sitting miserably in the barracks, aware that, in the end, he had been defeated. He no longer felt
safe and finally asked to be transferred out of the Vilayet of Aleppo.

A few days later, when Junaid came in to examine his friend, he found a short letter from Salih informing him that he had gone to wander the earth. He asked Junaid to look after his things, which he left in his care. They were the usual contents of the familiar sack, with the addition of some new notebooks.

Salih Azizi arrived in Istanbul in early January 1902. It was cold, but he had grown used to hardship during his journey there, which had taken place mostly on foot. Occasionally he had ridden with fellow travelers in a passing carriage. He had no money and subsisted on charity from other travelers, and on pickings from vineyards and fields along the way. He repeated Aisha Mufti's letters in a low voice; he was afraid of forgetting her words. He grew very thin, and his rough cotton thobe and shabby leather sandals made everyone think he was one of those Sufis. It was the first time he had traveled outside the environs of Aleppo. He watched the life of people along the way and he recorded everything he saw and heard. He convinced himself that he had to stay silent, telling himself that silence befitted the betrayer of the lovers. Salih Azizi reached Istanbul in the evening after a journey of three months. The large city dazzled him, and he slipped in among a crowd of dervishes who were crossing his path. He didn't stand out as he looked very much like them, but he was alone and isolated, without a group of his own. He spent three months in the Sufi lodges and received alms. Once he took part in a large celebration for various groups who had come from every corner of the country to celebrate the memory of their well-known sheikh from Antablay. Salih didn't care to know more details. He found himself among hundreds of skinny men, all speaking Turkish; in the daytime they recited the Qur'an loudly, and at night they recited the odes composed by their departed sheikh. Salih was enthusiastic; he stood up in the middle of them, they gazed at him intently, and everyone fell silent. Salih raised his hands, closed his eyes, and in Arabic, recited some of the passages from Aisha's letters that he had memorized. The eyes on him expressed warm admiration even though few of them understood Arabic. The impact of each consonant was powerful, and when Salih reached a certain passage, his voice shook as he intoned,

"I am your boat going to the end of the world, I am your star slipping into your heart at night to guard it, I am the rose that wilted yesterday because she did not see you, I am love that does not heal the sick—" He stopped suddenly. The eyes of an old sheikh were staring at him. He gestured at Salih to continue, but Salih couldn't keep a hold on himself; he burst into tears and fell to his knees. The elderly sheikh got up and walked toward him. He patted Salih's shoulder and asked him in Arabic whose words they were. Salih had no reply, but he repeated, "I am your boat going to the end of the world, I am your star slipping into your heart at night to guard it." He stopped, and the sheikh waved at everyone to carry on with the celebration. Tambourines were banged, and the sound of the ney was so heartrending that Salih continued with the rest of the letters under his breath. He reached the line "Take me, my beloved, to the green meadow, kiss me as if death were waiting for us around every corner, kiss me hard, dig a hole in my heart with the hatchet of your breaths, place your smell under my skin, and take me, a drowned woman, into the flames. Annihilate me, I died centuries ago, and I will not rise again unless it is for you, my beloved." Salih stopped and shook his head; his tears gushed in silence.

The following morning the sheikh asked for Salih, but when the students looked for him in his usual corner, he wasn't there. He had picked up his bag and disappeared in the alleyways of the large city, but the words remained engraved on the heart of the old sheikh.

The only place Salih could find to sleep was a gap between some sacks in the port, among the porters who were waiting for the ships to come in so they could unload their goods. He was miserable at having betrayed Aisha's words and cheapened them by speaking them aloud to others; struck by that deep emotion, however, he had had no choice but to lay bare his secret. He almost turned into a different person, a coward who didn't want revenge for his beloved. He spent six months wandering and homeless; no one understood why he had left Aleppo to live on a sidewalk in Istanbul. In his heart, his buried thirst for revenge gradually grew and fed on itself. Aisha's death was his greatest disaster; she had evaporated into thin air. At the end of those six months, he was ready to carry out his vengeance, and he searched in the enormous city for the address of Hikmat Dashwali, whom he saw swaggering on his horse in the entourage of Sultan Abdel Hamid as he made his way to the Sultan Ahmed Mosque. An officer of his standing was always accompanied, and Salih saw him again, surrounded by a gaggle of his friends on their way to a private celebration. Salih was pleased; he was starting to know the places that Hikmat Dashwali frequented, and he was determined that the officer wouldn't slip out of his grasp again. Hikmat was living in a house close to the Fatih Mosque. It was clear that he no longer felt threatened and felt no guilt over the murders. Every evening Salih wandered the area around the Fatih Mosque and watched out for Hikmat Dashwali coming home. He lay in wait and observed his prey constantly. Salih felt his opportunity had come when he saw Hikmat Dashwali climb into his carriage alone and drive toward a restaurant in a nearby neighborhood for dinner. Salih waited for him to return at the end of the night, drunk as usual. Eventually he saw Hikmat Dashwali's carriage rolling along in the distance. He was alone; it was one of the few times Salih had seen him without a guard or even his carriage driver. Salih didn't waste his chance. He took out the sharp knife that was tied to a leather belt under his clothes. He approached Hikmat slowly and deliberately, removed his face covering, dragged Hikmat off the carriage, and stabbed him three times. Before Hikmat Dashwali's soul left him, Salih looked into his eyes and said, "That was for Aisha. I told you not to kill her." He left Hikmat Dashwali only when he was sure he was dead. He put the dead man back in the carriage and closed the door. Salih walked away, utterly serene, heedless of anything around him. He didn't care if he was arrested. He wanted to die too; his soul would find peace, and he would consider it a fair price that three men had died on her account. Inwardly, he kept repeating, "What value has the morning without your words, what value has the river if it is not your mirror, what value has life if it doesn't take me to you like a boat sailing the three seas?" He didn't stop walking. When he reached the shore, he threw away his bloodstained clothes and went for a swim, despite the biting cold. He put on his unstained cotton thobe and turned his face toward Aleppo. He had been away for almost a year, and no one had known where he had gone. He missed his city, and so he returned on the first of October 1902. He felt that the city still held the breaths of the dead lovers.

Along the road, he stopped at many villages but avoided cities. He ate crusts of bread given to him by charitable people and received blessings from poor women; they believed that his silence revealed the strength of his faith. When he reached Aleppo, he kept going until he arrived at the lodgings of Junaid Khalifa, who found it painful to look at him. Salih's eyes were rolling in his head, and his body was emaciated. He had turned into a shadow of a man. Salih didn't say a word in response to his friend's questions; he didn't know how to explain that he was filled up with Aisha's letters. He picked up the things he had left with Junaid and left at dawn. He crossed the city more than once and circled the ruins of Hajj Bashir's house, where some poor families had moved in. He went into the house, and his feet led him to the place where, he guessed, Aisha's bedroom had been. Her breaths were in every nook here. This, all that remained of her, was enough for him. But he couldn't bear to settle in a place crammed with poor children in shabby clothes. He carried on to the river where, underneath a spring sky, he slept deeply for the first time in two years.

Salih woke at dawn. Hajj Bashir's house appeared in the distance. He returned to the lanes and alleyways, and before noon he found himself back at Junaid Khalifa's lodgings. Junaid looked at him, understanding his distress. He took Salih to his book-filled room and cleared some space so he could lay out a cotton mattress. Though he wasn't even thirty years old, Salih had completely renounced life. He became incapable of doing anything and stayed in his friend's house for several months. Occasionally, after persistent questioning, he made a brief reply to Junaid Khalifa, who wanted to know what had happened to Salih during those travels—which, Junaid eventually discovered, he'd documented in a battered notebook.

Salih's family tried to persuade him to come back with them to

Anabiya, but he had only one response: "I will never leave the land of my love. I will die here, close to her breaths." He came to feel that the city was choking him with its breaths; irritated, he declared that the city had changed. He went out into the lanes, into the coffee-houses, and recited Aisha's letters out loud as if he were reciting an ode. He wanted the letters to leave his core and thought that repeating them in this way was like a bloodletting. He had to remove it all from his life, he couldn't go on with it any longer. Memories hurt him: the memory of his betrayal, of Aisha's faint perfume. He didn't want to face Hanna, who had said he wished Salih would go back and live in the house at Bab Al-Faraj.

Aleppo meandered through the four seasons. Salih walked every single street, recited Aisha's letters to passersby, to the Sufis in their za-wiyas, to the worshippers in the mosques, but he was overflowing with pain. He couldn't endure the perplexed looks any longer. One day he slipped into the Umayyad Mosque after dawn prayers had concluded. He locked the door to the minaret from the inside and climbed the stairs all the way to the top. The inhabitants of Aleppo were surprised to hear Salih's sweet voice fused with letters from a female lover. He was weeping as he called their attention to one of Aisha's letters: "Your love is more valuable than the earth's precious stones, the asceticism of lovers who watch the flight of geese over the riverbank. Your love is stars rising from their own ashes. Lead me, my beloved, take me by the hand, and like I am a blind woman, lead me to the riverbank. There remove my clothes and drown me in the sweetness of your kisses, the sweet taste of your hands. After I die, you won't find anything of me but my scent that you love, the ambergris of my breast. I am earth, and you are water: make clay from my rib. Over my days, scatter de-tached time that stays apart and does not gather. I am earth, and you are water; water me so I will sprout sweet basil in the ribs of lovers."

Between every passage of Aisha's letters, he would cry and shout, "I am the traitor and the judge of love, I am the imam of the lovers." No one dared climb the minaret. Passersby gathered below in a large crowd, and it wasn't long before the Sufis emerged from their lodges and joined in these sweet, melodious recitations. The large courtyard of the Umayyad Mosque was filled. The soldiers were afraid of the ever-growing crowd, and Salih never interrupted his chanting. He was enraptured by the other voices, those that had heard these passages before and now joined in, and the city began to march to the Umayyad Mosque. No one knew the occasion, but when they saw Salih in his ecstasy, they understood that he had reached the end of his path. It was no longer enough to recite his texts to small groups in a few coffeehouses; he wanted to tell the entire city. The muezzin of the mosque begged Salih to come down, but he was ignored. Salih's voice was lost while thousands looked up at him in solemn submission. The vali arrived with some high-ranking officials and listened ardently to this grieving voice. When Salih briefly fell silent, the vali ordered his guards to bring Salih down and arrest him. The soldiers broke down the locked door and climbed the spiral staircase, but Salih, anticipating them, had tied a noose at the highest point of the minaret. Within a moment, he had hanged himself. Voices murmured in a hush, then rose. The imam of the lovers was dead.

The End

5

A Grave in the Cherry Orchard

Aleppo—1903

Hanna took the deaths of William Eisa and Aisha Mufti, especially their terrible circumstances, as a personal defeat. He still remembered Aisha Mufti's display of affection at his own wedding. He saw her standing by the church door with Sara and Souad, smiling. Souad had brought her because Aisha had wanted to thank Hanna personally for his help. She introduced herself by saying that she was their friend's beloved, and that she was there to share his joy. He smiled and made way for her so she could bless Josephine, who was taken aback at her costly gift: a zunnar of pure gold. As usual, Hanna didn't elaborate when Josephine asked him why some unknown girl had brought such an expensive gift; he said the gift came from Hajj Bashir Mufti, to whom he was connected by various business affairs. That winter, after Hanna's friend and his lover were killed, Hanna's troubled mood affected the guests at the citadel, who asked him to move on from the lovers' death. Enough had already happened on the lovers' account; Aleppo had almost burned to the ground, and Muslims and Christians had come to the verge of war.

In early December, the women arrived at the first gathering at the citadel. The guests were in high spirits, as usual. Shams Al-Sabah felt that in spite of the secrecy that surrounded them, the graves of Aisha Mufti and William Eisa would turn the citadel into a pilgrimage site for fans of peculiar tales. She had never grasped the secret of Hanna's buried grief. Several months had passed, but he still blamed himself and laid the responsibility for having failed to protect the lovers at his own feet.

When Shams Al-Sabah held him so he would fall asleep, his anxiety flowed into her. He didn't talk to her about Souad anymore; he had stopped describing her eyelids, how delicate and tender they were. Six in the morning would arrive before he fell asleep. During the night, not wanting to wake Shams Al-Sabah, he would pull her hand away gently and slip out of the bedroom. Once he left the citadel and walked in the cherry orchard until he reached their graves. Having woken up, she followed him, and before she could reach him, she heard his racking sobs. She understood that they weren't just a pair of coffins, but they represented an idea that Hanna needed, just like all of those who were still divided on its account.

Hanna stayed at the citadel for only a few days that winter. He spent most of his time walking in the fields around Hosh Hanna with Zakariya, who also didn't visit the citadel much, preferring to stay close to his horses and Shaha.

The pair remembered how, when Arif arrived and pulled back the blanket to reveal the dead faces of William Eisa and Aisha Mufti, they had felt cold to their fingertips. They didn't make any effort to return the bodies to their families, or whichever of their relatives remained. Arif said that he bore responsibility for their deaths; he hadn't offered them enough protection.

Hanna made no reply to the Greek Orthodox metropolitan who sent for him a few days later to ask about William Michel Eisa's body. Hanna denied knowing anything about the matter and asked him to consult the vali and demand that the murderer be brought to trial. Hanna added that William Eisa had done nothing for which he deserved to be killed. The metropolitan understood his anger and didn't reply to Hanna's barrage of questions. He asked Hanna to forget his request.

Hanna thought himself closer to the couple than either of their families and therefore that he had the right to bury them beside each other in a place that was neither Christian nor Muslim. Zakariya shared this mania. He dug a grave large enough for two people, and when the sun had risen, they lowered the two bodies inside and completed the burial. Arif Sheikh Musa Agha looked on, grief-stricken and filled with shame that he hadn't been able to protect his guests. He suggested to Hanna and Zakariya that they invite a priest and a sheikh to pray over the couple. Hanna replied that they were lovers, and no one was going to pray over their graves.

Over the following days, Shams Al-Sabah looked after the plants that Hanna planted on the large grave. He didn't answer the fellahin's questions when they pruned the cherry trees or harvested the walnuts. He made up a tale about Zakariya burying a particularly precious horse that had died in the previous winter's floods. As the gravestones were not facing specific directions and Zakariya's adoration of his horses was well known, it was a plausible story. Everyone forgot the matter eventually; it was just another one of Zakariya's inexhaustible stream of peculiar ideas.

A year later the tale of the lovers and their imam had disappeared from the city's conversations. Zakariya, Hanna, and their families decided to spend the Eid Al-Adha holiday at the family home of Ahmed Bayazidi. It was an odd sight to see them celebrating the festival at all, especially with the family. They undertook all their social obligations and didn't grumble once about visiting certain relations—on the contrary, Hanna and Zakariya were kind and affectionate and asked after everyone.

In the first days of Eid, the pair joined everyone at the dinner table. They swapped friendly chatter with visitors about horses and the seasons; they made a spontaneous visit to the family of Arif Sheikh Musa Agha and brought many gifts to Aunt Amina, who had gone back to her own house and hidden away from people. They accepted a dinner invitation from Josephine's family, and on the fourth morning of Eid, Hanna discussed the income from his investments with Ahmed Bayazidi. He listened gravely to the advice of the old man, who still went every morning to his office at the bank and received his workers in a bustle of activity. Whenever he saw rival families ascend in the accounting profession, he placed impediments in their way and mired them in swamps of figures, having no wish to depart this world until his own family was firmly placed on the throne he occupied.

He would gather the sons of the family periodically and ask their news one by one, to be reassured that a passion for numbers still animated the new generation. He made plans for them to inherit the sensitive centers of power: to serve as accountants of the vilayet, or the vali's personal accountants, or to take over administration of the new banks that wanted to open branches in Aleppo. Everyone kept these thorny and intricate relationships secret and did their part to strengthen them. They would make comparisons to the original Najib Bayazidi, who two hundred years earlier had said that family was like a notebook: if a single page was torn out, the rest would soon follow.

After a long night spent talking with Ahmed Bayazidi, Hanna admitted that he was enjoying his first taste of family life. He told everyone Josephine was pregnant; he had been charmed in recent months by the thought of an heir. He didn't want the church, to which he returned every Sunday to pray, to inherit anything from him.

That night he saw Souad on the way to her room. She stayed silent as she gave him a hard look, making no reply when he greeted her or asked her how she was. It was an indication of a breach he couldn't bear. He felt weak, superfluous. Her womanhood was perfect and complete, and he felt a deep, shadowy hollow in his heart. The loss of innocence in the later years of their relationship had created this wound that never stopped bleeding. In daydreams, he often imagined himself with her. They would be taking paths through the fields, walking to the end of the world. He was horrified at the realization that he was seeking out her scent in all the women he slept with. He wished he had been like William Eisa, who had surprised them all with his hidden strength when he told them, decisively, that he couldn't live without Aisha Mufti; all women, to him, were pale imitations of the girl he had met by chance in Istanbul. His friends hadn't believed him. Hanna had mocked him, Azar asked him to concentrate on painting,

and Zakariya just made do with laughing. But when William Eisa returned to Aleppo skinny and hungry, they believed him. They hadn't
expected the events that followed—it had been some time since a lover
had died so publicly in the city. All the lovers who had gone before had
died in secret, and everyone conspired to smother the stories of girls
setting themselves alight, boys committing suicide at the prospect of
life apart from beloveds married off by their families to avert scandal.
The sight of women, muffled in black clothes and headcoverings, did
not reveal them as lovers. The appearance of men, with their stupor,
their silence, and their secretiveness, did not indicate that they were
lovers. Love adores scandal, openness, day, light.

Hanna was overjoyed when Josephine gave birth to their son Gabriel a few weeks after they returned to Hosh Hanna, but within a
few days he was bored and annoyed. He considered escaping to somewhere no one knew about but couldn't think of anywhere he might relax apart from the citadel, and so back he went with Zakariya. Hanna
wandered on his own, recalling a picture of Souad that stopped him
from constructing his own image as a lover. He surrendered to the
idea of shame and weakness, of betraying a family that had raised
him as one of their own. The image of her as a sister had settled; she
was off-limits, and in his daydreams he didn't cross the line and think
about her plump breasts and her scent, but his dreams at night were
another matter. Souad's image never left him; he thought of her constantly. He was in agony, but at the same time he found some horrible
enjoyment in it. He thought he wouldn't be damaged forever, he knew
what he would say to Souad, but when he saw her, his thoughts dried
up, and he felt like an abandoned well clogged with dried-out grass.

Hanna walked from the citadel toward Anabiya, where Zakariya
had spent three days waiting for the birth of a rare and important foal
in his stable. Yaaqoub was occupied with delivering the foal, and he
was dripping with sweat. The birth, though difficult, was successful,
and Zakariya was overjoyed with the new foal. When he looked at
Hanna, his eyes were red, and it was clear he had been crying. The
pair walked through the cherry orchard, and in the shadows Zakariya

listened to Hanna's voice repeating that they could immortalize the memory of their friend and his beloved. Zakariya interjected that immortality didn't mean much, but they could at least prevent the couple's reputations from being defaced. Hanna held out an issue of the newspaper *Al-Medina*, in which Junaid Khalifa had published the first chapter of a novel he had called *Impossible Love*. He had changed the names of William Eisa and Aisha Mufti, but every reader would recognize the heroes and the imam of the lovers. Zakariya read the first chapter and said to Hanna that the writer hadn't known anything about their friend. The newspaper had sold out in the souqs, and the paper was inundated with letters expressing contradictory opinions. There were those who accused the newspaper and the writer of encouraging fornication, while another division of readers thanked the writer and asked for more. Some letters cursed the imam of the lovers and called him a traitor and an informant. Yet another group wrote their own personal stories of impossible love and sent them in hopes that they be used in the writing of the novel. Zakariya thought that the story would never end. The ripples of that stone thrown in the swamp were still growing.

In the morning they left the citadel and took the carriage through the alleys of the city. People were giving Hanna and Zakariya strange looks; people in Aleppo hadn't forgotten the story, as they had thought. The whole city now knew of their role in the kidnapping, and many made up stories about what went on in the verandas of the citadel, now a symbol of decadence.

They arrived at the Souq Al-Nahasin and soon learned the address they wanted. Junaid Khalifa was astonished to see Hanna and Zakariya leaning on the doorjamb and asking to come in. He knew them both well. They were taken aback themselves by a large portrait of Aisha, placed prominently in the middle of the room. They didn't ask why it was there; doubtless Salih had sold it to this man who was so obsessed with the story of the lovers. Junaid offered them sherbet blended with rosewater. Hanna and Zakariya exchanged a glance; it would be impossible to bribe an ascetic like this man, he made do with so little. Without wasting time, they said how much they liked his novel. Hanna explained that they were friends of William Eisa and his beloved, and that they could offer details no one else knew, if he wanted to write their story. Junaid listened to them and kept smiling when Hanna wondered out loud if Salih was really the one who had denounced the couple. Junaid said he was sure that Salih wasn't an informer, and that he knew that the pair had remained chaste, and he wasn't troubled by the stories in circulation that said otherwise. What did genuinely trouble him, however, was the disappearance of their bodies. Hanna thought quickly, and a quick glance at Zakariya showed that he had reached the same conclusion. He asked Junaid again if Salih had betrayed the couple's location, and Junaid denied it vehemently. Hanna asked him to come with them if he wanted to see the lovers' graves. Junaid got into the carriage with them without a moment's hesitation. On the way, they reached an agreement to halt publication of the novel until Zakariya and Hanna had put all the details in front of him and he had rewritten it, and in turn, he pledged to keep their graves a secret. He was the only person to enter the citadel from outside the charmed circle of chosen ones.

Hanna took Junaid through the cellar, past the platform for suicides and the press for striking silver coins. Junaid recognized the smell of arsenic. Together they went out into the cherry orchard and arrived at the large walnut tree. When they saw the graves, Junaid burst out into sobs and asked to leave at once. He also asked Hanna's permission to describe the graves without giving any indication about their location. On the way back, Zakariya drove the carriage, and Junaid told Hanna about Aisha's letters. He described her wonderful eyes, and her long hair, and after these few words, he fell silent. He said nothing about Salih Azizi's notebooks, where he had written at length about his shame at betraying the woman he loved, and other information that didn't explain the nature of his relationship with Aisha. Junaid seemed exhausted as he waved goodbye.

The carriage drove through Bab Al-Nasr and headed toward Jamiliyya on Khandaq Street. They picked up Azar, and Hanna asked

Zakariya to go back to Jalloum, where Michel Eisa and his four daughters had moved to a small rented house after fleeing his house in Farafra. Michel Eisa's oldest daughter opened the door to them and told them that her father was asleep and it wasn't a good time for a visit. She was very angry; her fiancé had left her over the scandal. But Hanna pushed past her, and Zakariya and Azar followed him. Michel Eisa, sunk in a drunken haze, was not overly pleased to see them, but Hanna didn't dawdle. He told Michel Eisa that he and Zakariya were responsible for helping their friend and that he was the reason the couple could have written to each other at all. Appearing decades older than he was, Michel Eisa looked at him and said, "I know you've buried him at the citadel. You did well; William wouldn't have been happy unless he was beside her. What would he do in a Christian graveyard? I don't want anyone to spit on his grave." Looking at Azar, he went on: "I'm like the sloping line of a building now, lost, hanging in the air. I am swinging like an old clock pendulum, like a scrap of fabric it's no use to dye." He spoke of the tragedy of his friend, Hajj Bashir, whose factory had closed and whose house had been set on fire, now fled to some unknown place. Lives had been lost, and no one would knock on his door to ask for the hands of his four daughters. He pointed at his eldest and said, "She is single again after an engagement of four years. All she can do now is become a nun."

Hanna sympathized with Michel. He believed the old man would calm down if they left, but instead Michel asked them to stay. He poured out some of the cheap brandy he was drinking and told them he didn't do anything now, he didn't leave the house, he couldn't stand the looks he got. He drank all the time and staggered to bed each night. He wanted to say the city would forget what happened, that it always did. But until that time, he had to either die or take his four girls and go somewhere far away. He waved toward the window, saying, "I'll do it at once."

That evening, as the carriage carrying the three friends crossed the city, Azar's head was filled with many things. They passed gardens full of flowers, and he saw the houses in the new quarters. They crossed the river into Jamiliyya, and Azar said, "William Eisa should have lived and carried out his plans and painted for a thousand years to heal our wounds. But he left everything and went away."

It was a difficult night for Hanna. He spent it by the lovers' graves. Zakariya left him there and went back to Hosh Hanna, where he would be alone with his horses and the river and Shaha. He wasn't in the mood to humor his drunk friends, who were opening the season at the citadel with a party graced by gauzy blue robes, at the suggestion of Arif Sheikh Musa Agha. A servant unloaded from his carriage three trunks filled with diaphanous blue dresses in various sizes and embroidered with delicate flowers, and the nine women who were sharing the rooms with the men donned these garments. The following night, Arif devised the idea of summoning a certain band he knew, three blind musicians who occupied the Umayyad Mosque, singing to barren women who had gone there to make offerings. The first night these musicians came, they played superbly, and the nine girls danced till morning. Arif seized his chance and contracted with the group to come and play three nights a week, and the blind men were delighted with these generous clients. The all-night parties were particularly shameless that year. Hanna would leave his guests and slip away into the cherry orchard, thinking about the dead who didn't need sun and didn't feel cold. He uprooted the grass that was growing over the graves and planted new flowers. The graves had been neglected as that second winter passed. Hanna struck silver pieces into commemorative medallions that bore a portrait of the lovers, put all the pieces into a box, and told the artisans to leave the citadel. He was bored with keeping a smith to cast coins for a nonexistent kingdom. He was delighted when Zakariya informed him that Shaha had given birth to a son, Ahmed. Zakariya was excited and asked Hanna to go with him to Hosh Hanna to see out the rest of the winter.

Returning to his family and passing the spring with Josephine and his son Gabriel gave Hanna an opportunity to reflect once more on how to calm his anxiety and live peacefully. The child's small fingers sent joy into his soul, and he would spend hours watching his son sleeping peacefully in his bed. But before too long, he had had enough of family life, and the desire to roam returned. He left Hosh Hanna and spent a few days as the guest of Arif Sheikh Musa Agha, who never stopped talking about trains, and the propositions he was studying in order to invest in this mythical iron mule that crossed vast distances in a flash.

Josephine was of the opinion that time would lead Hanna back to his rightful place. She made no objection to having more children, had grown used to life without him, and managed the affairs of her family smoothly, always under the assumption that she wouldn't find her husband beside her in the morning. She lived quietly, and her profound faith helped her to bear his absences. Deep down, she loved this tortured person whose heart was overwhelmed by worldly appetites. She believed Hanna was a true Christian, despite his love for a life of debauchery.

In the months before the flood, Hanna felt deeply bored with all this dissipation. He no longer accepted his friends' many invitations and searched for more exciting ideas. He was no longer tempted by breakfast with naked women, or a party with blind singers. He had been waiting for one of the gamblers to commit suicide, but he always intervened at the opportune moment and prevented any of his landowner friends from bankrupting themselves while gripped by their lust for gambling. His friends remonstrated with him, insisting that losing was all part of the excitement of the game, but Hanna remained determined not to see any of his friends go bankrupt. He asked everyone to think up something more exciting than cooking lamb in copper pots, or getting a girl to climb onto the table and remove her clothes piece by piece to the frenzied music that came out of those odd records from the West.

There remained a pleasure that no one else shared with him; sleeping in the arms of Shams Al-Sabah, who had by now conformed totally to the role he had wished on her. She stroked his hair, cut his nails, and asked him to look after his family. She would scold him whenever he talked about Souad and elaborated on the pain that kept him apart from her. She wished that particular tale would find its conclusion, because she felt how much pain it gave him. She asked him to bring his child to the citadel one day, but he always forgot. He thought about what Junaid Khalifa had said the last time they met, when he and Azar and Zakariya had been discussing William Eisa and Aisha Mufti. Junaid had surprised them all by talking for hours about his student, Salih Azizi, once Hanna's servant and now imam of the lovers.

Junaid defended Salih, but at one moment he almost admitted that Salih had left behind notebooks that laid bare his act of treachery. But in those years, he loved offering up Salih's tale. He didn't want anything to corrupt its purity; thus the imam of the lovers couldn't possibly have been an informant traitor.

6

The Hard Road

Aleppo—Deir Zahr Al-Rumman—1908

The last mourner left Ahmed Bayazidi's house. Zakariya looked at Hanna, who was silent and sad, utterly despondent.

Hassan Masabny had undertaken his duty flawlessly in looking after the mourners, especially the officials in attendance: the vali and his aides, the chief of police, the important traders. Trying to please Souad, he had opened his house to receive the female mourners, ordered the food, and in general handled every detail with the relish of one who adored mastering his social obligations. He loved it when people spoke of him with approval. Souad made do with sitting beside her aunt Amina, who kept her head bowed, reviewing memories of a lifetime spent alongside her brother Ahmed Bayazidi, who had feared her and so never failed to accede to her every request. He was a kind man who had believed he was created to correct the world, to straighten out its chaos by arranging it neatly in his precise ledgers. As for Amina, she didn't care about the many women who wanted her blessing. Young girls kissed her hand, and she rubbed their heads absently and made do with a few blandishments. Souad felt like an utter stranger, waiting for the rituals to come to an end so she could go back to lying alone on her sofa. On that last night, after the final mourner left and the servants began cleaning the house, she expected her aunt to get up and go to the bed Souad had prepared for her. Instead, she heard Amina ask why she wasn't happy in her marriage to Hassan

Masabny. Without thinking too much, Souad said it was impossible to explain misery.

She went to her room and heard Hassan come in late at night. When she woke up, she couldn't find her aunt. As usual, Hassan recounted every minute detail of his labors, and as usual, she didn't listen or care in the least about his description of the moment the vali arrived, or the compromise that had been reached among quarreling traders. She felt like a vase broken into so many shards it could never be reassembled. She didn't understand Hanna's transformations; when she looked out the window of her old room in her father's house and saw him rushing to join the other men carrying the coffin, he looked like a different person. She couldn't help feeling some sympathy for him; she used to want her hatred toward him to increase, but over the previous three days, she had thought of him continually. His image that day never left her: his thin face, the gleam of his eyes, the desperation dripping from his fingertips. She wanted to see him at any cost, she wanted him to go back to being the man she hated—arrogant, a coward despite his power—but seeing him crammed in among the coffin-bearers broke her heart. She returned to her old affection for him, to the days of their childhood she always tried to avoid remembering.

The previous night Hanna had ignored Hassan Masabny as he praised the 'aza, listing the important people who had attended and zealously explaining the implications of the family's covert influence. Hanna was distracted, and next to him Zakariya felt his own estrangement from what was being said. He was reflecting that his father had passed away at a judicious moment; he had been absolved of all duties. Hanna rose and left the house, followed by Zakariya, who hadn't understood that Hanna wished to be left alone that night. Zakariya saw him go inside a Syriac Catholic Church, and his heart sank; he didn't want his friend to end up this way, but he couldn't find the right words to deter him from the asceticism that threw him into the path of the church.

Hanna was exhausted, but he didn't complain. Inside the church, he put his hand on Mariana's head. She cried when she saw him; she had been longing for him, had no hope in this life apart from him. He asked to be left alone with Metropolitan Basilos, who led him to the hall of the library. Hanna told him about the visions that had taken possession of him for a hundred days, gradually growing clearer. He told the metropolitan that he was going to excavate the small hill facing Anabiya—which was situated on his own land—and there he would find a church buried underground. The metropolitan listened with interest and pity and told Hanna that the remains of the church he was talking about lay in the nearby village of Barad, not in that hill. If Hanna wished, he could go to that sacred ground; no one would stop him from restoring the ruins of the church and the houses of the early Christians, and beginning a new life there, but there was no church in the place Hanna described. The metropolitan was regarding Hanna with visible satisfaction: the runaway had finally run out of road, and he had nowhere to go but the church, to lay his soul on the altar.

Hanna went on with the details of his visions, annoyed by the metropolitan's doubts. He left the church at dawn, and after a few paces he realized that Mariana was following him. She told him that she believed him and would never leave him alone; she would follow him anywhere. She said, "Consider me a servant or a sister." She took his arm, and together they walked on. He asked her to go back to the church and said that his life was no longer what it used to be; he had lost all certainty, he didn't know what he was capable of doing at this surplus time in his life. But she wouldn't leave him. She carried on in silence after saying, "You can throw me out whenever you like, but let me see you now," and explaining that the church was no place for an orphan girl; she didn't want to be a nun, and if she went back to her uncle's house in Urfa, she would leave it only for her grave.

After the flood, Hanna had changed. His face became more serene, his pace grew slower. He had buried his past life in the depths of the river along with the faces of his loved ones. Mariana walked with him and asked him no more questions. She considered his silence permission to accompany him. He went into the Souq Al-Haddadin and explained to an old ironmonger that he needed sharp pickaxes, shovels, and other tools that would help him excavate a large hill. The man looked at him and said he knew him. Hanna ignored this and remained silent. The old man understood; he privately thought this must be some new caprice that would soon be forgotten, but whatever the case, Hanna Gregoros was a good client. He blocked the other traders from interfering; in his new clothes, Hanna struck them as half-deranged. The old ironmonger offered to make large spades specifically for this task, and Hanna agreed, agitated and annoyed—people were crowding around to get a glimpse of him, and he didn't want to talk with anyone. They looked at him pityingly; they couldn't believe the person standing in front of them, talking so softly, was the same man who used to set the city's imagination on fire with his scandals and his ideas, all crowned by the citadel.

Every winter, Hanna leaked the rumors he wanted to be spread about that building hidden from view by thickets of cypress and orchards of olive, fig, and cherry trees. Most of the stories were about lovers who had lost hope, women who bathed in milk and honey and wore clothes that came specially from Istanbul and London. Although no one had committed suicide, according to the stories, the Hall of Suicides (so named by Shams Al-Sabah) was adorned with a host of bodies, among them a group of artists, calligraphers, and poets who dreamed of residing there forever.

Hanna had been a participant in every unusual or peculiar event in this city. All eyes used to regard him with infinite admiration, not with pity accompanied by a sigh that a man no older than forty had come to this. His enemies thought the timing was right for revenge: Ahmed Bayazidi was dead, the flood had driven Hanna half out of his mind, and revenge could never wait very long. Everyone speculated about the tragic end that lay in wait for him, murdered at the hand of a vali, or a husband of one of the women whose lives he had ruined. His friends expected his end to come in the Hall of Suicides.

Hanna wasted no time on responding to his acquaintances in

the city. He hired a carriage, and Mariana sat next to him, struck by a strange feeling of sympathy with this being who now lacked any connection to the past. The carriage drove through Bab Al-Faraj and reached Ahmed Bayazidi's house. The driver asked Zakariya to get in, and the carriage continued on its way north until it reached Tel Zahr Al-Rumman. It stopped where Hanna indicated, and he took a few steps up the hill. There he planted a white flag and immediately began to dig and clear away the soil. To Zakariya, who was watching him in bewilderment, he said, "We will dig out this hill. There's a church buried under here. We'll uncover it and dedicate it to the memory of our dead, and our wanderings will be complete."

In the first few days, a large number of fellahin from Anabiya came to observe the folly of this man who owned more than half the village. The children were bold enough to pelt him with walnuts, the women mocked him, and the rival landowners in the area, the Khidr clan, came on horseback along with their men, all brandishing brand-new rifles, and tried to force Hanna to admit that he was looking for buried treasure. Hanna continued digging the ground in silence. Unable to abide the insults directed at his friend, Zakariya grabbed hold of the Khidr chief, Salim, and dragged him off his horse. He threw Salim to the ground and told him if his men didn't leave immediately, he would burn their houses down with whoever was inside.

Zakariya was deadly serious, and the Khidr clan knew it; he wasn't a man given to idle talk. Zakariya could ask for support from his brother-in-law, Arif Sheikh Musa Agha, and their friends, aghas from the Kurdish mountains who would instantly dispatch hundreds of their fiercest men, each one more than capable of burning their homes down and driving out the Khidr clan. Many doubts hovered over their holdings; over the years, the Khidr lands had been extracted by trickery from their original owners once their minds grew feeble in old age. The elderly landowners signed documents they didn't understand, and the Khidr clan went from tilling the land to owning it. But the clan lived in fear that the property deeds would be questioned, and only the Bayazidi clan could whisper in the ear of the vali and send word all the way up to the Sublime Porte, perhaps convincing the sultan himself to rectify the matter of the Khidr properties.

Salim Khidr reflected for a few moments. He understood that Zakariya was serious in his threat, and he concluded it wasn't yet time to appropriate hundreds of overlooked dunums from Hanna's lands and add them to the neighboring Khidr lands. Salim left with his fellahin and didn't come back again.

The events on Tel Zahr Al-Rumman were followed closely by spies planted among the builders who, on Zakariya's orders, now began to build walls around Hanna's lands in the region. His territories lay over four hundred dunums, not counting the small pieces of land dotted in between the possessions of Salim Khidr and his brothers, whom Hanna had never allowed to set foot in the citadel. He received them at the door when they thought of visiting; he offered them coffee there and listened to their point of view on building an aqueduct from the Afrin River. He was perfectly aware this was just a pretext; the river was much lower than the uplands they spoke of, and everyone knew it was impossible to raise water from the river to the mountains.

Hanna went on with his work, and Zakariya helped him move the earth and build walls that grew day after day until they blocked the view. After a month the fellahin forgot about it all, considering it yet another folly of huge landowners. Zakariya wouldn't allow them to work inside the walls facing his stable. He gave instructions to the wakil, who assured the fellahin that Hanna and Zakariya would go back to the citadel at the beginning of winter as they usually did, and everything would return to normal.

When darkness fell, Hanna and Zakariya slept peacefully in the old house by the hill, which Zakariya had left so he could relax close to his stables. Hanna dined at the table with Zakariya and Mariana; they all ate without talking, then each went to their own room. Zakariya, fearing the perfidy of the Khidr clan, decided not to leave Hanna for any reason. Mariana looked after the two men without heed to the rumors that, as a virgin living with two men who weren't her family, she was a fallen woman. As far as she was concerned, Hanna's visions were clearly true, just as they were for Zakariya. His friend's dream was beginning to work on him gently, and he thought that they should have dug up this hill a long time ago; even if they didn't find a church, they would certainly find statues they could sell to the foreigners who went on and on about ancient history and paid huge sums for statues buried in the ground. Hanna's fellahin often chucked statues into the stables or even destroyed them when they became caught in their plows.

Over those first three months, a new rhythm was established between Zakariya, Hanna, and Mariana. They exchanged few words. Both men were grateful for Mariana's presence and treated her with great kindness. She was grateful for Zakariya, who carried out all the practical matters efficiently and without being asked. One day Mariana saw him hide two middle-sized statues nearby and exchange a knowing look with Hanna. Mariana couldn't understand all the fuss about these statues; to her, they were nothing but big rocks, and Zakariya and Hanna had ignored many other big rocks they had taken out of the hillside. Zakariya kept an eye on their store of provisions, and he was the one to go to the city to fill the carriage with everything they needed. He sharpened the pickaxes and repaired the shovels and made no response to the derision of the Aleppans when they circulated what the metropolitan had said about Hanna: *he's mad.* He spoke more than once with the vali to prevent Hanna's property from being accessed or put at the disposal of the church, which was now the only heir of this member of its flock.

Meanwhile Shams Al-Sabah closed up the citadel. She no longer received anyone there and spoke only with the guards she kept on, just two out of the large number of men previously charged with guarding the citadel and looking after the grounds. She spent her time at the citadel with Shaha, working on the silk loom in a never-ending act of futility. She was waiting for Hanna's tragedy to come to an end so her own fate would be decided. The place was still in his possession, and if anything untoward happened to him, the church wouldn't waste a single day before taking possession of it. Then it would be destroyed, just as every man of religion had so often demanded.

The shovels scraped the first stones of the huge ruined wall. Hanna's eyes welled with tears, and he fell to his knees. Zakariya was utterly undone from the shock. It was the last day of April 1909. Hanna remained kneeling all night, while Zakariya was jubilant that his friend's visions had been proved right. He continued working, with calm but ever greater zeal, until the wall gradually appeared, like an island emerging from a calm sea in a moonlit night. He confirmed that they were not merely large stones but the remnants of a long wall. When Hanna saw them, he wept with the silence of an ascetic. Zakariya felt a sharp contraction in his chest. He said to himself that with this discovery, his friend's life had changed forever. The old Hanna was dead; a gaunt man bred from the corpse of his lifelong friend and the earth of the hill now stood in his place. He felt that he had to persuade Hanna to cover the walls back over, but he realized it was too late.

After being shown the discovery, Hanna spent the day on his knees, in silence. Mariana looked for Zakariya but couldn't find him. By that time, the sun had disappeared and darkness had fallen. It had been a warm spring day, and the stars shone like diamonds in a clear sky. Mariana reflected that the surrounding hills and the houses of Anabiya were composed of ruins and graves. She took Hanna by the hand and led him to the large fig tree, where she laid out a mat for him to sleep on. He asked her to leave him alone, and Mariana spent the whole night sitting by the window, watching him. She saw his face in the moonlight. When Zakariya came from his tour of the hill and saw his friend's new face, he couldn't bear to see him looking so frail. He left Hanna where he was and walked to the citadel, which was only a few hundred meters away. He knocked on the door and, without giving himself time to think, said to Shaha, "We've found the church." At first, she didn't believe him and thought he must have gone mad. She took him by the hand and led him to the bathroom, where the filth slid off his body. She brought him clean clothes and prepared a meal for him. She whispered the old words that used to make him stir; she said, "I want my horseman of the night." Zakariya was surprised at how much Shaha had changed. He had noticed her transformation over the last few days; she had started talking again, and no longer wandered so much. She seemed happy. He assumed that her conversations with Shams Al-Sabah had helped her to recover from the shock of the flood; a long time had passed since then, after all. Zakariya hadn't gone near Shaha, or any other woman, since that day. That night Shaha hurried him into her; she had missed him. She was another woman, more beautiful, her body softer, and she smelled of the perfumes that had belonged to the prostitutes in the citadel. She took him by the hand to the first room and asked him to sleep with her there. Zakariya forgot all about Shams Al-Sabah; he surrendered to Shaha, who was full of lust at that moment. She whispered, "I want a new baby," and Zakariya understood her desire. He thought she had come back to him. He embraced her and told her about the future; they would be just as they were before the flood, and he insisted that they would bear ten more children. But after their lovemaking, her grief returned. She wanted his sperm, and she asked him not to talk about going back to Hosh Hanna. She wanted a different life and whispered, "I can't bear living beside those graves."

Hanna stayed where he was, gazing at the moon floating in the sky. The night breezes revived him, and he would have liked to shout so that he would be heard by the jackals whose howls echoed in the valleys around Mount Simeon, but he stayed kneeling. He thought about the other life that he had discovered anew. He couldn't care less about his earlier frivolity now; he dismissed everything from his past, and he scorned the boy he had been. Next to him, Mariana was looking at him eagerly. His face radiated a light she alone could perceive. His laughing eyes gave her hope of new life; she didn't know what form it would take, but how she dreamed of being part of his life! In what capacity she didn't care—as long as she was beside him, she felt like the queen of the world. She had spent many nights dreaming of being one of his lovers or even his wife; now she reflected that Hanna might have been a lonely man and a wayward Christian, but he had found his way back to faith at last. The same passion he felt when he designed the citadel had returned to him. He lingered over settling his affairs and shut himself away in his room. Later in the afternoon, Zakariya returned with a trimmed beard and clean clothes, and Hanna learned that his friend had been in the citadel. He was glad to hear that Shaha wanted to have a baby; that meant she was healed. Hanna stopped listening as his friend chattered about the citadel. He considered demolishing the wall but the next day realized how absurd that would be, and so he went on calmly digging beside Zakariya. The walls around his lands were complete by now, and the curious could no longer sneak a look.

Two weeks later the church was clear. The walls were dilapidated and the roof destroyed, but the large stones, the columns, and the remnants of a dome remained. Zakariya dispatched his coachman to bring Azar, who arrived that evening. Hanna asked him to stay, and Azar made a tour of the place, inspecting the hill and the stones. From some inscriptions on the front, he understood that the building dated back to the fourth century. It might have been a large villa, perhaps the residence of some Roman officer, but it certainly wasn't a church, he told them. Azar stayed with Hanna that night, listening to his sporadic musings on annihilation. They were both woken the next morning by a horrified yell from Zakariya. He was holding human bones in his hand. There were more than thirty skulls, leg bones he hadn't counted yet, and many more bones that had crumbled away at a mere touch. Hanna went back into retreat, gazing at the sky. From where he sat, he saw Zakariya taking out the skulls and Azar helping him line them up carefully on the ground. No one had any answers as to who they were or why they were there. The friends tried to guess, but their imaginations were barren. In the end, Zakariya settled the matter. He didn't want Mariana to see them and argue about what should be done, so he picked up the bones and reburied them under the large walnut tree, not far from the grave of William Eisa and Aisha Mufti. It was an ideal way of preventing a dispute he couldn't bear thinking about.

Zakariya still considered Mariana an outsider, and Hanna agreed that the burial site should be kept secret.

None of them could guess why there was a mass grave there; it appeared that they had all died at the same time. Once the reburial was complete, Zakariya asked Azar to concentrate on this project of overseeing the walls and restoring the church. Azar repeated his opinion that it wasn't a church, just a dilapidated building, and it might even be a barn. Not wanting to argue, Zakariya asked him to build a church on the ruins of this building anyway. There was no way he could convince hundreds of devout Christians that it wasn't a church; news had already spread through the country, and their precautions would be of no use.

Zakariya finished the excavation, and the last wall appeared, covered in Syriac inscriptions. Azar brought a friend, a translator of Syriac texts, who looked at the writing carved in the stone and fell silent. Then he said that Hanna was right; it was a secret church, where early Christians had worshipped when they were being persecuted by the Roman emperor's troops.

Hanna ignored the animated discussions between Azar, Zakariya, and the translator. The whirlwind of activity made him determined not to let himself slip back to the concerns of the living, to the triviality of history and truth. He left his room wearing a clean linen thobe and leather sandals, with a bag on his shoulder and a staff in his hand. He asked Zakariya which road led to Bethlehem, and Zakariya pointed south. Hanna said he was leaving Zakariya total freedom to rebuild the church as it should be; the existing remains were enough to prove that it was a church. All Hanna wanted was to build a small monastery here, where he would live out the rest of his days.

Hanna left and walked toward the Church of St. Simeon Stylites. From there, he would continue to Jisr Al-Shughur, and then to Latakia and Qalamoun; then he would turn toward Hawran and from there to Jerusalem and Bethlehem. The way would be long, which would give him time to reflect on the contradictory ideas that were choking him. Mariana walked alongside him. When they arrived at Al-Dana, she told him that once they reached Damascus, they would be following Saint Paul's historic route, and so they were blessed. Hanna didn't care. He didn't want his spiritual purity to be polluted by the clamor of people searching for power they had no claim to; he was seeking hardship. He walked for more than ten hours a day and slept little. Whenever people asked what they were doing, Mariana informed them that they were on a pilgrimage to the Church of the Holy Sepulchre, but Hanna kept silent. He reflected that he was living in a labyrinth the end of which he never wanted to reach. If he walked until the end of his life, would he arrive somewhere different? He had no concept of what a different place might be. Margot's old stories came to his mind, the stories about cities of dwarves, and countries where the people had their eyes in the backs of their heads, and yet other countries where they never slept because the sun never set. But they were all alike to him: cities where the powerful strove to control people and turn them into servants and slaves, where men of religion doubted their faith but considered themselves intermediaries between people and God. Margot's stories about the massacres and mass graves of Syriac Christians were still carved in his depths. He wondered whether those skulls and remains were a mass grave of his own people, a group that was killed and buried at the hands of the janissaries. This idea pleased him, and he thought that the land must be crammed with mass graves where the mortal remains of the wretched had been flung carelessly; no one had buried them, no one prayed over their graves. He thought of his own estrangement and the estrangement of those dead people. He imagined their last gasps. It is impossible to beautify a massacre; nor can you forget the faces of the victims. A horrible death that no one survives. Margot's stories never left him, he recalled them in their entirety, they were stowed safely in some shadowy corner of his brain. There was no act greater than venerating victims and restoring their honor; they weren't merely remains but an entire life, forcibly buried. He wished Margot were still alive so he could tell her he was escaping from those terrifying pictures she had wanted to settle deep within him. "They are your ancestors, Hanna," she would have said bluntly. "And you must restore their honor." How to restore the honor of someone who died by the knives of a murderer? It was a question that deserved deep reflection. These thoughts—despite their cruelty—at least kept him aloof from Mariana's chatter. She was thinking of things that hadn't occurred to him. He wanted to live in the past with the victims, and she was going on about how he was going to become a saint: two ideas that were an utter contradiction of each other, impossible to reconcile. It occurred to him to go back again and raise an armed faction to take revenge on the Ottomans for all their victims, but really he was thinking of his other ideal, an ascetic who wanted only to live far from the reckonings of power. He was on the road to Maaloula now and thinking that he needed somewhere to rest his bones. He must surely be close to death, and these desolate mountains were an appropriate resting place for a man seeking his ancestors in obliterated footprints.

Hanna reached Maaloula and prayed in the church. Beside him, Mariana was exhausted, but she watched his every movement. This man had changed so much. The path of torment he was walking had, she supposed, given him an incandescent energy, and its glow touched Mariana. She thought he had finally reached a point of certainty.

Hanna spent a few days at Maaloula. He was deeply irritated by the questions of the priests, who didn't believe the story that had reached them. They laid siege to him, hoping he would confess that what he had uncovered wasn't a church but a ruin like any other, like the houses of the dead cities that had been destroyed by the wars on Christianity, the massacres, the continual earthquakes, and the wars between Christians themselves. Hanna refused to answer and asked them to excuse him from discussing his spiritual experience. He said his faith, which wasn't perfect, was different from theirs; he was still living through a harsh moment of rebirth. Escaping their questioning, he wandered in nearby regions and reflected on his fate. He felt lost, hanging in midair. He thought of sending Mariana away—she loved expounding his holiness—and going on to Cairo or anywhere far away where no one knew him.

He was gripped with longing for his room in Hosh Hanna. For the first time, Mariana urged him to hurry up so they would reach the Church of the Holy Sepulchre before Christmas, but he didn't reply. He thought he would be able to carry out his plan: he would restore the church and gift it to the believers, and he would build a monastery to serve as his final home. He would live there with his friends, who would eventually reach the stage of asceticism that he himself had. The monastery would be filled with them, elderly men who had once suffered from an excess of imagination, and no one would believe their stories about their bodies, now disintegrating, that used to walk tall on many roads.

It was a matter of indifference to him that some others appeared to worship his self-imposed isolation. Since he had not spent his life as a religious man, he didn't care about all the tales he was starting to hear, the legend forming around his church, the rumors that it was merely a flash in the pan. He remembered one occasion when Father Ibrahim, while spending a few hours with Hanna in his secluded room in Hosh Hanna, asked him about his dreams. Hanna replied simply that he had lost his family. The scene of the earth after the flood had inspired him to think that people who survived death weren't necessarily people who were still alive. Pointing out of the window at the flattened earth, he said, "Under this ground, my dead are resting." From that moment, questions of life and death dug deep within him. The few months he had spent away from people, watching the flight of birds and the turn of the seasons from his room on top of the hill, had revealed to him that life was just a long wait for death. He didn't care about questions of faith and heresy, nor all the works in church libraries about the birth of Christ and His miracles.

If he spent the rest of his life watching life and death from the window, in the land of the dead, he would find people repeating the same actions: building new houses, getting married and having children, then dying one by one, unless a new flood came and gave them the pleasure of communal death. Watching this perpetual cycle reinforced his conviction that everything was futile, impossible to bring under control. He came to this place to escape the throngs that would prostrate themselves in worship. People needed miracles, hidden tricks, delusions, dreams—things they couldn't understand. But he needed peace within, to die quietly away from the noise.

Hanna couldn't understand Mariana's behavior. Wherever they stopped, she would draw the bishops and priests aside for hours at a time, answering their questions and explaining his tormented past to them. Hanna had suddenly taken notice of her. She wasn't the simple, naïve girl who had made sugar brides for the children in Hosh Hanna and taught them how to write, but he was uninterested in this transformation. A novel fever had struck him—he was searching for something, but he didn't know what. He considered these days away from Aleppo his last chance to get to know himself. Mariana's words left him unconvinced; he didn't want to become a saint, he had never been drawn to the idea of miracles. Instead he used to be attracted by a life burdened with sin and foolishness, and even now he was still fascinated by the excitement of waiting for suicides. There were many things he didn't voice to anyone, and it was too late to admit to many of his fatal errors. He reflected that even in his dreams, he was running away. He loved evil and the devil more than the angels who drifted guilelessly around the heads of innocent children.

He didn't say goodbye to anyone when he left the church in Maaloula. He hadn't liked the daily derision of the monks at the dinner table, nor the hints that he was purchasing his sainthood. After a few days, he came to feel that the place was a beacon for charismatic religious personalities, and he didn't want to fight with them. He didn't have the energy to debate people who considered themselves the sole possessors of truth. He wished he had visited this place a few years earlier; back then he wouldn't have hesitated to crush the necks of some of these priests, to spit in their mocking faces and piss on their sanctity. But now his thoughts had become more remote, and he didn't want them to become corrupted by the opinions of others. Seeking the self did not require sitting at a filthy dining table in front of the general populace; all one needed was to curl up and throw your limbs away.

Hanna didn't stop in Damascus as Mariana wanted, continuing instead straight to Hawran. He was fumbling for the parts that were falling off him and that he couldn't catch. He told Mariana several times that his room overlooking the ruins of Hosh Hanna was the only suitable place for a new life. There he could practice his passion: observing life and death, the migration of the birds, the spring flowers quietly opening up and then dying in their turn. Nothing could equal this astonishing regularity. A flower never died too late, a bird never migrated after its appointed time. The joy of realizing how little he needed to live came as a shock. He felt his past life was a lie, although the citadel remained an exception. Skilled storytellers had made the place into a legend. Its greatest importance lay in its mystery, which aroused the imaginations of the city's inhabitants.

Hanna recalled the times when he used to lie next to Shams Al-Sabah, and he reflected that those moments restored much of his innocence to him. With her own hands she had bathed him, perfumed him, dressed him in pajamas, and led him to bed. She had told him stories until he fell asleep, and her scent became more like his mother's every day. Those moments, which he had never paid much attention to before, might have been the happiest in his life.

He had been supremely content whenever he felt her hands placing a cover over him, or adjusting his pillow. He would take her hand and feel the warmth of the old world that was lost, because Shams Al-Sabah was capable of quietly restoring it, without fuss. From the first moment, she understood that she too felt the happiness of the role she played and that she fully inhabited. She began to truly embody the mother. At the breakfast table she would hold him to account for a thoughtless act or phrase, and she made plain her severe opinion of the friends he invited to the citadel. She no longer entered the games room and left it all to the two elderly serving women and the women who lived at the citadel. She shut herself away in a private wing, refurnishing it as a small, cozy house where everything created an impression of innocence.

The closer they got to Hawran, the greater Hanna's anxiety. He had made up his mind: he would go back and live in his room looking out over the transient village of Hosh Hanna. He didn't want to live among crowds of people; he didn't possess any of the attributes that people assigned to him and spoke about as if they were facts. The heightened interest in Hanna and the rumors of his sainthood were all just a dream. Now he began to question whether what he had found came from his mother's stories; before she died, she used to tell him about a church buried underground in one of the hills on his father's lands around Barad.

Mariana was concerned about what he had said about Shams Al-Sabah and the citadel, but she couldn't do anything about it. He needed her—she would take his hand like a lost child and lead him along the path. She had found her life again; the flood was the Lord testing her faith. Mariana had also changed greatly. She decided she had inherited Shams Al-Sabah's role in managing his affairs and was determined not to let anyone dismiss him as ridiculous. While Hanna listened to her declaration quietly, he was thinking of the Lord's way of testing His worshippers by depriving them of everyone they loved all at once. Mariana never stopped talking about the signs they had been given in everything that had happened. She wanted him to live in his church, and she thought it wouldn't be hard to beatify him as a saint. He had all the requisite qualifications—the frivolous past, a lost lust for vengeance, a trial of faith (courtesy of the Great Flood). She told him that everything had to have happened as it did: the flood, the death of his wife and child, the total obliteration of the village, and most important, his visions that had been proved true—the church that no one else had believed was there. But she was taken aback by his scornful reply: "How expensive it is, then, making a saint."

In his prolonged silence throughout their journey, she saw healthy proof for her theory. Chatter was beneath the dignity of saints—it demeaned them. Hanna spent a long time observing the plants, birds, and reptiles along the road and ignoring the gatherings of people. He felt tired and informed Mariana of his decision to stop at the monastery at Hawran. He knew that in that isolated place, he would think for the last time about his life ahead. Mariana didn't want to stop there, preferring to continue on to Bethlehem and Jerusalem; his flock was waiting for his blessing in their churches along the way. Deir Hawran, on the other hand, was cut off from the world, concerned with issues that didn't affect the daily affairs of Christians. It was a retreat for monks, unsuitable for a person from whom everyone awaited more miracles once word of the church's appearance had spread. But she didn't dare stop him from taking the path that would bring him to the monastery in half a day's walk. She heard him say quietly, "Do what you want with your life, but leave me to mine." She didn't like it, and she thought everything she had planned for him might come crashing down. She was well aware of his rash thoughtlessness. His eyes still gleamed with that old lust for the pleasures of life, women, gambling, and strange ideas about dying and burial in pure silver coffins.

They reached the monastery a little before sunset. Father Ibrahim was expecting them and said he had been waiting for Hanna for some time. He had been absolutely certain that Hanna would decide to rest in his monastery during this difficult pilgrimage. Hanna replied that his pilgrimage was to this monastery; he wouldn't be continuing to Bethlehem. He added that from here, he would return to his last stopping place.

Father Ibrahim was kind and affectionate, and he grasped Hanna's anxiety. He had many ideas that he wanted to deliberate with Hanna, who himself needed to speak with an honorable man. Most men of the church hated him. He told Father Ibrahim that on the road he had discovered that Mariana was gripped by a lust for authority and added, musingly, "Is authority worth losing our pure souls?" Father Ibrahim observed her thoughtfully for a few days and described her thus to Hanna: Mariana was different from how she had been in Hosh Hanna. She wasn't some naïve girl but showed formidable intelligence and tenacity, and she liked to reach her goals by any means. He added that the church needed fervent believers like her. Zealots always provided immeasurable service, despite their rigidity and severity.

Hanna liked Father Ibrahim's clarity of thought; he thought a man could entrust his doubts to him. He thought of confessing to him but put it off until another day and decided to stay for longer than the fortnight he had originally planned. Father Ibrahim welcomed the idea, suggesting he move to the room by the library where he copied books and charts. Hanna agreed without demur. He wanted to get away from Mariana; throughout the journey, he had been exhausted by her presence and her constant chatter about the miracles he was capable of performing. From the first day, Hanna and Father Ibrahim easily returned to the feel of their few meetings in the past. They became friends, swapping points of view and speaking without restraint. They wandered the grounds of the monastery, and Hanna was greatly happy to be released from constraint. He regained the wish to speak, to question, to relate stories—most of which Father Ibrahim said he had already heard—from his past months of drifting. His tale had been told widely: here was a man who adored gambling and women, who had been transformed into a saint after the Great Flood. Skillful storytellers reworked stories of debauchery, invented years earlier by his enemies, according to their own imaginations; now they became stories of past infamy for which the Lord sent the Great Flood as punishment, but that also revealed the way out of sin into sainthood.

But Father Ibrahim, when he met Mariana, told Hanna that she was in some respects still that same simple girl, zealously committed to Christ—she was still afraid that Hanna would tell her to leave him alone. Hanna nodded in understanding, thinking that he had never before traveled with a woman who chattered all time, but he told Father Ibrahim about her great ambitions to have him beatified. He was surprised when Father Ibrahim advised him to keep Mariana beside him and told him he would often need her. Father Ibrahim repeated that she was still in a state of innocence and wonder at how her life had transformed; she was weaving her dreams in the air.

Hanna asked Father Ibrahim to persuade Mariana to stop telling stories about his miracles; news of them had spread around the country and begun to shape a new image of him. Once when they stayed overnight at the church in Yabrud, Mariana had been able to force him to pass his hand over the heads of three children suffering from paralysis, and afterward it was said that they walked without difficulty. Everyone present in those few moments said they had witnessed the light that usually shines from the faces of saints. Hanna didn't enjoy the turmoil and agitation of the crowds that swelled around him, and when women wept, trying to reach out and touch his outstretched fingers, he deeply resented Mariana; he wept and retreated inside the church. He gathered up his bag and left during the night after the people had gone back home. He wouldn't listen to Mariana when she pleaded with him to go to Damascus.

Hanna told Ibrahim that these miracles never happened. But Ibrahim explained the mechanics of creating a miracle. He said plainly that it wasn't important that a miracle had happened; what was most important was that people *believed* it had. This belief could not be stopped; humankind always needed miracles to alleviate the misery of existence. Father Ibrahim added that creating a saint required the collusion of the public: "Don't try to stop the stories. No one will walk on water after Moses, and no one will be crucified after Jesus; the image of Judas is complete in the minds of the people."

In the second week, Father Ibrahim offered Hanna some old plans of churches that had sunk into the ground or otherwise been erased. Some had been destroyed in earthquakes, others during the wars among the Christians, and Muslims had gained control of others and turned them into mosques. The plans were decayed, but the outlines were still legible. Ibrahim added that no one knew how Hanna's church had come to be interred, so he had to create it anew. Azar might be right that the place wasn't a church after all, despite the translator's confirmation that it had been dedicated to secret worship. Hanna almost told Father Ibrahim about the remains of the dead, but he stayed quiet; he wasn't ready to talk about victims of massacres.

Hanna's anxiety increased with every passing day. He felt he would never be able to escape the terrible collar that enclosed him. Only the thought of Zakariya's presence comforted him. Of course, Zakariya was looking after the place in Hanna's absence—he wouldn't let the mules urinate in the corridors. Hanna told himself that, of course, Zakariya would never leave him alone. He trusted Zakariya to finish building the church that would be turned into a small monastery. Hanna would leave it for the monks, and he would withdraw to his room in Hosh Hanna looking out over the graveyard and the river before he resolved what to do about his new life. Or later he might turn it into a center following the traces left by massacre victims. The center would count them and search for their graves, prompting a reconsideration of the anonymous oblivion to which they had been consigned. At the same time, it would identify the murderers by name so their heirs would feel shame forever. Hanna liked his strange ideas, but as he mulled it all over, he felt something was amiss. Why did he want the murderers' heirs to be ashamed, he wondered. What was their crime in all this? Could shame be inherited? Were our forefathers God-fearing, or were they also nothing more than a bunch of killers? More strange ideas about his new image entered the confusion. He reflected that most of the stories that Margot used to tell about the Messiah venerated tolerance, forgetting, and forgiveness. Yes, he thought; we are a blend of victims and murderers.

Ibrahim felt Hanna would never be right for the task of composing the monastery's story. But even so he told Hanna about the power of the faith in his heart, adding that his debauched life had given him the power of colossal insight and sensitivity—everything a man needed to transform. Standing alone and apart always requires strength, and Ibrahim felt that strength when everyone gathered at the dining table and waited for Hanna to address the monks who had been whipped up by Mariana's stories while Hanna himself was occupied with his friend Ibrahim, exchanging opinions and tales of the past and poring over the maps that astounded him. The monastery library teemed with thousands of these plans, which Ibrahim had organized over the twenty years he had lived there.

Ibrahim could feel how badly Hanna wanted to escape. One night Hanna told him about the wonderful feeling of living without expectation; waiting was the worst possible condition. He wanted to leave everything behind and go back to his room on the hill. There he would wake at dawn and inspect the trees and plants that had grown overnight, the daily transformations of the river. He would observe the animals growing older every day, and he would read books sent to him by Ibrahim, who tried to convince him that he could do all this at the monastery. But Hanna continued to describe Hosh Hanna after the flood, at the beginning of spring, when the grass revived and you could taste new life being restored, and within a few weeks the devastated ground had turned into a green meadow.

Hanna was dismayed at leaving Father Ibrahim, who said that Hanna would never be able to go back to his favorite place. He would spend his life waiting for death to turn him into a saint. Everyone wanted his death to achieve this; they were all waiting for him, this lonely man, to die, so their delusions wouldn't be ruined. There was no escape from the net that he had surrounded himself with. Father Ibrahim added that he would feel constricted at first, but soon he would quietly assume the soft power that surrounded him. No one would write a history of his doubt unless it was to thereafter establish his fervent faith, so they could say that the flood had transformed him from a shameless libertine, a powerful man who loved debauchery and worldly pleasures, into a young child who enjoyed playing with life.

At dawn, Father Ibrahim watched with sympathy from his window as Hanna left the monastery. Hanna felt a prodigious power, which disappeared shortly afterward. He felt he had entered a snare that he couldn't withstand and that he was walking to his own grave; his life troubled everyone around him, and his death would grant them new life.

After a journey of two months, Hanna and Mariana arrived at Aleppo. Hanna had missed walking through the intersecting alleys of his city and wished Mariana would leave him to himself so he could rove the alleyways alone, those well-known doorways and secrets. He was exasperated when people in the lanes pointed at him, reinventing the story of his visions. Everyone disregarded the original vision: that of a man who suddenly felt he was hanging in space, who renounced everything after he lost his son and his wife, and whose surplus years had thrown him into confusion. He felt the timing was suitable for his death. He didn't want to settle on the banks of a mysterious life that he felt burdened by.

No one had defended his father, and the flood reminded him that all his previous life had been trivial. The coins he had struck from pure silver had turned into scrap, a schoolboy's game. The silver coffins had tarnished; once symbolizing the freedom to choose to die with heroic chivalry, now they represented defiance against divine will. Everything that had happened was no more than a just punishment for his heresy.

Mariana wouldn't allow him to continue on to Hosh Hanna. She insisted that he consider his destiny once and for all, and she promised she would let him do as he wished. She had chosen her life, she would serve the Lord in the Church of Zahr Al-Rumman. Upon their arrival at the church, the great scene almost turned him blind. Next to him, Mariana's eyes were swimming in tears.

He couldn't believe what he was seeing. Hundreds of people—paralyzed, blind, suffering from leprosy; sick people on stretchers and donkeys—had been waiting for him for weeks. Shams Al-Sabah was there, wearing an abaya and a veil over her face, standing next to Shaha on the hill of Anabiya. From there they watched him make his entrance to the monastery through the prodigious crowd. Hands snatched at him. The place was drowning in tears. Hanna wept in silence. He didn't have the courage to tell these people they were seeking a delusion, that his soul was still stuck in the mires of this world. He gave up. He gave his touch to everyone, placed his hand on their heads, and drew back from the lips that strove to kiss his hand. He had never enjoyed this kind of slavish worship. He never used to think at all about human misery, and now he wondered secretly where all these wretches had come from.

He continued through the crowd, and silence saved him. The sheer number of tormented people surrounding him and grasping at salvation made him realize that everything he had done in his former life was worthless. What did it mean to live in luxury and build a citadel to pass the winter with friends, talking about the pleasure of losing at gambling, while all these suffering people lived beside you?

He completed his tour and felt himself slipping into a chasm with no way out. He couldn't tell these people that the help he was able to offer wasn't enough to make the lame rise and walk on their own two feet, and his touch wouldn't restore sight to the blind. His heart overflowed with pain, and deep down he was enraged because he wanted no part of this delusion. But this wish was destroyed at the cry of a blind man who informed everyone he could now see. The blind had been cured. From the other side of the crowd, a lame woman shouted that she was walking a few steps for the first time in her life. The miracle, embodied before his audience, locked every door for Hanna. Eventually he was able to throw off the crowd and vanish into the corridors of the monastery, which appeared untarnished in his eyes. Mariana led him to his room on the first floor. The principal part was finished, but some construction was still ongoing. Mariana shut the door behind him, and he threw himself onto the bed and slept for a few hours. When he woke at dawn, quiet pervaded the place. He was struck by a profound sense of contentment at having come back to the land he loved.

The dawn light coming through the gaps in the curtains colored the few things in his room as he slipped out the door. He reflected that Azar and Zakariya had shown great care in their preparations. The room was large, with doors that gave onto a hallway and another room. It was sparsely furnished, with a large walnut table circled by six chairs, a spacious bed, a bookcase, and a small wardrobe; it was simple, but great pains had been taken over every detail. He began to inspect the rest of the place. He walked through a passageway that led to five closed rooms. On the ground floor, there was a wide hall leading to a library and a large kitchen with a vast larder attached to it; that in turn led to a long stairway down to the cellars. He could smell lentils and onions when he neared the open kitchen door. He couldn't understand how this place could have been built so quickly. He opened the door and found a nun, who introduced herself as Sister Therese, preparing breakfast: lentil soup, delicious-smelling freshly baked bread, and onion. When Sister Therese saw Hanna, she bowed with great veneration and made to kiss his hand, but he pulled it back from her and asked straightaway about Zakariya and Azar. Yvonne was next to her, watching him. He didn't understand what she was doing there, but he was happy to see her. No one responded to his question, even after he repeated it. He heard Mariana behind him, saying that Zakariya and Azar had gone away. What, she wondered out loud, would a Muslim man and a Jewish man do in a Christian monastery?

Hanna maintained his silence and walked a few paces toward the outside. He was taken aback to find Mariana again, blocking his path. He couldn't go outside for at least forty days, she said. She gazed at him gravely. Everything about her was different. She ordered him back into his room and said the maidservant would bring him breakfast. Then there would be enough time to talk everything over. She added in a whisper that going outside would mean the death of his legend.

He found the gravity in Mariana's voice utterly horrifying. Even though he was no longer afraid of dying, the long journey to Deir Hawran had purified him. He walked back to his room. The servant Futaim came in with breakfast. She arranged everything for him on the table and left without uttering a word. Hanna wasn't used to living alone; before the flood, he had never eaten breakfast by himself. He left everything on the table and went out again. He wanted to inspect the place further. Mariana headed straight for him and said, "The most important thing for any saint is seclusion. The whole city has circulated stories of how the lame and the blind have been healed. The tale kept getting bigger and bigger, and now it is impossible to control. You can't convince anyone that you're not the long-awaited saint." She suggested that he devote himself to reading, and added, "From your room you can watch the birds, and the life and death of the plants."

Hanna mustered every ounce of his strength, came right up to her, and stated, coldly, that he didn't want to become a saint. What had happened was a delusion that he didn't want to continue. Everyone should forget him. He was well aware of how to reach the life he wanted, and he warned her against interfering in it, or trying to sell illusions to miserable people, or reaching an agreement with the patriarch and the metropolitan to rob him of his will.

He left her standing there and went on his way, trying to find the church. People he had never seen before greeted him, and he didn't bother to reply in kind. Agitation still dominated him. When he saw Yvonne, he stopped and talked with her about how she had lived after the flood. She told him that after being granted permission by Basilos, she had left her aunt's house in Aleppo to live in the monastery, adding that no one had ever forgotten the story of how her fiancé had taken her virginity. She asked his permission to move there, close to him, permanently, and added that she didn't want to live with her relatives or in any other place where there was no one to defend her. She asked for his total protection. Hanna knew her family well, and he recalled her fiancé, whom Zakariya had buried in Hosh Hanna. He smiled and told her she was welcome. Yvonne was glad and felt she had found her final place, here with this wonderful man. She added that everything she had learned from nursing the sick might come in useful to the residents of the monastery.

Hanna decided to go out, but from the small window he saw a crowd even bigger than yesterday's encircling the place. He felt deafened already by the imagined sound of their moaning. He found himself in a true dilemma: he would never humor them and sink into the role that others had drawn up for him, and no one would tell him anything about Zakariya and Azar and why they were nowhere to be found.

He went back to the kitchen and ordered Therese to feed the people waiting outside. She said they had brought all these provisions and hadn't come for food; what they were seeking was his healing touch.

Mariana watched his every footstep, heard everything he said. She recorded notes in a small notebook. He scrutinized her face and her body in detail, somewhat surprised to realize it was the first time he had spent any length of time really looking at her. Mariana was disconcerted but stood firm. She didn't want any detail to escape her. She knew him; he hadn't been saved from his nonsense quite yet. His imagination would lead him to ruin, and his lifelong sour relationship with the church meant that going out would put his life in serious danger. Confused and disturbed, Hanna drowned in a whirlpool of anxiety he hadn't felt since the day of the flood.

Mariana hadn't yet embarked on her chosen new life as a nun. She still felt estranged from monastery life. In the mornings, she missed the hubbub of the fellahin in Hosh Hanna, where everyone used to get up at the same time. Within a few minutes, every door would be open, the smells of breakfast wafting through the air. She had to forget her past life and kill her desires. She had to do something so Hanna would want to stay at the monastery, forgetting all about the folly of freedom and his former life among fallen men and women, among the landowners who adored his eccentric ideas.

Hanna didn't understand what had happened in his absence. He was determined not to allow anyone to plan his life for him. The sensation of those first few moments of the river after the flood still kept him awake at nights. He had never seen the truth as he saw it that night, when he climbed to his single room at the top of the hill. Everything had been in order at the place he escaped to every now and then—the manservant always looked after it well, keeping the room clean and ready to welcome its master at any time. Hanna opened the window and looked out at the scene he would never forget: a quiet river that for thousands of years had run along indifferently but that two days earlier had swallowed an entire village along with its inhabitants, cooking pots, beds and rugs, and livestock. It had left nothing behind. Even so, the river's appearance was charming, innocent. The full moon reflected in the river, and absolute silence, utterly soundless, drowned the scene. It took him back to the earliest moments of creation, and Hanna reflected that life had sprung forth in just this way, when beings emerged from the river and multiplied on its banks. He didn't look away from the river all night, ardently waiting for a miracle—for the river to return everything it had robbed on the night of the flood, to spew out the dead and their things—but nothing happened. In the light of dawn, the plants stretched out their heads, the green color spread and deepened throughout the day (the word *plant* meant nothing to him yet), and he kept his eyes on them until the earth on the riverbank crumbled, a riot of green, the sound of frogs, and he saw shoals of fish swimming in the river. One life had passed, and another went on. He thought how he had wasted the dawn all his life; it had been a long time since he had woken at sunrise. He hadn't reflected upon himself. He felt some regret; being a drowned man wouldn't be so terrible. There in the depths were many secrets that those strolling along the riverbank on summer nights had never seen.

He wanted to tell Zakariya all about the visions that never left him, but his ridiculous decision to excavate the hill had postponed the conversation. From that moment, he had withdrawn from everything, but surely Zakariya must still know that Hanna needed him. Hanna trusted that his friend wouldn't leave him prey to the coldness and ambition of Mariana, for whom he cared not at all, and the machinations of Basilos, who had once said, "If Hanna converted to Islam, it wouldn't be a great loss to Christians. On the contrary, it would mean we were rid of a lethal plague." His legs felt heavy; he walked to his room and opened his bookcase. He found some books he already knew and had no desire to read, and he thought that if this place was a prison, he would be saved only by Ibrahim, the holy man of Hawran, and his friend Zakariya. He was relieved to think that no one could possibly object to Father Ibrahim's presence here, and he wouldn't allow anyone to object to Zakariya's. He would defend his new life even if he was forced to burn down the house of worship. At that moment, he felt he had recovered his purity, his strength, and his reckless folly. He still had a deeply rooted wish to see that scene again, the upspringing of the earth on the bank of the river that ran with a strange calm, while in its depths, human corpses, household objects, and livestock from several villages meekly came to rest.

Zakariya would always remember Hanna telling him about the church buried in the hill. He had thought it one of the strange ideas that they continually batted back and forth and that afterward had become so mixed up they couldn't tell them apart. He used to believe that the flood was the upper limit of their tragedies, but it had been the beginning of a new life that neither of them knew anything about.

Zakariya still remembered a night, ten years before the flood, when he and Hanna were returning from Sharran after spending a full week drunk at Arif Sheikh Musa Agha's farm. The scent of pomegranate blossoms filled the air. Hanna asked him if there was any pomegranate on his lands, and Zakariya replied that he wasn't sure, but he didn't believe so. Essentially, Zakariya had no enthusiasm for land. At Hanna's insistence, he had bought a few dozen dunums, after his friend convinced him that they would come in useful later on, maybe as pasture for the horses. While they were traveling on that night, Hanna said that pomegranate aroused his craving for love. It wasn't the first time Hanna had spoken about craving love, but he didn't for a moment think he would be capable of it, while Zakariya used to believe that everything would work out in the end.

Zakariya remembered that day, the idea of love, and his friend's silence throughout the journey in their carriage, which was done up with the finest, most cheerful upholstery. When Hanna left Zakariya at the monastery, walking away like an orphan with a girl who knew nothing about their lives, Zakariya decided he needed to travel this road to its end. After all, he thought, nothing would happen unless he wished it, so he and Azar set to serious work, rebuilding the place as a church. The large stones had reliefs on them, and they stayed in place. Two months after Hanna's departure, the church was complete, and it was beautiful. Azar designed the small monastery that Hanna had described, employing hundreds of laborers who toiled night and day in unceasing shifts. Zakariya dug up some boxes of silver buried in the floor of his room and sold them, then emptied the wheat stores, all to pay for the building of the monastery, which he wanted to be worthy of his friend's new soul. Azar understood Zakariya's simple instructions. He liked both Hanna and Zakariya, and he still recalled William Eisa's stories about the madness of his childhood friends. The monastery was close to completion, the walls were finished, everything was almost ready, when Metropolitan Basilos arrived. In a resolute tone, he demanded that Zakariya leave the monastery and leave Hanna to his new destiny. He said that the Christians needed Hanna. The metropolitan went on to conclude that the drawn limits of the monastery were now the property of the church, and it wasn't permitted for a Muslim or a Jew to remain there without the express permission of the patriarch.

At that moment, Zakariya felt a large hole open up within him. He thought they wanted to kill Hanna and seize his property. He and his friend had never faced a moment more dangerous than this one; they both thought of religious men as horse ticks, parasites that sucked blood from beautiful creatures, and they often mocked both sheikhs and priests. Zakariya considered responding to Basilos and his entourage but felt that a battle without Hanna would be less forceful. Large numbers of Christians were beginning to make pilgrimages to the church; after Basilos broadcast the story of its founding, it had spread to every quarter. Storytellers added many details attesting to the holiness of the site, which was well suited to an atmosphere laden with respect for miracles. The church had been waiting for a miracle for some time, and Hanna had given it to them, however lacking and imperfect it might be. A miracle could never come to full fruition in the presence of a powerful witness like Zakariya who, everyone knew, shared everything with his friend: secrets, dreams, strange ideas. To perfect the tale, the witnesses had to be made to disappear, so that the storytellers' imaginations could weave the distant past and erase anything that impeded the lavish growth of happy endings.

Zakariya decided not to fight Metropolitan Basilos just then. He asked the man of religion to come back three days later so he could officially hand the site over. Basilos, for his part, was afraid of Zakariya. He knew he wouldn't give in so easily; Zakariya had no fear of the vali, because his influential family would guarantee his protection. The metropolitan accepted Zakariya's suggestion to return in three days' time.

Zakariya felt a deep void inside him as Basilos left. It had been a long time since he had asked himself if he had been right to want to remain alone, at a remove from his family. It occurred to him to go back to his father's house and rediscover his life. He spent that night at the citadel, trying to persuade Shaha to give birth in his family home, but she told him outright that she wouldn't go anywhere until after the birth. She liked the citadel; there her nightmares stopped, and she was no longer frightened. She had her freedom, and he had his—she wasn't waiting around for him. She added that she hadn't lost her love for him. She was waiting ardently for the new baby and hoped it would be a girl—there were so many things she wanted to teach her daughter.

The citadel had turned into a lodging house for retired elderly women of pleasure who had no way of supporting themselves in their old age. Shams Al-Sabah had invited Um Waheed first, and afterward she thought of turning the citadel into a place that housed them all. Hanna no longer cared what happened there. The idea might seem strange, but it filled the citadel with new life. Cooking smells wafted from the kitchen, and Jewish, Muslim, and Christian women lived side by side, reminiscing as they waited to die. They settled in quickly and admired the place. They themselves had never before set foot in it, but they had sent girls to it from all over.

Without Hanna, Zakariya seemed weak, a stranger to the place he had helped design. Shams Al-Sabah wouldn't let him wander through the citadel at will; she told him that now it had become a retreat, shut off from the world. Its gates were open only to women who wished to repent. He didn't understand what she meant at first and thought the citadel, in its oppression and emptiness, had driven Shams Al-Sabah mad with loneliness. But things were different under her new regime. The crates of fine wine, the neckties—everything to do with the men who used to live here for months on end was packed up in crates and moved to the cellar, which had previously been given over to sheltering the guests' horses and carriage drivers. Only Hanna's wardrobes stayed locked and untouched: the silk pajamas, the splendid suits, the pens, the shoes—and these things were few, barely enough to fill one small wardrobe.

Nevertheless, Zakariya had been secretly happy there with Shaha. She responded to him and wanted him to sleep with her every night. She wanted to become pregnant, as if she were bidding goodbye to life and pleasure. She told Shams Al-Sabah that Zakariya had asked her to become like the women at the citadel, and Shams Al-Sabah grasped the essence of her wish. She opened the Turkish hammam for Shaha, filled its three basins with hot water, massaged her body with rosewater, and put at her disposal a collection of revealing new nightdresses from Paris and Rome. She didn't stop Shaha from dressing up every night in the character of a woman of the citadel. She invented new characters and added them to Shams Al-Sabah's stories. Zakariya too wanted Shaha even more; she seemed more beautiful and more arousing when she dressed up in the character of those now-vanished women. They both engaged in a kind of mutual vengeance; she wanted to drive out the pus of all the women he had had sex with, and felt that she was joining him and Hanna on the wild adventures she had heard about from strangers.

They spent eight weeks wrapped up in their passion, and afterward, toward the end of the summer, she told him she was pregnant. She was delighted, and for the first time Zakariya felt there was still a possibility that life could go back to normal. Shaha picked up all the lewd underwear and burned it, and put on a loose purple cotton dress instead. She stopped matching him in inventing new stories. She thought about the coming child and spent a lot of time with Shams Al-Sabah and the old women, all of them preparing clothes, shirts, and nappies and speaking with total seriousness about "their child" who would be arriving next winter.

Zakariya refused Basilos's demand to hand over the site to the diocese and ordered the guards to lock the gates, but a few days later Ottoman soldiers stormed the place, arrested Zakariya, and fired shots into the air. A justice official handed the site over to the patriarch with a formal document while they took Zakariya to prison and threw him into a cold cell, threatening to transfer him to Istanbul if he persisted in defying the metropolitan. The interrogator told him that anyone who could have intervened on his behalf was dead.

Zakariya spent days in jail. He reflected on his fate and feared that Hanna was a vagrant, or dead. He thought about how he could get out of prison. He wanted to send a letter to his friends, but every path to do so was blocked. The guard would throw him his food in a shabby copper bowl and shut the door until the next day. Azar didn't abandon his friend; he asked Zakariya's brother-in-law, Hassan Masabny, to pay the substantial bail and conducted a negotiation that bartered Zakariya's freedom for four hundred gold liras. Hassan Masabny paid up with good grace and bribed the responsible officials and the judges to settle the topic once and for all.

Zakariya went back to the citadel but couldn't bear to stay there. The constant chatter of the retired women irritated him; they would cry all night long while they waited to die, and some took their penitence too far, in his opinion. But he dismissed it from his mind now that he was occupied with the approaching birth of his child and Shaha's refusal to leave the citadel. The place had changed considerably and now reeked of motherhood, but after the retirees from the brothels arrived, there was no escape from the storytellers' lewd new creations.

Zakariya spent the summer enjoying the extraordinary pleasure

and passion that Shaha gave him as he waited for Hanna, and the rest
of the time he traveled between his new stables, which had returned
to their previous glory as horse-fanciers began to flock back. But every
evening he climbed the hill and watched the monastery, where laborers still worked continually, building additional wings according to
the designs by Azar, who had spoken to Zakariya about his old passion
for openings in domes that held the light, like in the old hammams.

The metropolitan summoned an Italian architect from Beirut to
oversee the completion of the building and the furnishing and dec-
oration of the monastery and church. The Italian replaced Azar, who
secluded himself in his office, believing that it wasn't worth the fight.
But Azar's troubled eyes made Zakariya think they had lost both the
citadel and the monastery. If it was difficult to extract a bunch of
retired women from their places, it was no easier to extract a metropolitan. The graves of William Eisa and Aisha Mufti were all they had
left there.

Hanna's return and what it brought deferred any long discussion between Azar and Zakariya. As they stood on the hill, watching
Hanna as he cut through the crowds of the lame and the sick, touching them to give them his blessing, they were no longer sure that this
skinny ascetic was their old friend with the strange ideas.

Zakariya couldn't stand being so far from him. On the third day after Hanna's return, he headed to the monastery. He ignored Mariana's
instructions that it was forbidden to enter without permission, went
straight to his friend's room, and opened the door. Hanna burst into
tears when he saw Zakariya. He embraced him tightly and asked Zakariya not to leave him. Hanna was frightened of everything, he said:
of the air and the silence, of the people and the animals. He didn't trust
that they would let him live as he wanted.

Hanna didn't hide Zakariya from anyone and offered no explana-
tion as to how he had sneaked into the monastery. He asked Zakariya
to join them for dinner. Zakariya was welcomed by Mariana, who was
well aware that Hanna's agitation over Zakariya's treatment and im-
prisonment might bring everything crashing down. Over the last two

days, Hanna had regained his strength. He was no longer the man who accepted everyone's interference in his life, but Mariana was no longer afraid of anything. She felt she had profited from the battle, because she was on her way to being a nun, and the monastery was in the possession of the church. Her narrative of Hanna's sainthood and his vision of the monastery had made great strides around the region, and all that was left for it to be complete was some stopping points Hanna would have to discover for himself. No one mentioned Basilos's order to expel Zakariya from the monastery. Mariana inquired after Zakariya's horses and after Shaha, and he told her that Shaha would give birth in a few days, and that his stables had gone back to work. Seizing her chance, she asked for his help in establishing a stable at the monastery. She said she wanted the most important bloodlines in it, adding that many wealthy Syriac Catholic pilgrims would help expand the stables with rare bloodlines. She extracted a promise from him to consider her request. Zakariya was humoring her—he didn't want to ruin Hanna's happiness at having regained his friend—but at the same time he liked the idea, which stirred his imagination. It was the only way of staying close to Hanna, of protecting him and preventing murderers from infiltrating his life.

Zakariya didn't hide his happiness when Shaha moved into a room close to his in the monastery. Hanna persuaded her to stay beside them, away from those lost and ruined women. The upper floor now seemed to be set aside for Hanna and his friends, whom Basilos didn't dare to harass for fear that Hanna really was beginning to turn into a saint, or so said the believers.

Three weeks later Zakariya began work on the unusual task of establishing stables at the monastery. He promised himself they would be the most important stables in the East. He selected the northeastern corner of the monastery, where Hanna owned vast tracts of fertile land, and asked Azar to come back to work. They planned the buildings together, and the joy they had lost returned to them all.

On Christmas night, the church was lit by candles, a large crowd was waiting for Hanna to give mass, and Shaha went into labor. Hanna was standing with her by the door while the women assisted her. The contractions went on for six hours, and at daybreak the monastery was silent. The throng, having waited in vain to see Hanna look out over them, had dispersed after making do with praying in the church. Mariana's footsteps rang out as she emerged from Shaha's room with a baby boy and a baby girl in her arms. There was sadness in her eyes as she informed the two men that Shaha had died.

Stupor settled over everyone's faces. Hanna embraced the two children and said, "Shaha will be buried in the monastery." He left them and went to his room, carrying the two babies swaddled in pieces of cloth. He called for Yvonne to help him wash them and sprinkle their bodies with salt. It was a clear, unambiguous announcement of adoption. His angry, grief-stricken looks frightened everyone, and they complied with his orders without demur. The deacon, Boulos, who was among the residents of the monastery, dug Shaha's grave in a tucked-away corner by the wall that separated the monastery from the village. Zakariya asked Yaaqoub to go to his brother-in-law's house and bring his sister Souad and her husband. It wouldn't be difficult to find a sheikh among the inhabitants of Anabiya.

Mariana understood that it was a precarious moment—Hanna might be pushed to even further extremes if she wasn't careful. She joined the others in assiduously carrying out his orders and ensured that the church was prepared for Islamic prayer over Shaha's body. She asked Boulos to choose where the monastery's graveyard should go, because she didn't want Shaha's grave to be isolated. Mariana's tolerance broadcast an atmosphere of ease. She didn't hesitate to kiss Souad and offer her condolences, and then she supervised the opening of the 'aza and the cooking for the mourners who flocked from the nearby villages. From Aleppo came a crowd of Bayazidi family members, along with Arif Sheikh Musa Agha and his relatives, who considered Shaha's burial in this fashion to be an insult to their family. But Zakariya's grief suspended all discussion on this topic.

The only thing Mariana asked was that Hanna forbear from making an appearance, as the city would view it as an opportunity to come flocking to the 'aza in order to see him. This was a convincing justification, and Hanna made do with supervising the care of the two babies and making sure that everything was carried out in a satisfactory manner. He spent a long time with his friends, for the first time in a long time. He felt deflated when a young boy came up to him and held out a letter he knew came from Shams Al-Sabah. He didn't want to read it, and his lack of reply would communicate that the final break between them had begun.

In the evening, Hanna waited for Zakariya to appear. He held out the letter he had received and asked him to read it out loud. Zakariya was afraid of these strange moments. He opened the envelope; it was a short letter, the first Shams Al-Sabah had ever sent to Hanna. She requested that Shaha be buried in the citadel and that she herself be given care of the children. She said she was the most worthy person to look after the memory of her only friend in this life, and she pleaded with Hanna and Zakariya not to deprive her of her wish, which she said would be the last she would lay before them.

Hanna was silent, and Zakariya understood his wish for an end to this subject. She was the last person who could remind him of his former life. It was enough that the citadel was entirely given over to her; when the last woman died, they would find another use for the place.

No one spared a thought to name the newborns. Three days after Shaha's death, Zakariya felt as though he were unconscious, moved by an invisible force. He received everyone's orders and carried them out, but only Hanna's presence reassured him he was sane. Loss had crept into his heart. A furious Souad told him, after they came back from the burial, that Shaha should have died in the flood. She added that the babies should be made part of the Bayazidi family; monastery life would ruin them. But at that time, Zakariya wasn't thinking of anything but the coincidences that had turned everything and everyone's lives upside down. He regretted having allowed Hanna to dig out the hill, to discover the church and destroy everything. It was a bad omen that Shaha's death was the first to take place at the monastery. He felt he was no longer as he had been before the flood; something in his heart that he couldn't name or grasp told him he had to rectify this mistake. Narrow places at their widest filled him with horror. He didn't listen to Souad's monologue, or to Shams Al-Sabah's accusations that Mariana had murdered Shaha. He thought his head would explode. He wanted to go and live somewhere far away, where he could raise his horses and wander the earth with them and with his friend, never settling anywhere.

He paid no heed to a servant's attempts to prevent him from entering Hanna's quarters, nor to Mariana's insistence that he act with caution, that everything that belonged to their past lives had finished. Hanna was waiting for him and said, smiling, "We have to name the babies." He added that he had named the girl Aisha and suggested that Zakariya name the boy. Catching his veiled hint, Zakariya said the boy would be named William. Tears welled up in their eyes at the memory of their friend and of the moment that they still couldn't believe had happened, even after burying the lovers with their own hands in the cherry orchard.

There was nothing left for them to do but repeat the names, Aisha and William. Remembering their friend made them both happy. Zakariya thought it a feeble-minded idea to spend their lives here among all these people. He asked Hanna if they would be staying here much longer; he felt constricted by his surroundings, but he couldn't be sure of the reply he would receive. Hanna asked Zakariya to wait until the pomegranates were in bloom. Together they walked to Mariana's quarters, where she had allocated two small beds for the babies next to her own. The role of mother suited her well. The two children were frail, as if they would never be able to overcome the hardships of life, but a strange gleam shone from Aisha's eyes and face. There was no mistaking her resemblance to her mother.

They stood there just a few moments, but that was enough for both men to feel peace and a sympathy they often spoke about afterward. Mariana seized her chance and asked Zakariya either to take the two children so his family could raise them or to decide once and for all to leave them here. The nuns would look after them; she didn't conceal her own attachment to the two babies who, despite being somewhat sickly, smiled at everyone. Hanna settled the matter, saying, "William and Aisha will live here until they come of age." Inwardly, Zakariya agreed. He didn't want them to live in his family's house, where there was no one to care for them. His sister Souad was married, and his aunt Amina was absorbed by her role as a preacher. She was currently occupied with mourning for her greatest sheikh, Abulhuda Al-Sayyadi, who had been trampled by unionists in the streets of Istanbul, exiled to Buyukada in the Princes' Islands, and died there in 1909. Neither of them was available, so Zakariya didn't know why he still told Mariana that it was early yet to settle the matter of the children's life. The simple truth was that he wanted to contradict her. At that moment, she felt he hated her.

7

Hunger

Hanna's writings, No. 4—1915

Despite the war, Mariana was preparing a ceremony to celebrate the sixth anniversary of the monastery's founding. I didn't argue with the history she outlined, and I didn't care much about these special occasions that she was so bent on celebrating. She thought there was still a chance of my survival. I felt as though a new body had settled in place of my old one, and my sin-laden soul had crumbled. I scattered it, as I always wanted to, over the pomegranate trees—their wonderful wild blossoms have opened. Beauty allured me before; now I take hold of it and savor it at every moment. At dawn I leave my room and walk in the fields surrounding the monastery, and I see Zakariya hard at work, feeding the horses. I reach the top of the small hill clothed in cactus, and I see the citadel in the distance. I can feel its hungry emptiness. Strange that I don't miss it in the slightest; it has become a neutral place for me, as if it belonged to some isolated neighbors who don't care to bid us good morning. But still, it appears to me a marvel of engineering that Azar deserves to be proud of. It has been years since anyone has noted any movement or noise coming out of the place. Shams Al-Sabah has turned it into a place for Um Waheed's elderly companions to pass their old age, far from penury and the insults of people who would throw stones at them on the streets or spit on them in the markets. Those women have become a heap of eternal sinners, their repentance accepted by no one.

I imagined them to be broken-down, their bodies grown flabby, wearing loose dresses and no makeup. They bury each other without respect to religion. When the Jewish Widad joins them, it will give the place a new memory to reminisce about. I recall that Arif adored her soft fingertips and her white skin. He knocked on the door of the citadel one morning and told me, "I am going to marry Widad, I've bought her an apartment in the building that our friend from Antioch owns." He went on: "You have to witness our marriage contract." He sounded like a little boy. I said to him, "If you are still so determined to get married, and Khatoun Um Yousef allows you"—Arif's wife was ill with no hope of recovery—"I'll throw you a wedding like Aleppo hasn't seen for half a century." As usual, Arif turned the page on that story within a few days, and dust soon covered the furniture in that new apartment.

I thought about Um Waheed. They hadn't let her move her girls to another brothel when she finally lost her battle against the city's pimps. They took over the running of the place and ruled it with tyrannical force.

No one has accepted that these women have repented. How many of the people I welcomed in the past hid a thick rod in the sleeves of their flowing cloaks, declaring it to be the staff of God? I pity those men, but at the same time I always knew just how capable they were of destroying people. When Father Ibrahim explained the history of forgiveness to me, he knew that forgiveness is given by people, not by God. He wanted me to know that God cannot be unjust. One morning I opened the door to his library and found him sitting in his usual place, taking the first sip of a chamomile flower infusion, smiling as usual. I was in a dark mood and asked him outright, "If God doesn't exist, who will compensate the millions of people who spent their lives under a delusion?" He replied plainly, "We humans have invented God, and we defined his characteristics. If he doesn't exist as a tangible, material force, inventing him has given comfort to millions of people as they journey toward death."

It does no good to anyone to think of God's nonexistence. In recent months I have felt a strange comfort, I feel the taste of things again; the blind no longer expect me to heal them. I always wanted to be left in ob-

scurity, seen by no one. Disappearance is a speck of freedom. I have become a thread of light. The maidservants and nuns don't see me. I don't
require their greetings anyway, I have always hated deference. I fell in
love with the idea of disappearing, residing in a state of being forgotten;
it is the life I have wished for, all my days.

I don't occupy my thoughts with the matter of God's existence. I am
convinced that God is an idea, just like Jesus. He who has been struck
by the magnificence of that idea feels a secret happiness for that hidden
shadow that guards his life; he who hasn't, fears and reveres it. And he
who has no fear will feel his wretchedness and his vast emptiness, like
the dinosaur skeleton that Yousef, to my great pleasure, is so passionate about. The idea of God resembles the ideas of love and fear. When
I see Souad crossing the courtyard, I feel a breeze penetrate my soul. I
remember how she used to look at me before she saw the stain on the
silk shirt that she had asked me, in dead seriousness, not to let a prostitute unbutton for me. She didn't like sharing my love with anyone. It
was a very short moment, a fraction of a second. I would have liked to
embrace her and kiss her, ignoring the crowds around me. I had always
wanted that moment. I have never forgotten the fury on her face as she
looked at the shirt stained with wine and lipstick from women's kisses;
she spat on me and left. I have never forgotten her contempt, any more
than I have forgotten the rare times she touched me, or her fear that
I would suffer from a passing illness or even die suddenly. I will live
a long time, for her. The moment I left the house for Hosh Hanna, I
heard the walls of my heart shatter. That sweetness sank deep within
me. I have grown distant from her. I have turned into a stagnant pond;
frogs fill my ribs, and bats and ants divide up my empty spaces among
themselves.

I have savored love, I have experienced it throughout my life. I can
never convince someone who hasn't tasted love of its existence, not even
the closest of my friends. They used to say I was talking of some imaginary world, suitable only for children. Women, to them, were a collection of holes to be filled with their own holy water. For their part, they
failed to convince me that God, whom they knew, was the same one

spoken about by the men of religion. I always saw God as love, growing within my ribs. They didn't know Him. I have known Him in recent years. When I touched a pomegranate blossom for the first time, I wondered how I had lived for decades without a touch of the divine beauty that cleaves the heart.

Now I feel the necessity of going out into the wilderness and enjoying the power of disappearance. I feel the necessity of being forgotten by the world, of being alone with very few friends. I feel how right I was to keep Aisha and William living beside me, and Zakariya in the monastery—I cannot imagine life without them. I leap up like a small boy when six-year-old Aisha wraps me in her arms and whispers that yesterday she grew up and I grew down. Then she adds in a hushed voice, as if she were telling me a secret, that at night she goes to other places. Last night, for instance, I was a little child, and she was the grown woman, leading me by the hand. A little embarrassed, she said she was like her aunt Souad. She said we went to the banks of the Afrin River and jumped onto the back of a giant turtle and traveled on the river to another land. After a pause, she said, "I've forgotten its name now."

Mariana has ordered the servants to prepare for a special occasion to welcome the patriarch, who is coming especially to celebrate the monastery's anniversary. The celebrations have begun to exasperate me; the country is drowning in a grinding war, thousands of young men are led to the battlefronts and don't return. I told Father Ibrahim that sainthood is a delusion, and I am delighted that Mariana's spurious plan will never succeed in making me a saint. As he usually does whenever he wants to contradict me on some matter, he shook his head and said, "You are under the delusion that you are freer than ever before." He added, "You yourself have entered into idolatry." In my eyes, he can read the anxiety that has never left me as I think about escaping everything. He says, "You still have a last chance to run away. If you come back here, you will leave only to go to your grave."

I decided to escape alone. The earth is wide, and the world is bewitching; walking in the fields, watching and handling plants will give me pleasure as I live alongside people and grasp their pains. I have nothing more to lose; I have lost all my lands. Recently I thought about Salih Azizi, how he hunted down and murdered Hikmat Dashwali. His story has never left me; I always admired his passion. He had his revenge on all of us in the end. I think of the power of love that transformed a being from a servant into a wandering, ascetic poet, and then into an informer, a murderer, a suicide, and imam to the lovers.

At dawn I crept away from my room. I followed my own path that wound around the road. In my bag I had some bread and a few other items. I paused in the village of Barad and sought out those extinct footsteps that affect me greatly. The villagers are poor and couldn't care less that they live among the remains of churches and destroyed monasteries. They use the huge stones to construct their livestock pens, thinking of the crumbs that are their own lifespan, totally indifferent to the sanctity of history.

I thought of Zakariya, who would remain alone, but before I reached Deir Sam'an Amoudi, I noticed his footsteps behind me. He had been following me from the beginning. I asked him to leave me to my fate, and he burst out into the laughter that I had missed. He had instructed his carriage to follow us. He asked me when I was coming back, and I said, "I am not coming back." He replied, "I can't stay in the same place as Mariana. I might murder her and throw her body to the dogs."

I was overjoyed that Zakariya was accompanying me on my last escape. We had a long time ahead of us to speak about our childhood. I am afraid of life without him. No one in the world will rob me as long as he is beside me. He planned ahead, and when we stopped in Idlib, he procured some blankets for us to sleep under, some clothes, and enough food. On our first nights, we slept in the open air, and I watched the moon on those winter nights. I regained my skill at navigating by the stars; we shared reminiscences about our childhood, and we ignored inhabited places. We saw traces of the war and the terrible famine. The souls that were falling from starvation showed us the truth of our nature:

we are selfish people. We stopped at a crossroads to ask the help of some fellahin returning from the fields. They weren't stingy and were kind and generous to us, but our lack of direction irritated Zakariya.

I could feel his worry. He had something he wanted to confess, but he gave voice to it only when we reached a shrine on the summit of Mount Nabi Yunis, close to the village of Slunfeh. We decided to sleep there that night. Zakariya opened the door to the shrine; we weren't afraid, despite the bleakness of that clean place. We found some scraps of food and stayed there by ourselves for more than ten days. The February snow fell thickly; no one was going to venture out of their home to examine an isolated shrine on a mountain peak. On our last night there, Zakariya told me that the foundling child I had named Helen was his daughter. The mutterings of the monastery's inhabitants about an illegitimate re-lationship between Zakariya and Yvonne were true. Leaving Yvonne's name out of it, I said that Helen was happy with Futaim, her adoptive mother. Zakariya wanted me to chastise him, to blame him, but I found myself thinking, "Does what he did merit rebuke? What great sin has he committed?" I thought of the errors committed by my friend. Several weeks of wandering later, we came to Aleppo, and I asked him, "Is it true that Yvonne's fiancé took her virginity?" He looked at me with-out replying, as if he had forgotten that old tale entirely. Zakariya was always surprising me. He told me the story in full, as if he were in con-fession and asking forgiveness. I told him that the kindhearted Yvonne, who used to look after my affairs, had tried more than once to tell me something, but I had always been distracted.

The story of Yvonne, Helen, and Zakariya increased my pain. I remember the day Mariana brought the baby girl and put her in my arms, saying she had found her in a basket by the monastery's door. She asked me to name her and to allow Futaim, the servant who worked in the kitchen, to adopt her. Mariana wanted to expel the shame from the monastery, just as she had turned out the child's mother some months earlier. Yvonne wished she had drowned with her fiancé and her family; her luck in surviving had warped her life. The story about her fiancé still dogged her, and no one forgave her even the rumor of it.

Zakariya and I spent ten days contemplating the desolate forests of Slunfeh. At night we heard the howling of jackals and wolves as they circled us, looking for prey. The snow calmed, and omens of spring appeared. The few visitors to the shrine had thought we were the guards, and they left us a little food: a little bread, a slice of cheese. They apologized, telling us that they had nothing in this era of famine, but they blessed us and asked us to take good care of the holy saint of the shrine.

I felt a mental purity I had never known before. The absence of people wasn't such a bad thing. I undertook many different tasks: I gathered firewood and lit the fire, I cooked. Zakariya had been able to secrete a small quantity of bulgur wheat and olive oil in the carriage. I thought of how I was alone in the middle of these forests. What if I stayed here all my life, guarding a saint left alone by everyone during the winter?

In the first days of spring, the visitors multiplied, and we fended off a deluge of questions. Our wretched appearance helped to disguise us, but the carriage and pair of horses outside gave everything away. Zakariya took care of everything as usual; he spoke about fulfilling our vows through serving the shrine. We went back down the mountain with great caution and almost slipped more than once. We reached Hama but skirted round it and went in the direction of Salamiya instead. We wandered half-lost through the wilderness. The view was splendid; wildflowers were opening, and we were doused with morning dew. Our hearts were revived, and we joked around as we used to do in childhood, which we went back over many times, bringing up different moments and details.

Zakariya was driving the carriage, pulled by the best pair of horses in his stables. I whistled the melancholy tune we used to whistle as boys when we were coming back from playing on the riverbanks. Zakariya smiled. He gave me a searching look, examining what was left of my old soul. He knew I died some time ago and now I am someone else. I told him I wanted to go to Hosh Hanna. He mumbled something, and I understood that that same servant was still looking after my room there. I asked him to go back on the Aleppo road, the one the Bedouin used to travel. Reaching Hosh Hanna wouldn't be easy—perhaps we would be rich pickings for them. We no longer had any influence that might protect us. I have felt, recently, that we have thrown our entire past by the wayside.

I thought about my room in Hosh Hanna. I missed it. I had forgotten many things, and Zakariya believed that the time we spent on the road would be long enough for him to tell me about the situation with my properties, what remained of them. I didn't care very much. I knew I had nothing left but the land of Hosh Hanna, and I didn't know who was looking after it. The church had taken everything. In a moment of thoughtlessness, I had turned over all my bank shares and funds to Mariana, and she ceded the land and the monastery to the church. I told myself that I was giving to my people; they would respect my instructions that after my death the monastery was to become a place for the elderly to live out their final days. I realized that I venerate death and have feared old age all my life.

The way wasn't quite as we anticipated. I hadn't known that I had come out of one death and into another that was even crueler. Everything I felt in the previous months was a delusion. We cannot flee to ourselves. I still remember how, the moment we left the saint's shrine on Mount Nabi Yunis, I felt it would be lost forever. But it is a place that is not prepared to disappear.

Zakariya knew all the side roads leading to Aleppo. We arrived at Khan Touman but didn't care much for jt. We discussed making a surprise visit to Azar in his office, but I didn't really want to do anything other than reach my room in Hosh Hanna and watch the returning birds, whose flocks had begun to fill the sky. I was taken aback to see the streets of Aleppo abandoned and bleak. Surely it wasn't possible for all of a city's residents to disappear? A little farther on, battalions of young men, shackled at the wrists and ankles, were being led off to battle by Turkish soldiers. That was sufficient to explain what was going on. Mothers were begging the callous soldiers to leave their sons and their husbands, throwing themselves at their loved ones to touch them one last time, but the closely guarded train carriages soon swallowed them up and turned them into nothing more than plumes of black smoke.

It was difficult to see my city empty, frightened, and so utterly deso-late. I found it hard to breathe. I didn't know the reason behind all this misery. What had happened? A group of naked children were carrying empty bowls and cooking pots, and a group of sheikhs were distributing lentil soup and half a roll of barley bread, scolding the children who asked for more. Ottoman soldiers had raided every house and appro-priated everything there was to eat, and the famine had killed thou-sands. I had never seen starvation before, but the stench of it clogged my nose now. I hesitated to get down from the carriage; I was afraid of becoming visible again. Zakariya was miserable. He hadn't told me that the monastery had not escaped this campaign. The soldiers had seized all the provisions and left the cellars empty. I understood at last why we had seemed so very poor over recent months. I used to hear whispered discussions about the provisions running out and the redistribution of meals. Mariana was able to strike a bargain with the officer responsible for the region, and she held on to some sacks of bulgur wheat and lentils and a small quantity of olive oil in exchange for an enormous sum of money. She had held back this money from the last bond that the bank had sold for me. I deposited the money in the monastery's account, which Mariana ensured fell under her control. She used to say that I was incompetent, and besides, "It doesn't befit saints to possess filthy money, their pure hands should be kept unpolluted by it."

Mass funerals passed close to us, biers without mourners. The strong young men had disappeared—only old people and children were left. Soldiers kept watch on everything, searching carriages. There wasn't a single house left in the city that they hadn't searched. They plundered the warehouses filled with goods and grain and seized every animal that walked. We passed by them, and they gave Zakariya a savage look. He told me they wanted the horses. He went on to say that he had saved half the horses in exchange for a large payment to the vali, and another to the state treasury. I guessed that after paying those sums to save his horses, Zakariya was now a poor man. He added that he regretted it; he hadn't expected the famine to go on for so long. He assured me he wouldn't let anyone appropriate the carriage and the horses, but at that moment I wasn't thinking of anything but Souad: was she hungry too? I asked Zakariya about her, and he said Souad had a secret warehouse no one knew about, the entrance to which was stopped up with stones. There was only a little inside, but the provisions would rot if she couldn't find a means of bringing them out. Zakariya added that of course they would find a way of getting what they needed . . . Azar would help her. Zakariya tried to avoid going through Bab Al-Nasr, but it was too late. Our path was blocked by a large group of children, crying in chorus as if they were an orchestra playing a mournful tune. Their mothers were close by, holding out their hands to indifferent passersby. I got down from the carriage. I had nothing to give these children, but Zakariya gave me a handful of coins that I handed over to them. I couldn't tear my eyes away from the ones who were dying by inches, falling to the ground one after the other. I asked Zakariya if we had anything in our warehouses. He laughed and replied that we didn't even have the warehouses anymore; they had gone to the church. We were now as poor as these children. We might starve if we didn't reach Hosh Hanna; there, at least, we would find some provisions that the fellahin had buried in the ground.

I was distressed at seeing all these starving children with their rib cages jutting out, waiting to die at any moment. The alleyways of Bab Al-Nasr were completely empty. What was life worth if all this misery surrounded you? I asked Zakariya to stop at the corner of Khandaq Street. A dozen or so children came up to the carriage, and the rest followed behind. We arrived at my house in Bab Al-Faraj. I asked Zakariya to open the door, and when he did, there was a smell of mold. It had been years since I entered this house. Zakariya couldn't understand why I had brought the children there, to a house that had not a crumb in it. I asked the children to take everything away: the crystal chandeliers, the Persian carpets, the embroidered silk sheets, the sofas, the copper pots, and the bowls and the cups. The children loaded themselves up and left. I said to Zakariya they were things that could be sold, even if it was for a trifle. I had nothing else to give them. I couldn't stop myself from looking through the blinds at the entrance to Bahsita's general market. A small number of women were still selling their bodies at the souq, their hair disheveled and exhaustion plain on their faces. No one paid for sex anymore, there were no clients, no gifts, and no lingering perfumes wafting from the entrance. I left the door open, but Zakariya locked it after the house had been emptied of every object. We got back into the carriage and went on our way. I suggested we sleep there, but Zakariya wasn't listening—he was furious with me. In his opinion, those chandeliers couldn't be eaten, but they were a part of our old lives. He still hadn't lost hope that I would go back to how I was and our old lives would resume, but when he saw the children trying to carry out the sofas, he was finally convinced that I no longer cared about the few things I still possessed.

Before we left Aleppo, everyone watched the horses with surprise. People were picking through animal droppings, sifting out the seeds, and large cooking pots were boiling up leaves from the trees. The soldiers had raided everything and sent it all to the army's stores. They hadn't left anything behind. Chickens, lambs, sheep and goats, horses and donkeys—everything that walked on four legs, everything that could walk at all or be eaten had been moved to the front lines.

I didn't want to leave the city. For the first time, I understood the foolishness of what I was doing. This enforced isolation, these meditations on the origins of creation, on the concepts of God, beauty, and death—and here was death, walking barefoot, creeping over the earth beside me, and harvesting thousands of souls, slipping through the cracks in the doors. No one could halt its flood. Groups had volunteered to bury the bodies left on streets and in abandoned houses, but they couldn't keep pace with their task. Who can bury a dead city? I wasn't able to imagine the scale of the disaster when I was in the monastery. I had thought that the soldiers wanted their share of our wealth in their usual way. On our journey, I wanted to disappear. Zakariya told me that a year ago, when the war began, matters hadn't been this bad. Before we left Aleppo through Bab Al-Hadid, I saw some men trying to set fire to a pile of corpses. They waved at us to keep away, telling us they had died from the plague. Annihilation approached; whoever survived starvation would *die of the plague; whoever survived both of those would die of cholera; and whoever survived all that would die in the war. Zakariya told me suddenly that Hassan Masabny and his friend Raoul had been killed by the plague and their bodies had been burned. I reflected that it didn't matter what they had died of; it was all one, in the end.*

I saw furniture that had once been in my house wandering the city. The children must have sold it to a group of hawkers. They traded in everything now: souls, bodies . . . they wouldn't miss a rich opportunity such as this, but when I imagined them dying too, I felt sick. It had been a long time since I felt hatred. I thought I had forgotten rage and contempt, but they still scarred my depths.

We reached Hosh Hanna. The village graveyard was still the same, but no one lived there anymore apart from a handful of fellahin, who could farm only a few hundred dunums. Meanwhile the rest of the large territory had grown uncultivated and cracked, no plow had tilled it for years. The sight of a few cotton seedlings refreshed my soul. I went into my room. Zakariya had put away some meals for us, dried figs, raisins, meat jerky, and some rolls of barley bread. Despite the hunger that gnawed at me, I vomited. My insides contracted, and my breathing rattled in my throat. I threw myself onto the bed and couldn't get up when dawn came. Zakariya was fast asleep, snoring from exhaustion. I tried to go back to sleep. A little later I heard the clatter of Zakariya getting up, heard him speaking with the fellahin who had seen our carriage and congregated around the hill. Zakariya was furious and issuing threats; I realized someone had stolen the horses. I wasn't concerned, I closed the window and went back to bed. I could feel how powerless I was, but at the same time, I was thinking that things would be fine. The voices of the people surrounding the hill disturbed me. Zakariya came in and said, "They are your flock. They are waiting for you to go and rub their heads." The number of people had grown—I was afraid they would completely encircle the hill and the room within a day or two, and then we would have no escape. The famine was less severe in Hosh Hanna; there people could hide away food in wells or in treetops. The river had become a source of sustenance, and fishermen had resumed their activities, put-

ting up tents and diving into the river in search of fish and seaweed. Zakariya dealt with the matter by borrowing a horse from a landowner who complained that fellahin controlled all that was left of the lands. I had never allowed him to visit me; I always hated his greed and had known his intentions for some time. He wanted to annex the eastern part of my lands to his own vast territory. I asked Zakariya to find a way of fleeing the wretched, the blind, the lepers, and the lame, all waiting for a miracle I was incapable of performing. Zakariya said, "All you have to do is rub their heads." I won't sell a delusion to anyone, I told him as we left Hosh Hanna. I was grieved to my core, but the hot soup Zakariya had prepared the night before helped restore my health. Bodies were scattered along the road, and women were carrying their dead children. We learned they were Armenians, fleeing a massacre. Wild dogs gnawed dozens of corpses. We were approaching Aleppo again. I couldn't bear the sight of a vulture spreading its wings over the body of a child, probably dead of starvation, and devouring it with agonizing slowness. I could only let out a loud sob.

I thought for an instant that Zakariya would suggest that I spend the night at the family home, but he stopped the carriage in front of the Syriac Catholic Church. Souad had gone back to the Bayazidi family home after the death of her husband. His possessions, his factory, and his fine house hadn't survived the looting, Zakariya informed me. It suited Souad, who had hated that life of collusion. Hassan hadn't been able to flee the city as he had planned. She simply said, "Many people have died. Hassan, too, just like everyone else."

The church was deserted, and I felt like I was in the wrong place. I left before the metropolitan returned from inspecting his flock in Jazira province. Metropolitan Basilos had undertaken great work during the famine. In order to feed the people of his city, he had opened the church stores, sold some precious icons, and pawned others. The church had gone bankrupt and had nothing left to sell. The metropolitan had gone away on a tour to encourage his rich followers to open their storehouses to the poor. We knocked at Azar's door, and he was astonished to see us at such a time. The old fragrance of friendship came back to us. Azar had lost weight and, like many others, had received support from Jewish charitable associations. He hadn't escaped the tyranny of hunger and confiscations, but he thanked God he hadn't died of plague. We talked long into the night until I lost all desire to talk. I fell silent while Azar told us how David and many other unfortunates had died. Eventually I drifted off as I was thinking of a means of escape. I wanted to complete my journey alone and touch the plague myself. I had chosen my death; I was no longer enthusiastic about living. I felt great relief as I imagined my body burning alongside plague victims; it would be the peak of disappearance. I chuckled inwardly as I imagined Mariana's dilemma, speaking fervently about an imaginary saint. It is impossible to fully sympathize with those who have died of starvation unless you share their death.

We left Azar fast asleep. I was sad to realize there was no place left for me to disappear. I felt powerless. Zakariya was silent as he drove the carriage to Arif Sheikh Musa Agha's house, where the situation was no better. Arif was a broken man, utterly collapsed. They had led his son Yousef off to the war after he had been arrested in the monastery's stable, where he had been hiding out; afterward he had escaped and joined Sherko's men. Arif was deeply troubled. If he had had the money, he could have saved his son from military service. The soldiers raided the food stores and jars of olive oil and left him nothing, and now he was on the brink of starvation. In the large room, some Armenian families were taking turns to sleep. There were six young girls, survivors of the massacre that had killed their mother a few days earlier, and Arif had no idea what to do with them. I spoke a few words to them in Turkish, and one of them spoke up, saying her name was Maryam and these were her sisters. It was clear that they weren't really sisters, but Maryam had no time to explain. She was telling us in disjointed phrases about bodies hung from poles, and villages burned entirely to the ground, and the long distance they had crossed on foot. She said she had left Urfa a month ago. All her family was dead apart from her brother Harout, who had slipped through the soldiers' fingers and over the border into Kilis. Maryam burst into tears and begged us to look for her brother, *who was only eleven years old. She said he was too young for the war, and if they found him and realized he was Armenian, they would kill him like her uncle and his six sons, who had been buried alive.*

Arif was anguished as he brought china plates and set them down in front of us along with a little bulgur wheat, a small chicken, and a plate of yogurt. The six girls swallowed everything up in seconds. I made do with a few mouthfuls. Arif had aged; I had never seen him as depressed as he was that day. Four years earlier Zakariya told me that Arif no longer possessed a single thing and hadn't for some time. All he had left now was a little less than thirty dunums of land by the railroad. He had lost his standing among the aghas, whom he was too ashamed to see after his son joined Sherko's men. Every morning he waited for the train and waved as it went past, explaining to an imaginary audience that it was his train. He had nothing left but this house and the Aleppo house that had lost its value. Who would buy a house when people were starving to death? Money disappeared from people's hands without warning.

Arif didn't stop me from bringing the girls to live at the monastery. He was grateful. Before we said goodbye, we heard the sound of the approaching train. Arif smiled forlornly and said it was his train—if we wanted, he could persuade it to stop so we could have a tour. Even after all these years, he still didn't believe his dream was over. It meant nothing to him that the swindlers were arrested and put on trial, that all the money was gone without a trace.

When we arrived back at the monastery, I was at the end of my strength, though I reflected that it was impossible for humanity to be obliterated entirely. News of the war overshadowed everything. I couldn't bear to stay in the monastery and went out, wanting to walk to the end of the world. I hadn't asked anyone for anything. I wanted to lose my way and stray off the path, but I felt my feet were shackled to this place. The image of the vulture slowly tearing at the body of the dead child never quit my mind, the sight of the dead never left me for a moment. My memory was crammed with images of crows. I thought how they would look for me and never find me; in a few months' time, they would say that I had died, and I would turn the page on an oppressive chapter of my life. The night of my return, I spoke to Father Ibrahim, who had achieved great things in the last few months. He spoke to the metropolitan and obtained his blessing to sell the church's icons, he opened the kitchen up to the hungry, and he took care of Maryam and the other Armenian girls, assuring them they were safe now and that he would look for Harout and the rest of their families. Father Ibrahim looked at me pityingly; I had returned in defeat. I headed to my room and bolted the door shut—like all defeated persons, I didn't want to see anyone.

This was the beginning of the final surrender, despite my knowledge that I would disappear before long.

Deir Zahr Al-Rumman—1923

8

A World Subsiding

Aleppo—Deir Zahr Al-Rumman—1948

Childhood gets further away, but it never leaves us, Aisha repeated to herself. Two weeks away from her fortieth birthday, Aisha walked like a stranger through the passageways of the monastery. She was carrying her youngest son, Hasko, because she wanted a blessing from Grandfather Hanna Gregoros. For the third time, she had tried to see him without success; instead, Mariana had sternly told her to leave. Aisha's birth and childhood were painful memories for Mariana, in contrast to William's, which she considered good fortune. She always said that she would never stop rectifying Hanna's mistakes, not even for an instant. She believed that time killed all stories. She sowed doubts about Hanna's childhood and his life in Ahmed Bayazidi's house—a saint-to-be couldn't possibly have been raised by a Muslim family, she used to whisper to the nuns, who remembered everything Mariana told them about Hanna's childhood. In her retelling, it seemed as though Hanna had been abducted and forced to live with Muslims, and Mariana waxed lyrical about his torments as a young man before he was flooded with the light of Christ.

Aisha walked to visit Zakariya, who was silent as usual. He had stopped caring about what Mariana did. Aisha threw herself on his chest, and he hugged her and asked her to forget all about the monastery. The place was finished. She was upset to see that Zakariya had grown old, like his horses and stables. She asked him to move to her house, and he said, smiling, "Everyone left here will die here, and they will be buried without fuss." He added, "That applies to me, too." Zakariya's frustrated words hadn't changed in five years, and as usual, Aisha didn't want to believe what had happened. He never told her that he occasionally suffered from recurring boils. The doctor had advised him to learn to live with this illness, which he didn't name.

Aisha recalled when Father Ibrahim had come to live at the monastery thirty-five years earlier, when she was five years old. Hanna had taken her by the hand, and together they had walked toward Father Ibrahim, who received a warm welcome and a firm embrace from Hanna. William was lying in Mariana's arms, inseparable from her as always. Hanna and Mariana had shared the twins since their birth. When Mariana saw Hanna dangling adoringly from Aisha's eyelashes, she relinquished the baby girl to his care. She became William's mother instead, and every day she invented a different tale about carrying out Shaha's wish that her dear friend Mariana would adopt her son. Mariana's worry over William made him feel he had the best mother anyone could have.

In the spring of 1913, Father Ibrahim's procession entered the monastery, to a huge welcome from its inhabitants. It consisted of three carriages drawn by six Arab thoroughbreds, loaded with a large Esfahan carpet that still lay in the library, old manuscripts, many instruments for copying—papers and ink bottles, twine and English ink pens of varying shapes and brands—everything packed carefully into boxes of the appropriate size. William rushed to help the servants unload them, and Mariana watched him contentedly as he lost himself in the chaos, amazed at the sight of all these peculiar objects. She felt his eagerness that night when, before going to sleep, he told her about the large pens he used for writing. He told her they were like fish, then wondered if they could be eaten. She was used to his eccentric questions and, like any mother, praised his intelligence. She observed his development every minute and couldn't believe that God had given her such a precious gift. At times, she felt that she would pay any price for William to be her true son, but her time for having children had passed. She was more embroiled than she should have been in the plot to secure Hanna's sainthood, and she had to be satisfied with William, who didn't ask much about his real mother, content as he was with Mariana's prodigious affection for him. He felt special and behaved as though this sweet woman really were his mother. When he grew up, William found no difficulty in reconciling the contradictions that governed his life. He was scattered among everybody, but a secret thread pulled him toward Mariana, who felt safe within the strength of this connection. She reflected that to those He loved, God gave the things they lacked. If only William had been Christian and from an unknown family! The greatest problem was Aisha, William's strong-willed sister, who dominated his life.

The moment Father Ibrahim arrived at the monastery, William's life changed, and his passion for this new world was endless. Mariana assigned him to serve Father Ibrahim. William enjoyed cleaning his pens; he would bring him cups of hot tea, then wait for him to finish eating and sipping his water so he could wash the reverend father's hands and hand him a towel. He was always alert to any orders and carried out all his tasks with supreme gravity. On Sundays, Father Ibrahim would put William in front of him on his horse and together they would make a tour of the areas surrounding the monastery. Father Ibrahim loved William's artlessness and his affection for everything to do with writing, from paper and pens to the smell of gum and hides, and he loved William's wholehearted dedication to serving him. William accompanied Father Ibrahim on his rounds of the souqs, carrying his umbrella and making himself comical in his attempts to clear a path for him. Mariana was reassured that William would spend his whole life at the monastery, close to her; she couldn't bear being separated from him. She asked Father Ibrahim to teach him to read and write, and the very next day he asked William to sit down next to him at the large table and write out the letters ten times each. William drew them slowly, taking care over his handwriting. Mariana helped him go over his lessons and do his tasks. Aisha joined him, and the reverend father was impressed with the force of her memory, her ability to impose order on chaos. Within a few minutes, she was able to correctly rearrange a pile of scattered pages and documents and sort them according to type and size; she numbered them all and never mistook one folder for another.

Within five years, William and Aisha could easily read any kind of text and had memorized entire chapters of the Qur'an and the gospel. Given a couple of hours, William could draw a lifelike rendering of any person. His first efforts at portraits weren't to the taste of his teacher, who said, "Look for the hidden in people. Faces are flat and have nothing to do with our deepest selves." But he praised William's technical skill and bold lines, and he charged the boy with copying out a short text in which an anonymous monk had recorded his daily life in a long-forgotten monastery on the outskirts of Aden that disappeared in the tenth century. There wasn't much left of the monastery other than a long wall that formed the foundation of a sixteenth-century mosque. William sketched the monastery and its adjoining buildings, relying on the testimony of the unknown monk. He presented the new plan to his teacher, who didn't hide how moved he was by this marvelous work. Once he discovered William's love of painting, he conscripted visitors to the monastery to send paints, sparing no expense. These visitors dispatched the requested items to the reverend father, who in turn explained to William the different types of paint and how to use them.

Mariana still kept his first paintings in her own private cupboard. Among them was a marvelous portrait of Hanna and another of her; each portrait revealed his deep affection for the subject. He didn't need many notes in order to copy a particular manuscript onto a sheet of yellow card in skillful ruq'ah script; Father Ibrahim was proud of his student's accomplishments and patiently offered him more and more pages. Mariana almost wept with joy when Father Ibrahim told her, "Your son will do great things." He had thirty copies printed by the Shahba' Printers in Aleppo. The name *William ibn Mariana* adorned the front page, declaring him the copyist. Mariana kept the first copy for the rest of her life, and William kept another in a trunk in the cellar of his aunt Souad's house.

William spoke to Mariana every night about the dilapidated old manuscripts that emanated the breaths of their ancestors. Father Ibrahim was authenticating them, and it was hard for William to understand his mentor's desire to spend years of his life in such repetitive, tedious work, unsuited for the breadth of his knowledge. Father Ibrahim was fleeing from the struggles of the metropolitans and the men of the church; he wanted to maintain his inner peace. William couldn't extract his teacher's consent for him to write his biography, but the reverend father urged him to write down the story of Deir Zahr Al-Rumman. In doing this, Father Ibrahim was conveying a secret message to his pupil and also indulging Mariana in her capacity as a mother who wanted to keep her son close to her, in a place where the outcomes of its violent conflicts could never have been foreseen.

William understood his teacher's message and made do with drawing every detail of the monastery. He spent three years contemplating every nook and cranny. He made a large painting, eventually hung in Hanna's room, that distilled all the stories about Hanna's return from his pilgrimage with Mariana at his side. The painting was crammed with the blind and the lepers, the poor, the believers who were weeping and stretching out their hands for a blessing from their saint, Hanna. Mariana greatly admired this painting, in which she appeared in a simple, shabby white dress, an ascetic leading Hanna by the hand to give his blessing to the needy. The only thing she didn't like was that Zakariya was also present, tucked away in the corner of the painting, looking anxiously at his friend. Mariana ignored him in order to focus on the details that showed the strength of faith in Hanna's heart. William spent three months on this painting and wouldn't allow anyone, not even Aisha, to see it before it was finished. It was Aisha who had suggested that Zakariya should appear in the corner of the painting, but she went a little too far when she asked him to paint their mother Shaha as well. This he wouldn't do, but he painted a separate portrait of Shaha, just as he imagined her, on a huge canvas. Mariana was uneasy about this painting, which wound up in Orhan's house by means mysterious to everyone, including William. Most likely Mariana disposed of it in her perpetual effort to erase the relationship between William and his family.

William was growing up before Mariana's very eyes. His eyes gleamed with intelligence, and his achievements were made simply and without fuss. Absorbed in his sketches and paintings, he didn't even notice the struggles going on around him, and he believed everything he was told without question. The monastery's inhabitants loved him but they were afraid of his sister Aisha, who told stories as they happened, not as the storyteller wished to recompose them.

Mariana described William's childhood as the best time of her life. No one doubted they were mother and son. He slept in her bed, and she told him the story of Jesus, and long tales about virtuous people who had strayed off the path before repenting. (Repentance was a principal refrain in her stories.) At first these stories were thrilling, but as he grew older, William stopped caring about them. His life became a collection of images that had to be rearranged daily.

Left out of Mariana's plans, Aisha spent most of her time with Hanna. For his part, William walked down the monastery's passages and spoke about odd things, repeating scattered fragments of hymns he had learned by heart. He spent hours in the copyists' room, working alongside his teacher. Father Ibrahim wanted William to inherit all his knowledge, and he almost extracted Zakariya's agreement to send the boy to Rome to learn Latin. Zakariya was afraid of his son's notions. He didn't like the ways he was changing, and once his son had been seized by the idea of writing the history of the monastery, he feared his son would spend the rest of his life in this isolated place.

Mariana would have succeeded in obtaining a history of the monastery exactly as she wanted it to be written, if not for Aisha's interference. She scolded her brother vehemently for fabricating Hanna's history just to please Mariana. After he openly doubted Mariana's stories, she subjected him to rigorous observation. He questioned the nuns, who proffered the story that Mariana was determined should be the only one; it was already well known throughout the region. It was told and retold so frequently that it could be heard along any roadside. The only underdeveloped part was the tale of the Reverend Sister Mariana; most of the people who had known her in her youth had died in the plague that struck Aleppo in 1915. For years, her image remained an enigma that tempted storytellers to pad the details they already knew. As time passed, her true image disappeared beneath the accumulation of invented tales, just as she always wished. She constantly associated her history with Hanna's and wouldn't tolerate any error in the retelling. This suited her, but the story had become a muddle, immeasurably uglier than her initial inventions. According to the jumble, Hanna was now 150 years old and still cracking walnuts with his own teeth. In reality, he was no more than seventy-five. His skin was sagging and his hair was falling out, and it had been years since anyone had seen him in the prayer hall. Alone, he would cross the fields around Deir Zahr Al-Rumman to Zakariya's house, where he would spend a day or two before going back to his room.

Forty years had gone by, and Aisha still couldn't forget the light streaming from her window that looked out over the houses of nearby Anabiya. She had been walking in the fields, still a small child of six, to reach the citadel on the hill. No one had opened its curtains for some years. It was a mysterious place, half-abandoned, dogged by strange tales. No one, apart from Hanna and Zakariya, knew who lived there. The last person to speak of it was Teodor, the Dutch man who arrived at the monastery from Istanbul in 1919, loaded down with his suitcase, several cameras, and a collection of posters lauding the Russian Communist Party. He asked permission to stay in the monastery for a few days before continuing on his journey to India.

The day after he arrived, he went for a walk through the nearby villages. He took lots of photographs of the fellahin and fellahat harvesting lentils. He took pictures of church ruins, temples, abandoned stone bridges, paved roads, and wine presses carved with symbols of the sun god and Syriac phrases that no one had bothered to translate.

That night he went back to the monastery and told Father Ibrahim, who had invited the Dutch man to join him for dinner, that in the citadel he had seen women wearing white dresses, moving slowly as if they were walking on water or dancing to unheard music. He speculated there were more than ten of them, maybe more than twenty, but he didn't receive a satisfactory reply. In obedience to Ibrahim's wish, Teodor continued to prepare to photograph him with Aisha, who was sitting in his lap and smiling. Still ruminating on what he had seen, Teodor said there were three women, one of them very old; in her firm, strong voice, it was clear that she was begging to die. Father Ibrahim made no comment. He asked to see Teodor's pictures, including whatever photographs of the Russian revolution he still had in his possession.

Teodor went back again to the same place. He tried to enter the citadel, but the guard asked him to leave. No one could see what went on inside. He searched for someone to tell him what was happening in that strange place, but he found nothing apart from a few strands of a story, widespread in the area, that the citadel had been designed by a Jewish architect as a labyrinth for Hanna, the great landowner, and his Christian friend who fell in love with a Muslim woman, kidnapped her, and took her to this place. The girl's family had followed him and murdered both the lovers, and their graves could still be found in the abandoned cherry orchard, guarded by curses. No one went near them for fear of being struck down with leprosy. Hearing of Teodor's persistent questions, Mariana summoned him and demanded that he either leave or respect the monastery and its traditions, which included not talking about the citadel. Her tone was severe even in her limited French. He nodded to show that he had understood, but he could not forget the conflicting stories about the citadel that he heard in subsequent days.

Life at the monastery delighted Teodor, and he soon forgot all about his trip to India. He liked Aleppo and spoke long into the night with Father Ibrahim, whom he adored. William and Aisha grew attached to him, and he asked Mariana to be allowed to live at the monastery. He was a man who lacked certainty, as Hanna said when he met Teodor for the first time. He told everyone about his life and his childhood and his family, mourning his crushed hopes for Russia's October revolution, the great dream that was caving in before his eyes.

When Teodor was a young man of twenty, he had abandoned his studies in philosophy, certain that the world would wake to the dawn of justice when the Communists triumphed. He discovered a passion for photography when he met his first professional photographer, a Russian touring the villages of Holland and taking pictures of windmills. Along the way, he also photographed fleeting moments: drunks in bars, the funerals of villagers. The Russian photographer told Teodor, "The good life is a perpetual journey," and the camera was a passport that opened up every door. No one in the world could resist the temptation to stand in front of this miraculous device that stopped time. Teodor accompanied his Russian teacher on his travels and acted as his guide and interpreter. In return, the photographer taught him the basics of photography and spoke at length about the Russian peasantry and his faith in the upcoming revolution. It was a great moment of self-discovery for Teodor, who came to believe that he had been created to be a part of this new world. He despised his bourgeois family, who were astonished to hear their brilliant son repeating whole passages of *The Communist Manifesto* verbatim, speaking about the Paris Commune, and expounding on Engels's *The Origin of the Family, Private Property, and the State*. He asked them to redistribute their wealth to the poor, to rid themselves of the burden of oppressing the enslaved workers on their plantations in Africa.

Teodor lost no time. After the Russian photographer went back to Russia, he packed his own bag and left the family home. He showed his photographs to a well-known Dutch photographer who, on hearing his family name, decided to teach him photography. Teodor rented a room in the center of the city and looked for comrades who shared his ideals, eventually finding some young men from poor families who openly discussed Marx and Engels at the university. Teodor became a photographer; his talent amazed his Dutch mentor, although he disapproved of his student's notions, especially when he wouldn't stop preaching revolution. Teodor went to great lengths to seek out the poor in the factories and the peasants in the fields, the slaves, dock-workers, and prostitutes, and he took hundreds of photographs of them. He felt that the revolution in Amsterdam would be a long time in coming, so he traveled to Russia to take part in the struggle—the Russian Communist Party was attracting many revolutionaries from worn-out Europe. He arrived in Moscow and knocked on his former teacher's door. A haggard old woman answered and informed him that his teacher had died a few months after returning from Holland.

Nonetheless, Teodor became immersed in his new world. He rented a room in a student house where they all spoke constantly about the victorious revolution. His fervor reached its peak when he saw Lenin making a speech to the heaving crowds in Red Square. Voices were bawling, fists raised in the air. The revolution's victory was not to be doubted, but Teodor was a stranger. He walked through Moscow alone, looking for something that he didn't know how to define. He used to say, "When I see it, I'll know." An idea, a person, a gathering, a dream: he took pictures of every place and every face. He disapproved of executing the tsar's supporters without trial; his notions of justice were different. The weight he felt pressed down on his chest. His friends, intoxicated with victory, attacked and spat on him for talking like a member of the bourgeoisie. They wouldn't let him explain his point of view on justice, and they demanded that he leave their shared house.

He left all his things behind. He put a few items of clothing in a single bag along with his pictures and his camera and left Moscow. He didn't know where he was going; he couldn't go back to his family he had so abused; his break with them had been over more than a difference of opinion. He still remembered his Russian teacher's words about justice, that value to which Teodor was so drawn, and so he decided to go looking for it. He arrived in Istanbul, enjoying the idea of wandering at will. On the road, he felt that homeland and family and all the other things that implied an identity could easily be put up for debate, and so he simply relinquished them.

He arrived at Deir Zahr Al-Rumman one summer night and requested some food and a bed. The soft breeze at dawn captivated him. After his first week, he made an offer to Father Ibrahim: he would teach the children French, singing, and choral composition in exchange for food and lodging. It was a good deal and Father Ibrahim agreed to it, and he had no difficulty in convincing Mariana to set aside one of the second-floor guest rooms for the young man.

After he acquired the right to stay at the monastery, Teodor moved between Aleppo and Deir Zahr Al-Rumman. His feverish activity came back to him. Aisha taught him Arabic in return for teaching William photography. It was another good deal, and Teodor no longer felt powerless, homeless, and numb. He told himself he could work toward the realization of justice anywhere; the world was filled with injustice. He would be forty in a few months, and he still dreamed that Communism would bring happiness to all humanity. He ignored Mariana's entreaties to pray and teach the children religious choral music. He humored her by joining the ranks of worshippers at Sunday mass, but he told her that most of his students were Muslim and he himself wasn't Catholic. He almost told her he was an atheist but prudently held his tongue. He allowed the delighted children their choice of songs, and they sang folk songs with great zeal.

Every morning Aisha led him by the hand to a chair, where she taught him to read and write in Arabic. It was a ludicrous sight to see the eleven-year-old Aisha teaching this grown man, but Teodor persevered in his learning. He realized William had a passion for photography and taught him everything he knew, and he was a generous storyteller with the children of the village; they made a charming scene, gathered in a circle around their teacher under a large olive tree. Hanna would watch him from the window of his room, happy at the sight. Noisy life spread through the monastery; it was no longer rigid, silent, and sad. Teodor's piano could be heard for hours at a time, and the two children quickly learned to play. Within a few years, William and Aisha were traveling to the city to play in private concerts and sing in weekly choral concerts, and before long they were

earning money as musicians. At one concert, just as the choir was preparing to celebrate the end of the school year at the school run by the
Syriac Church in Aleppo, Helen approached the dais where the children's choir was standing and asked Teodor's permission to sing. She
was fourteen then, overweight and overlooked. She spent most of her
time with Maryam and the other Armenian orphan girls who lived at
the monastery.

Helen sang the first aria from *Aïda*. The choristers had failed to
memorize all the Italian words, and Teodor couldn't believe that this
overlooked girl, short and shy, was capable not only of memorizing
the words but of pulling out his heart from his chest. Overwhelmed
by the wondering looks on every side, Helen stopped singing the piece
(which she had performed in an imitation of Teodor) and fled to her
usual spot in the corner of the kitchen to continue peeling onions and
shelling lentils with her mother Futaim, the monastery's servant who
left every evening to go back to her home in Anabiya.

Decades later Aisha still remembered Teodor's time at the monastery. She smiled over the surprising turns that had befallen everyone,
especially Helen. Having been turned out by Mariana and failing to
see Hanna, Aisha went for a walk through the fields and was tired by
the time she reached Futaim's house in Anabiya. It occurred to her to
knock on the door and greet the kindhearted servant, who had grown
old by now, but she kept on walking. Suddenly appalled, she remembered meeting Yousef in the stable—she had never really thought about
it before, but a quarter of a century had passed since that meeting. . . .

When the First World War began, Aisha didn't understand why
Ottoman soldiers were attacking houses in Anabiya and the monastery, emptying out the cellars and leading the young men away in
chains. She saw these country boys walking with bowed heads to the
train station, where they would be taken to the front lines. Yousef
was among them, walking alongside hundreds of young men who
had been caught in the fields they had fled to. They dragged Yousef
out of the monastery's stable, where he had been hiding for months.
William tried to prevent the soldiers from taking him, but the coarse

troops hurled abuse at him. Aisha saw Yousef walking, head down and hands shackled like the others, but two days later he escaped from the convoy of forced conscripts. Along with some fellahin, he was able to jump from the train carriage and push deep into the fields around the village of Midan Akbas. They walked at night along familiar roads until they reached the caves of Mount Simeon. They decided to live in the mountains, where the Ottoman soldiers would never be able to reach them. Yousef and his fellow escapees knew all the secret paths between Qastal Jandu and Sheikh Al-Hadid. They continued through the rugged mountains. The fellahin opened their doors to them whenever they needed shelter, and from Sheikh Al-Hadid they returned to Bulbul via the Rajo road. They felt safe in those desolate places.

Yousef spent a year in the mountain caverns. He and his companions went out at night to look for food, but they found nothing, even when they attacked the houses of the rich. He missed his old life, reading in the library of Mala Mannan and studying Kurdish, which he was determined to learn to read and write. He missed the room of the dinosaur skeleton, which for him had turned into a teller of thrilling tales about the history of our distant ancestors.

Yousef and his fellow escapees walked through the ruins of the dead cities at night, hovering around nearby villages and going back to their caves at dawn. He asked around in search of Sherko, the legendary bandit, folk hero to the poverty-stricken Kurds. Yousef didn't have to wait long before three armed men led him to their leader, who did not hide his admiration of his old enemy's son. He listened to Yousef respectfully—after all, not only had he graduated from schools attended by the rich, and read many books from his grandfather's library, but he also spoke about justice, and the tyranny of the rich, and his desire to read and write in Kurdish. After that single meeting, Sherko decided to allow Yousef to join him and to speak in his name, unlike other escaped conscripts, whom he didn't trust.

This new life was harsh. Yousef was not used to sleeping in caves and fighting against the aghas and their men, and also against the Turkish soldiers who had been hunting Sherko for more than five years. He robbed the sleep from the government and the vali, and he struck terror into the hearts of the aghas. It was in a long speech of Yousef's that Sherko, for the first time, heard about the Kurdish people's right to an independent state. This huge, powerfully muscled man smiled like a child and nodded fervently when Yousef explained his views on their right to work toward this state, just as Arab intellectuals were working toward secession from the Ottoman state and founding a state of their own.

Sherko didn't grasp much of what Yousef said, but he enjoyed hearing the poetry of Mala Jaziri, most of which Yousef had memorized. He would stand at the top of the mountain looking out over Afrin and howl like a jackal as he reflected that fate was neither visible nor the stuff of daily life. He spent a lot of time with Sherko, joining him on his increasingly intensive raids against Ottoman convoys. The impossible, he reflected, had come to pass. By his third year, Yousef had started to enjoy this life. He no longer really missed his family home; he had slipped inside it more than once, but he couldn't bear seeing his father's grief at losing all his money and his land above the river. He decided to run the risk of going to see the dinosaur skeleton and paused at the monastery at a delicate moment. Occasionally he paid Hanna a short visit, during which he struggled to find the words to express the peculiarities of fate, both his own and Hanna's. He would make do with the little that Zakariya offered him on behalf of the monastery, but Hanna always asked him to come back if he needed somewhere to shelter; he admired Yousef's bravery, and his odd questions.

Yousef also spent a few nights in Zakariya's stable, especially during the winter, when life in the caves became precarious. It was impossible for Sherko's men to die of hunger, however; hard men, they were capable of swallowing dog or any living thing they could catch, and hunting was plentiful in the mountains.

Arif was worried about his son, whose power and thuggery increased. He was displeased that his son had joined Sherko. Like his leader, Yousef was now wanted for a number of crimes. The fellahin recognized him when Sherko's band waylaid a convoy of Ottoman soldiers leading a group of men in chains to the war. The convoy included seven large carriages filled with wheat, tomatoes, preserves, ground lentils, and flour, all seized from houses in Rajo. The ambush was carefully and precisely laid, and Sherko's men attacked at the crossroads with Kafr Janna. The troops were set free, their weapons were seized, and the band drove the carriages to Marimeen where, that same night, they distributed part of the spoils to the poor of the region, who knew them well. They hid the rest of the provisions in the caves around the village of Qibar. The operation was an act of glaring defiance, and Ottoman soldiers attacked the house of Arif Sheikh Musa Agha in retaliation. They smashed his water pitchers and insulted Arif, who threatened that his train would take them when they least expected it. The important thing, for Yousef, was that they didn't reach the dinosaur's room.

The Ottoman Empire lost the war. The campaigns came to a halt, and the Ottoman troops withdrew from the villages. The vacant cities and villages were instead occupied by the French in 1920, but the task of Sherko and his men was not over. Disagreement crept in among the outlaws at times. Some wanted to go home but didn't dare do so for fear of arrest. Sherko would repeat only that all men must die, and sure enough, his turn came, in the winter of 1922, at the hand of a masked agha who followed Sherko to the house of a widow he had married in secret; the couple used to meet from time to time on the outskirts of the village of Jindiras.

It was a sad day for his companions. Yousef thought it was impossible that anyone could inherit the mantle of Sherko's legend. He deliberated with his comrades over the offer of amnesty and pardon for all, in exchange for surrendering their weapons and pledging not to take up arms against the French state. Yousef carried on the negotiations from the stables of Deir Zahr Al-Rumman. He examined the guarantees carried by Mala Mannan, who was pleased to be made intermediary. Yousef spent most of his time reading and waiting. Every few days Hanna sent for him, and he slipped furtively into his room, followed by Zakariya and Father Ibrahim, and they would all have dinner together. Those were Hanna's favorite days. He urged Yousef to accept the pardon. Two weeks before Yousef left the stable, Aisha came in looking for her foal, and she saw him feeding the horses in his guise as a new groom. She looked at him for a long time. At fifteen years old, her breasts were small but full. She recognized him at once. Smiling, she went up to him and held out a hand to greet him, saying, "I know you're not the new groom. You're Yousef, you're the son of Uncle Arif Agha, who owns the long train that comes from behind the hill." And she pointed north.

His gaze clung to her eyelashes. She was wearing a dress patterned with roses. Yousef had thought she was a young girl, but she informed him she was a grown woman. She flushed and felt a light tremor befall her body, newly opened and daily developing in its curves. Speech came back to him. She told him not to be afraid, that she wouldn't betray him—everyone remembered how he had attacked the Ottoman convoy. She added, "You're a hero to the fellahin." Yousef was frozen to the spot. She left but came back a few hours later, carrying a basket of fruit; this time she didn't say a word, but before she hurried away, she let him look into her eyes. For two weeks, she kept bringing him special food. She was embarrassed whenever she looked at him in silence, and she never lingered long. He couldn't say goodbye to her. The amnesty agreement was concluded, dinner in Hanna's room took a long time that night, and Hanna warmly bade Yousef goodbye in the morning. Everyone bade him farewell, and the procession walked off behind Mala Mannan, who accompanied them to the saraya of Afrin as Hanna watched from a distance. Some of the outlaws had preferred to join Ibrahim Hananu's revolution. He turned to Aisha, who seemed to have taken the moving scene somewhat to heart, and said, "It will be hard to forget such men. I should have done what Yousef did."

There were more than thirty of them. They were amazed when they entered the courtyard of the saraya and saw a vast crowd of fellahin waiting for them, raising their fists in the air and shouting in Kurdish, "Long live Sherko," "Long live Yousef," and so on, naming all the comrades in turn. The women were ululating. Police and French troops encircled the place to ensure that everything went off peacefully. They recognized the difficulty of controlling an excited crowd that was welcoming heroes who had lived in the mountains, threatening the unjust aghas and the janissaries who had raided their homes for years.

Yousef never forgot that moment, nor the faces of the crowd. He decided that it was glorious to work on behalf of the oppressed. Wasting no time, he returned to take care of his father Arif, who had grown into an elderly man. Arif shared his tobacco with Mabrouk, his old servant, who preferred to live out his days with his master rather than returning to his family somewhere unfamiliar in Ethiopia, where he was originally from. The agha could no longer pay him but shared all the food and tobacco he possessed. The two old men spent their time talking about the past, watching the train, standing on the hill overlooking the tracks, and waving to the driver. Arif would give his instructions to the driver of his train, his words scattering on the air, and then they would go home to prepare some food. Every day, in total earnestness, they carried out the same actions. No one else was left from the family. Yousef spent most of his time in Grandfather's House. He couldn't believe the utter neglect into which his dinosaur had fallen; they had hung necklaces of dried okra around its neck and stuffed sacks of barley and jars of grape molasses by its feet. Yousef cleaned the place thoroughly and appointed a mason to block the windows and doors, and he stopped up every hole with stones and clay. He didn't want anyone going near his dear friend, the extinct creature.

Yousef never forgot Aisha's gaze, her trembling lips. He thought about her all the time, but he didn't dare ask for her hand. In any case, he had much to do in his new life, determined as he was not to succumb to the image of the former hero. He conferred with his father, who made no secret of his admiration for his strong son who had fought alongside his mortal enemy and spent nine years in the mountains living through danger and primitive conditions, experiencing cold, hunger, and thirst. Arif's lucid hours never lasted for long, and before long he would return to his delirium. He nodded in agreement

when Yousef made light of their having moved out of the agha class
and reverted back to being middle-class fellahin; despite their tum-
ble from the higher reaches of society, they certainly weren't paupers.
There was still some land scattered here and there that could respect-
ably support a small family, and a house in Aziziya that Arif had
bought on that long-ago evening of debauchery in order to please the
Jewish courtesan Widad. But his wife, Khatoun Um Yousef, had vehemently disputed this action. Already ill, she had died a few days after
that heated argument, and Arif forgot all about marrying Widad, who
had furnished the apartment in the Italian style. No one had entered
it since the flood.

Leaving his father in the care of Mabrouk the servant, Yousef
opened the door of the apartment, which was submerged in dust. The
sofas were eaten away, the bedposts rotten, the silk bedsheets yellowed
and foul-smelling. Even the mirror frame was decayed. Mice had
gnawed everything, and dead rats were scattered all over.

The apartment was utterly wrecked. Yousef threw everything away
and left the windows open for a few days to air it out. He stopped up
the holes and made some repairs, and in less than a month the apartment was habitable. It contained a small bed and a small desk where
Yousef sat for hours at a time, writing articles about the Kurdish question and attacking the Sykes-Picot agreement, which disregarded
entirely the right of the Kurds to a state.

His correspondence with Celadet Ali Bedirxan gave him great
hope and a conviction that the struggle for a Kurdish state was worthy
of great sacrifice. When darkness fell, he would sit on the spacious balcony for hours, watching the stars and remembering Aisha, her long,
deep glances and her quivering lips. He reflected that a single moment
could live within us forever.

Aisha, who would take her secondary school exams in a few weeks,
lived between the monastery and the house of her aunt Souad, who
occasionally welcomed Yousef to her atelier and called for the strong
coffee he liked to be brought for him. Souad enjoyed hearing Yousef
talk about the dinosaur and his life in the mountains. His visits to her

soon became regular. She liked his silence, the earnest way he dealt with weighty issues. She remembered when he was a boy and Hanna was looking after him at school. Now, in August 1926, she was thinking about her first fashion show. She spent a lot of time with Azar, sketching out the platform he would construct in her courtyard. Souad was exuberant as she remembered her teacher Hassaniya's words: "We create clothes for souls, not bodies. Bodies are idiots, souls are intelligent."

Aisha would always remember those days. She wasn't consciously thinking about Yousef, but he remained in her memory as a powerful and attractive man. She tried to support her aunt when she grew sad, burdened with worries after a visit to Hajja Amina Bayazidi, the preacher famed for her extremism. All through the city flew her harsh attacks against the municipality's decision against abolishing the regulation of prostitution, refusing the demands of the men of religion to close down the state-sponsored brothels, those dens of sin. She was known for a duaa she had written in which she eulogized Sultan Abdel Hamid II, the Ottoman Empire, and the Sheikh Al-Islam Abulhuda Al-Sayyadi, whom the unionists had beaten in the streets of Istanbul before he was exiled to Buyukada in the Princes' Islands, where he died in 1909. Just as well-known was her fervent farewell to the Aleppo soldiers heading to fight in the empire's army in Gallipoli in 1915, which saw a victory for the Ottomans. More than ten years had passed since she and many other women had welcomed what Aleppan troops remained on their victorious return from battle. The women let out ululations and prayed for God's mercy for the martyrs; they remembered Amina's declaration that the troops would be crammed in among the Prophet's companions on Judgment Day, to raise up the banner of Islam.

The old woman, an Ottoman partisan, didn't let much pass by without comment, the citadel included. She attacked Hanna and the myth of his sainthood, and she accused Ahmed Bayazidi, her own late brother, of heresy for having raised a Nasrany child and allowing him to mix with the Muslim Bayazidi children. She made the same accusation against her nephew Zakariya and her niece Souad and publicly disowned them after a stormy conversation with Souad, whom she summoned a few days before her fashion show. Amina's adherents had told her they had seen Souad walking bareheaded in the street for the first time; they also said she spent her evenings in Shahbandar Casino with her Jewish friend Azar and his family.

On that day, Souad went to her aunt Amina's house without a hijab. She sat down and waited for her to speak. Amina drew out the silence, looking at a large Qur'an that was open in front of her, while a servant scrutinized the Hajja for orders from time to time. Eventually, Amina lifted her head and closed the Qur'an. She asked for lemon juice for her niece. Amina asked Souad to take back her decision to remove her hijab; if she did so, it would be as if it had never happened. But Souad, who was now fifty years old, said calmly, "I am doing something even worse than uncovering my head." Hajja Amina didn't rise to Souad's provocation and calmly retorted, "Put your hijab back on and do what you like. Your Lord sees you in your bedroom, but we see you in the street." She went on to say that *they* would never allow bareheaded women to walk in the streets that were under *their* control, repeating the Prophet's hadith, "Whoever sees something abominable, let him change it by his own hand." She didn't complete the hadith but went on to say, "We will change it by our own hands, and we will not be content with the weakest faith."

Souad drank her lemon juice. She asked the servant for coffee and took out a cigarette case that her husband Hassan Masabny had bought for her when they visited London in 1910, when he obtained a contract to build a large textile factory that ran on electricity. This project, destroyed by the war before it took off, was the reason he went bankrupt and wandered aimlessly in the streets, only to catch from his Jewish friend Raoul the plague that turned them both into corpses that had to be burned.

Souad took a sip from her coffee and looked thoughtfully at her aunt, whom she loved. She didn't believe what she had heard about Amina's connections to extremist men of religion. Out loud, Souad said that forty years earlier Amina had predicted she would live a long time. She still believed it, just as she had when she was a child, so she wanted to live, as she understood the term, the life she deserved. She reminded Amina of the Bayazidi family inheritance of fear, despite their influence, and the heavy ledgers they were so proud of, and their life amid other people's numbers. Souad added affectionately that she had inherited everything that was strong and true from Amina herself— she didn't want to live like a number. What she was doing harmed no one; it was merely another way of understanding life. She reminded her aunt that she had never objected to Hanna's presence in their house and had even interceded to help complete his adoption. Hajja Amina was silent. She ignored what Souad had said about Hanna and, in a less severe tone, repeated her request that Souad put her hijab back on if she wanted to live in peace. She added that her other nephews, who heeded her, and their veiled wives who wore long, loose coats and covered their faces, were all the family she needed. They never missed any prayers and they didn't go around with Nasranys and Jews, unlike Souad and her brother, who had been so impudent as to join a Christian in building a castle for whores. How, Amina added, could these sins be wiped out without her intervention? What would she say to her Lord when she stood in front of Him on the day of reckoning?

Her tone altered again, growing tender. She begged her niece to respect her wishes, because her sheikhs were reporting back that Souad was mingling with French people and other foreigners, drinking alcohol and attending raucous shows at the theater. They considered her a fallen woman who was bringing shame on the Bayazidi family, which was known to have kept the secrets of the caliphate for decades. Souad responded by asking her aunt to return to her true faith, which respected others and showed them kindness. She reminded her aunt of the pain she felt after visions that prophesied a death.

Souad fell silent when she saw her aunt's closed eyes bulge in anger. She regretted having provoked her aunt, who warned Souad that rumors were circulating that she was thinking of holding a fashion show in her own home, to be attended by men and fallen women. Aunt Amina hoped she would reflect long and hard about this. Imitating foreigners to such a degree was dangerous, and only Christian or Jewish women, or apostates, could do it. The word *apostate* rang out clearly. Hearing it, Souad realized it would be impossible for her aunt to return from wherever she had gone. She had become a copy of those extremists who carried swords into shops that sold drinks and threatened to slaughter the proprietors unless they stopped serving alcohol. They would smash the bottles while French soldiers stood by, watching in silence. Amina added that God had accepted her repentance and she no longer saw the beyond, but she still knew she would die soon, even though she was strong and healthy.

Souad thought about this woman, whom she had known as abstemious, wonderful, affectionate. Isolation had turned her into a woman who openly declared the need for a return to the Ottoman caliphate, where sharia law was enforced in the streets by arm and sword. She remembered a visit her aunt had made to her when she was first married to Hassan Masabny. When Aunt Amina knocked on the door to Souad's pleased surprise, she welcomed her aunt and carried out her every wish, but she was astounded by the intensity of Amina's grief over Sheikh Al-Islam Abulhuda Al-Sayyadi's death in exile. She humored her aunt, sweetened her mood, and offered her condolences. Souad was even more surprised by her aunt's protégées when they came in a body to her house. They were different women from the ones she knew; they kissed Amina's hand, asked her for a duaa, and put their young children into her arms so she could spit in their mouths and bless them.

Then they didn't leave the house for three days. They donated their bracelets and their gold trinkets in a leather bag, which ended up weighing more than a kilogram, so that Aunt Amina could distribute these goods to any needy supporters of their martyred sheikh. Souad was baffled. She tried to draw her aunt to one side for some privacy, but found herself unable to do so. Her house turned into a shrine where Aunt Amina pronounced fatwas on sexual congress before wudu' to women loaded down with affectation and hypocrisy, wealthier and even stupider than they should be. They asked their brother Hassan to spend the night away from his house until they had squeezed everything they possibly could out of their seclusion with the saintly sheikha who was usually very reclusive.

Before she left, Aunt Amina showed her approval of the family that aligned itself with her views. She asked Souad to keep to her duties of obedience and prayer but whispered that if she had any complaints about her husband or his family, she, Amina, could intervene and protect her. No man or woman from the Masabny clan would dare cause trouble for the niece of Hajja Amina Bayazidi.

After this surprise visit, which had given her so much pleasure, Souad's sisters-in-law changed their treatment of her. They no longer showed any disapproval of Souad, they reduced their unannounced, critical visits, and before long they had stopped these visits entirely. Laughing, Souad told Hassaniya that a visit from her aunt was more powerful than one from the vali himself.

But today, on her way to her aunt's house, people looked at her like she was from another planet. For the first time, she was afraid to walk the streets. Her aunt had made it permissible to shed her blood. She felt trapped in this city and deeply regretted not having asked her husband if they could travel to Rome and Paris to wait out the war and the famine. Two days before he died, Souad had teased him by saying, "In the morning I'll cook you four carats of Bohemian crystal, and I'll put some Kashmiri silk on the side, and for dinner we'll have that sofa from Istanbul, the one inlaid with pure silver."

Her aunt's words had been cruel and resolute, like one of the fatwas issued by those sheikhs she worked alongside, the ones who praised her piety and her extremism in applying sharia. They called her Virtuous Sister of the Believers, Hajja Amina Bayazidi. Souad got up and tried to kiss her aunt for the last time, but Amina stopped her. She asked Souad to think carefully about what she had asked.

Sad and frustrated, Souad left her aunt's house. Her feet felt heavy as she regarded the locked doors around her. She remembered taking Grandfather Najib's hand on the day he taught her the names of each one of his doves, boasting that they would find their way back to him even if he released them in Istanbul. Today the streets were empty, and the few passersby looked askance at her for going uncovered in this district. She went on to Jamiliyya; the breeze was refreshing, and there was still some time left before it fell dark. She wanted everyone in the city to see her without a hijab. No one blocked her way. She arrived at Azar's office, where Sara kissed her warmly. In the few months since she had last seen her, Sara had aged considerably. She told Souad she was cleaning the office and that Azar wouldn't be long; he was with the carpenters, who were setting up the platform for her fashion show. Sara asked for two tickets so she could attend the show with Simon, a hawker of novelties in Sweiqa, who had been courting her recently. Sara added that he was sixty-five, but he was kind, and she would marry him if he asked her. She talked without stopping, and Souad nodded, smiling. She wrote a note to Azar, asking him to come to her atelier urgently—the fashion show wasn't going ahead.

In the preceding days, Souad had been very enthusiastic, flying around like a butterfly as she watched the volunteer models strutting in their first rehearsal for a show that she had waited to stage for over twenty years. She had been very grateful for her friend Azar's presence, although she was saddened by his current difficulties.

Azar had changed considerably after the famine and the end of the First World War. He became frightened of everything as he remembered the corpses of the starving that he had buried himself: people from his own sect, friends both Muslim and Christian. He returned dozens of times to David's last moments. David had knocked on his door after midnight and screamed in Azar's face that he was starving. Azar, who was carrying a gas lamp, was embarrassed and said that he was starving too; nothing had passed his children's lips in three days. David's eyes called him a liar, and for a moment, Azar thought he was going to attack the house and search for food, but he crumpled suddenly. With a sorrowful look, David said, "If I die tonight, it's on your head," then hurried down the stairs. Azar shut the door, frightened. He examined all the food he had left, but it wouldn't last his two children and his wife, the rapacious Misha, more than a few days. He

thought that in four days' time, he would think of something, just as
he always had in the preceding few months. He saw that he had to ignore appeals from his sect for donations on behalf of the starving. He
still had a fair amount of money, but if the prices of flour, bread, and
lentils continued to inflate, bankruptcy was inevitable. He still hadn't
forgotten that he had lived and studied on charity, and his liberal donations were necessary to expunge his painful memories. He never
forgot his mother's face when she answered a knock on the door and
reached out to take a bag, muttering phrases of gratitude. She would
open the bag to find a used woolen pullover that she would hide from
Azar. The next day she would alter it and wash it and convince Azar
that she had bought it from a hawker, that it would protect him from
Aleppo's gnawing cold, that he must look and admire how nice the
colors were.

Azar never forgot old images from his younger days; they kept him
awake at night. He remembered Hanna and Zakariya losing wagers and
pushing coins into his pocket, or sharing the notebooks that Ahmed
Bayazidi had bought them. His memories became even gloomier when
he married Misha, daughter of Raoul the goldsmith, who boasted that
he had paid part of Azar's school fees in Rome whenever someone
praised his work or his designs. Misha Raoul wasn't beautiful or ugly,
more the type who didn't attract anyone's notice, but she was proud
and haughty and could spend hours talking about all the things she
owned. Azar's father convinced him she was a suitable match, adding
that it lay within his grasp to lift the family out of poverty. Simply being a skillful engineer wasn't sufficient to save your family from the
bottomless pit that was poverty. Hayyim Istanbouli didn't conceal his
terror that Azar would be trapped into marrying Cosette; it was said
by the worshippers in the temple that, as was the custom among liberated Jews, Azar and Cosette didn't hide their relationship. Hayyim
Istanbouli declared that Cosette was more liberated than she should
be, and before long she wouldn't be able to resist betraying him with
a former lover.

Everything was settled according to the wishes of his father, who died within a few months of the wedding; he hadn't waited to see his family leave the bottomless pit. From the first day, Azar felt keenly the quandary of living with a woman who constantly reminded him of her father's generosity toward him. He tried to forget the matter and told himself she would be useful for hatching children. He wouldn't lack the means to live as he pleased. Before long, he felt that he didn't have enough time to see his two children. He was no longer surprised at Misha Raoul's transformations when, after the birth of her first child, she became an extremist. She made plain her hatred of his Christian and Muslim friends; she mocked haughty Souad Bayazidi and ridiculed Hanna and Zakariya and their citadel, calling them pimps. Not even David and Sara escaped her scorn. And all the while, she would enumerate the grants she and her father had made to the children of their sect and show off the few pictures taken on a visit to the orphanage that depended entirely on her generosity. On that occasion, she hadn't let the child to whom she was offering a meal eat anything until she had been photographed feeding him a crust of bread from her own hand.

Azar immersed himself in his office. He didn't want to go home and instead took his meals alone or with the atelier's laborers. Misha had become a stranger who shared his bed once a week, then once a month, and after that they both disregarded their connection entirely and spent what little time they shared discussing matters relating to the children. He realized he had committed a grave error and was glad to return to his secret life. For the first time, he felt he had been avenged for her arrogance and her putrid smell, her stubborn adherence to practicing every extremist Jewish rite without exception. When he saw her covering her hair and her face, he laughed inwardly but, as usual, made no comment. He wasn't really interested. He bought an apartment opposite the apartment of his friend Arif Sheikh Musa Agha and furnished it according to his own taste. It was a small apartment in a building where most of the residents were his friends, concealing their never-ending amours. He was delighted beyond measure in later years when Yousef married Aisha, who always looked after him so carefully. He often ate dinner with the couple, or Aisha would let herself into his apartment with the key he had given her and put some food on the table for him. She didn't care if it went moldy; she wanted him to always find some food when he came back to his little home.

Azar was fond of splitting his life into distinct eras: pre-Rome and post-Rome, pre-marriage and post-marriage. The principal division of his life was now pre-famine and post-famine. He felt truly paralyzed when he wandered the city and saw dying children, their bodies disintegrating on the roadside. Their breastbones stood out, their faces were yellow, and they hadn't had a full meal for months. Several times he considered moving to Europe but didn't have the courage.

The night of David's visit, Azar thought about sharing the little he had with him—how often David had been decent and generous to all—but fear of Misha let him down. It took Azar a while to fall asleep again, and he was woken at dawn by a knock on the door. He found some of his Jewish neighbors throwing themselves on his shoulder and mourning the death of David. They asked him to go with them to St. Louis Hospital to receive the body and bury it. On their way to the hospital, three men whom he sometimes saw at the temple on Saturdays told him that David had attacked the grain store in Sweiqa and killed the guard who seized him on his way out. The guard's companions attacked David and wouldn't allow any of the passersby, who were on their way to morning prayer, to step in and save him. They let him bleed to death. After the burial, Azar was taken by surprise when the family of the murdered guard attacked his house and David's. Both houses were looted, and the raiders threatened to avenge their relative's blood with Azar's. The only way he could think to extricate himself from this feud was to pay blood money of more than 30,000 gold liras.

Azar never forgot David's still face in the hospital. They had been childhood friends, and David had looked out for him on every occasion. He wasn't like the other boys of his generation, and despite being desperately poor, David had been sensitive and noble and had offered his services to everyone without expecting anything in return.

After David's death, Azar faced a worse turn of events. Misha began to gather up leftover food from the table and asked his clients for their old clothes on the pretext of donating them to charitable organizations. Instead, she was storing them in a warehouse until it was filled to the top. When she went to Souad's house with Azar, Misha asked for permission to take the leftover food to Sara, now a widow, who had fallen ill and hadn't cooked in two days. At first, Azar complied with his wife, thinking that the scars of hunger would soon fade. Souad made light of what had happened, told him this difficult period would pass, and advised him to be patient. But Misha's sickness of greed would not abate. She scolded Azar in front of others, reckoned up what he paid, and accused him of being a spendthrift. She went to clients asking to see his bill, presenting herself as a partner in the business. She scrutinized the prices of the little meat she bought each week and pored over the gas bills in the same way. She asked him to be more stinting; the world was hard, and she didn't want her children to die like David in the next famine. Sara, Azar's sister, hadn't been able to bear her hunger and wandered the streets with a shepherd she had met coming out of a brothel. She offered herself to him in exchange for two dinners, one for her and one for her sick mother. She traveled with him outside the city, struggled clumsily out of her clothing so her lower half was bare, and she slept with him on the back seat of a carriage. Afterward he was kind to her; he bought enough food to last her and her mother three days, and they arranged to meet in the same place in a week's time. That day, having arranged her dress so he could take her without needing to remove any clothing, she accompanied him to a house in Jalloum that he had borrowed from his friend. She spent three days there, eating whatever she liked. The nomad shepherd threw some food to the dog that was always at his side, and Sara picked it up to send some to her mother. When Azar discovered what was going on, Sara spat in his face for allowing her, her four children, and his own mother to starve. She said he was the reason David was dead. Shame enveloped Azar. He would always remember that he had lived on charity and stinted his people out of food during the famine.

Bitterly, Azar told Souad about Sara's story and Misha's thirst for revenge, cursing the circumstances that led an innocent woman to become the mistress of a shepherd. Souad faced the matter squarely and listed the girls from ancient families who now worked as servants in exchange for food. She tried to comfort him, but he just shook his head, repeating that someone who hadn't suffered had no right to talk about the pain of hunger.

Habit became gratifying for Azar as he received his wife's thanks for his charity whenever he "donated" money to her. In the months before he divorced her, she became frightened of everything. She would kiss his hand in exchange for the money he gave her for the household expenses (which had increased by more than half), thanking him and singing his praises as if he were a generous patron. He felt haughty and amused; her snobbery had been smashed to pieces, her spirit utterly broken. Since the famine, Azar had found life with her unbearable; he tried to save his children from her, but she took him by surprise, carrying them off to America after she secretly sold everything her father had left her.

Azar no longer took any care over his appearance. Though he wasn't yet fifty, he became middle-aged. He lost the gleam in his eyes and no longer quarreled or threatened if someone swindled him; he became totally docile. His clients made fun of him, but he didn't respond, and they didn't turn their backs on him. He had a genius for finding solutions to the hardest problems that arose during construction of large, beautiful buildings, and he was equally talented at finding the best architects to work alongside him.

When Souad told him of her plan to hold a fashion show, the gleam came back into his eyes. He spent an entire night thinking of the design; he wanted it to be a work of art whose echoes would reach the fashion houses in Paris. He asked William to paint all the work phases and lost himself in designing a platform to adjoin the large room where the models would emerge as, from the upper windows, colored confetti descended on them like late rain.

He was uneasy when Sara told him that Souad didn't seem quite well and was waiting for him in her atelier. He hurried out of his office and quickly walked the short distance from Jamiliyya to Jadida. Souad was expecting him and Zakariya was with her, trying to persuade her to cancel the exhibition; he took Aunt Amina's threat very seriously. Souad was of a similar mind, but she didn't like Zakariya's attitude of appeasing the old woman. She asked Azar to think long and hard about it all, and he lit a cigarette, and the three of them sat in silence. Azar no longer felt like one of the family; Zakariya was a stranger to him now, and it had been some time since they had met up and talked like they used to. Azar had changed since the night of Zakariya's surprise visit with Hanna; at least he had lost his old sense of fun. The death of David, followed by the death of his mother and Misha's bolt abroad with his children, had dug deep into his soul. The worst thing, which he confessed to no one, was how much he missed his children, Huda and Sami.

From Souad's hints, Zakariya understood that a battle had commenced. Though she had never been a fool, Souad was unafraid. She could easily spend hours bringing someone around to support an idea of hers, and now at fifty years, she was seeking out a battle that would set the city on fire. At that moment, Zakariya found her frightening, powerful, and reckless. The next morning she took her coffee with Maryam as usual, then asked her four models (one of whom was Aisha) to think for the last time about whether they still wanted to go on. They were all eager to continue, especially Maryam, who wanted to show off her figure. She was twenty and William still hovered around her, as he had since their days together in the monastery, although he went no further than a few words and some sick glances. Maryam thought the show would be her golden opportunity, one she wouldn't let slip through her fingers; she intended to net a foreign bridegroom and leave the city with him.

Aisha was working backstage in the large space set aside as a changing room. Each model would come out four times during the evening, and the show would last for three hours. An Armenian band would play classical music, and Teodor would accompany them on a grand piano that Azar had borrowed from Huda Shamoun, now Madame Giovanni, an enthusiastic supporter of the show. She had already offered to buy five outfits at whatever price Souad named, and she promised to stage the show in Venice, Naples, and Rome.

On the night of the show, everything was in order. Azar was examining the stage and the lights—he had asked William to design every detail—and the guests were beginning to arrive, the men in formal suits accompanied by their elegant, affected wives. It was the first time they had seen in Aleppo anything similar to what they had seen in Paris and Rome. Everyone was excited. In the first row were ranged the foreign consuls and their wives, including the Italian consul, who was joined by his wife, Huda Shamoun. Next came the new businessmen, with Orhan, chairman of the French Bank, in their midst. French officers and their wives occupied the far corner of the back row. Yousef Sheikh Musa was assisting William, who never stopped taking pictures. Yousef wanted to see Aisha strutting on the stage; he had spent many long nights thinking about her. At this point, Yousef and Aisha had spoken by themselves a few times, but his shyness prevented him from declaring his love, and his fear of marriage stopped him from saying anything about the matter to Souad. Yousef believed that Aisha would refuse him; those old glances she gave him in the past were mere signals of her approval of her youthful outlaw cousin who had been the talk of the city at that time, after he attacked the Ottoman convoy. Years had passed since that attack, and it had been three years since their meeting in the stable. Since then Yousef had done nothing that attracted any notice; the few articles he had published hadn't provoked any outcry. But many people hovered around Aisha, who had finished her secondary school studies a few days earlier. A newspaper had published a picture of her with her friends, presenting her as a symbol of modernity in a city that had spent centuries debating what was halal and what was haram, a city that had encouraged successive Ottomans over four centuries to increase the number of fatwas it issued.

Souad came out onto the stage wearing a long, modest black dress and a floral headcovering. Speaking in French and Arabic, she announced that her city would never die. Everyone felt she was on the verge of collapse despite her forceful front, and no one understood the connection between the undying city and the fashion exhibition. Souad thanked Madame Giovanni and Azar, and her team of models; she recalled her teacher, Madame Hassaniya, and wished everyone a pleasant evening, promising that the artistry would astonish them from the first number of the show. She descended from the stage and entered the room where the models were waiting to walk out, from which she could watch everything unfold.

The models went out, Maryam at their head wearing a belted linen evening dress, something like the robe of a seventeenth-century Italian barone. She was disconcerted, unsure how to endure all these stares, especially that of Orhan, who was struck at the sight of her figure, lost in the folds of the flowing dress. The models completed a circuit, went around again, and stopped, just as Azar had taught them; he had gathered his information about fashion shows from films, for which he had recently developed a mania. Murmurs of admiration rose from every side. William was taking pictures of Maryam and no one else. The second part went even better. This time the models' poses were more confident, less shy and trembling. Everything was exquisite, displaying the elegance that Souad had loved all her life. Everyone was eager for the show to move quickly so they could see more of these captivating designs, apart from William and Orhan, who were both staring at Maryam from different corners. Madame Huda Shamoun Giovanni stood to applaud more than once, repeating in Italian that Aleppo had a different flavor now. Teodor had begun to play the piano in the first part, and now, as he performed the opening from *Aïda*, the audience heard an entrancing voice—and after half a minute, Helen appeared, singing with all her might. Her emergence struck the consul and the foreign guests like a lightning bolt and aroused the amazement of the Aleppans, who had initially thought that the singer must be Italian.

Helen's voice touched them all with a special magic. The models came back to present the third section after a long ovation that had forced Teodor and Helen to take their bows twice. Suddenly the place went dark as the electricity was cut off. Bearded men carrying swords and knives and brandishing torches stormed in from all sides, from neighboring rooftops and the door and even scaling down the walls. Their apparent leader said they would never allow this depravity to take place in their virtuous city, and a man in a mask added that this was a message from the righteous to the infidels. They threw a flaming lump of pitch onto the stage and disappeared. Souad was afraid that the models would choke to death in their room, but Azar's design included an emergency exit through the room that Ahmed Bayazidi had separated off for Hanna's living quarters. The place was surrounded. The French soldiers fired into the air to disperse the attackers, but they arrested no one. Souad stayed in her seat, seemingly oblivious to the fire, while everyone else escaped and scattered through the neighboring streets. The terrified Aisha found herself next to Yousef, who took her by the hand. They went into a side street, then turned left to find themselves in Bab Al-Faraj.

The stage burned up entirely, along with the lemon tree and the rest of the nearby planters. Chaos reigned in the quarter, but Souad stayed where she was, arranging her clothes with silent, preternatural calm. Some of the young men who had been in the audience rushed to put out the fire, but within half an hour, the ground of the courtyard was no more than a ruin. Azar left everything and walked out. He got into the Italian consul's car with Madame Huda Shamoun Giovanni; it was she for whom he had named his daughter, in honor of their long friendship. He was silent. He was thinking of the girl who had sung the aria from *Aïda*, and of Maryam, whose dress had caught fire; she had been taken to St. Louis Hospital in an ambulance. Everyone had dispersed by now, and police surrounded the place, refusing to allow anyone near. Suddenly, in the middle of the street, Azar realized he had left Souad there alone. Fearing that someone might harm her, he asked the driver to stop and let him out. He had to share the wreckage with her, he decided. By the time Azar arrived back at the

Bayazidi house, it was almost ten o'clock. He found Souad sitting by herself, making no response to a sergeant who was begging her to reply to his questions so he could open an investigation.

She remained where she was, sitting in silence on the burned-out stage. Azar sat next to her and heard her mumble to herself, "The whole city should be burned to the ground to spread the scent of roses rather than rosewater." She appeared delirious. Suddenly she burst out laughing and asked the sergeant, who gaped at her transformation, "Why are you here?" The policeman didn't understand, but then he was no less shocked than the rest of his colleagues, whom the French officer stationed outside had prevented from firing on the attackers or even arresting them. Then Souad said to Azar, "Perhaps you remember when we were children. We used to send paper boats out onto the river, and now we have burned the city down. The fire should keep burning until the boats we've been expecting these forty years come back to us."

Zakariya couldn't ignore the attack on the family home, even though Aisha hadn't come to any harm and was now asleep in the next room. He had no confidence that this matter was over. Hanna was thinking of his own frailty, imagining Souad forsaken by everyone. He slipped out of his room in the morning and asked the carriage driver to head to Ahmed Bayazidi's house. No one saw him leave the monastery. The farther away he traveled from the place he hadn't left in ten years, the freer he felt. Souad was shocked when she saw him standing at the door. He seemed like a stranger to her, nothing like the Hanna she used to know. Souad walked through the destruction that the fire had wrought to the sitting room where she received her clients. He couldn't find any words to console her, and Souad was disconcerted. She suggested he join her for coffee and asked him if he was enjoying her weakness, to which he replied gently, "What did you gain by your strength?" It occurred to him to explain that there would always be someone stronger, but he stayed silent—he hadn't come to gloat. The previous night he had thought about her with great sympathy. Hanna went on to say that he had been reassured that she was unharmed, apologizing all the while that he hadn't been able to prevent the attack. He moved through the large house, trying to recapture memories from their childhood. In the courtyard, he was distressed to see the charred remains of the lemon tree. Souad watched him from the window, ruminating on the meaning of his visit. She had given up hope of seeing him, certain that he had disappeared and she could never regain him. She wondered if he was there to gauge her feelings toward him, whether she had grown softer toward him. Souad asked him to forget what had happened; she felt no regret, she had done what she wanted. She smiled and asked if he wanted to go back to his old room. Hanna smiled back and said the past wouldn't save him. What would she do with the wreckage of a man? Their conversation carried on in a desultory way, then suddenly he stood up and asked her to visit him; he said that everything was really finished.

She watched as he slipped away lightly, without saying goodbye. She felt as though she had let him down, but the surprise occasioned by his visit was greater than she could bear. She felt her old wish for vengeance flare up, though it quickly subsided as she repeated to herself his words: *What would you do with the wreckage of a man?* But the truth, which they both felt, was that neither of them needed words. Souad couldn't conceal her sadness and her defeat. She was in despair, lacking the energy to plunge into battle against her aunt and the sheikhs.

Over the next few days, Hanna never left Aisha's side. He bandaged her wounds and told her about Zakariya's paper kites; he wanted a cheerful tale from his childhood. Aisha felt that he, Zakariya, and Souad didn't like who they were now, but that all were incapable of recapturing their old life and strength. She asked Hanna to go walking with her in the fields. Ostensibly she wanted to tell him what it had felt like to walk on the stage, but really she wanted to talk about Yousef.

Meanwhile Zakariya saddled his horse and headed to Aleppo. His visits to Aunt Amina's house had become increasingly rare since his father's death. She had become someone else, nothing like the kindhearted woman he used to love. She entered into never-ending debates with certain sheikhs from the Rifa'i order, who objected to Sufis intruding into matters that didn't concern them. She cited Abulhuda Al-Sayyadi, who had once been a Sufi and head of the Rifa'i order, and whose Sufism hadn't prevented him from accepting the position of Naqib Al-Ashraf in Aleppo and becoming an official of the judiciary, before occupying the position he so eminently deserved: Sheikh Al-Islam, the Sheikh of Sheikhs of the Ottoman Empire and a trusted member of Sultan Abdel Hamid II's inner circle. Hajja Amina called on the Sufis to emerge from their apathy and isolation and go onto the streets to defend Islam by hand and sword if needed, demanding that the mortal remains of the martyred sheikh be moved to Aleppo for burial.

The last time Zakariya visited, a year earlier, Aunt Amina, though physically weak, had appeared to be the leader of a military squadron, no longer an ascetic content with milk and dates for her meals. The smell of roasted lamb filled the house, and the scent of rosewater, sprinkled ceaselessly by the maidservant, wafted into every corner. Rosewater was a smell that Zakariya detested, and he remembered how Souad had also commented derisively that her aunt's house was never free of it.

Zakariya reached Aleppo, tied up his horse in Khan Qadry in Bab Jnein, and continued on foot to Aunt Amina's house in Farafra. It was a long way, but he wanted to see the city again Here, he had passed his childhood with his friends, by the entrance to Souq Bab Jnein; there they had waved their knives in the faces of the janissaries who were stopping and searching passersby for no reason. He avoided the brothel by the clock of Bab Al-Faraj, which had become a signpost for the city of his memories.

Many people looked at Zakariya; the entire city knew about the fire at Souad's fashion show by now. Cruel glances besieged him, and many people he was acquainted with turned their faces from him. He arrived at his aunt's house and didn't bother asking the servant's permission to go in. His aunt was in bed, very ill. He sat next to her and did not hesitate before taking her wrinkled hand and squeezing it gently. He heard her say, "You're late." She went on: "If you want to walk in my funeral procession with your cousins, you have to cut Souad's throat from ear to ear." She took a dagger out from beneath the bed and held it out to him with a feeble hand. She was absolutely serious. She added, "If we couldn't prevent decay from spreading through the city, at least none of our kin will take part in spreading it." After a long silence, she spoke again: "There is a lot of gold in this box. You and your Nasrany friend Hanna can decide how much that citadel of depravity is worth and sell it to us at that price. We will donate it so it can be turned into a mosque and spread virtue and the religion of charity." Zakariya asked her dryly, "Where did you get all that money, Aunt?" She wouldn't allow him to deflect. "From benefactors. It's God's money." He asked her, "Are you happy to have set your brother's house on fire?" Smiling scornfully, she said her only regret was not having burned the whole place to the ground, brick by brick: "It's not the Bayazidi house any longer. It's a whorehouse." Zakariya wasn't surprised by her harsh tone, but he realized that any battle would be a losing one.

Hajja Amina closed her eyes for a few minutes. She had made her message clear. She asked him to leave and reflect on her instructions to wash away the family's shame if he wanted to hold her 'aza. Forced out of his aunt's house, he walked to see Souad, who had refused to speak to anyone since Hanna's visit.

Maryam had come back from the hospital with a bandaged arm and a few burns that would soon heal. Zakariya was taken aback by her beauty as she lay on a large sofa in the atelier. She had been assisting Souad, who was her teacher, before going back to the room set aside by Sitt Janette Antaky for Armenian girls who had survived the massacre and wanted to forge a new life for themselves by working in the city. Maryam was sharing a house with some other girls around her own age. They worked in embroidery ateliers and textile factories during the day, and they spent their evenings at the Association for Armenian Youth, hunting for scraps of information about their lost families. Maryam was one of the luckiest; Souad had agreed to teach her sewing and fashion design. Two years earlier William had told his aunt about a girl who had survived cholera, then escaped certain death a second time in being saved from the nun's life that had been planned for her. Souad understood that Maryam sought to flee a fate she didn't want. She decided to meet Maryam and discuss her experience before appointing her; when the two of them met, Maryam hastened to make herself agreeable and quickly won over Souad, who regarded Maryam as a potential friend more than an artisan.

After Hanna agreed that she could leave the monastery, Maryam was delivered to the association, which looked after the affairs of young Armenian girls who weren't able to reunite with their families. Mariana was silent on the matter. She felt that Maryam's departure was for the best; she didn't want the additional exhaustion of looking after this girl who was no longer a child. Maryam was proud of her slim body, openly discussed her wishes and desires, slept through mass, and even showed her resentment at communion.

For the first time in her life, Maryam felt free. She woke up in the morning and had breakfast with her friends, then at nine went to Souad's atelier. She tidied up, took her time over her coffee, and waited for Souad, who usually slept in and then also lingered over coffee. Every day Maryam thought of her distant childhood. She felt that leaving it behind had been like leaving paradise or abandoning foolishness; that first fresh taste of things was now lost.

She had nothing to say to Zakariya when he burst in furiously, cursing his aunt and accusing Souad of indifference. For the first time in his life, he also cursed Hanna, who had turned into a sick man who loved frailty and weakness. Zakariya spoke as though he had been forsaken by everyone, but he stopped suddenly and stared at Souad, who was still silent. She was avoiding a fight. She didn't want to lose him—her current misfortune was hard enough. She sympathized with Zakariya, who resumed his flood of words, as if he were reciting a monologue about everything that had happened since the flood. She tried to assure him that everything would be fine, that people would forget what had happened; the two of them would simply put their estrangement from Aunt Amina to the back of their minds, and there would be no need to ever mention her again. They knew that Amina was trying to please her sheikhs, who all sang her praises.

Zakariya departed before evening fell and went back to the monastery. Left alone with Maryam, Souad felt free.

Hanna was nursing Aisha through her shock. For a month, he never left her side; they would talk and walk in the fields, poking fun at Zakariya. August passed, and the fire eventually passed from their minds. And then one day Hanna was taken aback by word of Arif's request to meet him and Zakariya to discuss "a vitally important matter," as Mariana put it.

Arif had retained his laughter, but he couldn't hide his grief, his poverty, and his old age. He felt a deep estrangement as he sat in the chair Hanna offered him. Without overtures, he announced that he had come to ask for Aisha's hand on behalf of his son, Yousef. The matter had been prearranged; Yousef had exchanged a few letters with Aisha, and she was happy and in love, a love that grew day by day. She had liked Yousef since they first met in Zakariya's stable years before, and his few shy hints had reached her when he seized the opportunity presented by Souad's momentary absences. The first time he had pressed a letter into her hand, he was immediately overwhelmed with confusion. He glanced around to make sure no one had seen him, and then he leaped up suddenly and took his leave of Souad without finishing their conversation. Aisha stayed standing where she was and hid the letter from her aunt; she too was shaking. She didn't reply to the first letter, but when she saw Yousef again, she said she wanted to see the dinosaur skeleton. Yousef caught her allusion, and she added, "I want to share every secret with you." On the day of the fire, Yousef had tended to her and whispered in her ear that he loved her. Aisha had been expecting this, and she took his hand and squeezed it. Throughout her convalescence, letters had come to her regularly via a go-between, and they agreed to be married on the first of September.

Remembering the day he got engaged to Shaha, Zakariya burst

out laughing and reenacted the scene. Yousef, however, was no libertine but a serious young man of thirty-three who spoke with poise and gravitas. Hanna and Zakariya consented, and Aisha settled the matter, adding that she didn't want a wedding or guests. Hanna had been watching Arif from the corner of his eye throughout the meeting. The signs of dementia were plain as he spoke about his train that would soon be coming to take him away, and then he whispered to Hanna that they would all go to Baghdad in the royal carriage. Yousef hammered out the details of the marriage with Zakariya, Hanna, and Aisha, and he asked Zakariya's permission to speed up the process. Zakariya summoned a sheikh from Anabiya and sent for Souad, who arrived late that night with Azar and Sara. It was a simple celebration, and everyone was taken aback the next morning when Yousef and Aisha asked their permission to go away; a black horse was waiting to take them to Sharran. Arif was still asleep. When they arrived at Sharran, Aisha dismounted, hugged Yousef tight, and kissed him on the lips. He picked up the spade he had brought and shattered the stones that had blocked up the dinosaur's room for years. Together they went inside. Aisha was amazed at the sight of the huge skeleton, but within a few minutes, the dinosaur had turned to dust. It crumbled in the air as though a bomb had gone off, covering them in dust and ash while the couple just stood there, frozen with disbelief.

Aisha wasn't afraid. After a moment, she realized she was the last person to see that extinct creature, along with Yousef. They shared a great secret. Aisha's interpretation of the event delighted Yousef; it gave him the opportunity to investigate why the dinosaur skeleton, which had survived hundreds or thousands of years inside the earth, had turned to dust and floated away just a few years after the windows were blocked up.

He never forgot the incident, though eventually he stopped thinking of it quite so much. Instead, he would remember Aisha's face covered in dust, his clothes imbued with an unfamiliar smell.

Aisha set up her life with her husband. She found work as a teacher in a primary school near their house, and she talked about the children she would have, without prevarication or coyness. She visited Souad every day, looked after her affairs, brooked no complaints, and found a solution to every obstacle that lay in her path. She cared for her father and Hanna, choosing socks and thick pullovers for them that were made of the finest wool. She never missed her weekly visit to the monastery and only wished her uncle Arif had waited a little longer before dying; she thought he must have suffered from terrible loneliness in his final years.

A year after their marriage, Arif woke up from his deliriums and remembered that he had to invite aghas, relatives, and friends to the wedding of his only son. He put on his shirwal trousers, his embroidered sadriya, and his headcovering, and he sent for the musicians he used to bring with him to every wedding. The drummer arrived, bringing with him a young man who played the mizmar. The elderly drummer was overjoyed that Arif still remembered him. Arif rose with the two musicians, who were escorted by Mabrouk. The servant was delighted at his master's excellent mood and his wish to invite aghas and friends to a large wedding befitting the family's stature. Mabrouk also considered it Arif's final chance to recoup his losses; the aghas, especially Arif's uncles, would offer costly gifts to the newlyweds.

They walked in a procession, the drummer fervently beating his tabla and the young man playing loudly on his mizmar. Arif passed in front of all the houses of the village, and his servant distributed the gifts he had brought with him, while Arif decreed conflicting dates and times for the wedding. They reached the end of the few houses and turned toward the railroad. Arif asked the drummer not to stop hailing his train drivers and his friends. The children of the village had followed Arif, dancing and snatching up the sweets and chocolates scattered by Mabrouk while Arif was waiting for the train. He told them they would ride on his private train from Sheikh Hadid to Anabiya as he went to invite all the aghas. They would go through Jindiras, Bulbul, Kafr Safra, Jweiq, and Rajo. Arif reeled off names familiar to the drummer, places where he and Arif had often attended weddings that went on for days. The train came into view, gliding along in the distance. Arif ordered the drummer to play louder. The music rose, and Arif danced. The children formed a choir and enthusiastically sang all the songs they knew by heart. Arif stood on the tracks and motioned to the driver to halt. In a moment, it was all over. The agha was smashed to bits before the utter stupefaction of the drummer, the mizmar player, and Mabrouk.

Arif Sheikh Musa Agha's death was painful for everyone. The 'aza was concluded swiftly; no one wanted to tell the story of what had happened. As they learned, to general disbelief, Arif had lost his reason the moment the railroad company informed him that his documents were fake and worthless and that he didn't own a single screw of any train. He still waved cheerfully to the trains rushing past, offering advice and information to the drivers, who neither saw nor heard him.

Aisha recalled her childhood, when she and William would visit her uncle for days at a time. Yousef had been a youth then, spending most of his time away from the family in Grandfather's House, close to the library and the dinosaur. Arif used to take William and Aisha with him to see his lands, and he spoiled them rotten. While visiting the aghas in nearby villages, he would refer to them as "my dear children."

When Zakariya came back from Arif's burial, he told Hanna every detail, but Hanna was silent. He was thinking that their losses had still not come to an end. Zakariya asked him to stop punishing himself; time moved on, and it was impossible to regain the past. That night Zakariya said the place had become increasingly confining. He added, "Arif killed himself too late. His soul could no longer bear to be imprisoned in a body." He went on to say that they had built a platform for suicides in the citadel, but no one had used it. Everything came too late. Then Zakariya stopped talking. He wanted to rip up the notebooks where Hanna recorded his observations about botany and the migrations of the birds.

Hanna caught Zakariya's underlying meaning. He was afraid that Zakariya would leave the monastery and make a new life, one in which he would have his revenge on the instigators of the fire at

Souad's show and on all those who had ruined his and Hanna's lives. Hanna still feared the moment when Zakariya would rebuild his empire of horses, go back to Aleppo, and kick its doors open. But Zakariya's eyes, as he spoke about Arif's funeral and his last visit to Azar, revealed that he too was well on his way to surrender. He had nothing left but his few remaining horses. His stable had lost its reputation after the famine. He held back a sum from the sale of his final batch of horses and distributed it between Aisha and William, the latter of whom used his share to buy his own photography studio on Baron Street. Zakariya freed himself from his duties. He left everything to do with the monastery stable to his friend Deacon Boulos Hallaq, and he told Yaaqoub that he could leave the stables at Anabiya after hearing him grumble over and over that he had received offers of employment from the leaders of powerful tribes.

Zakariya remained alone in his house, close to the stable. He visited Hanna every day. They would drink coffee and speak about trivial matters, waiting for Aisha and William. William's visits became increasingly rare as he became preoccupied with his private world. Mariana asked him to come every week, and although he promised he would, he was often absent for several weeks at a time. Mariana would visit him and stay for hours, reassuring herself about his life. William still considered her his mother, but he could no longer bear to see the suffering of everyone he loved, the way they waited around for a death that seemed too long in arriving.

After Arif died, his servant Mabrouk had asked Yousef for permission to move to a hostel run by one of Arif's relatives, another agha. Yousef and Aisha stayed alone. They spent their summer holidays in the large house in the village. Yousef mended the roof, set up a bookshelf in the guest room, and turned it into an office where he received his comrades for never-ending discussions around the Kurdish question. On moonlit nights, Yousef and Aisha would walk to Grandfather's House and open the door to the dinosaur room, where only a few remnants remained.

Aisha reflected that she was reliving her mother Shaha's life. This made her very happy. She intervened in everyone's affairs, knocking on William's door spontaneously and asking him to put a stop to all his romantic exploits and get married. She didn't want him to end up like their father. William would ignore her advice, and they would plunge into a long chat, and then she would take him home with her to have dinner with Yousef's guests. William always wanted to escape to the printer's cellar, where he knew Junaid Khalifa would be waiting to continue their endless disputes over the manuscripts they were authenticating. And at the end of the night, William would seek out his friend Sam so they could drink themselves into a stupor.

Souad was quick to regain her vitality. She started to resemble her old mentor Hassaniya. She spoke fluently about love and feared nothing. She invited Azar, Sara, Aisha, Yousef, and William to dine in the casinos and openly cursed her aunt Amina and her sheikhs, calling for them to be arrested and executed. The only event that shook her was the birth of Aisha's first child, Hanna Sheikh Musa. Souad felt it was the momentous occasion everyone had needed, and she didn't bat an eye when she saw Hanna entering Yousef and Aisha's house. He was grinning like a little boy, and Zakariya was accompanying him. They all spent a wonderful day together, their first since the flood. Yousef remembered to invite Azar and Sara, and they were all amazed to be gathered together again around Aisha's three-day-old baby. Souad cooked, and Sara helped her. Everyone was exchanging mystified, incredulous glances. Hanna abandoned his caution and was almost like his old self, so much so that they felt that the twenty years that had passed since the flood had been nothing but a bad dream. But at the end of that day, everything went back to normal. They couldn't hide how much they had lost. Hanna took his leave and went back to the monastery. Impossible for the saint's bed to remain empty, Azar said sarcastically. But Souad defended Hanna and said, "He's still choking on the drowned from the flood."

Life returned to the monastery. Every week Aisha and the baby spent the whole day there with Hanna and Zakariya. Yousef and William were compelled to accompany her; the latter spent his time with Mariana, who was forced to consider family Sunday lunch a holy ritual. She prepared the food, and they all sat at the dinner table in Hanna's room. Hanna spent his time watching the baby.

On the twenty-fourth anniversary of the flood, Zakariya received news of Aunt Amina's death. He knocked on Souad's door, finding her, as usual, lingering over her coffee. He asked her to put on something modest quickly so they could join Amina's funeral, but Souad said dispassionately, "My aunt died a long time ago, and I'm not going anywhere." Zakariya went to his aunt's house but was astonished to be turned away by his cousins. They refused to allow him to bury his aunt, cursed him, and told him not to defile her sanctified house. Meanwhile hundreds of bearded young men waited outside, led by well-known sheikhs and accompanied by the nuba. The house was in utter chaos. Zakariya was prevented from arguing with his cousins. The women were wailing for Um Al-Fuqura', the "Mother of the Poor," and the mujahideen of Janaq Qal'a, and everyone else cried out in praise of Sheikh Abulhuda Al-Sayyadi, who had died a quarter of a century earlier.

Zakariya didn't much care about the insult, but he was alarmed. He didn't go back to Souad's house; nor did he tell her what had happened. Instead he went back to his stable, choosing to forget what had taken place. After afternoon prayer, the rain stopped. More than twenty men arrived at the citadel, bearing swords; these same bearded youths had brought the nuba and waited to pray over Hajja Amina's coffin, and now they were carrying out the promise they had made to her. Zakariya wasn't there to hear Shams Al-Sabah's pleas or the screams of the horrified old women. The bearded men stalked in, uncovering their faces. Without fear or hesitation, they forced the single guard to open the gate. They imprisoned the old women inside the citadel, stopped up the windows, and locked the doors. They poured gasoline on the furniture and in the passageways, and soon the citadel was a blazing lump of flame. The wooden ceilings fell in with a gigantic roar. Within two hours, the young men were certain that all the women had been burned to death. The fire had reached every room.

The victors departed after making sure that the citadel was reduced to ash. They passed in front of the monastery gates. The guards didn't dare challenge them when they released a flaming arrow and set fire to the furniture in a third-floor room. No one lived there yet—it had been made ready to welcome one of a new cohort of missionary nuns sent from Mardin by Deir Za'faran, after harmony reigned at last between the two rival monasteries.

The fire at the citadel died down sometime after midnight. No one dared to go inside apart from Zakariya, who couldn't sleep when he realized what had befallen. He sat on a boulder outside his front door and thought of everything that had come to an end. Everything he cared about was gone. He had considered the occasional secret visit to the citadel his last pleasure in life. He was the only man allowed inside. He used to visit those poor women spontaneously, or Shams Al-Sabah would send for him by way of the single guard whom Zakariya still paid to protect their cherished memories.

On those visits he would drink coffee and hear the complaints of the thirteen women who were gathered there, served by Shams Al-Sabah. When Zakariya turned up, they would smile, crack jokes, and laugh. On his final visit, they asked him to dig their graves for them and prepare them for burial. They were recalling Um Waheed, who had passed away two years before; no one had known how to bury her. They looked for a discreet man without success. They discovered the single grave that had been prepared for a suicide many years earlier, and so they buried her in that magnificent dome, but they asked for forgiveness at great length; they hadn't been able to find a sheikh who was prepared to pray over her, so they had done it themselves.

Zakariya had laughed to himself. He didn't tell Hanna that Shams Al-Sabah had become just as wretched as her charges: fat, her hands roughened by working in the ground like her fellaha companions, suffering imaginary ailments although she wasn't even fifty yet. Zakariya increased their provisions and always remembered the little things the old women liked; he brought them roasted walnuts and occasionally a few bottles of the fine whiskey he received as gifts from rich clients who adored their horses.

The old women had declared their repentance, but they still drank whiskey, and in fact they advised him on other brands that reminded them of their pasts. Widad, Arif's onetime paramour, was one of them. She had retired early after contracting incurable syphilis; the doctor responsible for overseeing the brothels in Bahsita wrote an order to withdraw her work permit, and she had nowhere to go apart from the citadel. After a lengthy correspondence, Shams Al-Sabah accepted her, thanks to the mediation of Um Badi', the procuress who never abandoned her role. She kept the place as clean as befitted these women who knew so much about the men of this city. Um Badi' occasionally used to threaten to write her memoirs and expose some of her God-fearing clients, and in this way they were forced to send her a little money. It wasn't much, but it helped her to buy the treatments for any of her women with syphilis or other chronic illness.

The police avoided investigating the fire on the pretext that there was no claimant or official complaint, and Mariana wouldn't let them question Hanna. She asked the metropolitan to intercede to close the investigation. She didn't want the fire at the citadel to be linked to the monastery; she considered it Hanna's last connection to his past. At any rate, the fire on the monastery's third floor was a small loss compared with the obliteration of the citadel.

Three days after the blaze, Zakariya quietly entered the ruins of the citadel. It was silent. The remnants of the fire's stench clogged his nose. He wandered the place, finding nothing. The women's bodies had been burned to ash, and he couldn't identify any of them. The few things that hadn't burned—the silver water pitchers, the silver cutlery, some of the gifts that had crammed the citadel's stores—had been looted.

Zakariya continued walking. The rain that had fallen in torrents for the last two days had worsened the smell of rot, and the wind scattered the citadel's ashes. The only thing he could find was Um Waheed's grave on the ground floor. Through a tumbled wall, he was surprised to see a bearded man in his seventies approaching, walking through the cultivated lands surrounding the citadel and bending low to avoid the intertwined branches of olive and pomegranate trees. When he eventually arrived, Zakariya knew him at once, despite how much he had aged. Salim Khidr bellowed, "The place had to be burned down for us to feel safe. And you should move the remains of your friends," he said, pointing to the graves of William and Aisha. The man left before Zakariya's fury rose to its full height, but not before he had been warned against coming near their private property again.

Zakariya spent hours gathering the women's ashes. He collected as much of their remains as he could find in a large canvas sack and buried it in a deep hole beneath a tree without marking the grave. He simply filled in the hole and left, grieving, secretly cursing Hanna because he had turned them both into men who could be insulted by a group of thugs, and now Salim Khidr had had his revenge on them.

Souad was not greatly distressed by the death of her aunt and she refused to hear about the burning of the citadel. She was constantly absorbed with recalling her past. She would listen to William as he told her of his love for Maryam, and she would answer, "You won't betray her any less than other men will." She added, "Leave her to her life. She's the survivor of a massacre and has no family." She considered Maryam her personal responsibility; deep down Maryam was weak, a girl suspended in space. She walked without touching the ground she trod upon, unlike Aisha, who was strong and self-possessed.

Three months after the fashion show, Maryam told Souad that Orhan had proposed. Souad was silent. She reflected inwardly that she didn't want to incite Maryam into any action that might ruin her life. Maryam might be lucky that a man of Orhan's attributes had offered marriage; she was nothing but a poor girl, after all. Keeping her own opinion of Orhan to herself, Souad encouraged her to accept but asked her to think carefully before making any decision. Maryam concealed from Souad that she had already met Orhan for several rendezvous after he made his offer. She had accepted his gifts and allowed him to hold her hand. She had listened, greatly impressed, as he cursed the Turks and told her in all seriousness that he disclaimed all association with them after the Armenian massacre. She believed him entirely when he said he lived alone and away from his large family, who had given up hope he would ever come back to Istanbul and in consequence had consigned him to oblivion. His siblings no longer mentioned him at family gatherings and had stopped expecting him for the Eid holidays.

Maryam admired Orhan's elegance and cockiness; William, in comparison, seemed like a sickly young man. When they met, William didn't talk about a future; he spoke about the turmoil of his soul and whispered to her that every morning, he waited for her to wake up so her soul would alight close to his. She would have liked to blend these two men into one, but this could not be. When she left her meetings with William, she hated herself and thought that if she said anything to him about her feelings for him, she would appear like some waif begging for protection and safety. She wanted to be rid of her endless nightmares about the massacre. For whole nights at a time, she still smelled the dead bodies that they had burned, ostensibly so as not to spread the plague, but in Maryam's view they had been hiding their crimes. All the way from Urfa to Azaz, she hadn't been sure she had really survived until Arif Sheikh Musa Agha had caught her, curled up with her six friends. They hadn't been able to find anywhere to sleep apart from the large mosque at Azaz that had opened its doors to receive survivors. Benefactors donated some items of clothing and a little food. Everyone had starved in those years, but despite everything, Maryam had escaped death. All her life, she gave thanks to the immense luck that had followed her when she moved to Arif's house, then to the monastery, and then to Souad's atelier. Her friends would live, miserable and grumbling about the boiled lentils and the heavy nun's clothing they had to wear, but Maryam was no longer a mere survivor; she was a girl who had received a marriage proposal from the director of a large French bank who lived in a splendid house, and she was loved by a young man who adored photography. She was afraid that everything would slip through her hands in an instant. She said, "A survivor has to hold on to something steady to increase her chances." She didn't keep Orhan waiting long before she informed him she would accept his proposal. Souad prepared her jihaz. Maryam told William in a few words that she was leaving him; she didn't have time to practice the luxury of love and ruminate on the weight of souls.

Maryam ignored the stinging criticism she received from her poverty-stricken friends at Madame Janette Antaky's house, who spat on her for accepting a Turkish man and a Muslim. She ignored Mariana's letter in which she said that Maryam had betrayed the message of Christ. She told no one that Souad had asked Azar for help in finishing the arrangements for the marriage; Souad couldn't stand talking to Orhan because, to her, he was still the same slimy man he had always been. Maryam kept her Christianity, and Orhan didn't ask her to convert. She was pleased with her large, splendid house and the substantial remaining balance of payment that Souad was determined to have recorded in the marriage contract. Accompanied by Azar, Souad discussed every minute detail that would protect a single woman with no family. Maryam remained grateful to Souad and Azar for the rest of her life.

She liked Orhan's aristocratic class, the way he had breakfast at the same time every morning, the exaggerated way he showed off his use of knife and fork; she enjoyed his admiration for the elegance she had reclaimed, and she bought lots of clothes. But William's dreamy glances still disconcerted her. In the first year of her marriage and after her pregnancy, she came to feel that she hadn't chosen anything in her tangled life; she had thought that marrying Orhan would certainly end her naïve little romance with William. But eventually she was forced to reflect on the mistake she had made. It would be impossible to spend years with a man who meant nothing to her but security. When she saw Aisha and Yousef, she envied them to her core, but she told herself that Aisha hadn't faced a massacre and lost her entire family. Nor had she lived on handouts; on the contrary, she had always been surrounded by love and care, the spoiled pet of Hanna and Zakariya, the desirable daughter of Mariana, Souad, and Father Ibrahim. Even Teodor had enjoyed it when Aisha played the role of the indulged daughter. Maryam was no stranger to saying a half-truth to mask her anxiety. At times her mood grew troubled, and she felt genuinely annoyed and upset by everything around her, especially by Orhan's little habits, which soon lost their shine. Out of all the aristocratic elegance she had once so admired, there remained merely the resounding pretensions of a man who considered his life worthy of a memoir, even though it was no different from the life of every other official who had ascended to his position through fierce opportunism.

At times, Maryam felt she was being unjust to Orhan and exaggerating her praise of William's piercing glances, his outlandish ideas about love. She would never forget the day he slipped into her bed in the isolation room at the monastery when she was gravely ill with cholera. He had wanted to share death with her; she had never known a lover who would share death with his beloved. She remembered him waiting in front of the door to the church for hours so he could escort her back to Janette Antaky's house after Sunday mass; the wildflowers he had picked for her at the monastery; all the times she had stood in front of his camera so he could take pictures of her in every conceivable pose and place. He used to say to her, "I will write our story in pictures—words aren't appropriate for love." She had believed him and admired his odd ideas about love.

She was burdened by the memory of past years, the memory of her misery. Deep down, like any survivor of a massacre who feels a new life has been born beneath her skin, she recognized her good fortune. But after a while, these feelings turn into a sickness, a chronic depression, because the survivor is alone, while the houses of her childhood burn and the rotting bodies of her loved ones convey nothing but pestilence. Survival isn't enough to make you feel lucky; rather, you feel genuinely, entirely damaged. Nothing of you has been saved, even though you continue to breathe and eat and drink. Survival is a journey through a trackless wilderness, and its pain cannot be calculated, any more than it can be summarized or spoken about lightly.

Sometimes Maryam would wake up early, put breakfast on the table, and leave, carrying her baby son, Abdel Hamid. She would go into the empty church and pray. She would make no response to the provocations of the Armenians when she was suffered to hear their inappropriate asides, but she went among them nevertheless to ask for news of her brother Harout, who she believed would come back to her and lessen the pain and shame of having married a Turkish man. On one of these morning rounds, three years after her marriage, she found herself in front of the door of William's studio in Baron Street. She took a seat and waited her turn like any other customer. It wasn't crowded. She looked at the few pictures displayed on the walls. She knew one of them, a picture of Teodor and Helen, who had departed only a few days earlier for Amsterdam, where Helen would sing in her wonderful voice. The picture was accompanied by an article, which the journalist concluded by musing on the apparent phenomenon of foreigners carrying off Muslim girls to turn them into Christians. The journalist's information was incorrect, but the article had sparked a number of responses, great support, and a debate about the role of missionary delegations operating under the auspices of the French occupiers.

Maryam thought about poor Helen, whom the article depicted as just such a victim—a girl smuggled away to be turned Christian. Maryam told herself it was fortunate that Helen's mother Futaim couldn't read and would never know what was being said about her sweet daughter, who had fled the prospect of a bridegroom who intended to add her to his collection of women who were forced to harvest lentils and chickling vetch in the summer and pick olives and feed livestock in the winter.

Maryam knew the true story behind Helen's travels. Orhan had often spoken about Helen's voice and how much he admired Teodor, who had discovered this miraculous talent amid the rubble, producing a diamond from the rubbish heap. Orhan had written a response to this article, clarifying that Helen had traveled abroad with her foreign husband, who had married her according to the sunnah of God and His prophet after converting to Islam. The journalist's boorish response spurred Orhan to go in person to the mufti's office to obtain a copy of the certification of Teodor's conversion to Islam; he also managed to obtain the deed of marriage from the sharia court in Aleppo. But the newspaper turned the page on the story, satisfied with a public response that granted victory to the journalist, who railed against missionaries who were evidently seeking revenge for the forced conversion of Christians to Islam over the centuries.

William left the studio, bidding goodbye to another customer. He was not surprised to see Maryam there; he had been expecting her since the day he opened the studio. He barely noticed what he was doing as he closed the outer door of the studio while she prepared to sit on the chair in front of the camera. He took her hand and smothered it in kisses; he kissed her lips and her neck. She responded at first, then stopped both herself and him. She held him away from her and sat back down on the chair, saying, "Take my picture." She looked at him as he moved calmly and with confidence. Her heart was thudding. He took his time bringing the lights, and she felt on the verge of attacking him and ravishing him on the bare floor. Her lust rose; she found him intensely attractive, despite his short stature. He was well dressed, and as for his perfume, Maryam would know it anywhere.

She rose hurriedly and said, "I want the picture to be ready next Saturday." She opened the door of the studio and rushed back to her house, her body burning in an unfamiliar way.

Orhan assured her that he was still searching for Harout and had sent details of the family to friends in Istanbul and Europe. Then he turned to his new tale about his "battle," as he called it, in defense of his friend Teodor and the marvelous Helen. Maryam couldn't care less about his fervor at that moment, but she smiled to humor him. She wanted him to finish his story now so it wouldn't continue when they went to bed; he often went on rambling after she had already put on her nightdress and slipped in beside him. That night she announced that for the first time, she would sleep in the second room, next to her son. Orhan didn't protest and kept talking throughout dinner about the day he and his friend Teodor went to Anabiya with a sheikh. They had arrived in the afternoon, and it wasn't hard for them to reach Diyab and Futaim's house, to which Futaim had just returned after working at the monastery. Diyab couldn't quite grasp the fact that these respected individuals were actually inside his house; he knew Teodor as the choirmaster with whom his adopted daughter was in love, but the sheikh explained to Diyab that they had come to ask for the hand of his honored daughter, Miss Fatima, as her parents called the girl named Helen by her godfather Hanna. Diyab ventured to ask for a little time to think. He consulted his friends and his family, who all gave their blessings for this marriage, as long as the man wanted to become a Muslim and would save the girl from spending her life working as a servant or a laborer in the lentil fields. They whispered to Diyab that his daughter would be a spinster, or the second wife of some old man looking for a servant, if she was lucky. Although they appeared to have the girl's best interests at heart, the truth was they simply wanted to be rid of a girl who was only adopted and to rectify the heresy that Futaim had committed—and Diyab agreed with their judgment. He hadn't listened to the sheikh back then, when he had declared that Islam forbade adoption and that this act of Diyab's had placed him in the ranks of the infidels. Diyab and Futaim hadn't cared at the time; they wanted a child at any cost and hadn't been able to have their own, and they considered the baby girl a gift from Heaven.

Teodor paid a respectable amount of money to Diyab and asked Helen to leave all her clothes for her mother to distribute among the poor. He laced his fingers through hers, and the entire village watched this beautiful man escort away their ugly girl with every appearance of love. Helen looked back at Anabiya for the last time and then got into the waiting car.

Helen dreamed of a world of music, of drowning within it, breathing it in entirely, and this was what Teodor gave her. A few days after they were married, he introduced her to the Dutch consul, who had held a private party at his house. Helen sang arias from *Aïda* and some old Arabic songs. The guests were incredulous that just days earlier this girl had been harvesting lentils and feeding livestock in exchange for a few franks. Shyness prevented her from ingratiating herself with the elegant people who formed a circle around her and questioned her about her life. Orhan and Maryam were in attendance; Orhan was swaggering about, and Maryam observed as he took it upon himself to explain to one and all the difficult life the girl had endured, just like all the greats, among whom, without a doubt, she was numbered. In phrases he considered the height of originality, he went on to say that her formidable talent was worthy of a Communist like Teodor converting to Islam, and Orhan also reminded everyone present that he himself had abandoned his family to become Syrian, then turned Armenian in order to marry the splendid Maryam, survivor of the massacre.

Orhan often repeated this story, then waited expectantly for gazes of admiration from his audience; Maryam had heard it a hundred times or more. Everyone flattered Orhan with dissembling smiles, chuckling and praising his courage in marrying Maryam, who was insulted although, deep down, she thought he was right. He had married her so that she might eat, and if he wasn't a courageous man, he wouldn't have abandoned his family because of his principles, just as he always said. Equally, with the passage of time, she was relieved that he had married her because of his principles and not because of her, Maryam, or because of any love for her that inflamed his bones. She had always found his few words of courtship so wretched that she pitied him. She hadn't understood Orhan at first, but after her second child was born, she finally saw clearly that he had married her to have children, and so that he could tell this story to the refined socialites that frequented her parties.

That party was Helen's last; she was content not to sing again at private parties for drunken men. It was the third time she had sung without the choir. The first time had been three years earlier, at Souad's fashion show; the second at a party Orhan held at his house after his son Abdel Hamid was born; and this last time in the house of the Dutch consul, who was entranced by her voice. He conferred with Teodor for a long time about how to manage their return to Amsterdam, and the consul himself wrote personally to the Dutch government, urging them to grant Helen Dutch citizenship and to bear her travel expenses.

Maryam developed a close relationship with Helen. She brought Helen with her to visit Souad, selected new clothes for her, and sometimes asked Orhan to dispatch the car to bring her mother Futaim for a Friday visit. Futaim would arrive loaded down with whatever was most abundant, whether cheese, bulgur wheat, or eggs. Futaim was poor and content with very little. She couldn't believe that her ugly daughter lived in a beautiful house and wore expensive clothes. In return, Helen would load her mother with clothes and woolen sweaters for her father Diyab, and in her hand she always placed some money— never much, but enough for Futaim's life to change. Futaim couldn't believe her eyes when she saw Helen's foreign passport. One day Helen asked Futaim to bring her father the next time; when they visited, she waited to tell them she was going abroad until it was almost time for them to go back to Anabiya. She was a different girl now, and she spoke confidently about her new world. She asked Futaim and Diyab to forgive her for mistakes she had not truly made, and she was affectionate toward this poverty-stricken couple who had wept over her if she so much as came down with a cold as a child. Helen promised to send letters and money, and to come back to visit every year, adding that she might return permanently, along with the child growing inside her, if Teodor joined the diplomatic corps and was appointed consul to Aleppo.

Futaim couldn't believe that her daughter might be the wife of the Dutch consul. In her entire life, she had seen Huda Shamoun Giovanni once, when she had visited Deir Zahr Al-Rumman years before. She couldn't believe it when her daughter's husband bent over and kissed her hand with every sign of deference, but she didn't stop weeping for months, despite the unceasing letters and the regular checks that arrived via Orhan, who would then suffer himself to the journey in his car to drink tea with Futaim and Diyab and hand over the money and the letters. Orhan would read out Helen's letters, in which she spoke of her happiness in her new country, or wrote bitterly about the child she had miscarried.

Maryam often thought about Orhan telling sentimental stories about Futaim's face, how she couldn't stop crying throughout the whole recitation of Helen's letters. Maryam knew her friend's secret: she wasn't pregnant, Teodor hadn't even come near her, she was still a virgin, and he had divorced her after they arrived in Amsterdam. She lived in a small room in the house of his family, who couldn't understand their son's latest caprice until they heard her voice. They were overcome with bewilderment and weren't reassured until the verified document of divorce reached them from the Dutch consulate in Aleppo. Their son's renunciation of his conversion to Islam, even though from the start it had been only a matter of form, meant a great deal to them; it had in fact been a primary condition for his return to the family home.

Teodor was no longer a rebellious youth. He bought a large shop in the center of Amsterdam and opened a private studio that he called Bolshevi in fond memory of former days. He attempted to procure work for Helen with various well-known music or theater groups but was surprised at how hard it was. First of all, it wasn't easy for them to accept her unusual backstory; they admired her voice, but her ignorance of the repertoire and lack of formal training were real obstacles. He had to retrain her, teach her Dutch, English, and Italian, and cultivate her afresh if she were to become an opera singer of note. Teodor's zeal increased; he began to teach Helen Dutch and paid to have her enrolled at a music school close to his family's house. He wasn't stingy with the money she sent to her family every month, nor with the small expenses of a girl who keenly felt the plight of her new life, especially when she stayed alone in her small room on cold nights, listening to the voices of the family upstairs, or when Teodor's brothers and parents avoided any conversation with her, just nodding whenever they passed.

Helen wrote a final letter to Maryam, saying that she wanted to come back but didn't know how. She had signed financial bonds that committed her to repayment from her forthcoming contracts, but those contracts never appeared. Her only opportunity was when she sang a short piece for an amateur company that was looking for an ugly girl with a beautiful voice. But she hadn't reaped the success that Teodor had expected, and even her voice was different now, not as powerful as it had once been. The music school informed him that his young lady was suffering from intense depression and homesickness. She would never reach the required level to ascend the stage, not even in the provinces. He had to forget any notion of her joining the royal troupe; there were dozens of stronger singers still waiting for their chance.

Throughout 1933, Maryam received letters from Helen almost weekly. In one letter, she asked Maryam to inform her family not to expect any more money or letters, and to tell them that they should forget her forever. Maryam didn't understand what these words meant until two years later, when she received a surprise letter from Helen. She wrote, *By the time this letter reaches you, I will have become homeless.* Maryam cried for days over the letter's conclusion: *I thought I survived a massacre, but that was a delusion. We never survive our past. I am still that filthy bundle, thrown in front of a distant monastery's door. In a few hours, they will throw me out of the house and out of their lives. There is no getting rid of the burden of living other than by suicide, but who is brave enough for that?* The family had told her she needed to leave. Teodor felt a burden lift from his shoulders, then in the next instant an oppressive loss, and he was filled with self-loathing. Helen wandered the streets, walking all day and returning at night to a charitable organization that offered food to the destitute and homeless. Eventually, she collapsed on the street, and in the hospital the doctor told her she was suffering from pneumonia and didn't have long to live. She managed to obtain a train ticket to Marseilles, and from there she was carried on a steamer to Beirut, and by the time she reached Anabiya, she was someone else. At death's door, she couldn't get up despite the care Futaim and Diyab devoted to her. She died three months later and was buried in Anabiya.

Teodor couldn't bear what had happened, but he always told the story in a different way, exonerating himself from the tragedy. When the Second World War broke out, he still hadn't managed to throw off the burden of Helen's story. He had let the frost bore into her bones in a mean little room intended for the family's dogs, before she became homeless on the streets, came down with pneumonia, and went home to die; so his friend Orhan told him, in a long letter that described Helen's emaciated face and debilitated body when she reached Anabiya. Teodor volunteered as a war photographer for a Russian magazine, which sent him to the front. He was out of his mind and wanted to die, but he was still seeking the immortality he had long dreamed of. Teodor was killed on a spring day in 1942. His name is still carved into a small memorial plaque on one of Amsterdam's narrow streets, while his pictures are published everywhere in the world. Underneath his pictures of Helen is the legend: *Girl from the East.*

Maryam remembered the moment, years later, when William had handed her an album of Teodor's photographs, published in Britain by the University of Oxford. They had bought the publishing rights from his sister, who had haggled with the university to give her oldest son a scholarship to study medicine in exchange for the pictures. The university published the rare images with a first edition in 1947.

When Maryam opened the album and read *Girl from the East* under Helen's portrait, she was furious. She considered writing to the university but eventually gave up that idea. She saw she had to move on. There in the photography studio, Maryam thought it was the last time she would see William, and all her past had to be forgotten. She wanted to be reborn; she was no longer the survivor of a massacre but a woman who wanted an entire world, rooted in the family. She decided to become a respectable grandmother. She had always liked grandmothers, though she was unnerved by Souad's utter indifference to

Teodor's pictures. One showed Helen singing onstage at Souad's marvelous, singular fashion show. Souad put the album away after flicking through it quickly, then said to Maryam, "One of the conditions of being a grandmother is to forget the painful past and remember only grandchildren's birthdays and happy occasions." She added a few words, praying for God's mercy for Helen and for her mother and Diyab. Souad was trying to keep her house from turning into a graveyard of all the belongings of the people she had known. Souad advised Maryam to forget her past—the massacre, Harout, William, Helen, the monastery, and Mariana—but Maryam couldn't forget anything. She thought she should follow Souad's advice, but her feet soon led her back to William's studio. She liked her first portrait, in which she seemed like a woman liberated from her past, the ghost of a smile on her lips. She tried to leave the studio but couldn't. She waited for William to get up from behind his desk and embrace her, but he didn't. He stayed where he was, pretending to be occupied with arranging the photographs of other customers. He didn't shut the door as he had done the previous time. When she left, he bade her a cold goodbye. As she walked away, she reflected that he too wanted to forget her. Her blood was on fire, boiling in her veins. That same night she left the bed, leaving Orhan to his undisturbed sleep. She longed for William and summoned up an image of him. She lay down on the mattress by her son's bed, her hand on her nipple, and gave herself to William. She drowned in this secret habit that she would regularly practice for years, recalling the scene when he held her tight and smothered her in kisses.

She went back to him a few days later. She had been thinking of him constantly, lying worried in bed next to Orhan, whom she no longer tried to entice with perfume or diaphanous nightgowns. The city had opened up, and its shops now boasted not only global brands but entirely new experiments in design and behavior. In fact, it was no longer improper for a woman to go out without a hijab; many women would go to the cinema and see a film in the chicest attire.

The city was a different place, and Maryam still remembered

Souad's advice about forgetting. But she couldn't do it; the past was heavy, it couldn't be simply erased.

She went into William's studio, determined to expel him from her life. She was taken aback at his coolness as he continued to work, ignoring her presence. She didn't stay long, but she felt her defeat keenly, and once outside she decided she wouldn't fall back into his trap. William didn't care; he was having a riotous time in the city and went to the bar at the Hotel Baron every night, avoiding the other customers and sitting alone in the corner.

That night he arrived at the bar at his usual time and asked for his usual—a gin and tonic—and reflected that he had been cruel to Maryam. He didn't know why he had ignored her a second time. He used to want revenge on her, having never forgotten how she had married in that peculiar way. He remembered how, more than once, she had ignored him when she met him at his aunt Souad's atelier. She didn't notice that his eyes swerved away, and she was indifferent to the letters he pressed into her hand. But now he had been cruel and deserved blame of his own; after all, she had wanted to talk for the first time in three years. He thought he would never be cured of her and had to learn to live with this sickness. On some level, he was gleeful that he had been able to ignore her. He had liked the advice of a young man he had met for the first time in this bar the previous week. When William was sitting alone in his inconspicuous nook, the young man had come over and held his hand out in greeting, saying, "I'm Sam, and you are the great photographer William Bayazidi. I want us to be friends, as close as we were two hundred years ago."

William said hello with his customary shyness. The Armenian waiter placed a glass of whiskey in front of Sam, who took the chair next to William and said, "You have to forget, my friend. Don't go near a woman you can't forget." Sam spoke in phrases that seemed to have been lifted from a book of ancient wisdom. William asked Sam about his claim to a close relationship, and Sam burst out laughing and said complacently, "The one skill I have perfected is knowing the lineage of every family in Aleppo." William couldn't care less about this and felt it had nothing to do with him. Sam proceeded to reel off a list of William's ancestors all the way to his great-great-great-grandfather, but his knowledge still didn't arouse William's curiosity. Everyone knew the information that Sam wanted to impart. Sam concluded by relating a story that was already familiar to William, but that he found interesting in Sam's retelling. Sam told William calmly that his great-grandfather was the full brother of the great-great-grandfather of Hanna Gregoros, his father Zakariya's friend. William was silent, feeling that Sam wanted to show off his imaginary information. William tried to brush Sam off but found himself unable to. He felt as though Sam's stories were helping him pass a hard night, even protecting him from committing an act of folly. He invited Sam to drink with him sometime, and Sam accepted with alacrity. He suggested they move to a new bar nearby and said, "You'll find some beautiful women there." William wasn't interested, but he promised Sam a night out there soon.

Now quite drunk, William went on his way to the press where he used to carry out work for his friend Junaid Khalifa. He found Junaid Khalifa struggling with asthma but still smiling as usual. He chided William for his delay in editing the book of an English explorer they had agreed to print. William told Junaid Khalifa that photography would be enough for him from now on, then both fell silent. Junaid Khalifa felt this as an enormous loss; William's enthusiasm had offered him an escape from the tedium of typesetting iron letters. He was old and tired and no longer a fervent participant in political proceedings. He decided to clear out this printer's cellar, which he had bought from his friend Amin Kahhala when he emigrated to Austria.

William's visits to his friend Junaid Khalifa didn't stop but became less frequent. On his final visit, he saw that the press had come to a halt. Junaid had gathered up his things and a bag filled with papers. He told William that he had decided to sell the printing press and go back to Anabiya. He would buy a large tract of land and make a living from farming it, and he would spend the rest of his life reading the books he loved. The city had betrayed him and had never appreciated him.

William felt he had come at a bad time; Junaid was clearly upset. Nevertheless, he carried out his friend's wish to photograph the place before it was handed over to its new owner, took several photographs of the printing press and Junaid Khalifa, bade him goodbye, and promised to come and see him in Anabiya whenever he visited the monastery.

Instead, William opened up his own studio, so he wouldn't have to go back to the monastery and be submerged again in the world of Mariana, who had begun to complain that he had abandoned her, and the world of Hanna and Zakariya, which had utterly collapsed after the fire at the citadel. Erasing the past wasn't easy. He heard Zakariya's harsh words to Hanna, saying that his weakness had made them both laughingstocks. He demanded that Hanna regain his strength and reminded him of their old dreams. Zakariya felt that his honor had been sullied. He had been waiting for the old women to die so he could turn the place into a home for the two of them, or give it to someone who needed it; that it had been attacked, burned, removed, its very stones stolen by the Khidr clan—that Zakariya couldn't bear. Hanna kept smiling as he listened to his friend's angry words, which didn't cease until Hanna finally interrupted, saying, "No one ever accepted their repentance." Hanna's refrain about repentance was what Zakariya hated the most. But Hanna's sincere grief made him feel guilty again.

He walked out of Hanna's room, mounted his horse, picked up his rifle, and left the monastery, determined to murder Salim Khidr. He found himself wandering aimlessly through the fields. He dismounted and stood atop a rise. In the distance, the moon was shimmering on the surface of the Afrin River. Zakariya didn't notice his own bitter sobs. He thought about killing himself. He too was full of sin—he had never forgotten the night he seduced Yvonne. He had stalked her through the passageways of the monastery for days, and it had come as no surprise to him when she came into the stable one night after learning that Deacon Boulos Hallaq had gone to Aleppo with Mariana. He shut the door quietly behind her, and she sat down next to the firewood brazier. She asked him, "What do you want from me?"

Without a word, Zakariya got up from his seat, took her in his arms, and kissed her. He led her to Boulos's bed and undressed her, and she didn't stop him—she wanted him, too. He arranged for them to meet throughout the winter of 1909. At that time, the monastery was going through an upheaval; Mariana hadn't yet gained control over the place, and Hanna's voice still held some sway. After several days, Yvonne had grown very familiar with the path to Zakariya's house, attached to the stable. She would cut through the fields around the monastery and slip into bed beside him every night. She believed his words of love and felt she had been created just to meet this man. After she fell pregnant, he fled; he was unable to rectify his mistake. The only thing he offered her in exchange for her silence was a rented room in a shared house, or to take her to Beirut until she gave birth, after which she could do whatever she wanted with the baby. Zakariya now accepted that he had been cruel; he didn't know why he had abandoned Yvonne so easily. She was a sweet girl, and during the months they had spent together, she had made him feel hope again. But he had failed her.

After the flood, Yvonne had had nowhere to turn. She asked for help from her childhood friend Mariana, and Mariana made it a condition of her help that she join the order of the nuns. Mariana wasn't content with obtaining the metropolitan's agreement to Yvonne's presence in the monastery, nor with Hanna's protection of her; she wanted to send a message to everyone that all matters in the monastery rested in her hands, and if anything was to be achieved, she had to agree to it. Yvonne had no choice but to submit to Mariana's conditions. Her dreams of creating a family and moving to the city were finished.

From the outset, she felt she was in the wrong place. She hated Mariana and missed Hanna. She had a terrible headache that persisted for many nights. She would leave her room and sit alone, breathing deeply. She didn't know what she wanted, restriction enclosed her, her body was on fire for a man. She thought constantly of how she had to leave this place, but her aunt's family was poor and hadn't welcomed the idea of Yvonne sharing their small house, and her uncles simply ignored what had happened. She had liked Zakariya for some time before; the girls of Hosh Hanna used to sigh and exclaim whenever he led his horses to pasture or came back from a journey, and they all envied Shaha to the core. Even now she didn't know how her feet had led her to the stable; all she had wanted was to talk to him, but she couldn't resist pressing into his chest. At that moment she needed him, and when she became pregnant, she felt the full danger of her predicament. When she shared what had happened with Mariana, asking for her help as an old friend, Mariana locked her up in the food stores. For the first time since the flood, Yvonne relaxed, certain at last that she had reached her nadir. She wandered through the shadowy cellar; she didn't know why she didn't just die now so that her tragedy would be over. But in the course of the seven nights she spent there, she regained her bravery. She asked to meet Mariana and informed her that she would confess what had happened in front of everyone—she didn't care about the scandal. Her remaining cousins would kill her, and that would put an end to the matter. Then she added, "Before they kill me, I'll kill myself." Her serious tone frightened Mariana, who didn't want a story like this circulating around the monastery. They came to an agreement that Yvonne would leave the monastery, abandon her orders, and disappear completely within the city. Yvonne accepted the offer but glared vindictively at Mariana, who had treated her like a servant and not like a childhood friend. Her swelling stomach soon threatened to betray her. She requested an audience with Father Ibrahim, confessed everything, and asked for his help. She was disgraced; she felt weak before the priest, who arranged every detail of her exit from the monastery. He advised her to accept Zakariya's offer of help, but to this she couldn't agree; she knew, in the end, that she was a sinning Christian, and she didn't want to rectify one sin by committing another, even greater. It had been a terrible moment of weakness, and it was over now.

Yvonne rented a room in the house of an old Jewish lady in the Jamiliyya quarter, close to Azar's office. Unbeknownst to her, Zakariya paid the rent. She gave birth to a daughter. Yvonne picked her up when she was four days old and, not caring whether anyone saw her, put her in front of the gate of the monastery. She gathered up her few things and left for Tripoli, where she found work through Father Ibrahim as a teacher in a primary school. She lived as a single woman in a rented room with some friends who came from nearby villages. Her only joy was her regular correspondence with Father Ibrahim. She wrote to him about sin and impurity and regret. He encouraged her, praising her extraordinary bravery in facing her fate. He visited her three times in the seven years of their correspondence. On his third visit, she had moved to a house composed of a bedroom and a living room in a rundown building close to the port. Father Ibrahim spent a week as the guest of the library of the Catholic church in Tripoli. He would finish his work at four in the afternoon and go to Yvonne's house, where she waited for him for lunch. She welcomed him in her own way and seemed in good spirits, as the chapter of her life involving the ugly baby girl, Zakariya, and the flood, had finished. She talked confidently as she laid out her plans for her future; she had a good relationship with a handful of kind families who included her in their special occasions, and she no longer felt homesick. When she talked about her family, she halted at the point of the flood, as if her life at the monastery and her relationship with Mariana had never happened at all, were just a terrible daydream. She hated Zakariya, Hanna, and Mariana. She believed nothing and lived in doubt, reading books and taking part in the cultural activities of the city. She wrote to Ibrahim zealously and sent him new books whenever she visited Beirut.

On his final visit, Father Ibrahim spoke for the first time about his life: about his mother, who had died while on a pilgrimage, and his grandfather, who had raised him and taught him to draw maps of monasteries and research their history. He brought the young Ibrahim with him on his long journeys and wrote outstanding books about the Christian pilgrimage route from Aleppo to Bethlehem, which he related in minute detail along with scores of stories, especially the curious anecdotes that he had collected over the ten years he spent as leader of the pilgrimage convoy.

Father Ibrahim, exhausted and approaching sixty, said he was bored with monastery life and the never-ending squabbles of men of religion. He wanted to leave and live a different sort of life, but he didn't know what form it would take. The night-long conversations he had with Yvonne gave him hope, and he colluded with her in her determination to forget about Helen. After his return, Yvonne received a long letter in which he shyly confessed that he loved her and asked if she would share his future life. She felt he was the right man for her. It didn't bother her that he was twenty-five years older than she was; he was a good man, affectionate and tolerant, and brought joy everywhere he went. He sent a letter to Cardinal Anton Deiry, a close associate of the pope in Rome. It wasn't easy to extract an agreement that he could marry and resign from the order. When the pope's decision reached him, he felt he had regained his freedom; he was being removed from the clerical state before he fell into sin. He arrived in Tripoli freed from all obligations and married Yvonne in 1929, and together they went to Beirut where Father Ibrahim found work he loved as a librarian in the Jesuit University. They rented a small house in Ashrafiyya and had a daughter whom Father Ibrahim wanted to call Aisha, after his excessive love for her namesake, but when Yvonne protested, he let it lie. He understood the sensitivity of someone who had long ago thrown her burdens off her back and walked a road of thorns to atone for her sin, and her regret was sincere. They agreed to name their first daughter Anthusa in honor of the mother of Saint John Chrysostom.

Father Ibrahim was still connected with the inhabitants of the monastery. Aisha kept sending provisions from Aleppo to Beirut, and she continued to visit him. She would book a room in a hotel in Al-Burj Square and spend a week in the company of Father Ibrahim, visiting restaurants, talking, and laughing together. Aisha understood Yvonne's sensitivity over her relationship with anyone from the monastery, but over the years she was able to convince her that their destinies were linked. In the end, Yvonne grew very fond of Aisha and no longer objected to having her as a guest in her small house with her own three children, but she never accepted Aisha's invitation to visit Aleppo.

Knowledge of the story of Helen, Zakariya, and Yvonne came late to Aisha. She was furious with Zakariya when she found out; she wept, pushed him away from her, and blamed him for having abandoned Yvonne and Helen, their own sister—but it was all over now. Helen had died, Yvonne had gone away, and Zakariya, like his horses, had grown old. Father Ibrahim never came back to the dilapidated monastery and seemed happy in his new life. He came home from the library for lunch every day, and Yvonne was a rare housekeeper. She left nothing to chance, looked after all her husband's affairs, ironed his shirts, polished his shoes, cooked, and concerned herself with her former students, who still remembered her with great respect. They remembered how sad she used to look, and her immense kindness and sympathy.

When Father Ibrahim resigned from the order and left the monastery, it came as a great shock to everyone, but for William it was a veritable catastrophe. He lost the spiritual mentor who had guided him through difficult moments to the hidden path of light that he alone could see. Junaid Khalifa couldn't fill the cavernous void in his heart. Junaid was more depressed and serious than was strictly warranted, and he was obsessed with his identity as teacher-turned-follower of one of his pupils, and with keeping the secrets of the imam of the lovers. On the night when William met his new friend Sam, he felt a new kind of cheer. Sam easily rattled off the life story of every person in the city, the history of every family, the connections between them, their economic misfortunes, and the secrets behind illustrious marriages. His prodigious memory made William feel that he needed him constantly; William himself was very forgetful. He lost things and forgot important appointments. He had never been much enamored of the world of light, preferring the shadows that he found in photography. He believed the story about his forefather, the Christian who converted to Islam to avoid paying the jizya, but he didn't understand why his ancestor had turned into such a fanatical Muslim, as the city told it. Sam elucidated this for him; to put it bluntly, Christians who converted to Islam were always under suspicion from Muslims. They didn't trust these converts, any more than the converts believed that they would no longer be forced off the sidewalk to make way for Muslims, or that they wouldn't be forced to wear clothing that marked them out. It was a sense of belonging to power. William was silent for some time, thinking about his grandfather Ahmed Bayazidi's relationship with Gabriel Gregoros. In the end, he didn't much care either way; he just wanted to tell Sam about Maryam. William had been drowning in loneliness, but from that night he became Sam's partner in his absurd adventures. Sam loved his life of idleness and was content with the little money he pocketed from renting out his shop in Khan Al-Harir, and his share of the profits from his father's shop, a well-known goldsmith's business run by his four siblings. He wasn't interested in the approval that everyone else was seeking, and anyone meeting him for the first time would think he was a prince without a kingdom. His small income was enough for him, and he had no ambition to found a dynasty; he spent his nights in bars and restaurants, enjoyed staying in hotels, and left his house for his unmarried older sister, who had chosen to live with him rather than dying alone, as she often repeated fearfully.

William liked him, even though he was ten years older and their temperaments were completely different. Within a short time they were firm, inseparable friends. William held his tongue about his relationships, rumors of which had begun to spread. He didn't want to work as a commercial photographer and instead established a studio in the European style—more like a gallery, bait for the elite.

This air of mystery made him enticing in the eyes of the society ladies who had dreams of immortality. He would gaze thoughtfully at clients with his wolflike eyes. Maryam had grown very far away in his memory now, and the instant he saw her come into the studio, he decided to expel her from his life. He grabbed her by the waist and kissed her with exaggerated violence. His message was clear: he was no longer that old romantic lover of fourteen who had brought her wildflowers every morning and declared his love, to the snickers of the girls who shared her room.

Those girls had regarded him as a nice boy who didn't enjoy the good looks a girl required in order to be lured to bed. But the women who stood in front of his camera felt for a few minutes that they were queens. Still, they didn't contradict any of his orders, and when he asked them to look in a certain direction, or to lie down on the red sofa, he knew what was going through their minds. He didn't participate in their schemes or favor one client over the others; he was stern in his opinion and admitted no conversations about others, only about themselves. He knew their inferiority complexes and crept inside their heads. They were astonished at his force and at the bizarre ideas about sex that he aired when he caught their conspiratorial glances, which he understood perfectly. He called them prey of the shadows. He told Sam about them without mentioning their names. He adored keeping his relationships secret and marked their pictures with ciphers no one understood apart from him. At first he pursued a French woman, the wife of one of the officers quartered in the garrison at Mount Zawiya. She loved showing off in front of the rich society ladies of Aleppo at the endless banquets where they cursed Ibrahim Hananu, Sheikh Saleh Ali, and Sultan Pasha Al-Atrash, who didn't want the French to "civilize" the nation. Madame Chevalier entered William's studio before sunset and looked at the wall crammed with mysterious pictures of women surrounded by shadows. Quivering as she laid bare her charms for the camera, she told him, "Suppose me to be Zenobia, queen of Tadmur, and take my picture."

He shut the door to the studio and poured her a glass of good wine. As he arranged the lights at leisure, he was watching her from the corner of his eye. When she sat on the chair, he asked her to bare her large breasts. She was surprised when her hand reached up and complied with his request, her eyes hanging on the click of the camera. It wasn't long before William took her to his house, connected to the studio by a narrow passage that only he knew about.

She was amazed by his virility and his frankly obscene way of having sex. He hurled vulgar insults at her, and she enjoyed it. She told her friends about him, and while she omitted certain details, they understood that he certainly wasn't the bashful young man who took care not to look at their chests when they stuck them out to exaggerate their femininity in their portraits.

William didn't care about the rumors surrounding him (that Sam played a primary role in passing on). He just smiled and said that what actually happened was far worse. Sam did his best to advertise his friend's magic. Maryam couldn't stand the legends about him. She was jealous when she heard women talking about William like a sorcerer, the way he spoiled his female customers and the way he so thoroughly understood them and their worries about getting older, about their mortality.

Returning home after their first meeting in his studio, Maryam felt utterly confused. He wasn't the lover she had known—clearly, he had slept with many women in order to perfect that kiss, which kept her trembling for days. She thought about him and the obscene words he had whispered in her ear. Unable to endure his rejection, she went back again, and this time he ignored her, then treated her with immense coolness, as if he didn't know her at all. He had turned his back on his old image as the unrequited lover, abandoned for a man Souad described as undercooked, banal, and wholly flavorless. Maryam remembered that she had never said goodbye to him. She didn't understand the messages he tried to send her during their repeated Saturday meetings. They talked once—when she asked him if he had loved her, he savagely replied, "A man doesn't forget a woman he gave all the flowers in the world." But she didn't grasp what he meant when he said, "You've become the shadow of other women." She always admired his peculiar way of expressing himself, the way he avoided touching her and photographed her using particular rituals. There was no end to his traps; every month he surprised her with a new photograph in which he read her lust, her longing, and her chaste restraint. At the same time, he hunted down every woman around her, especially the ones he knew would tell her about their escapades with him. He took particular care of them, knowing that Maryam would catch his scent in their conspiratorial smiles.

Many times Maryam reflected on the mistakes she had made in choosing her life. In William, she had had a chance at an outrageous life filled with folly and ecstasy, and every time she went to the studio, she resolved it would be the last. But she always returned, without understanding the attraction of a man who let her sit on a chair where no other woman was allowed to sit, but who avoided even brushing her hand.

After a year, Maryam sat down and spent a long time contemplating the twelve pictures he had taken of her. She was a different woman: a lover, reckless, living two lives without being able to choose either. She wanted to keep her family, and at the same time she wanted to be every woman he debauched. One day she couldn't stand it when her friend Narimane spoke about the unforgettable moments she had spent with William. She described his eccentric ideas in minute detail, praised the handful of pictures he had taken, and explained at great length his theory of shadow. As he had anticipated, Maryam understood perfectly that these were William's messages to her. She smothered her fury that he hadn't relayed them directly, just sat down at ten every morning to slurp his coffee with her phantom. He had turned her into a ghost, while she wanted to be a tangible being in his shadows.

One night William and Sam drank themselves into a stupor. William told Sam about Maryam and said she was the river he loved, and the city that increased his worries, and he never stopped fantasizing about her—she lived under his skin. Sam didn't understand his friend's torments and just asked coolly, "Why don't you penetrate her like the others?" William had no reply for a question he found so idiotic and simply added that when she left, it had meant death for him.

Sam couldn't understand the connection between her desertion of him and his unwillingness to penetrate her; he couldn't see how she was different from the dozens of women who had made his friend into a legend, a silent lothario. Over the following nights, William told his friend many details about his and Maryam's naïve love story; he had decided to leave it in the hands of someone other than Souad. One man alone couldn't love Maryam; she was a woman who needed crowds, hordes of lovers. Sam let him rant while holding the hand of Elizabeth, an English girl who had arrived in Aleppo the night before. She had sought out Sam on the advice of her friend, an archaeologist who had shared his bed and his nonsense for five months. Elizabeth was an amiable, well-mannered girl who used the formal *you* when speaking to both Sam and William. She came as a surprise to William; she resembled Maryam, but her lips were more beautiful. Sam didn't appreciate Elizabeth's formality, which he thought was a way of erecting barriers between them. Elizabeth had arrived with a mission to photograph the khans of Aleppo for the University of Oxford. She was an amateur photographer, and her limited knowledge was enough only for some unoriginal compositions, but her framing and lighting were sound. Sam was irritated by Elizabeth and William's conversation about photography; he was telling her about his mentor Teodor, and his relationship with old cameras came as a revelation to Elizabeth.

William was polite with her, and over subsequent nights the pair continued their conversation, the subject eventually turning to love. William didn't know why he was talking about Maryam with such passionate intensity, and Elizabeth didn't know why she was telling him about John, her boyfriend who had disappeared after sailing to Egypt as an infantry soldier. Sam would get bored with their animated conversation and wander over to another table to flirt with a woman he wanted to pursue, or he would leave them altogether and go to a brothel in Bahsita to keep company with the girls who were always waiting for him. William and Elizabeth would spend entire nights talking ardently about their thwarted loves, until they found themselves in bed. It was William's idea to swap their names; Elizabeth would become Maryam and he would become John. They allowed themselves to touch gingerly at first, then came moments of recrimination, when Elizabeth delivered a lengthy monologue about her agony at losing him, her joy that he had come back to her. William spoke about his endless pain when he imagined her in every woman that he took to bed. They enjoyed this game and identified closely with their new roles. William accompanied her to the markets and helped her take more original pictures. Sam looked on with glee as his friend and his guest blended together. However, he didn't like the thought of her staying on much longer in the city, and neither did Maryam, after William coolly told her she had been displaced by the Inkliziyya. There and then Maryam decided to distance herself from William forever. She was absent from the studio for more than six months, but in the end, she went back again. Every morning his image hovered around her with a greater urgency than before. She found him depressed after Elizabeth left; the English girl had given him moments he couldn't describe afterward. Maryam couldn't understand the blending of his memories. She realized her predicament; she was a married woman in love with a phantom who hovered around her and constantly occupied her thoughts. He enclosed her like a bracelet over her wrist, and she couldn't understand why she enjoyed it so much when her friends told her the news about scandals that had gained some embellishment in the retelling. In Sam's opinion, it was impossible to invent a legend without a few scandals; William would agree and subside into silence, waiting for Maryam to appear every Saturday like the apparition of a saint, and when she did enter his studio, he would treat her like a servant, an unwanted customer, and read her desire for him in the photographs he took of her.

William distributed his time between Aisha's house, the printing press where he met Junaid Khalifa, his shadow lovers, and his debaucheries with Sam. He had stopped caring about the monastery. He visited every Sunday morning, a tedious obligation to reassure Mariana he was still alive. Few details reached him about Hanna and Zakariya. Zakariya would hint to his son that he should get married, then ask to hear about his lovers. Their relationship was more like a friendship than that of father and son; they had never made a consistent life together but rather had been compelled by circumstances to live inside endless barricades.

By the time he was forty, William realized the delusion of living with shadow women. He kept up a few connections with a handful of women, who came more and more infrequently to sip fine whiskey and speak about the past. They endured his silences and his boredom until the few moments when they became Maryam, but those moments became as rare as his trips to the monastery.

On her own final visit to the monastery, Aisha lingered before leaving, holding her son Hasko, who would be ten the next day, by the hand. She had brought him so Hanna could give him his usual blessing, but Mariana's words had been unbearably cruel. Aisha realized that Mariana had been able to impose her authority on the monastery at last, and she was avenging the dead before they even passed. Hanna had seen no one but Zakariya for several months. Aisha dawdled as she walked. Zakariya had ignored her suggestion that they go together. Boulos the deacon sent her off with a sympathetic look; he no longer had much to say to anyone and was content to care for the few aged horses remaining in the monastery stable. He spent all his time cleaning the mangers and reciting the same few lines of an ode by Zuhayr bin Abi Sulma—*I have grown weary of the encumbrances of life*—whenever Reverend Sister Mariana passed by him. Nothing tempted anyone to stay. Mariana couldn't understand Aisha's adoration of Deir Zahr Al-Rumman, nor the fact that in spite of Hanna's wretched condition, Aisha still visited him every week. She wished, deep down, that William possessed such loyalty.

After she turned Aisha out, Mariana felt greatly relieved. Their thorny relationship was finished. She reflected that she had spent her life battling everyone in order to secure Hanna's sainthood after his death. She was secretly afraid she would die before him and everything would be destroyed. She herself played a principal role in the story she wanted to immortalize.

She was frightened that the stories she had spread to every corner of the country were now being forgotten and erased. Hanna's silence had turned the monastery into a ruin. She urged him to speak, to wander the surrounding villages and bless the many shepherds, and she invited him to appear at Sunday mass. But he only withdrew even further. As she watched Aisha walking away, expelled and humiliated, Mariana felt she had achieved revenge on yet another person who could destroy her narrative about the monastery and Hanna's biography.

Aisha was the only one who disregarded the teachings that Mariana issued on a regular basis. Although Mariana reflected with satisfaction on her victory over Aisha, she in turn had been destroyed by Hanna's silence. He had conquered her merely by sitting in his disregarded corner, in the room from which she had been barred for years. He had been utterly silent in response to her suggestion that the place be transformed into a pilgrimage site for Syriacs, who would never allow him to beg for alms to buy the lentil soup he gave to the people who had chosen to stay here until they died. These people were mostly nuns who had lived here all their lives and had no wish to explain themselves to anyone, and a few men of religion who yawned their days away.

Aisha found Mariana's cruelty unbearable. She sobbed in the back seat of the car that always waited for her when she visited the monastery. For the first time, she felt like an orphan. To be forbidden to see Hanna was unendurable; on her last visit three months earlier, he had told her that Mariana wanted to bury him alive. He was exhausted and sounded like an old man, dragging his feet with some difficulty. He told her how desolate he was in the absence of everyone he loved.

On that occasion, Aisha had looked at him for a long time. She offered to move him and Zakariya to her house; there he would feel free and could regain his vigor and well-being. It wasn't possible for two men in their seventies to live without their family's care, and she and Yousef and William and Souad were all the family they had. For some time, he had kept repeating, "Everyone wants me to die." He considered Aisha's spontaneous suggestion; why not really leave this place? But soon he retreated and convinced himself that he was there in order to be buried next to Zakariya in the neighboring graves he had dug for them many years ago.

For the last five years, Hanna had left his room only on rare occasions. His attendants stopped anyone from coming near him. No one dared touch him, although in all that time he was still a source of fascination, a genuine lure for his wretched flock, who still waited for his blessing. They would circulate his words and reverently tell his life story in its many and varied forms. They recalled his lecture at a Sunday mass five years earlier, when he had spoken for a long time about plants, birds, and animals, including, with great joy, the dinosaur skeleton in his friend Arif's house. Mid-lecture he openly doubted the existence of God and the myth of the resurrection.

That day Mariana had realized that he wanted to destroy everything and was determined either to restore the monastery as his own personal possession or to burn it down. He said out loud, clearly, that God was a delusion, adding that Jesus was greater than a mere prophet—he was a great idea that had been distorted into a pack of lies. Mariana didn't let him go on; she took him by the hand and forcibly led him out. She announced he had been suffering from a dangerous fever for days and had been delirious for a month, and the doctors didn't know why. For the first time in her life, Mariana was insolent to Hanna and stopped anyone from talking to him. Hanna no longer had the strength to fight. The faces of those he loved appeared to him, and he saw no way out. Mariana was no poor little girl anymore; now she was the reverend sister, absorbed in the struggles of the metropolitans and the priests and the patriarch. She was overjoyed by a few letters she had received from the pope, and she welcomed any invitation to the Vatican, which wanted her to complete her holy mission of running the monastery.

She ruled it with an iron fist. The last time she listened to Hanna had been a few years before, the day he decided to dig his own and Zakariya's graves in the monastery graveyard with his own hands. He repeated his last will and testament to everyone and, not content with that, wrote it down and sent it to Metropolitan Basilos. At that time, he had still been surrounded by a few friends and students, but now he was alone, half-imprisoned, cut off even from the people who circulated Mariana's invented stories. They all repeated her latest effort: he had doubted the existence of God and described Jesus as a mere idea, then the Light flooded his heart at night and woke him at dawn and he crawled on his knees to the statue of the virgin next to the altar, weeping from the strength of his faith. Mariana's story was a success, smothering Hanna's suggestion that Jesus was a luminous idea held up for all humanity. In the days that followed Hanna's zealous devotion to God (as Mariana told it), Mariana reflected that only a few steps remained for Hanna to be made a saint. An entire history couldn't be erased by a moment of folly. Still, she kept his friends away from him. Father Ibrahim had left the monastery a few months earlier, and now she prevented Aisha from visiting and ordered all the nuns to pray for Hanna to be healed. She summoned the most skilled doctors to consult them about a patient she wouldn't let them see or examine, because he was suffering from a luminous disturbance that rarely befell those not numbered among the saints. She told the doctors about nonexistent symptoms, and they offered expensive advice to preserve this sainted life.

After her exile, Aisha arrived at her aunt Souad's house, threw herself onto the sofa, and sobbed. Souad couldn't believe Hanna's isolation and his exhaustion; Aisha told her about the last time she met Hanna, when he told her that he could walk no farther than to Zakariya's house. He could sit by his window and watch the pomegranate blossoms turn into small fruits at his leisure, and the only pleasures he had left were chatting with Zakariya, and writing about the figs dripping honey and the cherry trees erupting into flower. He complained that Mariana read everything he wrote down and tore up whatever might contradict his saintly image. Just as Jesus is greater than an idea, so too is a saint greater than a man who rants and raves at will. Hanna had concluded by telling Aisha that, according to Mariana, saints had no freedom.

Souad sympathized with her niece. It had been some time since

she paid any attention to the tales surrounding Hanna; in her preoccupation with daily matters, she had forgotten how she had once loved
him. But that day she listened attentively as Aisha complained about
her loneliness, how she had lost everyone she loved. Aisha recalled
Teodor and his photographs; she was upset because he had stopped
replying to her letters even five years before he died. And Father Ibrahim spent most of his time in the library of the Jesuit University, finishing his magnum opus on the history of Christianity in the East.

Souad offered coffee to Aisha, who kept repeating that she didn't
want to go into a cocoon and hated butterflies, and she told Yousef
to be quiet when he teased her affectionately, calling her his butterfly. Souad laughed at Aisha's train of thought, at her mixing of things
that couldn't be mixed. She assured her niece that everything would
be fine—Hanna at his weakest was still stronger than Mariana, who
behaved like a woman still subject to a past that was burdened with
insults.

That night Aisha asked Yousef to think of some way to free Hanna
from his isolation. Yousef regarded her thoughtfully for a long time.
Eventually he remarked that she seemed like another woman altogether; powerless, lonely, pale, and frightened, she seemed as if she
were begging death to keep its distance. She told Yousef he was right;
she had seen apparitions of death hovering around her since daybreak,
when she had startled in terror from her bed. Yousef took her hand
and sat next to her on the bed. He whispered the words she loved in
her ear: "This weekend we will go to Sharran and open up the room
of the dinosaur. Only a few fingerbones are left, but its remains surely
miss you." Aisha smiled. Shaking her head, she said she would turn
to dust just like the dinosaur, then fell silent until she was completely
calm. She fell asleep holding Yousef's hand. Once she was asleep, he
covered her with a blanket and checked on their sleeping daughter,
Dilshan. He regretted having allowed their son, Hanna Sheikh Musa,
to travel to Britain to study textile engineering. He needed him close
by, and in recent days he had been thinking of how to tell his son that
he could no longer send him money. Yousef had sold the last piece of

land he had inherited from his father, and his income from translation and the articles he wrote on the Kurdish issue weren't enough to cover his children's expenses. But he put off thinking about it. Over the last two days, Aisha had gone back to her old fits, when she would press her whole body into his chest and tell him that she had seen death sitting on the edge of the sofa in her bedroom or, from the bathroom window, climbing out of the skylight in their imposing building. The apartment they lived in was the last property Yousef had left. It held all his memories of Aisha; he wouldn't give it up for any reason.

Yousef was terrified of losing Aisha. How he would live without her, he couldn't imagine. He opened the door of the bedroom where Aisha was sunk in a deep sleep. Her chest rose and fell with her regular breathing, and he was relieved that the angel of death must have left through the hole in the door. He slipped in between his daughter Dilshan and his son Hasko, put his arms around them, and slept till morning, when he was woken by his daughter demanding that he make them breakfast because her mother wasn't there—she must have gone back to the monastery to see Grandfather Hanna before they woke up.

Aisha had in fact woken at dawn and gone out. She slowly crossed the road to Baron Street. The city was still asleep; the only people around were some street cleaners and a newspaper hawker drinking tea on the corner of the Central Post Office building in Jamiliyya. She knocked on the door of her brother William's house; he was surprised to see her at that hour, even though he was used to her moods and the surprising turns of phrase that she had inherited from her aunt Souad. She asked him to get up—she wanted to talk to him about Teodor's pictures that he kept in his shop, the ones he had given her in exchange for teaching him Arabic. She said, "I want to see them, I miss my childhood."

Dawn was not William's hour. He usually woke up at ten for his standing appointment with Maryam, who sat alone at her dining table and poured out her coffee while he did the same at his own table

in his house, in a tradition they hadn't interrupted for twenty years.
Aisha realized he was a little befuddled. He looked at her with deep
love and suggested she prepare some coffee, but she asked to go down
into the studio right away, saying, "I don't have time for coffee." He
gave her the key and went back to bed, thinking of his evening as-
signation with Madame Mervet, who had promised him that this
time she would try to spend the entire night in his arms. She had assured him yesterday that her husband had gone to Beirut and that
she wouldn't leave him alone. He retreated back into his daydreams,
where the faces of Maryam and her dear friend Mervet became mingled. Usually nothing would make him get up early; he would wait for
the conclusion of Maryam's secret signs. He thought about his sister's
obsessive idea, which she must have clung to for two years now, that
the angel of death was perched on her shoulder. He brought his coffee
pot and his cigarettes back to bed. The clock was pointing to eight.
Right now Maryam would be sitting on the stone basin in the bathroom, stretching under the hot water, rubbing her armpits, closing
her eyes, and sending him the signals of her desire that he caught as
he lay in his bed. His sex swelled, and that hypothetical pleasure returned to him. At nine, everyone would leave the house and Maryam
would stay there alone, boiling her coffee and sitting on her chair by
the open window from which she could see the cactus and cypress of
the Franciscan monastery. She would take delectably unhurried sips
from her coffee, as if she were kissing him on the lips. It was their
secret hour, one that they had lived together thousands of times. To
them, nothing was equal to this love. They both reflected on their
longing, the invisible thread on which hung their burning, theoretical
kisses, their apprehensions, their buried desires—this invisible love,
which he noted in her eyes and between her breasts, which showed
from the necklines of the dresses she chose in order to sit in her special
chair, ready for him to take her picture, on the first Saturday of every
month. Afterward their coffee would be ready and waiting for them.
At times she felt she would swallow him whole, but she made do with

teasing him, telling him everything she had learned from the women whom she occasionally waylaid, so they would tell her in detail about what it was like to sleep with him.

He knew the women who would tell her every detail of his lechery. He sent messages to Maryam through their bodies, worlds were mixed, and women were intoxicated by their exciting experience with this bachelor. William spent his mornings daydreaming and his nights in the company of his shameless friend Sam, who made a ready audience for his tales about the anonymous women who passed through his life and his bed. Together William and Sam drank to the health of thigh and breast; then William would fall silent as he listened to his friend, after a short while, cast his net like a skillful hunter around whichever foreign woman was currently patronizing the bar of the Hotel Baron to round out her experience of The Orient.

The sound of Aisha moving around reached William from the studio. She took out Teodor's pictures and contemplated them, as she usually did whenever she was struck with longing for the days of their distant childhood. And as she usually did, she spent a long time looking at one particular picture of her, William, Hanna, and Zakariya, taken when the twins were eighteen. Hanna was smiling and hugging her, and she was leaning her head toward him like a caress. Zakariya's face shone with contentment and a profound sadness. She hadn't hung the picture on her living room wall; she believed it to be part of the personal secret that the twins shared, and that others had no right to see or know about. Despite her pale face and her unconcealed anxiety, William guessed that his presence would ruin those moments of recollection and disturb the silent tears that Aisha habitually shed whenever she was eulogizing the past. She always said, "What fools we were to leave our childhood. We left Hanna and Zakariya behind for Mariana to quietly destroy."

Aisha didn't know why she came to the studio at that early hour of the morning. She had spent a bad night and couldn't bear the thought of no longer seeing Hanna. She didn't want to visit Shaha's grave by herself—she wanted to repeat the ritual that had become holy: she would arrive at the monastery before sunrise, take Hanna by the hand, and together they would walk the short distance, leisurely and in silence. On reaching Shaha's grave, they would clear away the dried plants and adorn it with the olive branches, pomegranate branches, and wildflowers that they had picked on the way there.

Hanna would close his eyes for a few minutes, and Aisha would do the same. Then together they would go back to Hanna's room, have breakfast, and speak about their lives. Aisha encouraged Hanna to travel and see his flock, who always spoke about his blessings. She knew he loved walking in the fields. She suggested he come and live in her house, and as usual he smiled and looked at the photographs she took out of her bag. They were pictures of her family, over which William had taken great pains to perfect the angles and lighting. In them, Aisha looked like a lady: angry, powerful, filled with longing. Her husband Yousef stood beside her, both of them still deeply in love; their son Hanna Sheikh Musa and daughter Dilshan were never absent from these photographs, the likes of which William had taken many times over the years. More recent photographs had seen the addition of Hasko, her youngest son, whom Hanna doted on. His grandfather Zakariya used to joke that Hasko looked more like Hanna, and that Hanna's genes had routed even those of their friend Arif Sheikh Musa Agha. Aisha used to say to Hanna, "Ya Abati, children grow up in photographs." Sometimes, with a wickedness Hanna appreciated, Aisha would slip a photograph of her aunt Souad in among the collection of pictures. She still retained that haughty look, and despite the passage of years, she was still attractive. Every day Souad grew further and further away from the heedless child she had once been.

In the studio, Aisha brought out the photographs, which had been carefully wrapped and arranged in a large binder. She threw herself onto the long sofa that William often employed for his fleeting sexual adventures, and she tossed an album of Teodor's photographs onto the small table beside her. She suddenly knew that the angel of death wouldn't be satisfied with feeling the lines on her palm this time; she could feel him seeping through her pores into her blood, rising through her arteries into her heart; she felt him in her sap. It was all over quickly. She wasn't even forty. She leaned her head back and surrendered without a fuss. At ten o'clock, William got up and went through the hidden corridor to the studio. Thinking her asleep, he came close to her and took her hand. The coldness he felt there crept into his heart. Aisha was dead, and William learned that their connection had betrayed him for the first time in his life—she hadn't sent him a final sign.

He picked her up in his arms and carried her to his bed. He thought of keeping her beside him, but the clatter of customers coming into the studio prevented him from giving in to his thoughts. William's apprentice, Khalil, knocked on the door to his apartment. The door was open, and in the deep silence, Khalil felt afraid—William's rooms had never been like this before. Khalil went into William's small apartment and saw his elegantly clothed mentor kissing his dead sister's hand, his body quaking with silent sobs.

9

The Lover's Apparition

Aleppo—1951

Maryam used to watch William from her seat by the window over-looking the Franciscan monastery in the upper-class neighborhood of Muhafaza. She saw him wandering the streets and bars with Sam, then go into his aunt Souad's house, where he would sit in the printer's basement for hours at a time talking to Junaid Khalifa about the manuscripts he had to verify and print. When he cried from longing, she saw him, and when he was struck down with lethal anxiety, she could see it as if it were a material substance, a clot of feelings flying in the air. An image of him came to her, vague; he was embedded in her pores. His desire tore at her when she saw him drawing on other women to supplement the image of her in his daydreams.

William was Maryam's other face. She realized that her fate was linked with his and with his genuine connection to Aisha and his aunt Souad. Their personal history took on a single meaning, four people cheating death, correcting the stories all around them, planning their lives and dreaming that they would live for ten centuries, then just melt away. Their heads would shrivel, their bodies would disintegrate, and they would disappear. They decided the dead were in error when they surrendered their bodies to the worms in the ground; they spoke passionately about everything, except for death, as if it didn't exist.

At first, Maryam was dismayed by the idea of cleaving to one man all her life. She didn't know how she had become attached to him. He didn't ask much from her, however, and she relished her predicament. She heard how the city circulated the stories of his amorous outrages; for his part, he was annoyed by the questions that besieged him on all sides. He lived only for Maryam, and communication between them was never interrupted for a moment, and in the end they were both resigned to their shared fate.

Maryam never allowed the thread of secret love connecting them to be interrupted. She felt the burden of emotion and responsibility for his life, the threads of which she held in her hands. Their meetings on the first Saturday of every month were tempered by her jealousy; she wanted him for herself alone, to be her lover. Still, she was constantly overwhelmed by the profound sensation that he had abandoned everything and subjugated his whole life to loving her.

One day Maryam woke up early, drenched in her own fluids, her body trembling with lust, missing William. She knew these depressing moments all too well; she feared that one day she would open the door and go out onto the streets to hunt for him like a madwoman. As usual, she went into the bathroom, sat in the stone bath, and sank into cold water to extinguish herself. She closed her eyes, determined that her day would be completed just as she had been planning for weeks. She would see William—she wanted to see the new photograph—and tell him not to wait for her, that she had had enough. Then she would continue on to the church. The Armenians would be commemorating the massacre that day, and she would ask the metropolitan about reclaiming her identity as an Armenian Christian. She didn't know if this would help rectify her history; she knew what the Armenians said about her, but she didn't care. She wanted to light a candle for her mother, her grandfather, and her aunt. And she would resume her search for Harout; no sign of his death had ever reached her, so surely he must be alive in some distant land. In the previous two weeks, she had concluded that she had been through enough. She was no longer concerned about the image that Orhan had so carefully guarded: that of a good Muslim wife, devout, soon to be a distinguished grandmother. Her childhood besieged her, left her no opportunity to forget. Well, she was no longer a tattered doormat. Orhan had died the previous year, and the mourning period was over. Mornings weighted with obligations had come to an end. She had been determined to carry out his wish to be buried in his family grave beside his mother; she had gone to Istanbul with his body and transferred all care of it to its owners. She remained silent in the face of unceasing insults from his family; she endured the burden of being alone in a group of men and women who were mostly strangers to her. At night she slept in a room hung with medals and pictures of Ottoman officers. Perhaps one of them had killed her family and burned down her house.

After a full year of absence from his studio, Maryam stood silently in front of William. She allowed him time to contemplate her as much as he liked, and he quietly gestured at her to enter the photography studio and sit on the chair. He hadn't sought her out over the past year, but he had waited for her at the same hour that hadn't changed in twenty years. She removed her coat and hung it on the hook. She left the special chair empty and instead sat on the chair for general clients, as she had done the last time she was there. Both easily understood the unspoken messages that flowed between them. She looked into the camera and attempted a laugh, reconsidered, and pursed her lips instead. She decided that he no longer deserved her light spirits. Now, for her, William would be just a photographer, one who should be grateful that Madame Orhan Al-Din Urfili was one of his clients. Her silence disconcerted him; she was an expert at torturing him. Secretly she was pleased that he was still waiting for her.

Everything was ready, as it had been for twenty years. There was her chair, with a history of their first meeting, on the seventeenth of January 1931, carved on the right armrest. She had inquired about him in the isolation room in Deir Zahr Al-Rumman, a distant memory now. He had carved the story of their meeting using an intertwining line, a secret code no one could crack. On the chair's second armrest, using the same intertwining pattern, he carved a history of the thirteenth of February 1933, the day he had seen her in the shadows of the basement in his aunt Souad's house. On that day, she had been waiting for him in agony. She opened the buttons of her fur coat and was completely naked underneath. She embraced him and whispered shamelessly in his ear: *Take me.* She added a plea that he carry her to the bed to smash open her ribs and rip her body apart. Her knees were breaking. She had waited years for that moment, and when he laid her on the bed, she panicked. The daydreams she had had for years evaporated; she felt the ceiling was too low and would only hold them back from taking flight. She tried to explain to him, but he was content to draw his fingers over her body, he promised. He just wanted to savor the smell of her, to examine her every pore with his palms and fingertips. Gently, he took hold of her nipple, and then his touch descended over the edge of her breast, carried on to her stomach. He inhaled her deeply so her scent would permeate the depths of his soul. An hour later she got up. She felt relaxed and rested. He kissed her, their second kiss. It was long, he didn't want to leave her lips and her tongue. She was feeling for his sex with her knee, and this increased her fear. After she kissed him, she expected him to enter her, but he threw a blanket over her naked body and sat, smoking, staring at the weak light that seeped in through the low windows. She left him in the cellar and went out, alarmed. He stayed alone in bed, looking at the point of light. Reinvigorated, he left his aunt's house and walked through the empty new quarter. He left the wool market and headed to the Hotel Baron where, in a corner of the hotel bar, he burst into sobs like a small boy while Sam was convincing a French tourist that he had seen an enormous crocodile in the Euphrates. William listened to Sam, who appeared utterly serious, and to the giggles of the reckless bar customer, who required no fairy tales to go to bed with him.

Maryam arrived home, trembling with fear. She went to her room but couldn't bear the enclosed space, nor the worried looks of her husband and young children, nor the sympathetic gaze of her maidservant. She thought they all knew what had happened. She thought of going outside, anywhere; she suggested to Orhan that they go to Restaurant Old Town to have dinner. As soon as she sat next to Orhan in the car, she realized it was a disastrous idea, she didn't want to meet anyone, but in the end she went on foot through the crowds and the traffic. William didn't come to the restaurant that day. She was dazed, assailed by images, she thought she had come here to see him. She missed him, she wanted to see his ribs groaning. She tried to relax and asked the waiter for a table away from the crowd; she didn't want to play along with the other customers, most of whom she knew. In a shadowy corner, Orhan's hand squeezed her thigh, but she felt nothing. She couldn't change the pictures in her mind. Calmly, she ate a plate of Armenian salad and a cut of pork. She had ordered it to annoy Orhan, but he was affectionate and, as usual, didn't argue the necessity of adhering to Islamic customs. She thought, whenever William was late to meet her, that those images would never be usable again. They were faded and smudged, and at that moment she was no longer anything like the woman who wept from an excess of love, and William wasn't the reckless lover who had slipped into her bed-room one wintry day a year before and stood beside her bed. He had climbed the bank manager's fence; any slip might have cost him his life, but he was prepared to pay it for the chance to slip into bed beside her and stay until morning. She was alarmed when she found him gently stroking her arm, reaching the roundness of her breast with his finger. The window was open, and he was smiling. He gestured at her wordlessly, but her pleasure was mingled with horror when she recalled he was in her husband's house. Furious, she escaped his arms and ordered him out at once. He didn't care what might happen that night—as he told her later, he was craving to see her stomach and hold her hips. He touched her bare right breast and inhaled the scent of her body, brimful of sleep. For him, his life was a just price for all this. He merely said to her, "I want to smell the scent of you sleeping." She was incredulous when she saw him leaping lightly off the fence like a highwayman. Sam was waiting on the other side; he took hold of his friend, who was waving a gun around, and the two of them walked off around the corner as if they hadn't done a thing. She couldn't believe he had done it.

Sam took his arm, giggling, but the night didn't end well. Sam

wouldn't let William go and took him to the Show Night Bar near
the train station. The Turkish band was playing songs Sam loved, and
after their third drink, William was convinced that everything had
gone off safely, and he wasn't going to die. He relaxed and remembered the warmth of sleeping beside Maryam. He thought he must
have lost his mind to have stormed her bedroom that way, but he was
extraordinarily happy; the feel of her breast had had a peculiar savor. Sam got up suddenly and walked to the band. He slipped five
liras to the bandleader and stood in the middle of the dance floor. He
asked them to play any song about impossible love. As he pointed at
William, Sam declared that this song was dedicated to him, the most
important photographer in the world. Then he added that William
had slaughtered his beloved two hours ago and thrown her body into
the River Qweiq. He added, "From an intensity of love, we have to kill
our beloveds—love is worthless without murder." He added, loudly
and clearly, that William's beloved was floating on the river in a white
dress under the moonlight of that beautiful night.

There was no moon that night, but for Sam, every night was moonlit. Most of the customers were aware that his stories were mostly
invented, but a frightening silence dominated the bar. Sam's utter dis-
regard of the stares of the crowd filled William with a sense of danger.
But the band played on, and with all his might, the singer sang three
Anatolian songs about impossible love and added his own extempo-
rizations, echoing the sentiment that love was worth nothing without
the risk of death. Sam liked the singer's improvisations and asked the
band to play a fourth song that corresponded to that evening's tragic
events.

Maryam later heard details of this story, which spread all over the
city. She quite sincerely felt that she would be killed that very night
and her body would be set afloat on the river. When the band began to play, William closed his eyes, and his mind replayed, as he
relished to the last note, the songs that Maryam had given him on a
record. The other customers stared at him enviously, just like all the

men who contemplated the pictures hanging on the wall of his studio and reflected that he had probably bedded all these lovely women. Even Orhan, every now and then, used to repeat the legend that Sam propagated about the man who had won the adoration of every beauty in Aleppo in exchange for capturing her immortality in entrancing photographs. Not content with spreading the legend of this Don Juan, Sam had invented a whole different life for him, just as he had invented his own earlier life.

Before the night ended, William found a police car waiting for him outside his house. The police sergeant gripped the steering wheel and told William to be silent. He was brought to the guardhouse, and a boorish policeman threw him into a cold cell. Another policeman spat on him and called him a fugitive and a murderer. Sam was so drunk he couldn't walk home and had to take a room at the Hotel Baron. He didn't wake up until after the call to afternoon prayer, by which point the entire city was talking about the photographer who had murdered his beloved and thrown her body in the River Qweiq. The police were searching everywhere for Sam to take his witness statement, without success.

In the morning, a police patrol accompanied William to the forensic medical center. When they uncovered the face of a woman in her thirties and asked him to identify her and describe his crime, William realized he was in trouble. On the advice of the lawyer his aunt Souad had engaged for him, he maintained total silence apart from a few words, which he kept repeating: he didn't know who the victim was, the story was the invention of his friend Sam, heir of the well-known goldsmith Baron Mikhail Musa, and it was one of a thousand stories Sam told every night.

The officer on duty was an admirer of William and his myth. He didn't believe that a poor woman in a peasant's dress would attract the notice of a man like William. The officer had no doubt it was an honor crime, especially as the woman, according to the notes of the forensic doctor, displayed signs of having undergone excessive violence and sustained beatings in the days prior to her death, and she hadn't been slaughtered with a knife, as the person who informed on William had reported.

Maryam had an anxious few days, but she secretly enjoyed the romance of it all: the idea of a lover killing his beloved from a surfeit of passion. The image with the most artistry and finesse, however, was that of two lovers who died together, in the same moment, in a single bed, each of them inhaling the scent of the other as they slept.

On every one of those mornings, Orhan would curse William, pray for God's mercy on the soul of his own mentor, William's grandfather Ahmed Bayazidi, and ask Maryam not to go to the studio again. He found the scandal an excellent opportunity of revenge for the upper-class women's admiration of William's camera angles, which made the shots look like something out of a film. Orhan found it an equally opportune moment to cut the tie between Maryam and the monastery, between her childhood and her current life. She kept her counsel on his comments, but Orhan spent days blathering on about William's supposed guilt, and he wouldn't have appreciated her making the truth known to him, to say the least. In moments of fury, Maryam wanted to say that she was the lover from Sam's story. A few day later a fellah recognized the picture of the murdered woman that was published in the local papers, and the official report was closed when the family came forward and received her body, saying only that she must have slipped into the river and drowned.

After three days in prison, William was released. He locked up the studio and slept at the house of his aunt Souad, who informed Maryam that she needed to visit him. In a brief note, Souad wrote to her that he might vanish within days—"vanishing" being the generally accepted term between the three of them for "dying." Maryam went to Souad's house that day. She sat on the bed next to William and gave him her hand. He took it and kissed it and repeated what he always said: that he was no longer capable of withstanding the torture. On her way to see him, Maryam had decided that she would be harsh, she would scold him and break his nose—she was furious and had no sympathy for him or his situation. But when she saw him lying there, speaking about disintegrating and vanishing in that grief-stricken way, she remembered the iris flowers he used to leave by her window in the room for quarantined patients at the monastery. She was just a poor girl who had survived a massacre; she didn't deserve all the feeling that he showed her.

She suddenly found herself in a moment of unique emotion. She groped for his legs; they were cold, and his nails uncared for. She blamed herself for having neglected him, for having left him alone. If only she had allowed him to spend the night in her bed. He had wanted to inhale the scent of her sleeping; how cruel that a man had spent half his life without inhaling the scent of the woman he loved as she slept. She kissed his legs, locked the door, and slipped into bed beside him. Taking off her clothes, she dug her tongue into the tip of his nose, sank into his chest, and hoped to sleep. Just then she wanted to make all his wishes come true. He was delirious from the fever. His body was drenched in sweat, his eyes wandered aimlessly. All night she was thinking how, if he died, she would throw herself into the river so she would be swept away from this city. There was a void in her body, her soul was weighed down with matchless inanity; she wondered what on earth she was doing in Orhan's house. Who were these children who wandered so confidently through the large house, jabbering in French in the morning, and joining their father in the evening to listen to Turkish songs and discuss the glory of their people?

As she walked along Baron Street, Maryam remembered the first time she had stood in front of William's camera. She had been sixteen, amazed, and she still recalled William's gleaming eyes, Teodor observing him from afar with total satisfaction. By that point he no longer corrected the lens for William or advised him how to look at the light. She was brushed by magic at that moment. The negative of the most recent picture, the one he had taken a few minutes earlier, hadn't been developed yet. Now she was forty years old, struck with a peculiar indifference. She had become a widow at thirty-nine, free of commitments, and instead of thinking of how to set up a life with William, she had gone in the opposite direction.

With William, she had lived an entire lifetime as half of this pair of withered lovers. They had never spoken about love, they simply lived it, steadily and persistently, as though the innocent conversation of their childhood were still ongoing. Maryam felt as if she were merely an album of the photographs that kept accumulating in the corner of his large shop, and she grew furious at the notion of steadiness and persistence. What did it mean that your life was propagated in photographs, photograph after photograph, so you made an album, and then album after album, filling up space in a vacuum? At one time, she had believed William when he told her they weren't just pictures but a document of their silent love.

After Maryam was widowed, she thought of escaping everything and traveling, to what destination she didn't care. She reviewed her possible escapes, and memories of the depressing places she had lived came back to her. In spite of the space that surrounded her, she felt confined; the breezes in the monastery oppressed her, as did the larder and the cold kitchen, the ponderous movements of the nuns, and the Syriac language classroom; her mother's grave tucked in among a few vine trellises along some anonymous road; her grandfather Gregor's house overlooking the square in Urfa; the streets and squares of Aleppo. Her chest tightened as she visualized these places. She decided that the cellar in Souad's house was her favorite place, although she hadn't been there for several years. She couldn't have cared less about anywhere in this city apart from that place, where she had discovered her femininity for the first time. She had carried out an experiment, putting on the long black dress in which she had strutted about in the fashion show, drawing the eye of Orhan, who wasted no time and proposed to her a few days later. And after her marriage, she had found herself drowning in continual nightmares.

Two months after Orhan's death, she went outside for the first time with Souad, after the older woman had come to visit her and teased her about her determination to complete her 'idda to please her children. Souad left her in her house on that visit but said she would be expecting Maryam the following day. Maryam reflected that Souad always saved her at difficult moments. She took off her black dress and informed her children that she wouldn't be observing the full 'idda period, adding that she wasn't even Muslim. She left the house without listening to the protests of her oldest son, Abdel Hamid. She let herself into Souad's house with her key and passed through the threshold, after giving her usual signal of three knocks. From the window looking out over the courtyard, she saw the shadow of Souad in her room, arranging her clients' dresses, as she usually did on a Thursday evening. Souad saw Maryam crossing the courtyard quickly, heading for the cellar. As if Maryam could see her, she laughed softly. She wasn't surprised that Maryam had come back. She had been expecting her for some time, but she had been late, as usual.

Maryam didn't stay long in the cellar. She realized how absurd it was to seek a fleeting memory in a place full of mannequins and boxes of old dresses. It looked like the disused storeroom of a seamstress who had no longer cared about boasting to others. Maryam felt hope sputter out, her delusions frittered away. She wished she had died in the cholera epidemic thirty years earlier, at the moment when she saw William's eyes keeping watch over her as she lay on a filthy cotton mattress in an isolation room at the monastery.

She crossed Baron Street and seemed to be seeing Aleppo for the first time. When she arrived at the church, a huge crowd of Armenians had gathered, exchanging news as they waited for mass. She walked steadily to the front pew and sat there alone. She could feel the stares of people she knew boring into her; no doubt they were wondering what she, a Muslim woman who had married a Turk, was doing here. But she was Armenian and Christian still. Mass began, and amid the wailing of old women, tears flowed over her cheeks. She was remembering her brother Harout, and his buzuq with the broken strings. She didn't wait for the end of mass; she rose from her seat and left, feeling it wasn't the right time to talk to the metropolitan about such a delicate matter. Overcome by memories of the massacre, she drowned in tears, her speech was confused. She reflected that massacre survivors did not suffer from forgetting; instead, their chests were inscribed with bitterness and a wish for vengeance.

She arrived back at the house at eighty-thirty in the evening, weighed down by depression. She went to her bedroom, lay down on the bed, and tried to expel the images of burned Armenian women, the face of her mother in her last moments before starvation propelled her to her last gasp, the little girl they had tried to save, the burned-out houses. It was impossible to summarize the massacre, especially for a woman who had spent her life trying to learn how to forget. She had to admit that she hadn't succeeded; instead, all the vanished images had come back. A long time might have passed, but not long enough for the blood to dry.

If William died tonight, then everything would be ruined. It would take her back again to zero, to the anxiety that had never left her since Orhan's death. She used to think that she would be a free woman as a widow, but right then she certainly wasn't. She was suddenly convinced that it would all be over only when both men were dead. Deep down, she wished they had both died on the same day. She decided she would live her life as a comedy, not a tragedy, and she would look for Harout. She would burn William's photo albums and scatter their ashes over the River Qweiq. She would burn the hundreds of handkerchiefs she had kept so that William, as he used to tell her, could breathe in her perfume, recomposing the scent of her neck and the beautiful valley between her breasts as he recalled the memory of their touch. She thought she might go and live with Souad and try again to seek the definition of happiness, recalling the memory of exhibiting her figure onstage at the fashion show.

She said to herself, "Those images of the massacre aren't lethal." She left her room. She didn't want to be alone. She prepared dinner at the usual time and calmly fried meat fillets, put pickles on small plates, and sliced tomatoes. She was imagining it was Orhan's body she was slicing, and that she was frying the eyes of his hateful uncle who had banned "the Armenian" from entering the family home on the only occasion Orhan had mulled going back to live with his family.

Everything had passed now. The only thing she was sure of was that she had never felt any emotion whatsoever toward Orhan. The only man she had ever loved was William, even though she had tried to deny it—the image of William as a man lost in silence. He was a man who didn't want to live. He wanted to turn this weight into colorful balloons, light and transparent, that would go flying through the air, to be gleefully pecked by birds until the balloons exploded and their pieces scattered over the ground.

Still, the memories of the massacre sent her back to the black hole that was always waiting inside her. When she heard Armenian youths talking fervently about taking revenge on the Turks, she was horrified, and her feet suddenly became very heavy. She thought that family produces cowards, even as it creates attachment to objects. Whenever she started drowning in lethal pictures, her painful memories, she thought that family life wasn't so bad; the successes her children presented her with were an additional reason to sink into forgetting. Her oldest son, Abdel Hamid, would go to medical school at Harvard in two months' time, and in a few years he would be an American citizen of note. He loved this image of himself. Her younger son Uthman would go to Istanbul next year to study at the Military College. He had arranged it all with his father's family; a few years earlier he had reclaimed his Turkish citizenship and started spending his holidays at his grandparents' house, and now he spoke with an accent that resembled that of his father's upper-class Istanbul family. Her daughter Gulnar would soon be completing high school. She was the only one who had mastered the Armenian language and never missed Armenian youth clubs or meetings. She would have no difficulty selecting an appropriate bridegroom. Maryam thought everything would be fine when she was a grandmother, spending her time between her house and the house of her daughter, who had inherited Maryam's long neck and shapely chest; she was nearly a carbon copy of her mother.

A year before Orhan died, Maryam had said to William, "You won't see me again after today. I want to become a grandmother." Satisfied, she went away and started sleeping in Orhan's bed again, but she couldn't stand his coughing at the end of the night. The smell of his skin didn't give her the intoxication she craved, the thrill of slipping into bed next to a man, and the few times his organ had briefly straightened up inside her after much coaxing and caressing, it hadn't been enough to bring her to orgasm. Orhan hadn't given her the happiness she had imagined when she agreed to marry him. For him, sex was a burdensome act, and her attempts to press into his side and arouse him only made him complain that the bed was too small and she was bothering him. Several times she thought that he had married her to assuage his own guilt; he used to feel as though he had committed the massacre himself, and saving a girl like her was an act of charity that would grant him peace of mind. But being in her life in that capacity only increased his guilt. He kept seeing her as his victim. His mind was not on love but on the task of raising this girl himself, bequeathing to her his tastes and the fundamental ways of Istanbul families who spent their days extolling their ancestors.

A year after they had married and she was pregnant with Abdel Hamid, Maryam asked his permission to sleep in her own room. He was keen on the idea and built her a bedroom with a private bathroom, furnished with a spacious bed and heavy curtains. It was some distance from Orhan's room. She felt free there, half cut off from the house. No one could hear her when she undressed herself and reclined on the bed, recalling the nights of the stone isolation room at Deir Zahr Al-Rumman. She never forgot the smell of the sheet, damp and stained with William's sweat, from when he crawled into the room and lay down beside her, wanting to share her sickness.

In her dreams, she desired all men. She couldn't forget what it was like to touch William's sex, nor the stories of her friends who slept with him. But she made do with some affectionate stroking from the old man she had married, elegant enough to attract a deep sleep and reassurance in his embrace. Both of them found the attempt at passion troubling, and she soon stopped this game, as they had done in all previous attempts. It wasn't possible for a light caress to set her body on fire. She had to kill what was left of her sensations in order to be able to live with the calm and resignation that was appropriate for grandmothers, among whom she would be ranked within a few years.

On the morning that Maryam made her first visit after being widowed, Souad told Maryam that William had spent the night talking about loss and disintegration. He hadn't believed the void in her eyes in the most recent photograph. Yes: she had lost her old shine and become a sack of moldy potatoes. Despite the fur coat, fundamentally she was a different woman; her desires had prematurely come to a halt. She didn't want to explain the terrifying idea that had come to her while she was traveling back from Istanbul after burying Orhan.

After his burial and the 'aza in the large family home in Şişli were over, Maryam hadn't waited for permission to leave, as was expected of her. The following day she had simply packed her bag and departed for Aleppo with her daughter Gulnar and her sons Abdel Hamid and Uthman. On the way, she was agitated and disturbed: for the first time, her fate was in her own hands. No one would impose anything on her. Waiting for her in the mailbox were three letters from William, the first he had ever mailed to her. He used to leave letters for her at Souad's house, but now he thought she belonged to him and he had the right to propose to her without fear.

After she entered the house, she felt a horrifying blank and said to herself, "William has disappeared too." The two men were connected, she felt; the absence of one meant the absence of the other. She didn't grasp what that meant at first, but in the end, she accepted it as fact: with Orhan's death, William had become part of the past. She didn't care very much what people said about her. She emptied the wardrobe of Orhan's smells. She was indifferent to the suits of fine English broadcloth that he had adored; she had never liked them. She renovated the house and moved things around. It became a different house, but the memory of Orhan lay in wait for her in every corner—killing the past wasn't as easy as she had thought. She was determined to expel every object that reminded her of him. She sent a letter to William through the mail, telling him not to wait for her. She thought that a few harsh words in a letter would be enough to expel him, too, but still she remained under siege from both men. She felt, for a brief time, that William's death might mean the end of her own life. Souad told her that he had recently left the city. He had been more serious than such a move really warranted and had ignored Souad's scrutinizing stare and her questions. He had been talking about death, which she refused to acknowledge; Souad was afraid of being left alone, and an early death in the family would bring her to despair.

William told Souad that he would restore the cellar, adding, "No fear of rot for those pictures and documents." He insisted he would rearrange everything. She didn't believe him and told him that for the first time, her things no longer held meaning for her, that he could dispose of them as he saw fit. She wanted to lighten the load of the past. Souad ignored that part of their conversation; he didn't want to be her heir, and in fact, on some level he wanted to reverse their positions and leave his things in her custody forever. She was the only person who would be fit to dispose of his thousands of photographs, his many possessions. He still had the documents he had brought in three large tin suitcases when he fled the monastery for the last time: maps and a collection of files in ancient languages, the text and illustrations of which he had spent twenty years helping Father Ibrahim Hourani to copy. There was a collection of old newspapers and books he had collected from Junaid Khalifa, when William had convinced himself that Junaid Khalifa might compensate for the huge loss that Father Ibrahim's departure had left behind.

For the first time since Aisha's burial, William spoke in riddles to his aunt in a conversation filled with allusions. Each of them wanted the other to inherit their belongings, and both wanted a reckoning of their past. They thought that immortality could be achieved through what they left behind. Souad grieved, deep down, as if everything had assailed her at the wrong moment. She wasn't ready to die; nor was she ready to bury William. In a moment of levity, she told Maryam that they both should die at the same time, adding that there was no point for either of them to be alive when Aisha was dead. The Bayazidi children would toss all these shabby old trunks to the junk hawkers. What use would either of them have for the leavings of a couple of eccentrics? In her conversation, she made no reference to Maryam, but Maryam understood herself to be among these leavings.

Maryam considered the dismal ending of a man and a woman who had sought immortality in a city like Aleppo, where all inanimate objects were immortal: the ancient souqs, the famous citadel, the houses built over a thousand years earlier. It was frustrating to her that mere things achieved immortality while everyone conspired to erase the great stories, to disdain and sneer at the pain and uniqueness of their heroes. Retelling a story over and over is nothing but an attempt to distort its heroes.

Maryam hadn't turned into an ethereal apparition, as William once expected; instead, she had become a woman burdened by the worries of her family. She moved slowly through the large house and retold to herself the story of how she arrived in Aleppo, inventing her past. She tried to forget Harout's buzuq, which she had held on to despite its broken strings. She tried to convince herself that everything she told herself was no different from the happy childhood stories she and her children fabricated to pin their memories in place. She kept repeating that happiness was clean children, and a warm house with a well-stocked cellar, and a respectable husband who, at precise and strictly defined times, went to his office at the bank crammed with auditors, and who received praise wherever he went. Happiness, she decided, was being envied for one's many possessions. She was turning into Mariana, whom she still hated, although she never mentioned her; William's persistent defense and Maryam's disdain eventually drove her out of their conversations altogether. Secretly, though, Maryam wondered about the purpose of the ornate bedside table. What sensations did a silver dinner service provoke? *Nothing* was the answer— everything is dead in the end, however hard we try to imbue it with a soul.

Maryam no longer considered William one of her reasons to be happy. Her passion was finished, along with the feverish languor on the sofa, the dress designed especially for the monthly photograph, the fevered emotions that struck her when he breathed near her. Today she felt everything was over. She had aged enough, her presence was no longer needed in his life—or rather, he was no longer needed in hers. And besides, William was no longer himself. After Aisha's death, he had become distracted and withdrawn. He couldn't believe that he hadn't died alongside his twin. At a moment's notice, he would call a taxi, go to the monastery, and seek out Hanna to discuss his obsession with dying at the same time as his sister, as befitted their connection. Then he would spend a long time with Mariana, behaving like a prodigal son who wanted to compensate his mother for his long absence. But he soon vanished again. Mariana couldn't understand his transformations, but she was happy at his renewed attachment to her, even though Hanna concluded that William had lost half his heart with Aisha's death.

Maryam had stopped expecting William to turn her into a woman hovering in the ether, entering through gaps in the windows and passing a divine hand over the brows of tortured lovers, granting them the hope that all torn and anxious people were in need of, as William always used to say. Maryam found that she was repeating everything from the years of her married life and getting the same results. Waking up at seven, preparing breakfast, sitting down with each of her family members in the same places. (After he died, Orhan's chair at the head of the table was left empty, Maryam on the opposite side, the three children distributed over the rest of the chairs.) At midday the family returned to the same places to eat their lunch, and the same thing was repeated at dinner. They worked silently in their rooms and observed each other, and none of them noticed that they had grown older. In the years before his death, Orhan was no longer able to read for hours at a time, and the postman no longer brought Maryam fashion magazines and her favorite Armenian books. One day Orhan stopped talking about his dream, which he assumed Maryam shared, of going back to Istanbul and spending the rest of their lives in the family home in Şişli. Gulnar's enthusiasm for her maternal family and her forceful-ness in speaking of the massacre had caused a deep rift in the fam-ily. Orhan stopped thinking of going back to Istanbul. He imagined the furious looks that would surround him—what would he say to them about his marriage to Maryam? Or about Gulnar, who wanted to murder Turks in revenge for the death of her mother's family? He could say nothing. He had not prayed with his family since the day he chose to stay in his beloved Aleppo and not to travel on with the rest of the Turks who fled the city when the last Turkish troops withdrew.

Now the past had grown distant. Maryam believed that she was approaching old age, and as she had always thought it would, this helped her achieve happiness. The periods of distress that had driven her mad—when she had dreamed of escaping everything and running away with William to some far-off place, or spending their remaining years in Souad's cellar, away from prying eyes—now came to an end. But recent months gave her a profound sense of peace and assurance that she had never known before.

On her last visit to William's studio, her manner had been cold. She didn't tremble when she sat in the chair all his clients sat in, neutrally facing the camera. She scorned her warm feelings of the past. At last she was content, she had conquered her anxiety. Troubling, lewd im-ages no longer came to her, and she no longer left her bed at night like a madwoman to stand under the cold shower, heedless of her soaked clothing and the wondering glances of her family, especially in the winter when she was trembling with cold. Unable to explain what was happening to her, she had always simply gone back to her room with-out a word, trying to forget it even though it kept on repeating. A seasonal fever afflicted her; she feared she would lose her reason and burn everything down. She convinced herself it wasn't madness—she was afraid of being homeless again, of having to rely on benefactors from mosques and charitable organizations. She thought she had to escape the warm house and take Harout's buzuq with the broken strings with her. But it was too late. It was all finished now; she was finally approaching forty; the lethal pictures would finally let her live in peace.

She left the studio, determined to visit the church and speak with the metropolitan about her Christianity, which she hadn't abandoned, whatever the Armenians said. But when she saw the crowds, she felt oppressed. She went back to the house along Baghdad Station Street and decided that she had to hold on to all those possessions for which she was envied. At last, William was merely a skillful photographer who courted her passion for taking photographs and piling them up in albums. She was merely a mother who would soon celebrate her children's weddings, and who carefully guarded the memory of her late husband, who had spent his final years without dreams, supposedly thinking up many projects but in truth just waiting to die. He hadn't established a corner for his family in the city's graveyard, he had never once listened to a single piece of music to the end, and he never wrote down his memories of the turbulent era he had lived through, nor any of his observations of the Armenians who survived the massacre. Instead, in his last days, he began to deny the slaughter, cursing the Armenians and praising the Ottoman life. He had passed away at the right time, which was before Maryam ripped out his guts and tossed them to the wild dogs in the street.

In the past year, during their final meetings when she was sitting in her own special chair, William told her that he could no longer wait. He stopped caring about his beloved places, Aleppo and his studio, and could no longer sustain himself with the tales he had invented about their shared life over the last twenty years. Because of Maryam, he no longer woke up laughing; instead he entered the kitchen quietly so as not to wake her—he always used to imagine that she was sleeping next to him, and he inhaled the scent of her sleeping. He made coffee for two and put hers on the small table in the corner by the window looking out over Baron Street. He brought the coffee cup to bed and asked her to take her time over it, adding that it was still too early for her to disappear just yet. When he was angry at her, or she was scolding him for his scandals, he would wish he was living in the monastery once again, carrying out Mariana's wishes without fuss. He would pick eggplants from the monastery grounds and gardens, scoop out the gleaming back seeds, and take the vegetables to the large cellar to be preserved and pickled for the winter. And every morning he would tend Aisha's grave.

Maryam did not share William's wish to go back to the monastery. She thought of herself as a venerated grandmother to a collection of grandchildren. She stopped receiving his daily letters, which instead went flying off into space. She no longer wanted to cry when she was struck with a fever of desire, spending the night nervously pacing between her bedroom and the kitchen, suffering from a headache that had no cure, for the three days before her period was due.

On her last visit to the studio, William was afraid of what Maryam would say. He knew she was going to tell him this was the last picture in the album, that it was time to stop the photographs, their only remaining means of communication. He was afraid of her request, which she repeated, to take her to the monastery for a final visit. When he withdrew to the darkroom, leaving her alone on the chair, she knew that he was thinking of his sister Aisha and her sudden disappearance. He missed her greatly. He was frightened of going together to the monastery after all these years and hearing bad news that his heart could no longer endure. What was left of his life had been plotted out carefully, but everything had vanished now. There was nothing left to do but die, which he didn't think would be so bad. He regretted not having gone to Beirut with Father Ibrahim. There far away, he would have been able to spend his life among manuscripts written by unknown people about a bygone life. He could have joined in composing stories about people scattered and lost in the desert. Surely, she knew how hard it was for him to get up from his bed every morning and prepare coffee for one person.

Souad had already told him that Maryam had informed her of her final decision to escape William. He expected Souad to mock him, but she said no more. She left him alone and withdrew to her bed on the upper floor. Her body was sluggish as it crossed the courtyard with slow footsteps, and her hand, clinging to the staircase, increased his misery. The princess, on whose account most of the city's men had lost their dignity, had grown old.

On the day after Maryam's last visit to William's studio, and for the first time in years, she didn't sit at her table at ten in the morning, after she finished in the bathroom, to drink her coffee and receive William's letters that from now on would go swimming in space. She felt a slight light-headedness and a deep contentment as she listened to the music coming from a nearby street where a brass band was playing nationalist songs and military marches, cutting through the crowd that was advancing on the train station to welcome Shukry Al-Quwatly and the delegation from the National Bloc that was accompanying him. She guessed that William, just then, would be looking for a vantage point from which to photograph the Father of Independence the moment he arrived. He wouldn't miss this historic moment, she was sure. But instead, just then, William was packing everything into a large trunk. He threw away hundreds of photography journals and newspapers that had published the photographs he had taken at various social events. One newspaper had run an image of a small child gripping a French soldier and crying for his murdered father. The author of the accompanying article had pressed William for the child's words, but he had simply left the photograph with the journalist and walked out without a word. The following morning, the photograph was published above a bold headline: *Syrian Boy Hero Says Death to the Colonial Oppressor.* Maryam still remembered William's distress at this editorial manipulation, the attempt to exploit the emotions of a grieving child to create a stir. Besides, it was foolishness to seek out this child's words when his tears so clearly expressed his horror.

Heroism meant nothing to William. He didn't approve of photographers who believed that their pictures created heroes and so boasted of their relationships with politicians and socialites. He was constantly mocking those who sought out the camera and then complained of the hardship of life in front of it.

After Maryam's last visit, the world became a narrow place for him, and he decided that would be his last photograph. For her, he had become a photographer, but in that final photograph he didn't feel her longing for his hands that lingered as they passed over her thighs. Her eyes were neutral. For her, he had become a photographer, and now he had immortalized her as she was at that moment: an honorable grandmother-to-be whose photo would live in the album her proud grandchildren would one day inherit. She wasn't a lover. Everything in the final photograph betrayed the fact that he had no place in her life anymore. The dress she wore had a staid, motherly demeanor, not a lover's folly; she hadn't even left a button undone so the shadow of her concealed breasts could scorch him in the darkroom. In this final photograph, when the lines of her neck and the details of her face became visible in the development fluid, she wanted to appear to him as a client no different from the others: all those wives of high-ranking officials, doctors, and lawyers, who explained that they wanted the photographs to reveal their happiness to their grandchildren, emphasizing that modesty was a sign of belonging to a family that, they were always determined, should be considered old and respectable— even though some of them came from humble origins. They were the daughters of minor officials, or fellahin who had moved to the city, but through their marriages, these women were able to weave new tales about their enhanced circumstances.

Months later Khalil told Maryam that on that day, William had walked through the crowds that were trying to greet Shukry Al-Quwatly and his companions from the National Bloc. He stood at a distance, looking for Khalil and finding him, as expected, hanging off a big tree in utter absorption in his task, greatly excited by this historical event. He tried to attract Khalil's attention, without success. William approached the stage, stood under the large tree, and shouted so that Khalil would notice him. Khalil didn't pass up the opportunity of photographing his mentor at the moment when Shukry Al-Quwatly and his delegation came close. He snapped six photographs in quick succession, and in one of them, William was so close to Shukry Al-Quwatly that he seemed to be part of the delegation as it walked through the hubbub welcoming the Father of Independence.

William quickly made himself understood to Khalil and tried to get out of the crowd. Always afraid of falling into some snare, he waited for the delegation to pass. Then the crowd receded and left him standing there alone, watching from a distance as thousands of people followed the procession. Khalil didn't miss this opportunity either, and the photograph he took then was most expressive of William's situation at that moment: a lonely man, left behind by the crowd. The quick-witted Khalil guessed that this picture would be of interest to a French journalist he knew who was always staying in the Hotel Baron. It didn't require much effort on Khalil's part to sell the photograph; the journalist had often tried to curry favor with William through Khalil, but William had always kept his distance, repeating that he was a photographer of shadow and didn't appreciate what foreigners said about and looked for in his city.

The same night William met Khalil and Sam in the Bab Al-Faraj coffeehouse. William asked Khalil to work exclusively for him for three days. Two of those days were devoted to putting the shop's affairs in order. William recorded the rental deed for both the shop and the house in Khalil's name, and they both signed a contract of partnership stating that Yousef would manage the finances. William bequeathed Khalil his valuable negatives; Khalil knew their worth, having spent years archiving them. Most inhabitants of the city had passed through this studio, and many of them had returned years later, struck down with yearning, asking for photographs of their childhood or their very first portrait, for which they were prepared to pay an exorbitant price. On the last day William, alone, occupied himself with arranging Maryam's photographs, which he kept in a locked box. He already kept a second set of printed copies in another trunk, which Maryam knew was squirreled away in Souad's cellar. That second box also contained her handkerchiefs and her openwork gloves, which still retained her perfume, all of which she had helped him pack carefully, according to the history of their meetings.

William considered leaving his boxes in Souad's cellar, but he couldn't bear to have them so far away. All that was left to him of Maryam were the photographs he had taken of her and the belongings in that second box. She had known that he wouldn't be able to lock away those memories in boxes; he wanted to send them off to unknown destinations, like his father Zakariya with his paper kites. William imagined the boxes floating away on the Euphrates; he liked the idea of his memories setting sail on the great river. Khalil finished helping him move the boxes from his aunt's house, and on the third day, everything was done. William went to an undertaker and bought a sumptuous coffin, refusing to answer the questions of the carpenter, who knew all his Christian clients; William simply said he needed to put everything in order for his death. He put all the boxes in the coffin and bought a strong carriage and a pair of horses, which he selected with the care befitting the son of an expert.

He slipped out of the house at dawn. Maryam imagined him as the carriage set off through the city. She was certain of his feelings of emptiness, of a strange desolation in his heart. It was certainly a surprising scene for the inhabitants of the villages he passed through: a well-dressed single man, driving a beautiful new carriage that held a coffin. The villagers surrounded him and asked him if he needed any land for the burial. William only ever thanked them with a nod and went on his way after a short rest. He needed silence, having always considered words unbecoming for an abandoned lover. It was difficult to retell a love story to strangers.

The following week Maryam kept examining every Arabic and French newspaper for pictures of the delegation's welcome, searching for William's photographs. She found Khalil's picture of him, alone, watching the procession as it passed him by. She felt a deep sadness over this image of her angel, who looked like a forsaken man seeking to die.

She cut out two pictures and hid them inside an Armenian edition of Omar Khayyam that she had found in a bookshop in Beirut twenty years earlier. She carefully placed the book among her underwear, even though no one but her would care about a book like that. Her two sons hadn't learned Armenian, making do with French and, later on, English. They couldn't care less about the poetry of Omar Khayyam. Her daughter Gulnar was more interested in reading about the history of the massacre than poetry or literature.

Maryam didn't feel the relief she had thought would follow William's departure. She would get up from her bed in the middle of the night and nervously open the book to gaze at his photo. In his eyes, she saw the bleakness that he had once told her about as he placed her picture in front of her and asked her not to inquire after his other women. She thought that he would never die without sending for her, nor that he could die suddenly, as if he were just anyone. She could understand the despair in his face as he looked at the delegation and the crowds receding from all around him; he had never been very fond of protests or heroes. She blamed herself, because in her last session with him she had only wanted him to be a photographer. She didn't take off her coat, and she didn't select an angle from which to look at and seduce him. Staying away from him for an entire year without reason had been cruel, she realized, and at that moment she loved him to the point of worship. But she had ruined everything. She didn't want him to die in front of her, she wouldn't be able to endure losing him.

In the days after he left the city, she didn't sleep well. She didn't prepare breakfast for her children as she usually did, nor offer any reason for not doing so. She thought she wouldn't be able to lie and conceal her enormous secret; she felt ready to commit an act of madness that could ruin the family's image.

A few days after his departure, she left the house early, before anyone else was awake. From afar, she saw the shop was open. Once she had opened the door and looked at the walls of the studio, she didn't need Khalil to tell her that William had gone away. The photographs on the wall declared plainly that he no longer had any relationship to this place. Khalil had taken down the portraits of mysterious women who shared knowledge of themselves with William and replaced them with pictures of hordes of protesters. There was even a gold-framed clipping from the French newspaper that had published the photograph of William. Khalil had kept only one other token of his mentor, a photograph he had taken of William, sitting at a table in a coffeehouse with Junaid Khalifa, who seemed like an old man now, constantly smiling and his hand never without a cigarette, as he carried on a conversation with a friend he truly thought of as his son.

Now Maryam understood what William had meant when he said that walls portrayed our identity. It looked like Khalil hadn't even waited for William to leave the city before he announced his own identity on the walls, hiding any sign of his mentor's. She accepted a coffee from Khalil; she wanted to stay awhile. She understood that William had gone and left everything to Khalil; he would never come back to her. But she was pleased that he had found an heir to maintain his legacy—the thousands of negatives stored in his archive. She didn't ask what had happened to her pictures, but Khalil told her anyway. She had been frightened that her pictures had been left behind with the few sofas and the huge bed and the trunk of elegant clothes; but on reflection, after being told, she decided that it wasn't really important what he had done with them. She went on to Souad's house and thought that this too was one of the places William had had to escape. Fleeing the places, colors, smells, and symbols of those we love is a sign that we want to be rid of everything that hurts us.

Maryam waited for Souad to finish her appointments with her morning clients so she could open the spoon drawer in the kitchen and take out the key to the cellar. Souad opened the cellar door for Maryam. It was unusually tidy; Souad's mannequins and the old bed on which she had formerly lain naked looked out of place. Souad took Maryam by the hand and sat her down on the long sofa. Maryam was relieved when she didn't see the boxes in their usual place. She lay down on the bed, then got up immediately as if she had been stung. The moment she closed her eyes, she had felt his fingers slipping over her right thigh; a mere brush there with his fingertips used to be enough to arouse her. She missed him. She cried in front of Souad, who looked at her compassionately, but then stated baldly, "He went back to the monastery. He went there to die. After Aisha died, he never really believed he was still alive." She added, "People saw him leaving Aleppo with a coffin." Then both women were silent. Before Maryam left, Souad asked her to take the key to the cellar. She too wanted to be rid of her legacy and her many belongings. She wanted to spend the few years she had left with the butterfly lightness that she had clung to throughout all seventy years of her life.

10

A Saint's Soft Bed

William had come back at the wrong time. The monastery had become a half-ruin. He discovered that Mariana was on the verge of blindness. He hadn't stayed away from her for long, but he hadn't kept a close eye on her. Hanna spent his time at Zakariya's house, where no one else but Boulos was allowed.

Deacon Boulos informed William that prayers and mealtimes continued at their usual times, but everything else had changed. No one had seen the reverend sister for several months—she had instructed Boulos not to give William any hope of meeting her. Boulos took his arms and shook him hard and said he wouldn't be able to live here again. He knew the monastery was no longer a place for living, but a place for intrigues, settling scores, and waiting for death.

While waiting to meet Mariana, William passed some time in Zakariya's house. Zakariya did not invite his son to stay, however; he didn't want to see William so defeated. Depressed, William returned to sit by the coffin with Deacon Boulos, who recited memories of Zakariya as if he were giving an elegy. Mariana saw William from the window of her room. Boulos conveyed her words to William, claiming them as his own. In the first week, he told William that everyone had expected his return for a long time. If it was life he wanted, he was too late, he said, but he had come far too early if he wanted to die. William replied solemnly that if he died, he wouldn't want to be buried at the monastery. He would instruct everyone to burn his body and scatter his ashes over the fields, but, he added, pointing at the coffin, his things should be buried with all due reverence. William added that contrary to common belief, the things a person left behind were not trivial. Boulos was silent and did not report this answer back to Mariana, but he admired William's strength and his reverence for the memories and the objects left after a person was gone.

Mariana didn't ask about William's reasons for coming back. She was delighted he had returned at last, but a loved one's ill-timed return is tantamount to them coming back dead. She sent him a large jar of apricot jam and ordered Boulos to fetch William's meals straight from the kitchen so he wouldn't be forced to talk to anyone. She sent for news of everything that had happened to him in the past years; she wanted him to be part of the life of the monastery once more. During his visits over the years, he hadn't bothered much about the stories of the monastery, content with merely checking up on Mariana, Hanna, and Zakariya. He behaved as if he had moved abroad and visited his family only on his holidays. For so long, he hadn't wanted to link his life to the monastery, but after Aisha's death, he thought that he couldn't live away from it.

Mariana wanted to make sure he stayed in the monastery and didn't leave again, but William was indifferent to his fate. He already knew it all; fundamentally, he had never really left. He remained immersed in his daydreams and his internal disputes; he was searching for the inner peace he had lost over the years. One look at the monastery, meanwhile, told him how everything had changed; the passageways that used to smell perfumed and clean had become moldy. The locks were broken on the imposing doors to the monks' and nuns' rooms. There were no more voices in the copyists' room where he had spent ten years helping Father Ibrahim verify and copy manuscripts from Deir Najran. Dust covered the binders and the manuscripts.

William remembered his happiness in the old years, when his eyes met Maryam's and he felt the odd quiver that began the strange story of their lives. He thought he had plenty of time stretching out ahead of him, certainly enough to put his memories in order. During the first week, he felt that time was passing slowly, and he worried it was a bad omen, but the open spaces, his closeness to Aisha's grave, and his memories of the places of his childhood all gave him a feeling of safety.

Mariana knew that William hadn't returned with his coffin of belongings just to listen to Boulos chatter, but equally she didn't know why he had come back to this depressing place. Nothing was left that might tempt passersby to stay the night, and the constant fare of lentil soup and boiled potatoes betrayed the poverty within its walls.

When Mariana used to visit William, she had thought that he had a different life, a happy one, but she had underestimated the extent to which his life was intertwined with his twin's. Burying Aisha at the monastery had been the right decision after all; now Mariana saw that her grave had brought William back to her again.

Every morning William saddled his horse and rode out of the monastery's wide gate to wander through the nearby regions. He reached the outskirts of Azaz and Afrin and came back along the same road, recalling his cherished memories of Father Ibrahim.

Mariana didn't know what she wanted from him anymore. She kept changing her mind as to whether she wanted him to stay, yet she felt a secret joy she hadn't felt in years. Finally she decided she wanted him to stay close to her till the end of her days, to care for her as a son would his mother, but she decided to test his patience by making him wait to meet her. Boulos relayed to her that William was considering replanting the extensive grounds, which had been neglected in recent years. The monastery had been forgotten by all its former donors. Boulos encouraged him to undertake any work he wanted and not to hesitate to revive the monastery's stable, of which nothing was left but a pair of aged horses that could no longer reproduce.

Keeping herself hidden away from prying eyes Mariana depended on glimpsing William from her window. She couldn't see him clearly, but she felt she was seeing his ghost in the twilight before dawn, rolling up his sleeves, harnessing his horses to the plow, and cultivating the land with great care. He spotted her watching him from a small opening, although she didn't wave; he didn't know that she couldn't see very well. Through Boulos, she sent him word that she was expecting him to go back to Aleppo, didn't want to see him, and no longer had time to take care of him. Everything was finished as far as she was concerned. She paced sluggishly through her quarters. In truth, she would never forgive herself if he went back to Aleppo, despite her perpetual complaints that he had abandoned her and was a constant disappointment to her. She had told him once, when he visited at Christmas several years before, that she regretted having allowed him to go away. Deep down, she knew she wouldn't be able to prevent a lover from joining his beloved. She had been waiting for him to come back for all this time, but she was still surprised when she saw that carriage of his, loaded down with a coffin. She told Boulos to tell William that it was still too early for him to die. Boulos almost told her about William's insistence that his body be burned and that they should be content with burying his objects, but he kept silent. He wouldn't give her any additional reason for alarm.

Mariana recalled Zakariya in his prime. William wasn't like his father—he was more graceful and less athletic—but the same strange blood ran through them both. As the days went on, she grew less wary about observing William and hearing his news. Finally, when the seedlings of green beans and tomato began to flower, she sent for him. She decided that he would see her face only if she felt convinced that he wanted to stay permanently. She didn't want him to see her wrinkles, her scrawny body, the hollows around her eyes. She would speak to him through the barrier that she had taken to using for any necessary dealings with strangers in recent years. There were only three people who had the right to speak with her directly and to see her shriveled, puckered face: Hanna, who hadn't spoken to her for ten years; her maidservant, who occupied the room close to hers on the upper floor; and Boulos, who was in his eighties but still flourishing. He still dreamed of living for many more years and reviving the glory of this great monastery. The three of them ignored any question about how she was, or what she was doing up there in her quarters. If it weren't for the sound of her movements on the upper floor of the monastery, and the occasional times she sat on her small balcony on scorching summer nights, everyone would have thought she had died some time ago. The eras of the monastery had blended together and her narrative had conquered, just as she had always wanted. The only tangible material thing that couldn't be shifted or storied away was the place marked out for Hanna's grave, next to where he had buried Aisha. When he died, Mariana could finally begin the process of having the pope declare him a saint. She chose the place where they would both be buried next to each other, under a lone fig tree that loomed over the horizon at a distance, and dug the new grave there. She used to feel that the tree resembled her and Hanna in their shared history, in their loneliness. The faces of her brothers and sisters, her father, her mother, Hanna's and Zakariya's sons—they all floated on the surface of the Euphrates and kept her awake at night. Forty years and more later, she still couldn't forget the details of the flood. It remained in her memory, a scar that couldn't be erased.

Boulos led William to the upper floor, sat him on a chair, and left him alone to listen to Mariana's heavy breathing behind the wide wooden partition. William remembered when he used to clatter and crash through the silent passageways as a child. He could enter every room, including hers, and play with everything. He spent his childhood in her lap, smelling in her body the scent of the mother he had lost. He still recalled every moment of his happy childhood, but now he was a stranger, speaking from behind a partition.

Before long, she asked him how he was and offered him her condolences on Aisha's death, denying that she had ever forbidden her to meet Hanna. She neglected to ask about his aunt Souad. William replied tersely that Aisha was gone, just as Mariana had long wanted. It felt like an exaggeration, but he had no time to enlarge on the thorny tale of Aisha's life. He told Mariana briefly about Aisha's marriage and her children. He wanted to talk about Maryam, about Aleppo, about his wish to write the history of the monastery and restore the stables, about undertaking any project that might speed the slow motion of time. But Mariana's short, intermittent phrases and the barrier between them made this impulse fade, and instead he made do with asking her permission to bury the coffin of his things in a place of his choosing within the monastery walls. She asked him to choose a burial site for himself, not for the coffin. He told her that if he died here, he wanted his body to be burned and his ashes scattered by her own hands in the pomegranate grove when they were in blossom. She told him that she couldn't endure the idea of burning a man's body; it was a sin she wouldn't commit. She didn't ask him what the coffin contained and refused to respond when he brought up the topic of cremation again. She was frightened of such a conversation; she knew very well when William was in the grip of a strange idea. She set aside the matter of death and burial and tried to talk about his life. William's tone of bewilderment made Mariana feel that she was reliving a conversation she had often had with his father, who had been angry when she hadn't allowed him to bury his black horse after it was poisoned. William was different from Zakariya, but, she reflected, echoes of the past remain inside us. She didn't want his heart to be broken, she wanted to embrace him, but she stopped herself. She advised him to leave the coffin of his things nearby, and said some final words to the effect that while the okra and green beans were flowering, it was still too early to be speaking about graves. His plants should give him hope. She begged him to understand her message—her little speech about his plants coming into flower was her way of welcoming his life, not his death. Before she put an end to the meeting, Mariana asked him outright if he was dying. Her heart was reassured when he told her that his health was fine—it was his soul that was exhausted, and he was suffering from despair and loss. Mariana was silent, determined not to enter into a lengthy discussion that might lead her to sadness or cruelty. She felt that he really was her son, and she wanted him to live.

She ordered that a spacious room by the library be allocated to William—the room that Father Ibrahim used to work in—so that

William wouldn't leave for Zakariya's house. She gave him permission to request another meeting with her in a few days' time. Via Boulos, she told him that she did not wish to see horse traders in the monastery; she wanted those who had remained at the monastery, including Zakariya, whom she visited several times, to die in peace. She was gentle with her old adversary and wished him a speedy recovery from his mysterious ailment. She had stopped caring what the church would do with the place once she and Hanna were dead.

Mariana couldn't sleep that night. What would William do with the old people left behind, too few of them to fill even a single pew in the small church? Boulos pointed out to William that he enjoyed a great honor; he had permission to reside in the ranks of monks and nuns, companions of the great Reverend Sister Mariana, and the right to wander freely through the monastery and its surroundings. Boulos suggested that William might like to turn part of the stable into a place where he could paint and added that in nearby Anabiya lived a Muslim man, one of the best icon painters, whom he could invite to share his studio. But William decided that painting belonged to his past, and he wished his past into oblivion.

Mariana asked Boulos to look after William, record the details of his movements in the monastery, and tell her all his reactions. Boulos told William that Mariana still considered him her own petted child whom she had raised here; he was her son, and she wanted everyone to know.

From her refusal to let him look in her eyes, together with her feeble voice from behind the screen, William suspected that she was in her last days. She didn't want to ruin the arrangements made for her death; she loathed living. In their second meeting, he was sad and sympathetic toward Mariana, his mother. He told her about Souad, that she enjoyed good health and would live a long time yet. They both avoided talking about Zakariya's illness. William explained at some length that if he had stayed behind, so close to the perfume of Maryam and the cellar, then he would fall apart; he too would loathe living.

This was the right place for a man without ambition, who wanted to distance himself from lethal images, and whose every belonging was gathered in a coffin that accompanied him wherever he went.

After that conversation, Mariana woke the next morning full of zeal and activity. She asked Boulos to instruct the maidservant to clean the deacon's room attached to the stables, and she gave him permission to cook in his own room from now on. Boulos welcomed her idea, which he wouldn't have dared implement on his own; he could no longer endure eating his food with a group of people who hated spices and passed all their time in prayer.

After moving to his new room, William sat with Boulos and reminisced about Father Ibrahim. He had spent some of the best years of his life in the room where he now slept. Mariana knew it was his favorite place. At its door, he had seen Maryam for the first time; she had offered flowers to Father Ibrahim and then walked on without a word. William hadn't been able to stand, as if he had just seen an angel. His knees betrayed him—he didn't notice Father Ibrahim as he looked for a vase or a jug for Maryam's flowers and mentioned that the Armenian girl had recovered from the fever thanks to the doctor's medicines and the care of Father Ibrahim and a nun. They had both stayed by her bed for seven days and nights, the nun helping her to eat boiled potatoes, and Father Ibrahim singing some Syriac songs to her. She didn't understand them, but she had looked at him in a friendly way. She hadn't really believed then that she would recover and tend to the flowers she had planted underneath her window.

William kept thinking about her and looked for her everywhere. He slipped into the maids' rooms but found no trace of her. He didn't dare ask anyone about the apparition who had stood there for a few moments, holding out a bouquet and smiling. Her clean dress couldn't conceal how poor she was, but at that moment he saw only the face of an angel, handing out flowers to lonely people in a place burdened with sin.

His strange movements had aroused Mariana's misgivings, and she worried he had come down with fever when she approached his

NO ONE PRAYED OVER THEIR GRAVES   377

bed, and he kept his eyes closed. After she left his room, she saw him go into the monastery's kitchen without permission; a stare from the servant preparing lentil soup stopped him in his tracks. She heard him ask in a trembling voice for a little salt to treat a wounded horse. At other times Mariana saw him spying on the girls' room. Aisha told her sarcastically that he was looking for an angel. Mariana knew the face of every inhabitant of the monastery, and so her best guess was that this was a case of mental disturbance, not an angelic visit. Aisha told her the story, but in such a flippant tone that she raised no alarm: the flowers currently wilting in the copyists' room, she said, had been presented by one of Father Ibrahim's Armenian girl students. He was determined that they would all learn Arabic grammar, and he wouldn't leave them alone until they learned how to read and write. But Mariana allowed no one to trifle with their soul. She watched William covertly, and eventually he confessed that he was looking for an apparition, a girl who had offered flowers to Father Ibrahim.

Three weeks later, on a scorching dawn in the summer of 1922, when he was saddling a horse so the reverend could visit Jisr Al-Shughur, William saw the apparition again, now crossing the balcony of the room where the girls of the monastery sat in silence to knit woolen sweaters and socks. They were the poor Armenian girls who had decided to become nuns. William's angel was sitting among them, meticulously working a heap of wool with excruciating slowness. She was wearing the same blue dress dotted with yellow flowers. A few moments were all that he needed to confirm that she really existed. Maryam stood up and went inside. He waited for her to come back and join her companions for the rest of their vigil on the balcony looking out over the vast fields. When she didn't return, William picked up a large basket of grapes and went up to the second floor. He knocked on the girls' door, and the oldest opened it. She was surprised to see him there. He held out the basket of grapes to her, glanced furtively through the open door, then left without a word. That night he decided that he would sneak into the girls' room when they left for their Arabic lesson the next day.

Through the window, he saw Father Ibrahim reading from a book while the girls yawned in their chairs. There were six of them this time, not seven. He had no doubt that the angel was staying in one of the monastery's rooms, but he couldn't ask anyone about her. He had stopped telling Aisha anything since she made fun of him and shared his secret with Hanna and Mariana. His alarming movements were attracting attention. Mariana laughed to herself and said it was a little adolescent fantasy and would soon be over. But his condition worsened, and the symptoms of love appeared. Father Ibrahim warned him about the deluge of desire in a place that didn't celebrate it; his father suggested he travel to Aleppo and escape monastery life. William just closed his eyes and told Father Ibrahim about an angel who distributed flowers all over the monastery. He spoke for hours about an angel no one else seemed to have noticed. But he had seen her, distributing flowers and scattering joy.

William stopped working with Father Ibrahim, making do with helping his father carry out the demands of his many customers for perfectly crafted saddles. He loved watching the foals gambol around, and he would herd the horses to the reaped wheat fields and watch them for hours. His father didn't want him to turn into a horse herder or a saddle maker; neither did Hanna, but he said that being with horses would help cure him. William's listless movements and hollow eyes had alarmed them both in recent weeks. Mariana was terrified he had come down with tuberculosis. Zakariya felt utter dread; he couldn't endure more losses. He considered escaping the monastery for good and going to Aleppo, but he couldn't face establishing a new life yet again. The truth, as he was well aware, was that he couldn't abandon Hanna or the stables in Anabiya.

Everyone took notice as William grew thinner and thinner. He led the herd to pasture in silence every morning. The herd had grown considerably, and the monastery's stables, along with Zakariya's own, had acquired a widespread reputation. Every Tuesday traders came from all around the country to barter over the horses for sale, thoroughbreds that Zakariya had raised and looked after with care, using the skills that once upon a time no one would have imagined he possessed.

William didn't care when the young foals wandered away from the herd. When he went back to the monastery at night, many horses still hadn't eaten their fill, or some would be missing, and Zakariya and Boulos would be forced to go out and search for them.

By the end of the month, William would sit in the large room where Father Ibrahim worked. The servant offered him lentil soup and a piece of bread, and he made do with a few mouthfuls. He no longer went up to Mariana's room as he used to do every day, not even for a short time. He made elegant copies of pictures of long-gone monasteries from the Arabian peninsula, drawn by monks who had died a thousand years ago and left behind them plans for the buildings that had been lost to raids and the desert's shifting sands.

William was lost himself, in a maze he couldn't get out of. The only thing Mariana remembered later was that he had told her he couldn't stand this place any longer, it had become so bleak. William spent all of August looking for his angel with increasing hopelessness. One night he saw the doctor's carriage stop in front of the monastery, and the doctor descended with his bag. Behind him came the municipal carriage used only for carrying away the bodies of cholera victims. The doctor walked straight to the copyists' room and put his large bag down on the table. William saw him through the glass as he spoke to Father Ibrahim and Mariana, seemingly explaining something to them. William thought it must be serious, otherwise he wouldn't have come so late at night. The doctor and Father Ibrahim left the room and walked to the isolation room some distance away from the main building of the monastery, and Mariana went to Hanna's room after summoning Zakariya and Boulos. William walked behind the doctor, and when he left the main building with Father Ibrahim, he knew where they were going. William arrived at the same time as three municipal orderlies carrying stretchers. He peered in through the large window down the main corridor and was astonished to see his angel lying on a cotton mattress in a bare room with an earthenware pitcher filled with water next to her. The doctor was examining her and pouring out a spoonful of medicine, which a nun helped her to swallow. The nun was wearing a tightly sealed dress and rubber gloves. The doctor left his patient and went to supervise the removal of three bodies. One of them belonged to the angel's friend, the one who had taken the basket of grapes from him a few days earlier. The orderlies placed the three bodies in sealed bags and closed them tight. They carried out their work very quickly; they had buried many bodies over the past few weeks.

The doctor continued with his round of the large ward. William's heart sank; his angel was withering and slowly dying. He walked back to his room, dragging his feet. Aisha looked at him, frightened. He was crying silently, and when she hugged him and held him close to her chest, he exploded into loud sobs. He freed himself from Aisha and walked aimlessly through the passageways. Mariana saw him wandering in the monastery's fields, climbing the walls, running away through the fields of pomegranate, olive, and cherry. Everyone looked at him sympathetically from the windows, apart from Father Ibrahim, his mentor, who couldn't bear to, suspecting the painful fate in store for him. William returned to his room to find Aisha crying silently; she believed that their twin-connection had been lost forever.

Now, in the weeks after William's return to the monastery, he noticed that Hanna's movements had become slow. Every day he would walk the distance between his room and Zakariya's house unhurriedly, leaning on his cane, not allowing anyone to accompany him. He would go into Zakariya's house, and the two of them would pass the time in sporadic conversation. Boulos helped them prepare the ointment the doctor prescribed, and Hanna rubbed it on Zakariya's body, but the pustules of his illness that was left unnamed neither stopped nor retreated. Zakariya would grind his teeth in pain, and Hanna prepared sedatives for him and sometimes spent the night at his bedside. Boulos would help him reach the bench in front of the front door of the house, where Zakariya would sit, relaxing in the sunlight. He feared that death wasn't close. He closed his eyes, not wanting to see anything; every corner in this place reminded him of his defeat, but he didn't want to burden Hanna, who seemed to have disintegrated after Aisha's death. Hanna sat close to Zakariya, and to anyone who didn't know them, it was a strange sight: two old men waiting to die. After William came back to the monastery, he joined them, but Hanna wouldn't allow him to help anoint Zakariya's sores. Hanna assured him that Zakariya would recover. On the day they buried Aisha, Zakariya was very thin, having lost his appetite—not uncommon in old men—and three months earlier he had had small-pox. The pustules split his skin, and he wished they would penetrate all the way to his heart and stop it.

Every moment Hanna thought about Souad, who had nothing left but the possessions of the dead. And every morning Souad wondered what all the people from her past were doing. She no longer trusted life, but she didn't trust death either. She felt that time, which never stopped, was a great lie. She shut her door in the faces of her clients and welcomed none but a small number of women who resembled herself. Although twenty-five years had passed since the fire at her first fashion show, she could never forget it. She remained a captive of that moment of destruction, wondering deep down, "Why did those young girls, so proud of their bodies as they strutted back and forth on a wooden stage designed by an engineer suffering from loneliness, cause so much harm in the eyes of a woman who would die within a few years, and a group of men who believed that burning the place down would open up their path to Heaven?" Souad remembered the horror on Maryam's face; she had survived a terrible massacre and didn't want to die amid all that splendor. That day Aisha ran out sob-bing, and Yousef went looking for her through the fire. It was a rare opportunity to tell her how much he had loved her from the moment they met, when Aisha turned from a child into a young woman. Their love was born among the ashes. Aisha told Souad that when Yousef embraced her to protect her from the fire, he had encircled her life forever. She could feel his heart thudding, and despite being a former guerrilla fighter, with all the strength and bravery that entailed, he was crying like the women.

Souad reflected that the cellar in her house had become a graveyard of things, and she was nothing but their custodian: William's pictures and old cameras, his paintings, a few clothes from his many women, old mannequins, and whatever clothes still remained from that orphaned fashion show. Souad was no longer quite so eager to listen to Maryam when she came as usual to talk without stopping about the void inside her, about her wish to reestablish her relationship with the church, about William, whom she no longer missed.

In recent days, Souad had grown sad enough that she felt no interest in others. Her dear friend Azar had died two months earlier, and she still couldn't believe he had died so utterly defeated. Sara had called and asked her to come to his house at once, adding that she might be too late. Souad rushed out of her house, but by the time she arrived, Azar was already dead. She hadn't been able to reach him. In the last weeks of his life, Azar could no longer walk to the bathroom. He had suffered from sudden renal failure and left the hospital paralyzed; after a photograph of his son and daughter was published in an Israeli newspaper, he simply gave up. The picture, which was secretly circulated among all the Jews in Aleppo, had shaken him. His wife, Misha Raoul, had been one of the first to move to Israel after it was declared a state on May 15, 1948. She called the Jewish Agency for Israel in New York and begged them to expedite her travel to Israel with her son and daughter. The photograph printed in the newspaper was clear: a Jewish woman proud of her new nationality, her son standing next to her wearing a military uniform, holding a gun, and raising his hand in a victory salute.

Azar couldn't stand the shock. He had planned to meet his son and daughter in New York the following summer, to suggest that they return to Aleppo. He had become an old man and wanted to spend his last days with them. He had always believed that his daughter Huda would come back with him; in her letters, she would write about how

bored and frustrated she was by her mother's stinginess and her difficult temper. Misha stayed awake to turn the electric lights off after her
children, insisted they both make do with a single lamp, and wanted
them to talk only to Jews. He felt he had lost everything. Within a few
months, their letters stopped coming, and they didn't reply to his ur-
gent telegrams. Souad understood his worry and fear and did her best
to help him, as he reflected that what remained of his life would be
spent away from his children. He kept repeating that they had gone
beyond his reach.

Azar was no religious bigot. He had always believed that Aleppo
was a magical city, and no one who had been born or lived there
could possibly exchange it for another. On the day that Israel was
declared a state, he told Souad that the Jews would go through another, eternal Exodus. Within a few years, he said, she wouldn't find
a single Jew here; they would pluck them out from the places of their
childhoods—by force if necessary, they wouldn't lack the means—so
their sons could forever inherit the shame of having shed the blood
of the Palestinians.

Azar clung to his house. He didn't go outside unless it was absolutely necessary, didn't participate in the discussions between other
Jews who were gathering and arguing about Israel, furtively compar-
ing the offers from various Jewish agencies to help them emigrate. The
dream of his old age, of opening a night school to teach architecture,
was over. He kept saying, "Everyone has surplus imagination, and it
should be invested in crafting beauty."

Now, laid out on his bed, his body betrayed his wretched condition. He hadn't shaved in months, and his shirt smelled revolting.
Souad realized that he had never worn the new shirts she brought him
on her last visit, after he had left the hospital.

She took his hand and squeezed it. Coldness crept into her fingers.
Large groups of people trooped into the house, and Souad left them
and went out of the room to sit in the living room, waiting for his body
to be brought out so she could walk behind it. She felt distinct among
all the mourners. David's and Sara's children were rushing around,

arranging the burial rites. She felt superfluous and went out to wait for the funeral procession on the balcony of Sara's nearby house, determined to wave to the coffin as it passed. She had lost a piece of her soul; Azar could never be replaced. The bier came outside, and Souad looked at it in silence. Amid the howls of the women, she waved to him as if he were going on a short errand and would be back in a couple of hours. She watched steadily until the funeral turned the corner by the post office. Souad went back to her house, closed the door, and wrote a long letter to Hanna. She didn't know why she sat down that night to write to him, sixty years after the night she spat in his face, when she saw the lipstick and wine staining his silk shirt.

She didn't read over her letter so she wouldn't tear it up, as she usually did. Walking to the post office, she reflected that the letter might fall into Mariana's hands. She found a taxi driver she knew well and asked him to deliver her letter, giving him a double fare and an instruction not to put it into anyone's hands but Hanna's.

The letter rested on Hanna's table. He didn't dare open the envelope. When he thought of her certain forgiveness, the letter turned into a terrible nightmare. Eventually, a month after it arrived, Hanna woke at dawn, sat in his chair, opened the envelope, and read Souad's letter.

My dearest Hanna,
I won't trouble you. Azar has died, defeated, ulcerated. In his last days, he punished himself for things he hadn't done, and following his death I have become a lonely woman, waiting to die myself. Azar has died, and William Eisa died before him, and Aisha, the darling of everyone's heart, is dead. So what is left for us?
Nothing.
I write this letter to you, and as yet I have no confidence that I will complete it. It is hard, as you know, to write a letter you have been thinking about for sixty years, and for nigh on sixty years I have been thinking about writing this letter, ever since

the day I opened the door to you when you came back from Venice with Zakariya. When I saw your face, I knew you were the angel I had been looking for.

I couldn't tolerate the alteration in our image and relationship to each other. I wasn't capable of deceit. My life was divided into two parts, neither of which I chose. The first part was before your return from Venice, during our childhood, the happiness, the joy of which I have only recently realized—but equally, I realized it was a deceptive childhood. We were brother and sister; I used to feel that, sincerely. I divided my love equally between you and Zakariya, whose life ended, I believe, the moment you entered our house, and you both cut your fingers and swore eternal brotherhood with me as witness. You have both become one person with two bodies; yes, it was eternal brotherhood between you both, but I was the one who paid the price of it.

I will briefly explain to you how we all suffered from the change that the three of us experienced, in that second part, which began after your return. I will summarize it with a few images that still arise in my mind: we are all, Azar and Sara and William Eisa and Zakariya, and you and I, crossing the bridge to go to Mount Jawshan so we can fly Zakariya's kites. And before that, we six friends sent our paper boats forth on the river. Another image: you and I are in the middle of the large courtyard that I can see now from where I am sitting as I write to you. I was standing on the sixth flagstone from north to south, third from east to west, and I was standing in front of you. You weren't my brother who had been traveling for two years. You were someone else, someone I didn't know, and that night I couldn't sleep. I spied on you breathing, and I sat on the step and wept.

Now I know that at that moment, I was signing my own death warrant. A girl like me couldn't live two lives. But as you see, all these years later I have come to realize something, too late. I did live two lives, divided by a shadowy passageway that I crossed through every moment. Imagine living in a shadowy tunnel . . . that was where I lived. I lived my forbidden love all alone. I received a word of encouragement here, another there; every woman I knew could see you traced on my skin, hidden in my palm. The looks of commiseration ate me up; pity is all you can feel for a woman living out forbidden love in a tunnel.

At that moment, I felt you had slithered inside me, and when I realized I was stuck inside your labyrinth a few days later, I tried to escape, but I couldn't. Every day I tried to take you out of my womb but failed. You have lived in that warm place ever since. Through hundreds of nights, thousands of nights, I have had no means of defending myself other than weeping. Even when my husband Hassan Masabny was lying next to me in bed, he could sense a strange, invisible being lying in between us. He feared going to the sheikhs to ask them to drive out the evil spirit that separated me from him. He was afraid that the umbilical cord would be cut and my insides would gush out and drown the whole world.

The few times I went to bed with men, I was expecting it would satisfy my ravenous appetite for pleasure, but at the pivotal moment, you would rise from my womb and lie down between us. True, those encounters were not many, but it was the fiercest pain that can happen to a woman. I used to tell Azar about those few lovers, and he used to encourage me toward connection and love, like any good friend, but he was miserable when I told him that I turned into grains of sand in bed, slipping through the cracks. I was sad and felt that it wouldn't be possible for any woman to carry that weight, of a ghost making itself at home in her body.

I am trying now to put the images in order, but I feel wasted and weak. There are only a few, in any case, but some I have never forgotten: I was cooking beans in my family's house, and I put your bowl on the table. My father couldn't understand why I was placing an extra bowl there. I would repeat to myself that I loved you and wanted you to taste the beans that I had cooked with my own hands. I went into your room and arranged your clothes. Every day I did the same thing, and you understood that you had to leave me some trace of yourself. I was resigned to my fate, and when Josephine put her hand in your arm and the metropolitan declared you husband and wife, I saw your other image. It was to my indescribable joy that my brother, which you were at that moment, was married to this good, kind woman. And when I went back to my room that night, I intended for the first time to extinguish my lust and my longing for the two men you were. But after I lay down naked in bed, the images of you as my brother wouldn't come, and I felt utterly sick. I didn't know why, or against what, my body was rebelling so openly.

I didn't try to do that again. When I lay in bed naked after that, I would summon up other men—your image was not allowed to slip into my bed. After I slapped you, I regretted it for a long time, because for me, you weren't a man made of blood and nerves but an apparition, hovering around me and refusing to leave my womb.

You were with me every moment, you have never left me, and now I think that everything had to happen as it did. I must thank you for everything you did for me. When I used to watch you getting out of your carriage in front of the house, standing downwind from you was enough for me. I pity those women who experienced all your brief, quick pleasures. I thank them for leaving me your apparition, which was what I wanted, and for taking away your bones, which are like the dinosaur bones I saw the remnants of, the ones Yousef told me about so many times. Bones can't slip into a womb.

If you were beside me, I would ask you to move away. I don't want to lose the wonder I feel at turning into a being that can open itself whenever it wants, taste the honey of love, and then close it back up again, just as we used to do when we were children wolfing down honey in the larder.

You won't leave my womb until I die. You will delight in that wonderful moisture, swim in that pure water, fall asleep on the soft saint's bed, just as you have done for fifty-five years—not quite sixty, as I wrote above. Sleep, my darling. No one will see. No one will see your apparition except me.

Souad

February 16, 1951, Aleppo

Unable to bear Souad's delicate words, Hanna sobbed bitterly. Over the following nights, after a short, restless sleep, he would startle, full of anxiety, and leave his room to walk to Zakariya's house. He would sleep on the mattress laid out next to Zakariya's bed, listening to the moans of his friend, staring at the ceiling, feeling powerless. He couldn't bear the thought that Zakariya would die. He stayed in this condition for weeks, struck by a sense of loss and futility. He felt he was hanging in the air of a room that had its windows stopped up, only to become a tomb. Worms would scent his corpse and Zakariya's and emerge from the ground to devour them. He thought about disappearing all the time. The monastery had become wretched, lime flaking off its walls, dampness spotting the cellars, its windows ripped out. And the image of living in Souad's warm womb never left him.

Hanna didn't wait long. The winter passed, and Zakariya still hadn't recovered. He had improved, said the doctor, who nevertheless cautioned Hanna that Zakariya might still be infectious. At the beginning of spring, Hanna spent an entire night in conversation with Zakariya. Three days later he sent for William. Mariana sensed that Hanna was plotting something and thought that one of them would soon die—herself most likely. Over the previous winter, her health had declined, and the doctor's visits to the monastery had multiplied. Everyone had grown old. She guessed that Hanna was right to refuse the church's offer to renovate the monastery and its environs. He asked Metropolitan Basilos, who by now had become a friend, to let him die in peace among these elderly people. The metropolitan listened to Hanna calmly and sympathetically, musing on their relationship, which had altered greatly after the famine. Back then Hanna had admired the metropolitan for opening the church's stores and selling off its valuables in order to offer food to the needy. Basilos no longer dreamed of being the patriarch, and his debates with Hanna and Father Ibrahim had changed him. After the famine, he saw that death harvested everyone, and he reflected on Hanna's transformations, reminded of the lives of the saints who experienced pain.

When William first entered Hanna's room, he seemed like a sick man; his eyes had lost their gleam, his face was a jaundiced yellow, and he spoke slowly, as if he were plucking every word from his own throat. In a friendly tone, Hanna asked William where he was going to bury the coffin he brought with him, and William replied coldly, "I don't want anyone to see my past or my things. I want to bury them close by."

Zakariya joined them. He wasn't like a father to William at all, but his libertine past reminded William of his own, although he himself had been more discreet. In that first meeting, William just wanted to leave. He was bewildered when he saw Zakariya's sores and Hanna's decrepitude: his clothes were unclean, his face was wrinkled and shriveled, his lips were trembling, and there was dust everywhere. Clearly, it had been a long time since Hanna had seen anyone but Zakariya and Boulos—silence turns every being into a piece of rotten sponge.

William said that he missed Father Ibrahim. Hanna fell silent and then, sensing William's discomfort, gave him permission to leave.

William's mood improved in his next visits. He had read Hanna's writings from the previous forty years and had them delivered to Junaid Khalifa, to join the suitcase filled with some of Hanna's belongings that he had sent Junaid years before. Junaid was very thankful that William had moved to the monastery and was now closer, even though they met only a handful of times. He too wanted to bury these writings in a graveyard of things, along with his own novels about the imam of the lovers. Junaid looked sorrowfully at the old notebooks. He admired the sketches of plants, then set them aside on the chest of drawers. Looking out from his room over the fields of Anabiya, he considered rewriting, editing, and publishing them. The title "The Dinosaur Skeleton" occurred to him as an appropriate one for the thrilling confessions of a man with such an odd life story. He liked what Hanna had written about the dinosaur and Yousef. Still, Junaid was perplexed. He no longer had enough time to do anything with them, but he didn't want these writings to fall into oblivion; he was persuaded that Hanna had written them so that someone would publish them. He didn't want to become a saint by means of invented stories—he wanted to tell a truth of which Mariana would never approve. Junaid rose and opened the large bag. He emptied out everything that was inside and selected a new, permanent spot for it in his library.

Hanna felt delivered of a weighty burden. He felt light. Junaid wouldn't care about his writings; he would just toss them all into the fire. A sense of great power welled up from deep inside him, and he decided to go away with Zakariya. He asked William to accompany them both on their final errand and then to leave them after they reached their destination. He wouldn't die here, he would die in the place he had always dreamed of: in his own room in Hosh Hanna, on the banks of the river. William wouldn't let him down.

They arranged it all. Hanna met William at Zakariya's house, where Zakariya lay on a litter. Hanna and William helped Zakariya into the carriage, and William covered him up with a blanket and settled a cushion under his head. The carriage passed through the fields and arrived at the grave of William Michel Eisa and Aisha Mufti, where it paused.

Hanna stood humbly in front of the graves, and from his spot in the carriage, Zakariya looked on and muttered something no one could hear. The dawn was chilly, and Hanna was wearing only his thobe. He used his stick to lob at the plants on the road. He seemed strong as he walked barefoot alongside the carriage, along the road to the citadel. William, driving the carriage, glanced over at him occasionally, utterly incredulous that this delirious man was going to walk the more than one hundred kilometers to his rooms in Hosh Hanna.

They arrived at Souad's house. She was astonished to see Hanna barefoot. William waited on a side street with the carriage while

Hanna had breakfast with Souad, Yousef, and Hasko. He didn't give Souad time to offer him pity or anything else that might give him pain. He rose and, leaning on his cane, prepared to walk out alone. He embraced his three companions affectionately and went out the door that he had entered seventy years earlier as a child and the survivor of a massacre. Souad closed the door behind him; she didn't want to receive anyone that day. On the table she noticed a sealed envelope marked "Hanna's last letter to Souad." Her hand shook. She hadn't noticed him leaving the envelope—she had tried to avoid watching as he left. She thought of calling him back, but to where? Hanna would never return to the monastery. She had known very well that now he was wandering the earth, as was right for him. She put the envelope on her chest of drawers; two days later she found herself sitting on her bed, opening it up, and reading it.

My darling Souad,

By the time you read these words, I will be well on my way to disappearance. I confess to you that my greatest moment of happiness will be when I return to you in a short while as a mote of dust clinging to your clothes. It will find its way into your blood, my place that I will never leave, just as you have always been in my blood for the last seventy years. I must tell you that Zakariya's festering body is waiting to die. We have both agreed, without a word exchanged, to stay together until the very last moment. We no longer care about the graves. No one knows that the ulcers invaded Zakariya's body three months ago, and as usual with this disease, treating them has been very difficult. He won't allow anyone to anoint his pustules but me. Can you imagine it? Zakariya—our support, our wall, our protection, our master, our leader—is begging for death, which turns him a deaf ear. We agreed not to tell anyone about our catastrophe. I haven't left him alone—I was never afraid of being infected— and he wouldn't allow me to leave by myself. He said to me, "Let me disintegrate by the river." Nothing has flavor anymore. After

Aisha died, the arc of the circle remained open, waiting for my death or Zakariya's—or yours—so we can close it. But as you see, it never happened. When you brought Aisha's body, you and Yousef and William, we didn't grasp what had happened. I didn't believe it. Every day I still ask Zakariya, "When is Aisha coming?" He tells me, "She died. We buried her in your grave." But I don't stop asking, and Zakariya gives me the same repulsive answer, that she is dead. I want to ask you, for the last time, if Aisha really died, or is this another one of her childhood games? You won't remember because you lived apart from us, but I used to wake up at dawn and find her looking at me and smiling. She would order me to get up and say the sun had been asking after me, then she would add that the wind was sad because it couldn't find me anywhere. Then we would walk together along the passageway to the breakfast table and begin our day. I always used to think about the heavenly gift that Shaha gave us before her death. I always thought that I woke up only on account of that innocent smile.

So we have buried our loved ones, as you said. William Eisa died, and so did Aisha Mufti. Our friend Azar has died, David has died, Arif has died, our father Ahmed Bayazidi died, and before him our mother Radia died, and before them all, my mother, my father, and my four brothers and sisters died. So many of our loved ones have died. We thought we survived the flood and reached a settlement with death, but death cheated us by coming for Aisha. I couldn't believe how cold her body was, how rigid her smile. I couldn't believe your yellow face, or the tears of Yousef, Dilshan, and Hasko. Everything passed like a nightmare; when Zakariya and I laid her in my grave, after making sure it would fit her, we thought it must be a game that you all had invented to reclaim us. That grave was all I had left to give her. And after you all left, I felt a terrible void within me. Zakariya and I kept meeting at her grave at dawn. Now we have nothing left to say. Zakariya walks slowly, with help from Boulos, who has also grown old. Since then I have realized that I am the reason for each of our losses. I entered your house seventy years ago and destroyed your lives, and here I am, going out the same door for the last time, leaving everyone in ruins behind me. Even you are destroyed, there is nothing left of you but memories.

The first night after the flood, as I looked out on the anni-hilated village, I felt like there was nothing left of me. I tried to walk, to go back to Aleppo, but I couldn't. I was stupefied at how quickly I had changed, as if I had reached out my hand and pulled off my mask to reveal my new face, my new life. I peeled off my skin, everything vanished in a matter of moments—but those moments seemed like an eternity. My feet couldn't carry me anymore, my eyes didn't want to see anything, I hoped I was blind, had lost all my senses, but by good fortune I wasn't forced to answer people's questions, which I didn't care about. My new image, heart, soul, were perceptible to me alone. The moments that brought the change lasted an eternity, an entire century. I heard my old skin shedding, crawling into the river. I could see it all, but I couldn't stop it, not my transformation, and not the new soul that came to alight in my body.

A seed of doubt sprang up within me, questions prolifer-ated. I have not found a single answer for them, but they still dwell within me. Why were we created if misery and suffering await us? What is this "joy" that people speak of? I can reel off hundreds of questions. For a moment, after the flood, as I was looking from my window at that blighted place, I believed I had found answers to my questions about joy, ownership, death, and nature—but the questions always come back, like a flock of sheep wandering lost in the desert. Or like a storm battering down my windows. We can't see God, so we must grow accustomed to the absence of those we love. Many times I came close to believing Mariana's claims that I was a saint who could reach the spirit of God and Christ, and that there really was a connection be-tween Him and me. I used to lie down, watching the stars and the changing colors of the sky, and fall asleep believing that dreams were the only suitable place for my delusions, but in my life I have seen nothing but nightmares. Whenever I threw off a burden from my sinful being, new sins would grow. Everything I thought after the flood, everything I believed to be true, was scattered in the wind. I used to see the image of God and the saints scattered over the surface of the river, in the pomegranate groves, in your coursing through my blood, in my perpetual lodging in your blood. Nothing helped. Death is our only truth, and the emergence of life in the pomegranate blossoms each year, and their death, is the truth of eternity without beginning or end.

I have stopped reading the books that Father Ibrahim sent me. I believed for a while that it was absurd to understand God's truth and the multiplicity of religions. I feel I have done many things to atone for my misdeeds, but what I have done to you requires many lifetimes of atonement. You were my joy that I squandered, you were my certainty that I needed every instant, but I have been scattered all this time. The more I contemplated, the more bewildered I became. Why am I not a pomegranate flower on your branch—and you, the tree that I love?

How wonderful it would have been to weep when they plucked me, to leave you in order to return the following year, having longed for you. I embrace you, I cling to you as befits a beautiful flower slowly becoming fruit. No one sees us as I enter your sap, and I hide away from everything that is visible. If I were a fruit, we would have lived more innocent lives.

I often think of you as an image of God, whom I love. I have thought of you as an image of certainty, which I seek. You are not a woman but a river in whose depths I am delivered from questions that burn. Yes, perhaps love is the only happiness close at hand that can't be caught.

I won't take up more of your time. I have left my notebooks with Junaid Khalifa; I didn't want to burden you with them. I wanted to be lighter, but I don't want my things to weigh you down. For what good would they do you, a few pages of confessions heavy with regret? Regret is no good for anything. In the last sixty years, I have been unable to endure losing you, losing Aisha, or Zakariya's pustules, for which I am responsible; I weakened this colossus, he has been swallowed up by degradation because of me. I used to see him concealing his anger with me, but I was powerless to take off my ascetic's robe and return to our old selves, when we were children infamous for our knife skills, seeking out a victim. If I was still filled with greed, with a love of possessions and the perfumes of prostitutes, you would be justified in slapping me again. But even of that justification, I have robbed you.

There are thousands of images in my memory, which has never suffered from forgetting. Our images when we were children, our images when we used to look at the world from the top of Mount Jawshan as Zakariya's paper kites crossed the city. Our images have never ceased reproducing in my memory, and my questions will go unanswered for centuries. Humanity accumulates questions and doesn't attempt answers for the enigmas that multiply every instant. A delusional person is one who believes he will see the face of God or who awaits the resurrection of Jesus. Every instant Jesus rises and searches for someone who needs him, but a cruel wall is raised between him and those who reach out to him in agony.

I am one of those in agony. I can feel the wall between him and me in every moment. I am not strong enough to knock the wall down, but I hear his breaths encircling me from afar, and that is enough. You too—your breaths encircle me from afar.

On my way to disappearance, I leave you my erased footsteps, my breaths, and my regret, which will do no good. Forgive me; I am weaker than the image of me you drew in your mind. All my life you were the apparition that overwhelmed me with love. Do not stop giving it to me with the generosity of the sister and mother I lost, and the friend who became lost among other identities, and the beloved, into whose blood I slipped to hide away. Zakariya and I will disappear; we have lived together and we will die by each other's side.

I embrace you,

I love you,

And what is left of me isn't enough to regret . . .

Hanna

March 22, 1951

Calmly, Souad returned the pages to the envelope. In the morning she woke up and put a few clothes in a small bag. She sent for a car, which wasn't long in coming, locked every door of every room, and closed the door behind her without turning around. The car reached Hosh Hanna before midday and continued to Hanna's room, which could be seen from everywhere in the village. She went inside. Zakariya was lying on the wooden litter, staring at a point on the ceiling. He didn't ask why she had come; he was expecting her. Hanna was sitting in his usual spot. Souad took Zakariya's hand and burst into tears. She heard Zakariya's dry laughter and his voice, saying, "Everything has finished. Death, who I considered a friend, has betrayed me." And he suddenly stopped talking. Souad uncovered his pox-riddled body. She got up and spoke to Hanna, who fetched some cloths steeped in a tisane. The voices of the fellahin, on their way back to work in the fields, reached them. Souad decided to stay, against their wishes. She tidied the room so there was space for the three of them. Zakariya was turned over, slowly and gently, and she could smell that his skin was beginning to rot.

All the way to Hosh Hanna, Hanna had talked cheerfully, telling William many stories about their childhood. He avoided people, walking along the side roads, enduring the pain. They slept at night in an olive grove. The March cold was biting, but Hanna made do with a light blanket. They slept for a couple of hours, then woke up to continue with zeal, keeping parallel to the riverbank. They reached Hosh

Hanna on the evening of the second day. The room was ready. William dusted it down and drew some water from the nearby well. Hosh Hanna was the same as it had been ever since the flood: abandoned. A few families had attempted to come back and live there, without success. The lands were now subject to the church and had been rented out to an investor who planted them with cotton. Hanna's place was as clean as ever; the children of his old servant cleaned the room now, just as their father had done for over twenty years. Hanna was reassured to see that his bed and his few things were exactly as he had left them in his last visit with Zakariya.

Hanna asked William to leave. He wouldn't even allow him to stay the night. He instructed William to tell Mariana not to send anyone after them, adding, "She won't have time to, anyway." He hugged William, who leaned over and kissed Zakariya as he lay on the wooden board. Zakariya whispered that Maryam was still waiting for him, and it was still too early for him to die. William needed those words. He returned to Aleppo and sent Maryam a short letter asking her to come to the studio; Khalil might have made it hideous, but Maryam's chair was just as it was. William was furious with Khalil who, crestfallen at his mentor's reaction, labored for days to restore the place to its former appearance.

Maryam received William's letter, but she didn't come. He waited for days, but she didn't come. He went to meet Sam and found him repeating the same old stories, having added the tale of William and his women to his trove. Bored, William went home again. The walls were cold. For the first time, he realized his leftover food was moldy. He wandered through the studio and thought that the place was destroyed; it couldn't be truly restored. Moments streamed out of his memory that he used to believe would remain there forever. He looked thoughtfully at the photographs of women that Khalil had returned to their previous places. There was nothing left of these women but a painful shadow, the delusion of youth, the stopping of time at a moment of squandered beauty. He decided that Hanna's room in Hosh Hanna was the only suitable place to live. He left the studio at dawn and found a bus that would take him to the junction for Hosh Hanna. It was crammed with passengers, but he took no notice of their noisy chattering. William reached Hosh Hanna at night and climbed the steps to the room. Hanna was in the corner with Zakariya next to him, and Souad was looking after both men. Hanna said, "I knew you would come back, but you're not too late." William didn't reply. He fell into a deep sleep beside the litter where his father Zakariya slept. In the morning, Zakariya refused to have William there and demanded that he leave them to themselves. William went back to the monastery, and within two days the lives of all three were settled.

After William left, Souad sat on the chair, looking at the night. She asked the others if they remembered their letters on the river. The three of them gave themselves up to conversation and laughter, and then a silence fell and lengthened. Souad dozed off briefly, and when she woke up, the dawn was magnificent. The plants were in bloom, the colors were new, everything was new. She couldn't see Hanna; Zakariya was crawling toward the chair. Souad stood next to him; Zakariya was moaning in pain. She asked him about Hanna, and he said he had seen him walking on the riverbank. Hanna had been walking slowly, and Zakariya had watched him from his window, crying bitterly. Then he stopped crying. Hanna reached the river, where the waters had begun to overflow their banks at the beginning of spring. Hanna walked forward and plunged into the river, and Zakariya saw the powerful current sweep him away.

Souad didn't believe or understand until she looked out and saw dozens of young men conferring on the riverbank and then diving into the water. The colors seemed new to Souad, changing every moment, and Hosh Hanna, which Zakariya and Hanna and Mariana had never stopped talking about, appeared as a lost paradise, of which nothing remained but this room on the hill.

Before midday, Zakariya was sitting in place on the chair, watching everything. Pieces of his body were falling off, but he paid them no attention. Souad saw thousands of people unloading from a sea of buses and cars, and they were all heading for the riverbank; an entire city seemed to be springing up anew. Dozens of young men were diving into the cold water in search of Hanna, who had vanished within the depths he had walked into shortly before dawn. The moon had been full, floating on the calm surface. He hadn't lingered—he had plunged straight in. Down there were his son Gabriel, and Josephine, and Zakariya's son, and the priest and Yvonne's betrothed and his father who owned the mill, and all the rest of the drowned, who rose joyful from their death, took him by the hand, and led him to their kingdom where life is fresh and tender and the fishes never die.

Damascus—Cambridge—Boston
Summer 2015–Spring 2019

Acknowledgments

I feel immense gratitude and esteem for my friends who have been generous as always in reading the drafts of this novel at various stages. Their painstaking comments left their mark on me and rid the text of many defects; if any remain, they are my own personal responsibility.

First, I feel continual gratitude for my very great friend and literary agent, Dr. Yasmina Jraissati, whose generosity with me does not stop at this novel but extends to all my books, over my entire life. With respect to this novel, she has been with me from the earliest moments, the very initial idea of it, over a decade ago. Throughout the years of writing, she listened to my misgivings, bore with my anxiety, and read the initial chaotic drafts and the final drafts more than five times. She followed the work in its various stages and forms and wrote long, profound reports about every detail. She has given me many hours of her precious time to speak honestly when we meet in person or over Skype. Her work as an editor and reader has had a profound influence on me.

Likewise, I give thanks to my friend the lawyer and book lover Jean Masry, a classmate in the College of Law at Aleppo University, who even now retains his elegance, his generous spirit, and his passion for the history of our city. He read an early draft and made vital notes, answered my questions during the course of a long interrogation session, and generously supplied me with essential references.

Thank you to my friend the critic and writer Sobhy Hadidi, who, despite having little time, undertook a careful reading of the last-but-one draft and offered important feedback on the body of the text, language, and structure.

Thank you to my lifelong friend the poet and storyteller Ayed Abu Hassoun, who read the text with great and minute scrutiny and drew my attention to errors in an early draft. He drew up an index of the characters and mapped out the relationships between them with his famed accuracy, and his observations and our conversations had a great effect both on the novel and on me as a person.

Thank you to my friend Wael Farouq, writer, critic, translator, and professor of Arabic literature at the Università Cattolica del Sacro Cuore in Milan. He made some inspiring notes that were of the utmost importance, and my conversation with him about this book lasted three years.

Thank you to my friend Dr. Hussein Jawish, who taught me so much when I was a young man, and who continues to teach me. He never stints the time he gives me. He studied all the characters through the lens of a psychologist, and his valuable feedback illuminated the narrative structure, the history, and the implications of each character. Our long conversations in Berlin in the spring of 2018, as well as his emails since, have had a great effect.

Thank you to my friend the great director Haitham Haqqi for his feedback and for the generosity that I have exceeded over the course of our entire relationship, which reaches back twenty years.

Thank you to my lifelong friend the journalist and writer Sayyed Mahmoud, who honored me with a close reading and feedback, and who gave me his time for a long and minute discussion.

Thank you to my friend Rana Hayek, editor at my publishing house Hachette-Antoine-Naufal, who has shepherded me through the work, borne up under my chaotic moods, and never despaired in her diligent pursuit of bringing the text to its best possible version.

Thank you to my friend Arij Jamal, writer and editor at Dar el-Ain, whose painstaking notes, conversations, and discussions were of great help in ridding the text of many errors.

Thank you to my friend Dr. Sarya Marzouq, who offered valuable information about horses and was generous with her precious time when answering my questions.

Thank you to my dear friends Ali Abu Hassoun, the translator Ibtihal Mahmoud, Lama Muhammad, and Fatima Judayna for their interest in the text, for playing the role of reader at various stages over the last four years, and for allowing me to direct many questions at them over the course of long sessions about the novel and its characters. Their feedback has had a profound impact on my attempts to take apart and understand the text.

Likewise, I must thank my friend the American writer Jane Unrue, director of the Harvard Scholars at Risk Program, along with everyone else who works at the program, which hosted me while I was writing part of this book. Jane was a wonderful friend who enveloped me with her friendship while I was going through the hardest time of my life in 2015.

Thank you to everyone working at the Institute of International Education, which offered me a writing grant in cooperation with Harvard University, so I could dedicate myself to writing part of this novel.

Thank you to all my friends at the Passa Porta program for writing in Brussels, which hosted me for five weeks in the spring of 2016 so I could revise the first chapters.

Thank you to everyone working at the Santa Maddalena program in Florence, which hosted me for a month and a half in the spring of 2018 so I could work on the penultimate draft.

Thank you to my friends who have endured me for the past four years while we walked through the dark streets of Damascus. They listened to me rant and rave about the novel and its characters, just as they have done for my previous novels, and they do it all out of intense love. Particular thanks are due to my dear friend the theater director

Osama Ghanam, my dear friend Boulos Hallaq, my dear friend Lina Antaky, and my lifelong friend the sculptor Safaa' Al-Sitt.

My deepest thanks go to all these friends, who have immersed me in love and given me their valuable time with such abounding generosity.

A NOTE ABOUT THE AUTHOR

Khaled Khalifa was born in 1964 near Aleppo, Syria, the fifth of thirteen siblings. He studied law at Aleppo University and participated in the founding of *Aleph* magazine, which was closed down a few months later by Syrian censors. Active in the arts scene in Damascus, where he lives, Khalifa is a renowned writer of screenplays and novels. His novel *No Knives in the Kitchens of This City* was awarded the Naguib Mahfouz Medal for Literature and was a finalist for the International Prize for Arabic Fiction. His novel *Death Is Hard Work* was a finalist for the National Book Award.

A NOTE ABOUT THE TRANSLATOR

Leri Price is an award-winning translator of contemporary Arabic fiction. She is a two-time finalist for the National Book Award for Translated Literature for Samar Yazbek's *Planet of Clay* and Khaled Khalifa's *Death Is Hard Work*, and winner of the Saif Ghobash Banipal Prize for Arabic Literary Translation for *Death Is Hard Work*. Her translation of Khaled Khalifa's *No Knives in the Kitchens of This City* was short-listed for the American Literary Translators Association's National Translation Award.